SADDLEWITCH

Brian Rider

Bannerman Press

© Brian Rider 2001
Saddlewitch

ISBN 0-9540541-0-5

Published by Bannerman Press
Littlenook
Chapel Street
Hook Norton
Banbury
Oxfordshire OX15 5JT

The right of Brian Rider to be identified as author of this work has been asserted by him in accordance with the Copyright, Designs and Patents Act 1988.

All rights reserved. No part of this publication may be produced in any form or by any means – graphic, electronic or mechanical including photocopying, recording, taping or information storage and retrieval systems – without the prior permission, in writing, of the publisher.

Design & production co-ordinated by:
The Better Book Company Ltd
Warblington Lodge
Havant
Hampshire
PO9 2XH
Tel: 023 9248 1160
e-mail: editor@better-book.co.uk

Printed in England.

Cover design by Richard Draper

ACKNOWLEDGEMENT

Grateful thanks are due to my editor, John Wheatley,
for his valued, expert advice, time and patience,
also to my proofreader Geoffrey Lilley.

This book is dedicated to my wife, Sheila

Author's Note

Any resemblance to persons living or dead is entirely coincidental, as is the village of Saddlewitch and other places mentioned in this book.

CHAPTER ONE

Sasha Paget's mind was far away from her present activity of walking her retriever bitch, Bess, along a woodland path. The rough track, for such it was, meandered through the woodland on the eastern side of the village of Saddlewitch. It was a fine warm July day, and the sun filtered down through the thick verdant canopy of foliage above her. Bess ran ahead enjoying the numerous aromas of the woodland wildlife. Sasha never had to worry about her and knew that she would return instantly when summoned. A rabbit ran across in front of Sasha but today she hardly noticed it. To her left, running parallel to the rough path was a steep incline where, some sixty feet below, a little brook bubbled and gurgled. The waters merrily twisted and turned through the wooded valley. Every hundred yards or so the trees were interspersed with the mighty stone pillars from an old disused viaduct, covered now in ivy and creeper so that they stood as ghostly sentinels – monuments to a bygone era. Before the days of the Beeching axe in the sixties, they had carried the track of a proud Victorian railway, running right across the valley basin. Now deep in the undergrowth they resembled something akin to Sleeping Beauty's castle.

Summer birdsong and the far off cry of a rooster today barely interrupted Sasha's thoughts. Her mind was on her daughter Debbie's problems at school and getting home to collect her other child Annabel, aged three and a half from play school. Bart, her husband of seven years, was at home today, but she knew he would be far too involved with his business calls on the telephone, to think about collecting Annabel. Life for Sasha had changed dramatically over the last three years. Once Bart had been a normal loving husband, but so gradually had the change come about, that she couldn't put a date or time on it. Of late he had no time for her or the two girls and at times was quite tyrannical. True, he had never actually hit her although twice had raised his hand in threat. Sasha wondered if it was something she had done. Was she no longer attractive to him? Only that morning she had stood naked in front of the bathroom mirror taking stock of herself. Although not in any way conceited, she liked what she saw in the reflection. At twenty-seven her figure was as good as it ever was before she had had the children, the oldest of whom, Debbie, was five and at primary school.

Sasha was fairly tall at five feet seven with a slim waist and well rounded hips, tapering down to a shapely pair of long legs, which she considered her best feature. Long dark shoulder length hair framed a face that was not pretty in the chocolate box mode, but definitely attractive. Even in her depressed frame of mind she had been forced to admit that to herself. Pale blue grey eyes looked back at her from a solemn face. She had forced herself to smile and the mirror had responded with fine even teeth between full red lips. Little dimples in her cheeks and fine lines round the corner of her mouth had reluctantly appeared. Her nose was straight and even her worst enemy couldn't have faulted it. Eyelashes were naturally dark and long and her eyebrows fine and well cared for. True she could perhaps have afforded to lose two or three pounds from her hips, but that was nothing a good week's dieting wouldn't have taken care of.

Continuing her walk, she thought about her wardrobe. Bart hadn't bought her any new dresses for ages and wouldn't give her any extra money to buy them herself. She had suggested going out to work but Bart had bellowed in horror.

"No wife of mine is going out to work. I've never heard of such a thing."

Sasha wandered on. She could hear Bess barking up ahead, probably a squirrel up a tree, she thought absently. Her thoughts came back to her current situation. Why was she so depressed? Hadn't she two lovely daughters and a handsome husband, five years older than herself with a highflying job. Perhaps he had a mistress at the office, she mused. Was that why he had seemingly lost interest in her and the children? Lovemaking with him these days was almost non-existent, and when it did happen, she recalled with horror it had almost amounted to rape. The last time, two weeks ago, Bart had returned home late at night the worse for drink, virtually tore off her nightie and forced himself upon her. She had cried herself to sleep.

Now these problems with Debbie at school were simply the last straw. The child's form teacher had requested to discuss it with Sasha and Bart, but he had simply said "Your problem, not mine."

When Sasha had talked with Miss Morris, the young teacher, she had been told the child was frequently in tears at school and could she think of any reason for this. Sasha had promised to talk to Debbie about it. When she had, all Debbie would say was, "I hate daddy. Why don't I have a nice daddy like Rosemary's?" Rosemary was Debbie's best friend.

Even in the cooler temperature of the woods, Sasha was regretting the jeans and trainers she had dressed in. Without thinking about it, she pulled the sweatshirt over her head and tied the sleeves round her waist, leaving her upper half in just a white cotton tee shirt. Probably because she was busily involved in tying the garment around her, she didn't notice the tree root exposed on the dirt path. The toe of her right foot caught under it, sending her sprawling. Unable to stop herself she tumbled over the edge of the path, rolling over and over down the steep slope towards the stream at the bottom.

Crashing through some bracken she came to rest against a small tree that arrested her downward plunge, growing at an oblique angle about half way down. She was temporarily winded and suffered a few scratches from the brambles, but otherwise appeared unhurt. She lay still, breathing deeply, trying to recover from the sudden shock of the fall. After a couple of minutes, she heard barking above her, and on looking upwards from her prone position, saw Bess, her black coat glistening, looking down at her. Standing on the path the bitch wagged her tail furiously and barked excitedly, obviously thinking this was some sort of new game her mistress had invented.

About thirty feet separated the two of them and, at this stage Sasha saw no cause for alarm. She called out for Bess to stop barking, which to her credit the dog did instantly.

"Bess – stay!" Sasha called up to her.

It should be easy enough to half crawl and climb up the steep slope with the help of the small saplings to pull her up on, she thought.

It was then, as she went to put her weight on the right foot, that she felt the searing pain in the ankle, crying out aloud with the sudden pain that weight bearing had exposed. She collapsed back in a heap on the dry earthen slope. Bess barked again.

Sasha realised, with horror, that she would never be able to climb the steep forest slope on her own without help. The movement had caused the ankle to ache and throb painfully. My God, she thought, it's broken. Whatever will the children do? It was perhaps a characteristic of her that her first thought was for the children. In half an hour she should be back to go and pick up Annabel from the playgroup. She began to panic and tears ran down her cheeks.

Bess was slithering down the slope on all fours, whimpering now, sensing that something was very wrong with her mistress. A few moments later she lay beside Sasha licking her face. The dog's action seemed to restore Sasha's mind to the reality of her situation. This was a lonely path. It was quite possible nobody from the village would even come this way today. But then, when she didn't appear back at home with the dog, surely Bart, even in his present frame of mind, would miss her – or would he?

Sasha had told him often enough where she went to walk the dog, because he had always demanded of late to know where she was at any given time. Not, felt Sasha, because he cared about her, but she was his possession and he should know where she was just as he did his car, computer, Financial Times and the like. Sasha knew she would have left him, but for the girls and anyway where would she have gone? She had no job, and therefore no money. Her parents had been killed in a motor accident three years earlier and Bart didn't like her to have friends of her own.

She choked back the tears and tentatively tried to put a little weight on the foot again, but collapsed back in a heap, sobbing with the pain. Already she could see that the ankle was swelling ominously, pushing against the denim of her jeans.

"Think girl, think," she said aloud. Bess licked her face again. Tears mingled with perspiration on her face and she felt sick both from a mixture of apprehension and pain.

The only sound came from a light breeze in the high treetops and a distant knock, knocking sound of a woodpecker in one of the woodland trees. It was only the tree in which she had lodged against in her fall, which had prevented her continuing downward for another thirty feet or so to the stream at the bottom. She realised with newfound horror if she crawled away from that, there was nothing to prevent her tumbling down further into the stream.

Nothing for it then but to stay where she was and trust someone would miss her even if Bart didn't. Surely when she didn't turn up at the playgroup Pat, who ran it, would telephone Bart to see where she was. Yes, she reassured herself that is what would happen. Then again, sometimes on her walks through the woods, she had seen Job Parrott, the local poacher, known in the village of Saddlewitch as Digger.

Maybe, just maybe, he was around somewhere or there was young Bessie Pepper, the barmaid at the local inn, The Black Bull. She didn't work until the evening and sometimes Sasha had seen her in the woods walking her little white poodle.

Sasha began to call out for help, shouting loudly at the top of her voice.

"Is there anyone there? Please help me." The only result was that the woodpecker ceased his tapping and the only reply that greeted her was the gurgling stream below, waiting to drench her if she fell any further. Several times she repeated the call with the same dismal outcome. On the perimeter of the wood she could hear a sheep bleating.

In frustration she beat the earth with her bunched fist. Bess now had laid alongside her and turning her head from side to side, trying to understand why Sasha was not getting up. Sasha reached out and stroked the bitch's glossy coated head. Bess turned and licked her wrist.

"Go for help, Bess. Go on. Good girl."

Bess looked confused, seemingly unable to comprehend the command. Why was her mistress sending her away?

"Shoo, shoo Bess. Fetch help. Go Bess go."

Twice Sasha repeated the command indicating with her hand for the dog to go back to the path above them.

Suddenly the bitch seemed to grasp the need and slowly at first backed off. With one more turn and an uncertain look back she stood for a moment watching Sasha.

"Good girl. Get help. Up girl, fetch help." Sasha waved her hands in an upward motion towards the pathway. "Go!"

Bess scrambled upwards on her belly until she reached the path and on arriving there, turned to look down at her mistress again.

"Good, Bess. Now go."

Slowly at first, with several backward glances, Bess ambled off, breaking into a run, and disappeared from Sasha's sight.

For a period that seemed eternity Sasha settled down to wait, there being nothing else she could do now. With difficulty she pulled herself up into a sitting position against the trunk of the tree that had arrested her fall. In the pocket of her jeans was a wrapped boiled sweet, slowly unwrapping it she placed it in her mouth. Somehow the sweet sugary taste seemed to renew hope and confidence a little. All too quickly it had gone, time dragged on and, in spite of the heat of the day she found herself shivering. The sweatshirt she had been tying round her waist when she fell had come away. In fact she could see it caught on the brambles just below the path at the top.

Once more she began to call out at intervals. A grey squirrel scampered down a nearby tree and watched her for a few seconds before scuttling away. Once she dislodged a stone by her foot, which bounced off down the steep slope to finish in the small brook at the base. She looked round her trying to calmly take stock of her surroundings. To right and left on the dirt slopes grew small saplings. These were interspersed by fallen and rotting trees with numerous ferns and brambles. At least she thought, I should be seen from the path above if anyone goes by and I can call out.

At first she had heard Bess's barking, until that, too, had receded into the distance muffled by the thick vegetation.

She began to feel very alone. It wasn't just her situation here in the woods, perilous as it was. It was the overriding feeling that nobody gave a damn about her, least of all her husband.

She had had lots of friends once, but when she thought about it, she realised that Bart had chased them all off. True, she knew people in the village, but none of them in any great depth.

There was the Reverend Grenville and his wife. She only ever saw them at church on a Sunday when she took the girls. The Parson and his wife, both in their thirties, were fairly new in Saddlewitch, having taken over the Parish last year at St. Martin's.

John and Betty Durban were a middle-aged couple who ran the local grocery store, and there was Dorothy Sheridan the postmistress, a kindly soul who knew everything and everybody in the village. She was a widow in her fifties. Then there was the local constable – quite a character she had been told, although she only knew him to say good day to. George Fenning by name, a tall lean man.

Sitting there alone her mind began to wander further. Once she thought she heard a sound and called out anew, but presumably it had only been a rabbit or something moving about above her. Soon all was quiet once more and she was left to ponder her predicament.

Twice more she tried to struggle into an upright position with the help of the tree trunk supporting her, but the pain in her ankle caused her to involuntarily cry out in anguish. She slumped down onto the earthen floor beating the ground with her fist in frustration.

An aeroplane droned by overhead. A fat lot of good that was! She couldn't even see it through the canopy of the trees and even if she had done, the pilot would never have seen her, a mere speck in the woodland scenario. Another sheep bleated a long way off and once she heard something that sounded like a shot, but it could have been a car backfiring way off in the village.

Her wristwatch told her she had already been there for thirty minutes, although it seemed more like hours. Poor Annabel would soon wonder where her mother was, and why she hadn't arrived to collect her. Never could she remember feeling so helpless. Her arm felt sore and for the first time she found, on examining it, that it was badly grazed. She tried licking the superficial damage, which gave a little relief. Of Bess there was still no sound. Perhaps if the dog went home without her even Bart would realise something was wrong. That's if he even bothered to let the dog in when she barked at the back gate.

The minutes ticked on, forty-five of them now on her watch. With another monumental effort she tried to rise, but nearly slipped further down the slope, only at the last minute grabbing the trunk of the tree to steady her.

Sasha gritted her teeth and resigned herself for a long wait. She continued to call out at intervals to no avail. Even her throat felt sore from the effort of shouting. Why oh why didn't somebody come?

* * * * *

In fact she had surmised correctly. Her dog Bess had, on deciding to leave her, sprinted for home. Charging through the village to the amazement of all who saw her, she arrived home to find the back gate locked. She began to bark furiously and went on for fully ten minutes.

A window upstairs in Bart's study opened and he leant out cursing her, commanding her to 'stop that bloody racket'. She continued to paw the gate and bark even louder. He hurled a marble paperweight at her. Fortunately for the dog it missed and clattered off the wooden gate onto the grass.

A further stream of oaths and abuse followed and then the window was slammed shut. Bess ran off and barked outside the post office. By now it was lunchtime and Dorothy Sheridan, the postmistress, was just showing the last customer, Burgess Steele, the local farmer, out before locking up for lunch.

"Isn't that the Paget's dog, Dorothy?" he enquired.

"Yes, it's Bess. She's always inseparable from young Mrs. Paget. I've never heard her bark like that," she replied, looking concerned.

"Certainly seems agitated," grunted Burgess, getting into his Land Rover. When he drove off, Dorothy stroked the dog, which seemed to pacify Bess.

"Good girl, Bess. Run home." With that she went back into the post office and locked the door. Bess looked to right and left and ran round the village barking excitedly and then headed back for the woods.

CHAPTER 2

When Sasha Paget didn't arrive to pick up her young daughter Annabel from play-school, Pat Lambert, who ran the little group became concerned. When the other children had all been collected by their mothers and a further twenty minutes had elapsed, she telephoned Annabel's home.

The telephone rang for quite a long time and Pat was beginning to think that no-one could be at home. Then a man's voice answered, obviously by his very tone irritated by the disturbance.

"Yes, what is it?"

Somewhat taken aback, Pat explained the problem adding, "I wouldn't normally mind but I have an appointment in Grantfield this afternoon." Grantfield was the nearby town, where most of the village folk did their big weekly shopping and banking, etc.

In a very bad grace Bart Paget reluctantly agreed to come and pick the child up.

"I'll be there in about ten minutes," and then more to himself than to Pat mumbled, "Where's the silly bitch got to?" Pat heard the receiver slammed down at the other end.

"Well really!" she exploded, then remembering Annabel tugging at her skirt, knelt down and wiped a tear from the child's cheek. "Daddy's coming. Don't cry, dear."

"Don't want daddy … Want my mummy," protested Annabel, before dissolving into tears again …

Back in the woods Drew Thorpe ambled along, his attention momentarily caught by the ivy covered pillars of the old railway viaduct. He looked up studying a noisy confrontation deep in the creeper towards the top of one of the stone towers. The commotion was explained when two wood pigeons emerged and flew off. Drew's Alsatian dog, never far from his heel, watched with equal interest.

"Come on, Caliph, time to go home," he said to the dog, turning round on the narrow path. Obediently the dog turned almost at one with him. New to the village, Drew Thorpe had caused quite an impact amongst the villagers, a young man of thirty-one renting Briar Cottage on the edge of the village with apparently no wife, no children and no job. Speculation ran rife in such a small community. Several people put their own interpretation on his arrival; others added spicy gossip of their own.

"His wife has left him and taken the children, I expect," ventured barmaid Bessie Pepper. Gardener Jake Cutter and his drinking mate Bert Thorogood reckoned Drew Thorpe was a Russian spy.

"This is just the sort of place they hide, yer know," he informed all and sundry. Nat Browning, a regular at The Black Bull, reckoned 'a criminal if ever I saw one. You can never trust these quiet ones.'

Gudgeon, the local gravedigger, decided "Ee cum ere ter die, that's wot ee as." Postmistress Dorothy Sheridan scolded all the gossipmongers.

"Leave the poor man alone. Everyone deserves a little privacy in life."

"Well, I'll be keeping a careful watch on him," confirmed P.C. George Fenning. Not just a few of the female hearts in the village had been seen to flutter at the sight of Drew. Tall and well built with dark brown, wavy hair, he was most of the village girls' idea of the prototype matinee idol. When he smiled there was a little dimple that appeared between mouth and chin.

"Such a strong mouth," murmured village man-eater Barbara Lake to her friend Sally Greves.

"It was his eyes I noticed. Lovely they were, clear blue, almost danced they did, when he looked at you," put in Sally.

"I saw him first remember, Sally."

"You want to watch out Barbara Lake. Your husband is a respected bank manager in Grantfield … . If he hears you talk like that . . You ought to know better, a woman of nearly forty."

"I'm only thirty-eight Sally, as well you know. We went to school together — remember?"

"Anyway, he's too young for you. Can't be more 'n thirty if he's a day."

"Just the way I like 'em," grinned Barbara, rolling her eyes dramatically.

Drew couldn't have gone more than another hundred yards when a black retriever ran up to them barking loudly. Caliph made as if to intercept but was quickly brought to heel by his master.

The retriever continued to run round the pair barking, then ran off a little way and looked at them before repeating the whole scenario.

Drew watched the agitated performance with interest and then continued towards the village along the path but the retriever followed them, barking loudly in their wake. Drew turned to shoo the dog but the animal was having none of it, running away to their rear then returning.

Drew scratched his head.

"I believe she wants us to follow her, Caliph." He half turned and the animal ran off down the rough narrow track, still barking loudly. "Come on Caliph, let's see what she wants." Wearing only trainers, jeans and tee shirt, Drew was very fit and set off at a run after the dog, Caliph still keeping pace at his heels. Every now and again the retriever would stop to make sure that they were following, then raced on again. This must have gone on for the best part of three quarters of a mile before Drew was halted by a plaintiff cry.

"Help! Can somebody please help me?" He isolated the sound and dashed on. The cry was coming from somewhere quite near now. The retriever was standing on the edge of the woodland track about fifty yards ahead of them. The animal was looking down at something below Drew's line of vision. Quickening his pace, together with Caliph, they raced up to join the retriever still barking. It was then he saw her, about thirty feet below, down a steep fern and bracken covered slope. Wedged against a small tree, about half way down, to where a little brook wended its way along the valley floor.

He stopped in amazement. She saw him at the same moment and called out, her voice nearly breaking in the middle of the appeal.

"I'm hurt ... my ankle ... can't move ... . Please help."

Drew saw that she was an attractive young woman, probably about his own age, or possibly younger. Her face looking up at him was streaked with dirt and tears and her hair disarranged with strands stuck to her forehead.

"Stay where you are. I'm coming," he responded. Then realised how ridiculous this must have sounded. She couldn't do anything but stay where she was. Caliph was sliding down the slope on his belly towards her. "Stay!" commanded Drew. The retriever had already joined her mistress, licking the girl's face. Without too much difficulty Drew half slid and half scrambled the thirty feet or so down to the girl. "What happened?" he enquired as gently as he could.

Half sobbing, Sasha explained, more concerned about her child's pick up from playgroup than herself.

"Calm down. I'm sure she will be all right until we contact them. The main thing is to get you out of this predicament. How long have you been here?"

"Nearly two hours since I fell ... It's my ankle – I can't put any weight on it."

"Let me have a look. I may be able to see what damage there is." Shifting his position round the trunk of the tree he carefully raised Sasha's foot. The retriever growled and bared her teeth at him, eager to protect her mistress.

"Good girl. It's okay," reassured Sasha, and Bess immediately lay down on the dry earth once more.

Drew could see that the ankle was badly swollen and puffy and the jeans were painfully cutting into the flesh above the ankle. He reached into his pocket and produced a Swiss army knife.

"W...what are you going to do?" stammered Sasha, thinking he was going to cut her foot.

"Don't worry," said Drew with a reassuring smile. "I'm only going to cut the leg of your jeans. The tightness is interfering with your circulation." So tight were they that he experienced considerable difficulty in achieving it, but eventually a nine-inch cut to the denim material taking it as far as the calf was effected.

Immediately Sasha felt the pressure ease, but a few moments later came an uncomfortable pins and needles feeling.

Drew saw her distress and explained, "Don't worry ... quite natural. It's the blood getting back to the area ... It will go off in a minute or so." With strong gentle fingers he explored the ankle and foot. "Bend it down," he said firmly. Sasha eased her toes downwards. "Now pull the toes up." Again she complied. "You're doing well. Now try to turn the foot inwards in a circular movement."

She gasped with pain on trying to obey and leant back against the trunk of the tree, a tear rolling down her cheek.

"Fine, just breathe deeply." Drew stroked the back of her hand in a comforting gesture. "You are going to be all right. I don't think anything is broken, just very badly sprained, but you won't be walking on it for a couple of weeks at least."

"Are you a doctor," Sasha enquired.

"No – my name is Drew Thorpe, by the way."

"I've never seen you around the village before ... oh, sorry. I'm Sasha Paget."

"You wouldn't have. I only came to Saddlewitch two weeks ago. I rent Briar Cottage – but enough of this. I've got to get you out of this and back home or better still, to hospital. That ankle should be X-rayed just to make sure nothing's broken."

Sasha could feel some of the tension going out of her. This stranger gave her a reassuring feeling that she couldn't explain. He was so calm and in control, that in some strange way she never even thought to question him. Drew looked about him.

"I'm going to leave you for a few minutes. We need to splint that ankle before I try and move you." Alarm showed on her face and Sasha grabbed his arm.

"No ... Don't leave me here ... Please." He smiled, and with the back of his fingers brushed her cheek, which seemed to ease the momentary feeling of panic.

"I'll be within sight, I promise, but I need to find a suitable piece of wood to make a splint for that ankle of yours."

"Okay, I'm sorry to have panicked and to be such a wimp, but I began to feel that nobody was going to find me down here."

"Not surprising … . Two hours can seem like eternity sometimes. Now just rest and breathe easy … I shan't be long." Drew scrambled up the slope after ordering Caliph to stay with Sasha and the retriever. Sasha could see him rooting about along the path above her and to the right of her position. A few minutes later he scrambled down the treacherous slope with two pieces of wood in one hand.

"Right, now this should do as a makeshift splint … Hmmm! Now we need something to use as a bandage."

Without more ado he pulled his tee shirt over his head exposing a well-muscled bare chest. He then began to go to work with the Swiss army knife cutting the garment into long strips. Sasha watched his biceps flex as he cut through the flimsy material, experiencing a strange warmth that she hadn't felt for a long time.

Amazed at her own reaction she tried to cover it up by countering with, "Your shirt! . . You shouldn't have."

"Oh, it's only an old one and it's going to be more use to you like this," he said laughing. Going to work with a will he set about securing the makeshift splint. When the work was complete he leaned back to examine his labours. "Nothing special," he commented, "but it will stop any further damage whilst I get you out of here, Sasha."

It was the first time he had used her name and she felt herself blushing like some silly schoolgirl.

Drew explained to her how he was going to get her up to the path once more. The plan was for him to go up backwards with his arms under hers, pulling her on her back after him. It was to be slow and she was to cry out if it hurt too much.

"Once back on the path, I'll be able to carry you home … Okay?" Sasha nodded. It proved quite difficult for Drew to turn her round so that she now faced the tree that had broken her fall. In getting his arms under hers and across her body, his fingers brushed her right nipple and instantly ashamed of herself, Sasha felt it harden beneath his touch. In a fleeting second the moment passed and ever so slowly he dragged her backwards, a few feet at a time, then a few moments rest in between. Sasha's tee shirt rucked up out of the waistband of her jeans and she could feel the rough ground on her back. Five minutes later they flopped onto the path and lay on their backs for a minute or two to recover. Shafts of sunlight bathed their faces through the canopy of the trees.

Sasha wanted the moment to continue but all too soon Drew scrambled to his feet saying, "Well, that's the hard part ... Now all that remains is to get you home." Stooping, he scooped her up in his arms.

"You will never be able to carry me all the way," Sasha still found it hard to say his name out loud.

"Want to bet?" he replied, his blue eyes twinkling merrily. With that he set off along the path with Sasha in his arms and the black retriever Bess running on ahead of them. As always Caliph kept to Drew's heel. Once they stopped for a rest in the woodland when he found a nice grassy and soft mossy area for Sasha to sit. "When we come out of the woods you will need to direct me to your house ... Will your husband be at home?" Drew enquired.

"Today he is," she replied.

"That's good news anyway. He will be able to look after you ... Drive you to hospital for an X-ray perhaps?"

"Some hopes," said Sasha too readily. Drew looked at her curiously. "No, he's all right really, just very preoccupied and busy to have much time for me and the girls." Why had she said that to a perfect stranger? Sasha was quite amazed at herself.

"Oh, surely not. I can't believe he wouldn't be interested in you," Drew replied. Sasha didn't answer. Perhaps she felt she had said too much already. There was an embarrassed silence, finally broken by Drew.

"Well, if you're rested enough Sasha, we had better be getting on." She nodded and once again he scooped her up and it felt good to have his strong arms around her. She wanted to let her head rest on his shoulder, but fought the impulse, holding her neck stiffly rigid. Once out of the woods, they came across the village green with its War Memorial and onto the road.

Suddenly there were people about and Sasha began to feel acutely embarrassed as folk began to stare. Drew, however, marched on calling a cheery good afternoon to all who stopped to watch them.

Sasha whispered, "I think you ought to put me down, or you will be talked about."

"Nonsense. You can't even begin to walk and anyway it's easier this way. Now which way is it here?" he enquired as they reached the forked road by the village store.

"Right and up the hill," urged an embarrassed Sasha. Whatever would Bart say when he saw her arrive carried by a stranger. Ted Sewell, the plumber, was just pulling away in his van but stopped again to gawp at the strange spectacle before his eyes. Drew however marched on, oblivious to all but getting Sasha home.

By the village hall, they turned left and nearly bumped into Hortense Hyde-Potter, the president of the W.I, who physically recoiled aghast at such a phenomenon.

"Stand aside please madam," commanded Drew as the bespectacled woman in her felt hat blocked their path.

"Well really! Such goings on ... I must speak to the vicar about this!" With little mincing steps, wielding her handbag, nose in the air, she hurried off in the direction of the vicarage. Even Sasha was forced to giggle.

"My God, Drew," she used his name for the first time without thinking. "You've done it now, as they say. Hortense Hyde-Potter virtually runs this village. Even tells the vicar how long his sermons should last, I'm told."

"Chairman of the Parish Council, I expect, as well," laughed Drew.

"How did you guess."

Past several quaint thatched cottages, the fire station and the post office.

"Turn left here," prompted Sasha.

"Your wish is my command, fair lady," quipped Drew. They were now in an area with open countryside to their right. On the left Drew saw expensive looking large houses standing in their own grounds.

"Ours is the one at the end," Sasha pointed it out to him. "Please, Drew, put me down before we turn in or my husband will ......" she let the sentence tail off.

"Your husband will be delighted that some kind soul has returned you to his bosom unharmed." In spite of Sasha's protests, Drew's grip remained the same, and she was powerless to do anything about it, even when they turned into the driveway of their black and white gabled house with its spacious lawns and rose beds. A man was just coming out of the garage. On seeing his wife in the arms of Drew, his face turned as black as thunder and he stopped dead in his tracks.

"What's the meaning of this?" he virtually roared, a moment later rushing forward to confront the pair. Drew made no effort to relinquish his hold on Sasha.

"Your wife has badly hurt her ankle. Luckily I found her ... She needs an X-ray."

"What do you mean, you found her?.. Who are you anyway, and why are you handling my wife?.. Put her down this instant. Where did you find her?"

Faced with this aggression Drew was quite taken aback. He had obviously thought any husband would be relieved to see his missing wife safely returned. Sensing the aggression, Caliph snarled at the man and began to look very threatening.

"That will do, Caliph. Heel." Drew's call immediately relaxed the Alsatian, who lay down instantly.

"Put my wife down at once," commanded Bart Paget again.

"Now Bart, please don't be so rude. This kind man has helped me and brought me home," said Sasha, still in Drew's arms trying to pour oil on troubled waters.

"I suggest you take her. She is unable to stand on her foot," said Drew, his voice now turning to ice. Bart stepped forward and roughly

Saddlewitch

virtually tore his wife from Drew's grasp. Turning, he headed for the house, half carrying, half dragging, Sasha.

Sasha called out, "Thanks for all your help, Drew. I don't know what I would have done without you."

Drew heard her husband say, "Oh, so it's Drew is it ... Know him well, do you?" A moment later the front door slammed behind them and Drew was left standing in the drive.

He thought about going in after them and intervening, but decided it might only make matters worse for Sasha. Reluctantly he turned and left the scene, totally amazed at her husband's reaction.

CHAPTER 3

Early on the same warm summer evening, the young Reverend Mark Glenville closed the door of the old Norman church behind him, regrettably being forced to lock it, due to recent vandalism – a mark of the times. He walked slowly down the path to where a large chestnut tree bordered the churchyard.

From this vantage point he could look down on the village of Saddlewitch nestling in the valley. He could make out the crossroads in the centre of the village where the old Black Bull stood, a fifteenth century inn. Surrounding it were several black and white gabled houses of only a slightly later period. Sounds of happy children's voices floated up to reach him from the valley.

Between the churchyard and the village were two fields of now almost golden corn, the heads of which swayed slightly, wafted by the light summer breeze. A pigeon cooed in the tree above him. What a peaceful scene it all was.

He was a troubled man, having only taken over the parish some three months before from a Rector who had been the incumbent for longer than anyone could remember. The Reverend Wesley Pendale-Cummings, the old man, for such he now was, had been an advocate of the old fire and brimstone sermons. Mark, however, was a modern thinker, realising that if the church was to succeed then it must appeal to a younger element of the parish. The Parochial Church Council made up of the likes of Hortense Hyde-Potter and her ilk was opposing him and his wife, Mary, on every issue. It would probably have been easier to have relented to their demands and given in gracefully for a quiet life. Mark was only too aware that he couldn't expect to change things overnight and he didn't intend to try.

Many of the old ways were good, but surely there must be room for the new. The 'die hards' however, opposed change in any shape or form. Only last week he had virtually been instructed by Hortense Hyde-Potter that he should preach exclusively from the Old Testament and that the sermon should not exceed ten minutes in length. His wife Mary nearly fell about laughing when he had discussed it with her, but she hadn't been quite so amused when he had gone on to tell her that Hortense had also drawn his attention to the length of his wife's skirts.

"Far too provocative for a clergyman's wife, rector," she had said. Mark didn't tell Mary that bit. He knew only too well what her response would be. After all he had to live with these people.

"Silly old moo," snorted Mary, who was not a bit like one's imagination of the archetypal rector's wife. Tall and slim with flame red hair, she was only one inch shorter than Mark at six feet. Mary's temper, when roused, Mark knew could match the fire in her hair. In spite of this, she was incredibly supportive of all he tried to do and very mature for her thirty years. Mark, two years older, for the first time in his life was faced with responsibility for making his own decisions. Up until three months ago, he had been a curate in a large parish and had therefore complied with what the incumbent said or did. A modest man, caring and thoughtful, with nothing flamboyant about him, Mark had a fairly laid-back approach to life that appealed to his peers. Some of the young women in his last parish had thought him very attractive, not that Mark had really noticed any of them. Mary, however, had and she had informed him in no uncertain way of the fact. An early receding hairline did little to age a warm friendly face, with eyes that lit up when he spoke. His problem now was how he, so comparatively young, could win over those people long since set in their ways.

"Where yur be wantin' it Rector?" He was shaken out of his reflections by the voice of the gravedigger, Gudgeon. He had been so deep in thought that he hadn't heard the old fellow approach. He knew, however, that the gravedigger referred to Friday's coming funeral and wanted to know where the grave was to be sited.

"Oh yes, Mr. Gudgeon. Come this way. I'll show you." He was probably the only person in the village who addressed Gudgeon as mister. To everybody else he had only a surname, by which he seemed to be known.

Mark led him down a grass path and past several graves and pointed out the area that was to be designated for the burial.

"There will be fine, I think," he said.

"Lordee, no parson. This area is reserved for them of the manor house family. Yur can't put 'e' thar." Here we go again, thought Mark, feeling his heckles rising.

"And why not, Mr. Gudgeon?"

"Cos 'im that's gone 'n died, like, well 'e was only a farm 'and like." Mark, trying to keep his voice calm, reasoned with Gudgeon.

"And you think this deceased gentleman doesn't have the same rights as the manor house family?"

"Wot ol' Ted? 'E warn't nobody," grunted Gudgeon, stubbornly.

"Everybody is somebody in God's eyes and has a right to be buried." Gudgeon gave a hitch to his baggy trousers and laid his spade on the ground defiantly.

"Well parson, I tells yer ... They won't loike it ... Not a bit they won't. Yur needn't think they will ... T'aint roight."

Mark decided to make his stand. After all he couldn't let a gravedigger say what should and shouldn't be, he thought.

Facing Gudgeon with his firmest face switched on, he retorted, "Dig where I've told you, Mr. Gudgeon please. I will decide where Edward Dimmock should be buried."

Gudgeon continued to argue, spittle running down the heavy stubble on his chin and on to an already heavily holed and stained waistcoat. He narrowed bushy eyebrows that seemed to merge with his long white and unruly hair. The colour rose in his cheeks.

"'E wus never Edward. 'E wus ol' Ted ... 'E never amounted tur much, did ol' Ted." Mark let out a long sigh of exasperation.

"I won't discuss this further, Mr. Gudgeon. Mr. Edward Dimmock will be given a Christian burial like anybody else ... Dig the grave where I say." Turning on his heel, he strode purposefully away and on up the path. In his wake he could hear Gudgeon still muttering to himself.

"'E will see o'im roight, 'e will. They manor 'ouse people will be after 'e, wun they 'ears aboot it."

★ ★ ★ ★ ★

On his way home, he passed what was once the old rectory, a large house in its own grounds with large white double gates. Mark smiled to himself, thinking how times had changed. The rectory he now occupied was a semi-detached three-bedroom house. Not that he resented the fact. Both Mary and himself had settled nicely in the house and they were both very content to live there.

On arriving home, he found Mary doing the ironing and watching the television at the same time. He told her about the encounter with Gudgeon.

She laughed and said, "Oh well, that's not the end of your troubles. I've had Mrs. Ponsonby-Forbes on the telephone complaining that somebody had been in her pew. Apparently she found a sweet wrapper in it when she arrived last Sunday."

"Her pew, indeed," echoed Mark indignantly. "And there's me thinking that the pews belonged to the church ... Anyway I expect that it was left there by one of the Sunday school children from the week before."

When they had first arrived in Saddlewitch and he had taken his first look at the church, he had been amazed to find several of the pews had little doors with bolts fitted. When he had enquired about this phenomenon, the retiring rector Pendale-Cummings had tapped each pew in turn proudly naming its Sunday occupants.

Oh, I see ... You mean each one pays for the privilege of having a designated place?" Mark had said.

"Certainly not, young man," the old fellow had replied. "This is the way it has always been and will be so." He had glowered at Mark reproachfully, for questioning what in his eyes was obvious. Mark, however, needled by this attitude had not been prepared to accept the obvious.

"Are not all men equal in the eyes of God, rector?" Pendale-Cummings' eyebrows drew together and he had peered at Mark from under a furrowed brow.

"You would appear to be a socialist, young man. My advice to you is not to flout convention."

For the time being Mark had taken the matter no further, merely saying, "My beliefs are strictly non political, as it happens." Very slowly he was implementing changes well aware of the old adage 'softly softly catch a monkey'. Although aware that a lot of the old guard resented change, he had been encouraged by a few new young people beginning to attend church.

Mary had teased him that most of them were village girls, and that they had only come to flutter their eyelashes at the new young vicar.

"That may be so," he had replied, "but they are coming, and that's a start." None of the older ones had actually stayed away, merely showing and voicing their disapproval at the changes he made.

Mark helped Mary fold a couple of sheets whilst they discussed village news.

"Take them upstairs will you, love, if you're going up to your study," she said, handing him a pile of tidily folded clothing.

* * * * *

Sasha's problems had only just begun when her husband Bart had dragged her inside, slamming the door behind them. By the time that Drew Thorpe had left the driveway to the house Bart had begun to berate her.

Not even enquiring how she was, or what she had done to herself, he was far more put out by having had to collect Annabel from playgroup himself. He looked at his watch.

"And now, I suppose, I'm going to have to collect Debbie from school in half an hour, woman."

"Well, it's either that or we send a taxi to get her," put in Sasha. Coming across the room, he pushed Sasha roughly down into a chair.

"Well, I suppose you are going to try and lie your way out of this," he retorted, pushing his face into hers.

"There's nothing to lie about," Sasha responded and tried to tell him what had happened in the woods.

Long before she had finished Bart flew into a rage. Grasping her by the shoulders he pulled her up out of the armchair. Sasha cried out in pain at the sudden movement of her ankle. Little Annabel, playing with a dolly on the lounge floor, began to cry. She reached protectively for her mother. Once more Bart pushed Sasha back into the chair.

Almost black with rage he roared, "Who was that man? Carried you all through the village ... You think it's funny to make a laughing stock of me, do you Sasha?" She tried to explain further, but he wasn't going to listen. Striding around the room he continued to lambaste her. "For all I know you were carrying on with this – man – and that's how you came to hurt yourself ... If I thought he'd touched you, I'd take a gun to him ... You belong to me and to me alone ... I've a good mind to go after him now. Where does he live? ... Tell me," Bart commanded.

Sasha thought it was prudent for Drew's sake not to know. She merely said, "How should I know? He is just a kind person who helped me, that's all."

"Hhhh! You knew his name – Drew somebody or other. I'll ask round. Somebody will know." Bart smashed his fist down on a coffee table so hard as to make the flower vase on it jump up and down. Sasha looked at him coldly.

"Yes, you should go and find him and thank him like any normal person would, but perhaps first you might deign to telephone the doctor for me ... It may have escaped your notice but I can't walk or even stand."

Bart continued to roar on for a while and then, as his temper began to cool, resorted to innuendoes and veiled threats. Sasha was greatly relieved when it was time for him to go and pick up Debbie from primary school. He went out, slamming the front door behind him and a moment later she heard the car go out of the drive with a screeching of brakes as he rounded the corner into the road.

Annabel ran to her, jumping onto her lap. The child was still in tears. Sasha stroked her hair and gave her a kiss.

"I wish daddy would never come back. I hate him," sobbed the child. Sasha thought to herself, my sentiments entirely, but it wasn't fair to say anything to the child. With her free hand she reached for the telephone and called doctor Denzil Davidson, the local GP. He was a kindly middle-aged practitioner who had been the village doctor for a good many years. Everyone said he was as much a friend to them as a doctor. He was very concerned when she explained what had happened.

"I'll come right round Sasha, before I start the evening surgery. Sounds as if I ought to have a look at it."

Ten minutes later his car drove into the drive, followed by Bart returning with Debbie from school. Bart used his keys to let him in to the house, behaving like the perfect gentleman so concerned about his wife.

"Poor Sasha is in a great deal of pain, doctor," he began as both men, together with Debbie, walked into the lounge. Debbie ran to her mother.

"Are you hurt, mummy. Poor mummy."

"Hello darling. I'm all right but please go and play with Annabel, whilst the doctor looks at mummy's ankle," urged Sasha. Doctor Davidson knelt down on the carpet, thoroughly examining Sasha's injured ankle. He made her move it in different directions and press against his hand.

Finally he pronounced, "Well, Sasha, it's very swollen so we can't be sure without an X-ray, but I don't think it's broken." He reached into an inside pocket producing a prescription pad and began to write. Finally he turned to Bart handing him two note lets. "Get your wife to casualty at Grantfield hospital for an X-ray. On your way, pick up this prescription for her; it will help with the pain. I presume you have already applied an ice pack to reduce the swelling?"

For the first time Bart looked embarrassed.

"She didn't want one, doctor."

"I don't recall being asked," retorted Sasha coldly. Doctor Davidson looked from one to the other and then again at Bart.

"Well, I suggest you do so now, Mr. Paget. It will help to control the swelling. Make sure the ice doesn't touch the skin. Put a damp flannel between her skin and the ice, or she will get an ice burn ... do you understand?" Bart was all courtesy and solicitous now. Sasha thought that Bart was behaving like two different people. This seemed very odd indeed, but she decided not to say anything.

He hurried off to see to the ice pack and left doctor Davidson talking to Sasha. When he returned, the doctor supervised the application of the ice and seemed in no hurry to leave. Finally, after showing the GP out, Bart declared that he would bring the car right up to the front door to take Sasha to hospital.

"I'll ring Clare next door and see if she can have the children for us."

Sasha listened to Bart on the telephone to their neighbour. Butter wouldn't melt in his mouth, she thought. Clare said yes, she would have them whilst he took Sasha to hospital ... Poor Sasha, was there anything else that she, Clare, could do? And yes, bring them round straight away.

★ ★ ★ ★ ★

At hospital an X-ray revealed that there was no fracture but that the ankle was very badly sprained.

"No weight-bearing for at least a week. Ice packs twice daily and pain killers every four hours," said the doctor at Casualty. They provided Sasha with elbow crutches and, as they were leaving, the nurse said to Sasha, "It may take two or three weeks to get right, so be patient."

Bart heard and said, "Don't worry, she's got me. I will do everything for her. Nothing for my wife to do but get well for us all."

The nurse smiled and replied, "Oh, how lovely. I wish my husband was so thoughtful and kind."

Sasha just grimaced and stumbled out on her crutches to the car park.

Saddlewitch

CHAPTER 4

Later that same evening police constable George Fenning took his usual seat in the saloon bar of the Black Bull. George could usually, mornings or evenings, be found there. Even the divisional police station in Grantfield always knew where to find him. His capacity for consuming the local ale was legendary. It said much for George's genial character that nobody either reported him or took him to task for it. More often than not he would be dressed in civvies rather than his uniform.

At least four times every day he would be seen riding his 'sit up and beg' black bicycle between the police house and the Black Bull. His long cream coloured mackintosh always looked as if it must surely catch in the spokes of his rear wheel. The village children would bet on it, but they were always disappointed for it never did.

George was a tall lean man with a long mournful angular face that completely belied his genial nature. Nobody could ever remember him ever booking anybody for anything. After about nine thirty in the evening, George would spend the remaining opening hours seated on his bar stool in a kind of happy haze. A favourite pastime was to sit under a sign situated over the bar, which had printed in large capital letters

W Y B M A D I I T Y

He would patiently wait for a stranger to appear to order a drink from the barmaid, Bessie Pepper. In his slow mournful drawl he would enquire if they knew what the sign meant.

Always the answer would be 'no idea.' George, with some alacrity, would then respond with his favourite line.

"Will you buy me a drink if I tell you?"

To which, somewhat embarrassed, the stranger would usually reply, "Yes."

"Well, that's what it means." George would then spell out the letters concluding with, "Mine's a pint of best bitter, thanks." He would finish his glass pushing it forward for a refill, happy like a child winning a game against an adult.

Although they had seen it happen more times than they cared to remember, it never failed to amuse the regulars. George had another favourite trick to which he was a brilliant exponent. This one was reserved for the village regulars. When someone he knew came in, he would jump up from his stool and shake hands saying, "Have a drink with me."

"No, that's all right, George, you have one with me."

The normal answer with most people would have been, "No, I asked you first." With George it was "That's very kind of you. I'll have a pint of bitter." Should all else fail, George would produce an old leather purse from his Mac pocket, and take so long sorting out small change, that the regular would become embarrassed and say, "Let me, George," and produce a note for the barmaid.

"Very kind," George would say. "I'll get you one next time." He never did.

Near closing time three weeks earlier an incident had occurred. The Superintendent of police had telephoned the Black Bull to speak to constable Fenning. A bus had overturned on a sharp bend approaching the village. George, however, by this time, was so much in his cups that it is doubtful whether he could have held the telephone, let alone speak into it. There was a quick conversation between some of the regulars when Bessie Potter told them who was on the line.

John Durham, who ran the local grocery shop with his wife Betty, was amongst them.

Attempting to impersonate George, he picked up the hand-piece and replied, "Constable Fenning here sir. What appears to be the trouble?"

The Superintendent had outlined the problem concluding with "Now get your arse off that bar stool and get down there and take charge, constable."

"Yes, sir. Right away, sir," John Durham had replied. Two more of the regulars had helped John get George Fenning into John's car and they had proceeded to the site of the accident. Fortunately there were only minor injuries and the ambulance had already arrived. Once out of the car George stood in the centre of the road, tottering from side to side, waving his arms in all directions.

"I'm in charge ev…, everyone I…leave this to m…me."

"That's right, George, you're in charge," said John Durham, winking at Ted Sewell, the plumber, who had accompanied them in the car.

Together they escorted or rather half carried and dragged George to the side of the road, concealing him in a nearby ditch. George sat down heavily and continued to wave his arms wildly. John Durham and Ted Sewell had then completely taken over the incident and dealt with it. Luckily the ambulance men both knew George's reputation and nobody was any the wiser, at least no one that mattered anyway.

★ ★ ★ ★ ★

This evening it was the turn of Drew Thorpe to be caught by George, as Drew paid his first visit to the Black Bull. When he had bought the constable the regulation pint and purchased his own, the two men fell into conversation. Although well into the evening George was not yet drunk and proved a mine of information about the local village, so much so that Drew bought him another pint of bitter. After they had been talking for half an hour, Drew told him about the strange reaction he had received from Bart Paget after helping his wife.

"Not a bit surprised," said George. "Rum one that Bart Paget is for sure."

"How do you mean?" enquired Drew. George coughed, looked to right and left in a secretive fashion, then ran a bony forefinger up and down alongside of his nose before replying.

"Well, he used to be quite a good egg, when he first came here with that pretty wife of his, that is."

"So?" prompted Drew.

"Got in with a bad crowd if you ask me. That's what did it …

Changed completely over the last two or three years. Don't know how that wife of his sticks it ... Puts up with it for the kids sakes I suppose," said George, answering his own question.

"What does he do?" queried Drew.

"For a living, you mean?" replied George. Drew nodded. George eyed his pint pot, which was once again down to a mere half inch of ale. "Thirsty work all this talking," he commented. Drew smiled and bought the constable another, omitting to order for himself. George took a long swig of the new offering, which depleted the contents by a good third. Drew waited patiently, by now intrigued by George's revelations concerning Bart Paget.

Finally, after another pull on his rapidly diminishing pint of bitter, George continued.

"Quite a high flyer he is – travels into Grantfield and catches the train up to London most days. Something big in the city – stockbroker or the like, I'm told. Odd days he works from home." George laughed at this point, a strange phenomenon quite altering the usual mournful features he showed to the world, and then added, "Unluckily for you lad that you picked one of those days to bring his wife home."

Drew ignored the jest and probed further. "What did you mean when you said that he ran with a bad crowd?"

"Oh that ... yes ... well, he meets up with a wild bunch in Grantfield about once, sometimes twice a week. They call it a luncheon party, but it goes on till the early hours of the morning, I'm told ... Gambling and the like. You know the sort of thing." Drew didn't know, so he pressed George to elaborate further. George, however, was not so drunk as to become a little suspicious. He eyed Drew down his long, bony nose. "You seem to asking a lot of questions young fellow. New in the village – renting Briar Cottage, I'm told."

Drew was quite taken aback. This man was obviously not the buffoon that he had taken him for, and evidently knew everything that was going on in the village.

"Yes, that's right," Drew replied, ignoring the first part of the question. It was George's turn to probe.

"What is it you are occupied in here, then . . .? In Saddlewitch, I mean?"

"Oh, yes … I'm a journalist – freelance, you know."

"Ah, that's why you keep asking questions, I expect." George seemed satisfied with this, but no matter how much Drew tried to ferret out any more information about Bart Paget, the constable always managed to find a question about Drew's reason for asking. It was soon obvious to him that a stalemate had been reached and that he wasn't going to find anything else out from George that evening.

It was about ten o'clock when he left George at the bar. The constable's parting shot worried him more than he cared to admit.

"As far as the Pagets are concerned, lad, it might be better for Mrs. Paget if you forget the incident." Drew, his hand on the exit door handle, half turned back. George went on, "Mrs. Paget, like everybody else about Bart Paget is his possession, so don't go getting out of your depth and into hot water."

Drew simply nodded and closed the door behind him. Now he was even more intrigued. There and then he decided to call round the next day to enquire after Mrs. Paget. Surely Bart couldn't be as bad as the constable had made him out to be? No, that was it, he had just caught the man on a bad day, he mused.

★ ★ ★ ★ ★

Sasha Paget probably wouldn't have agreed with Drew's conclusions about Bart had she known about them. That evening he had been in an angry sullen mood, with bouts of accusations interspersing the long periods of sulky silences.

Most of the time his anger had been directed at the extra things he would have to do for the children because of her accident. Even tomorrow he would have to stay at home until something better could be arranged. It was all her fault, he exclaimed. For all he knew she had been monkeying about with that fellow that brought her home.

This sort of thing went on until she declared for an early night, thinking to escape into sleep. Then with horror, she realised she would need his help to climb the stairs.

"What," he bellowed, "after all the trouble you have given me."

Ignoring him, she defiantly crawled on all fours to reach the stairway. Once there, she managed one step at a time, going up on her bottom to reach the top.

From the lounge, still seated in his armchair, he watched her every step of the way, lips pursed tightly together and eyes like cold flint. With difficulty Sasha dragged herself across the bedroom floor. It was an arduous effort but loosening her belt she managed to wriggle out of her jeans and haul herself into the large double bed. Too tired and exhausted from the happenings of the day, she didn't bother with removing her panties or even the grubby torn tee shirt. She pulled the duvet up round her chin and tried to shut out the world.

It didn't work. She thought back over the years, to when Bart had been a kind, thoughtful, husband very much in love with her and, to be fair, she with him. Was it her fault? Had she failed him in some way? Was it the pressure of his work? Certainly he had no time for her or the children these days. Yet if she even looked at another man or smiled at someone, he flew into jealous rages. Sasha tried to analyse herself. She certainly hadn't let herself go. What clothes she did have, were well chosen, with the limited money he allowed her. True she spent most of the meagre allowance on Debbie and Annabel. After all, she didn't want them to suffer and feel inadequate at school or with their friends.

When she had asked Bart for more money he had simply said, "Make your own clothes, woman like anyone else." Sasha had tried to reason with him, to no avail. Perhaps he has a mistress at the office. Yes, that must be it. Then she dismissed the idea as quickly. Only last week he had come home at night with a wrapped present for her. She knew at once he hadn't wrapped it. A red professional bow secured the expensive gold foil paper. Excited, she had slowly unwrapped the parcel to expose a large white cardboard box.

Standing over her, Bart commanded her to open it. He had been virtually leaping about with excitement. Sasha, despite a momentary joy at the gift, suddenly had misgivings.

"Go on … . Go on, open it." Bart had barely been able to conceal his impatience. Sasha removed the lid of the box to reveal, all carefully folded, a little black mini dress in wet look leather. Also in the pack, were long thigh length red high-heeled boots to match.

"Put them on now," Bart commanded. Sasha tried to make light of the moment.

"It's very nice of you, Bart, but when I said I needed new clothes I didn't exactly have this in mind … Where do you think I'm going to wear this sort of stuff – round the village?"

"Certainly not. You wear it for me now, woman." By now Bart had already worked himself into a rage and she had seen his expression turn to menace. It had been easier to comply than to fight. She slipped out of the cotton dress she was wearing and donned the ridiculous apparel.

When the transition had been completed, she turned and said, "Satisfied?" The sarcasm heavy in her tone.

"Strut woman … Walk up and down," Bart commanded. Sasha, feeling ridiculous, looked at her reflection in the full-length bedroom mirror.

"I wouldn't look out of place in King's Cross," she snapped. The wet look leather clung to her figure in a sensual provocative manner. The long leather high-heeled boots leaving a large area of her thigh exposed between skirt and boot top.

"I told you to walk, Sasha." Again Sasha detected the undertone of menace in his voice.

She looked at him defiantly and said sarcastically, "Perhaps you would like me to swing from the chandelier or climb a pole."

"No, just walk," he replied coldly. Sasha walked up and down the bedroom doing an over exaggerated swirl and curtsey at the end.

"That enough for you? What do you think I am, a tart?" In a normal relationship Sasha wouldn't have been adverse to a bit of bedroom fun but she sensed this was something quite different.

Then came the real bombshell when he said, "I want you to wear that when we entertain my friends to dinner in two weeks time."

"The hell I will," objected Sasha. "Just what do you think I am?" For a moment Bart's tone had changed to one of gentle persuasion.

"I'm so proud of you, Sasha. I just want to show you off in front of my friends."

"Oh, do you? . . Well, in that case you can buy me a decent cocktail dress and not this tart's rig." Sasha had moved to unzip the garment.

"Leave it on," Bart screamed. He moved towards her and Sasha was sure he was going to strike her, but instead he pressed her against the wall and ran his hands up and down the leather dress. She tried to edge away but she was pinned in the corner between the walls. His eyes were boring into her and she could see the cold fury written there. Sasha met his gaze and forced him to drop his eyes, but his hands were under her skirt, tugging at the waistband of her panties.

"Not like this," thought Sasha. "No way buster." She brought her knee up sharply and Bart let out a yell.

"You bitch!" A moment later he was curled up writhing on the bedroom carpet. Sasha ran out of the room and locked herself in one of the spare rooms. That had all been a week earlier.

Now, lying in the bed, she thought about his planned dinner party for his friends. At least now, she mused, my damaged ankle will get me out of that. He will have to entertain them out somewhere now. Sasha knew that there was no way that she would have entertained them, dressed in that ridiculous garb that he had given her anyway.

That night, a week ago, she had finally decided that his behaviour was the last straw. In fact, she had made an appointment to see a solicitor tomorrow. That too, would now, due to her ankle injury, have to be put on hold until she was more mobile.

It was only the children that had made her stick the marriage this long. God knew though, how she was going to manage. Everything had been organised with the house and money in his name. She had no parents living and hardly any friends. It was going to be extremely difficult, but surely anything must be better than this present existence.

Saddlewitch

A few weeks ago, after a tremendous row, Sasha had tried to get Bart to seek medical help, but his temper had merely worsened at the suggestion and she hadn't mentioned it again. With his violent mood swings, Sasha knew it could only be a matter of time before he struck her or one of the children. For their sakes she must get them out of this unhappy environment. No doubt a lot of the problem with young Debbie at school was due to the home life.

Her thoughts were interrupted by the bedroom door being pushed open. She was relieved to see that it was only Bess the retriever who had entered. The dog curled up at the foot of the bed. Ten minutes later she heard the front door slam, and a few seconds after, their car driving off.

Bart had gone out and Sasha experienced relief at the thought. She realised that she wasn't interested where he had gone, at this late hour, as long as it was far away from her and the children.

Turning over on her side, she was asleep in minutes, exhausted by the events of the day.

CHAPTER 5

The following afternoon the weather was equally hot and sunny, with the sun beating down on the village from a clear blue sky.

It being late July the school holidays had just begun. For those people living on the local council estate, living near to Dennis Madely and his friend Billie Tate, a time of trepidation. Young Dennis, aged twelve, had a reputation as the local tearaway. Nearly every sign of mischief in Saddlewitch was put down to Dennis and his friend Billie, who was a year older, but was led by Dennis. True, it wasn't always the two rascals at fault, but it was probably a fair assumption that ninety per cent of the time it was.

Old Rowley's wood lay on the other side of the valley to where Sasha Paget had had her unfortunate accident. Open countryside of hedges and fields separated it from the village. Amongst other things, the large wooded area contained two gigantic bomb craters, a residue left by World War Two, fifty-five years earlier. A badly damaged German bomber turning for home had jettisoned his two massive bomb loads at random. Fortunately, the explosive impact had fallen harmlessly into Old Rowley's wood.

Although no harm had been done to the population thereabouts, the end result was two enormous craters, each some thirty metres across. About a hundred and fifty metres separated the two huge rents in the earth. Due to the very chalky soil of the area, the water that in time had filled the craters was grey/white in colour. Local parents had always warned their children to give the area a wide birth. The two craters were known to be some three metres deep in the centre and because of the steep sloping sides extremely dangerous. This warning, of course, did not apply to Dennis Madely or Billie Tate. It was a favourite haunt of theirs, especially since one day earlier that summer they had seen Rachel Steel, the local farmer's daughter, skinny dip in one of the pool-like craters.

Today they lay concealed in the undergrowth waiting for a repeat performance. It appeared Dennis had seen Rachel leave the farmhouse with a towel under her arm. Without more ado he had raced round to Billie Tate's house and the two had run all the way to Old Rowley's wood to arrive and hide before Rachel came to take her swim. The woodland there was on her father's land. Burgess Steel was a gentleman farmer owning several thousand acres including the woodland on this side of the village. His daughter Rachel was tall and dark and at twenty-two quite a renowned local beauty, with half the local lads setting their caps at her. Rachel however, never had time for any of them. She was much more interested in the men from the national hunt and point to point circle. It was well known in the village that her current boyfriend was Toby St. John Vandervell, whom, it was rumoured, was related to a duke.

The boys lay amongst the bracken and fern, half screened by brambles from the crater. They waited with baited breath. The seconds ticked by.

Billie whined, "I've been stung by these stingers ... Look at my arm." He pointed at the nettles close by to his left.

"Shut up, she'll bloody 'ere yur," whispered Dennis.

"Are you sure she's coming, Dennis? Maybe she's gone to the other crater."

"Naw, she alus comes to this 'un."

"We've only seen her once before so how do you know that?" queried Billie. Dennis scratched his head.

"Tell yer what, Billie. Yer run up ter uver crater ... See if she be thar, instead of 'ere." Billie looked doubtful.

"But you said she always comes here Dennis, and if I go round there I'll miss her if she comes here ... Why don't you go and look and I stay here."

"Yur chicken, Billie Tate, that's wot yur are. Shut up anyway. I can 'ere somebody coming, fur Pete's sake."

"Who's Pete, Dennis? I don't know any Pete." Billie was not blessed with exactly the highest I.Q.

Dennis gave him a fierce dig in the ribs and when Billie grunted, Dennis snarled, "Shut up will yur an' watch."

Definite sounds of twigs cracking underfoot could now be heard approaching from opposite to their position in the bracken. A few moments later they saw Rachel Steel emerge from the tree line. She crossed to the rim of the crater and stood looking down. Dennis placed a hand in the middle of Billie's back and pushed him flat, whilst craning further forward himself.

Rachel was dressed in a pale green patterned frock and just a pair of sandals on her feet. She began to work her way round the rim of the crater, obviously looking for the least steep point of entry.

Dennis muttered, "Sod it. If she comes round 'ere she'll see un … Keep yur 'ead down." He increased the pressure on Billie's back virtually squashing his friend's head into the green mossy floor of their hiding place. Luckily for the two boys Rachel stopped diagonally to them and sat down on the crater's rim to remove her sandals. This accomplished she stood up and pulled the green dress over her head. A moment later, reaching round behind her, she unfastened her bra, exposing firm young pointed breasts.

Billie, pulling his head up from the soft moss, audibly gasped a half choked "Crickey!"

Dennis ran his tongue round his lips and whispered, "Cor look at them tits."

Rachel, oblivious of the presence of the two boys hooked her thumbs under the waistband of her white bikini style pants and slid them down her long shapely legs. Adroitly she stepped out of them and bent to fold her clothes in a neat pile. Billie looked across at Dennis to see what his friend was doing.

"My mum says you'll go blind if you do that Dennis."

Dennis, too involved with his present occupation and his eyes on corn stalks, merely snarled, "Shut up, can't yur."

Rachel slid down the slope and entered the murky snowy coloured water, very gingerly at first. Near the edge it was quite shallow, covering no more than her knees or just below. She turned her back to where the boys' position was, giving them a good view of her well-rounded and firm buttocks. Wading round the edge she turned inwards towards the middle, and they were offered a good view of her profile. Another step and the water came up to her waist. Throwing herself forward she began to effect a strong over-arm crawl to the other side of the crater. Once there she turned turtle onto her back and floated lazily on the surface for a while. After a little of this, she swam round the crater pool on her back, finally finishing with some accomplished breaststrokes.

After about ten minutes Rachel headed for the easier shelving of the pool to climb out. Dripping wet from head to foot, ringlets of wet hair sticking to her forehead, she scrambled up the dry slope and reached for her gaily-patterned towel.

"Cor blimy, will yur look at that 'un." In his excitement Dennis had raised his voice above his normally almost inaudible whisper. Rachel, in the act of towelling between her legs, ceased abruptly and wrapped the towel around her.

She called out, "Who's there?" panic and anxiety in her voice clearly evident.

"That's torn it ... she's dun seen un. Run Billie." Without waiting for his friend, Dennis leapt to his feet and bolted, crashing through the undergrowth. Billie, almost too terrified to move, climbed to his feet and stood for a moment, almost rooted to the spot. Rachel, wrapped in her towel, was looking right at him. Then he in turn, after staring transfixed for a moment at Rachel, rushed after Dennis. Rachel, relieved that it was only the two youngsters that had been spying on her, yelled after them.

"I know who you are Dennis Madely and Billie Tate and my father will be round to see your parents about this. You are also trespassing on private land."

The retreating boys heard every word as they crashed off in indecent haste. When they had put a safe distance between themselves and Rachel and out of breath from their headlong flight after detection, the two boys stopped.

"I've got bloody stitch now, 'aven't I?" moaned Dennis, clutching his side and doubling over.

"Perhaps that's what you get before you go blind, like my mum says," said Billie.

"Shut up, yur don't know nuthin'," snapped Dennis.

"I know that I'm going to get a hiding from my dad when farmer Steel comes round to complain about us trespassing and spying on Rachel," moaned Billie.

"Do wot I dus ... Stick a bit of cardboard down yur pants ... It don 'urt so much then." Dennis had had so many good hidings that he was virtually immune to them anyway. He went on, "Wul I reckon t'was wurf it to see 'er loike that."

The two boys, reluctant to go home for a while, continued to mess about in the woods, but eventually, like all boys, their stomachs began to tell them that it was getting on towards teatime. They left the woods and walked across the fields to the village. On their way home, however, they came across the old derelict windmill that stood to one end of the village. The sails had long since rotted and disappeared leaving only the stumps where they had been. The door at the foot was kept padlocked with a very heavy lock, but Dennis noticed that one of the lower windows, about six feet from the ground, had been broken. It didn't take him long to find a nearby stick to knock out the remaining fragments of glass.

"If'n I stand on yur back Billie, I can prob'ly get in thar," said Dennis. Billie protested that he was more interested in going home to tea, but as usual his argument carried little or no weight with Dennis. "Bend over and I'll cloim on yur t'ur reach sill." Billie, as usual, obliged and a moment later Dennis hauled himself up through the broken window. His friend stood and watched as Dennis' backside and legs disappeared from his view over the ragged sill.

All was quiet for a few moments, then a rope was thrown out through the aperture, or at least one end of it was. Dennis' voice from inside stated that the other end was secure and that Billie should climb in and join him. Wary of Dennis' temper and wrath, Billie thought it best to comply with alacrity. After all, Billie had gone to all this trouble for him. Two minutes later found the boys both inside.

Several of the floorboards were broken. Cobwebs hung everywhere and there were rat holes evident in the planking of both walls and floor. A pile of dirty old sacks stood in one corner and in another an old empty petrol can. A few strangely new looking planks of timber were leaning against one wall. Propped up against them was a fairly new toolbox. Dennis opened it, surprised to find it wasn't locked. Inside were a hammer, chisel, screwdriver plus some screws and nails.

"Finders keepers," proclaimed Dennis.

"You will be a thief, Dennis, if you take those," argued Billie.

But then Dennis' attention transferred itself to the rickety stairway. One or two of the steps had vanished, but several still remained. Dragging himself up and across the gaps the old boards loudly creaking, he edged his way to the top. It took Billie a shade longer but he too managed the climb to the top floor. This was in no better state than the lower, and they could see the remains of the spindle and workings where the sails were connected to the internal mechanism. An old rusty crowbar lay on the floor and to their surprise, a gleaming steel cage with a padlock holding it together. The sunlight, through an upper window, reflected off the metal. The cage was empty but gave the appearance of being new.

Dennis trod warily between the broken floorboards. Then a commotion above them caused both boys to start with alarm, but it turned out to be nothing more than a wood pigeon obviously disturbed by their entry. It flew out through a gaping hole in the roof accompanied by a flurry of feathers. It was then that Dennis made his real discovery, an old chest stowed away behind some wooden beer crates. It was padlocked and the lock was obviously new.

"The crowbar, quick Billie," commanded Dennis. Billie looked anxious, but picked it up and handed it to Dennis.

"Somebody might know it's us. I shouldn't, Dennis," he pleaded.

"Rubbish man, this ol' thing aint no use t'nobody." So saying, Dennis rammed the crowbar through the U bend of the padlock and levered with all his strength. "Don't just stan' thar Billie. 'Elp me wi' this 'un."

The combined weight of both lads on the heavy crowbar succeeded in jemmying the lock. It went with a large metallic twanging sound. In a shake Dennis had the lock off and opened the chest slowly. All they could see at first was a mass of black cloth. Dennis knelt down and rummaged with his hands beneath. Then he began to extract the black cotton material from the chest. It wasn't one but several black cloaks or gowns. Beneath these were as many black hoods with eyeholes cut into them.

"Wonder who these belong to?" queried Billie.

"Local drama group, I 'spect ... Yer know that ol' woman runs the village shop, she runs drama group, too."

"You mean Mrs. Durham ... She's not old. She's the same age as my mum." Dennis broke off from examining the contents of the chest and looked up at Billie.

"Well, so wot ... Yer mum ain't young, is she?"

Billie added, "Well, I can't see Mrs. Durham coming up here to this old windmill with a trunk full of clothes."

"Naw, now yer comes to mention it, naw can I." Dennis went back to foraging in the chest. "Cor, look at this!" he exclaimed, extracting a large curved knife with a jewelled handle. "I bagsy this."

"Don't be daft Dennis. You go flashing that thing around the village and somebody is sure to recognise it." Dennis looked thoughtful and replaced the fierce looking blade back in the chest. He stowed the other garments back on top of it.

"We'll keep it 'ere and get it out w'en we needs it, eh Billie?"

"Best you do Dennis, or your dad'll thump you if he finds you with it. Let's get home to tea. I'm jolly hungry."

"S'al yer ever think aboot, yer tummy Billie. S'no wonder yer fat."

"I'm not fat. My mum says I'm just well covered," exclaimed Billie indignantly.

"She's old, your mum. Jes' loike Mrs. Durham at the shop," said Dennis. The two boys left the windmill by the same way they had

Saddlewitch

entered and continued on through the village still arguing. They split up when they came to Dennis' house, four up from Billie's.

Dennis' mother was standing at the door waiting for him. One look at her face and the arms folded across her ample chest told Dennis he was in for it.

"Wot yer been up ter, boy," she growled as he came up the garden path.

"Nuthin' ma. . Just playin' round wif Billie, loike."

"O'il gi' thee playin' round wi' Billie. Oi've 'ad farmer Steel round 'ere only 'arf 'our ago. Sez yer bin spying on his gel Rachel on 'is private property. Wot yer got tur say fer yerself, 'eh?"

By this time Dennis had reached the front door, and was well within reach of Jean Madely's backhander. His evasive action was too late and he caught a stinging slap across the face.

Cowering back against the door frame he countered with, "It twern't me, ma."

"The 'el it twern't, yer lying little sod … Yer jest wait 'til yer father gits 'ome … E'll tan the 'ide off yer." Dennis tried again to lie his way out of trouble, to no avail. "Git off upstairs ter yer room. Yer needn't think yer gonna get any tea today, boy."

Dennis knew far better than to argue further. He trailed off upstairs to search for some cardboard. Four houses along the street Billie was receiving a more refined version of the same thing, his mother having the advantage of a better education.

"I've told you before Billie about playing with that Madely boy. That family can't even speak the Queen's English. First thing tomorrow morning you're going round to Rangeway Farm and apologise to Mr. Steel and his daughter. You will be lucky if they don't prosecute you or us … I don't know what your father will say when he gets home? Brought shame on the whole family, you have … Now get to your room, Billie."

Billie trailed off upstairs without another word.

CHAPTER SIX

Two interminably long weeks dragged by for Sasha, and July gave way to August. The weather continued hot and dry. The harvest this year was early, due to the fine weather and the combines were very busy reaping the barley and wheat in the fields to the rear of the Paget household.

Although her ankle had only turned out to be badly sprained and the daily ice packs had helped she was only just beginning to walk again without a limp. Unable to do much, she had spent most of the time reading and sunbathing in the garden, enhancing an already golden tan. She hadn't seen a great deal of Bart. Some nights he hadn't even returned home and when he had come home for dinner he had gone out again soon after. Still, at least she had to admit to herself he had arranged for a woman from the village to come in and clean three times a week and help with the children.

The biggest surprise had been the additional arrival of an au pair. Without ever having discussed it with Sasha, Bart had arranged for a Swedish girl to come and live in. She had arrived in the second week of Sasha's incapacity. Her name was Olga. She was nineteen, fair and very pretty and most of all easy to get along with. When Sasha had taken Bart aside and remonstrated with him for bringing the girl in without consulting her, he had simply shrugged his shoulders and turned his palms upwards.

Infuriated, Sasha enquired just how he had managed the paper work involved, without her signature. Not even blinking, he had looked straight at her and told her that he had forged her signature on the forms. She was doubly furious, but he had intimated that she should be glad of the extra help.

Like many women, she thought at first that perhaps there was a sexual involvement between the two, but soon realised this was not so. Bart hardly took any notice of the girl at all. Sasha felt quite ashamed when she found that she didn't care in the least if he had.

It was then, probably for the first time, that she accepted she felt nothing for Bart. In fact, if he had run off with somebody she would have been relieved.

Saddlewitch

Several times her mind had wandered to Drew Thorpe. She remembered his thoughtfulness and kindness, so alien from Bart. She had looked him up in the telephone book thinking that she would ring up and thank him properly. Alas he was not listed. She had rung enquiries but they had been unable to help. She mentioned it to the cleaning woman, Carol Bannerman, who was married and had lived in the village for some years. Carol said yes, she had seen the man, and she believed he was renting Briar Cottage.

"Yes, that's right," exclaimed Sasha. "Would you take a thank you note round for me, Carol?" To her surprise Carol had looked embarrassed and muttered something about it being out of her way. This was surprising as normally she found the woman most obliging. "I'll pay you, Carol."

"No, it's not that, Mrs. Paget. I don't want to get involved."

"Come on, it's only a thank you letter I'm asking you to take."

"I'd rather not, if you don't mind." Sasha was cross, but there was no way she could have driven or walked herself and she was even more furious when Carol followed this last remark with, "That would be the young man who called the day after your accident to enquire how you were, would it?"

"That's right – Drew Thorpe," replied Sasha excitedly.

"Oh well, Mr. Paget answered the door to him. Told him, we didn't want his sort round here and it was no business of his. If he saw him again he'd have the police onto him and prosecute." Sasha could hardly believe here ears.

"What!" she yelled.

Carol went on, "Said on no account was I to let Mr. Thorpe in, and if he ever came round again to let Mr. Paget know if he was even near the place."

"The swine! I can't believe it."

"Who? Mr. Thorpe?"

"No, my goddamed husband." Carol looked sympathetic but wasn't going to budge, so Sasha hadn't pressed her further. The woman was clearly frightened stiff of Bart.

In the end, she wrote a note and addressed it to Drew at Briar Cottage. When Strimmer the postman called with the morning mail she asked him to post it for her. Unknown to her it had been one of the mornings when Bart had been home. He had met Strimmer on the way out, having seen Sasha hand the note to him at the front door. Quickly Bart had headed the postman off, intercepting him in the road, behind the high front hedge surrounding the property. Sasha, at the front of the house, hadn't seen a thing. Putting on his most affable manner Bart had approached Strimmer, as he was about to cycle off.

"Hi there, postman. I think my wife just gave you a letter to deliver."

"Yus sir, that's right. Ter 'im at Briar Cottage," replied Strimmer innocently.

"Oh well, I'll save you the trouble because I'm gong there myself now … if you like to give it to me."

"I don't mind delivering it, sir. Your wife has stamped it anyway."

"No, that's quite all right postman. You give it to me and I'll take it myself." Strimmer mopped his red face with his handkerchief and propped his bicycle against the fence, which ran along the lower part of the high hedge. He fumbled about in his inside pocket and finally produced the envelope.

"Here it is, sir."

"Thank you postman." Bart stuffed the letter into his jacket pocket and Strimmer didn't see the sly smile on his face, as he rode off in the direction of the war memorial.

Sasha, of course, knew nothing of this and assumed that Drew would have had her letter. She had hoped that he would reply, but realised that due to the reception her husband had given him, on two occasions, it was no wonder that he had decided discretion the better part of valour.

She had thought of Drew often over the last two weeks, and couldn't seem to put him out of her mind. She was being silly, she knew. He was obviously the type who would have done what he did, for anyone in trouble.

Now her ankle felt better. True it still ached a bit, but the swelling had gone, and it looked quite normal. This very afternoon she would go and call on Drew and thank him personally. That was the least she could do, she decided.

Why was her heart beating faster at the thought of seeing him again? Once she had made her mind up to go, she went upstairs and put on a little yellow dress that enhanced her now perfect tan. Carefully she applied her makeup and did her hair with infinite care. She would take Bess for a walk to the post office and go on from there. It would give her an excuse to call. Why did she need an excuse she told herself? This was ridiculous. What if he was not in? Her heart sank at the thought.

She told Olga the au pair that she wouldn't be more than an hour and to give the children their tea if she wasn't back. Foolishly she had put on black high heel shoes. Within a few steps, she realised she shouldn't have been so vain, her ankle hurt again. He had only seen her in old jeans and a torn tee shirt, and she didn't want him to remember her like that. Fortunately, Bess walked to heel on the lead otherwise she couldn't have managed. She gritted her teeth against the aching ankle and kept on going. She called at the post office and had a chat with Dorothy Sheriden, the postmistress. Dorothy said she had heard about the accident and how glad she was that Sasha was better. Sasha thanked her, bought some stamps and envelopes and left.

As she neared Briar Cottage she felt her pulse quicken and quite forgot her ankle. There was no outward sign of life. The cottage was a pretty thatched one, and was well named. Several varieties of roses flourished in the small front garden, whilst others bloomed on trellis affixed to the white plaster walls. The windows were of the old lead latticework type. In suspense Sasha walked as boldly as she could up the little paved path to the front door. She grasped the handle, which was in the shape of a lion's head and knocked on the door. Sasha almost startled herself by the hollow noise that resulted as the knocker met the woodwork. No-one came to answer, perhaps he wasn't in. She knocked again, and waited a further minute. Disappointed, she turned away and retraced her steps down the garden path.

Just at that moment a small silver sports car, a Mazda, she thought, drew up by the gate. The engine was switched off and the driver got out. It was Drew Thorpe. They both saw one another at the same instant. Sasha's hand was still on the gate latch.

"Hi there ... I see you've recovered." His eyes went down to her ankle.

"Yes, I came round to thank you and to apologise for my husband's rudeness to you ... It was unforgivable."

"Think nothing of it Sasha ... Wasn't your fault. You're not his keeper, are you."

"No, but he sometimes thinks he's mine." She felt herself blushing at Drew's use of her name. He had remembered!

"I came round to call the next day, but I'm afraid I didn't get further than your driveway ... What's his problem anyway?"

Sasha looked embarrassed.

"Yes, our 'daily' Carol told me you had called; that's why I wrote to you apologising."

"You did? Well, I never got the letter. Did you post it?"

"No, I gave it to Strimmer the postman to give to you by hand."

"Well I never got it," explained Drew.

"I'm not surprised really, poor old Strimmer is past it. Should have retired years ago. Probably had one drink too many at the Black Bull and clean forgot about it." Sasha laughed. "There was a story going round the village last Christmas, that he had been found with his bike, dead in a ditch. Turned out he was only dead drunk. Most people had offered him a Christmas drink and old Strimmer never could refuse one ... Bit like George Fenning the local bobby," Sasha added.

Both laughed spontaneously and Drew followed this by saying, "Yes, I've made the acquaintance of the constable."

"Bet he caught you with that trick sign at the Black Bull. He catches every stranger to Saddlewitch with that one," quipped Sasha. Drew laughed again. Sasha liked the way his eyes lit up when he laughed.

Saddlewitch

"There's one born every minute, they say. I'm one of them … a real sucker."

"Well you will have the consolation that there was an awful lot of people that fell for the same trick before you came along."

Drew cut in, changing the subject.

"Look, let's not stand here. Come in and have a cup of coffee or tea." Sasha smiled and looked up and down the road, the only person about was Jake Cutter the local gardener. He was working in the garden of the house opposite, but she could see he was taking more than a lively interest in Drew and her.

"Well, yes, I'd love to, but this is a village, you know. Do you mind being talked about?" She nodded her head towards where Jake was leaning on his spade. "Old Jake's the prize gossip in Saddlewitch. Some people reckon you don't need a local newspaper. What Jake doesn't know he makes up, they say."

Drew smiled.

"Well, I don't mind if you don't. I may not be living here that long." He led her up to the front door, foraged in his pocket for some keys and opened it. Stepping back he waved Sasha in. When the door closed behind them she saw that they were in a small hallway, with doors leading off. There was a small table with a red telephone on it and some old Constable reproductions on the walls. He ushered her into the lounge and invited her to sit down, then enquired whether she wanted coffee or tea, or possibly something stronger.

"No, coffee will be fine," she confirmed. When he left to prepare it she took stock of the room. Mostly old fashioned furniture typical of an old rented country cottage. The sofa she was sitting on matched a couple of paisley armchairs. An old walnut sideboard and bureau completed the furniture, apart from a coffee table. The carpet was rust coloured and had seen better days, slightly threadbare near the door where numerous feet must have trodden on over the years. On the walls were more old Constable paintings.

"Only instant, I'm afraid," said Drew, setting down two steaming mugs of coffee on the coffee table. He went out of the room and returned with a sugar dish and some biscuits on a plate. "Sugar?" he enquired.

"No thanks, this will be fine." Drew helped himself to some and stirred it into his coffee. Without taking his eyes off Sasha he sat down beside her on the sofa.

"So, you're really okay now ... Your ankle I mean?"

"More or less. Aches a bit sometimes, but I suppose that's only to be expected," she replied. He nodded.

"Help yourself to biscuits."

"No thanks, I'm on a diet." Drew's eyes travelled up and down her and Sasha felt herself blushing.

"Rubbish! You look absolutely great to me. Not a spare inch on you."

Sasha was about to say, 'not if you saw me without clothes on' but simply said, "Thanks for the compliment."

Sasha felt very relaxed in Drew's company and they went on to discuss the accident and how much worse it might have been. All this time Bess, Sasha's retriever, lay curled up at Sasha's feet. She remembered Drew's Alsatian Caliph, and asked him where the dog was. He explained that he was going away for the weekend and had just come back from taking Caliph to the local kennels.

"You said that you might not be living here in Saddlewitch very long, Drew?"

"That's right. I only rent the place on a short lease," he replied. Sasha didn't know why, but she experienced an empty feeling, a kind of numbness.

"Is it your work that brings you to Saddlewitch?"

"Sort of." For the first time Drew looked slightly uneasy.

"What do you do? I think you did tell me but it must have slipped my mind," she prompted.

"I don't think I did ... but I'm a journalist." The last bit of the sentence came too suddenly. In spite of several questions, Sasha always found that he seemed to be able to switch the conversation back to her and her husband. She decided that he must have been running away from something. A wife perhaps, or the law. Whatever it was she would have liked to tell him she was on his side.

Gradually, without her really realising it, he had dragged out of her the details of her unhappy marriage.

"This Bart sounds a perfect swine to me," he said. "Why don't you leave him?" Strangely, Sasha found herself trying to exonerate Bart.

"He wasn't always like he is now. Once he was as steady and good as any husband."

"When did you first notice this change in him?" Drew prompted.

"Over about the last two years. Now things are so bad I would leave him, but for the children and the fact that I've nowhere to go and no money."

"Haven't you got any friends that would take you in?"

"No, Bart has been so horrible to them all that nobody comes near anymore."

Saying all this to Drew brought back the reality of her circumstances and without meaning to, she found herself crying, the unhappiness within her boiling over. Putting his coffee cup on the table he put his arm around her shoulders and drew her head onto his chest.

"Come on, love, let it all out … You can't go on like this, you know. We have to do something about all this," he said trying to comfort Sasha.

That word, we, seemed to give her hope. Suddenly she didn't feel so alone. She looked up at him through tear filled eyes.

"You said, we," she murmured.

"It's about time you had a friend … Come here and talk to me whenever you want to."

"I'm sorry, I've burdened you with all this Drew. It's terrible of me, but I just had to talk to somebody," she blurted out between sobs, "and you've probably got your own troubles anyway." Gradually Sasha began to compose herself. Eventually she just had to ask, "When are you leaving Saddlewitch?" She wanted to ask if he had a wife or steady girlfriend but found it difficult, not wanting to seem too pushy. After all she hardly knew him.

"That will depend on the outcome of my work," he answered.

"Do you write novels or something like that," Sasha prompted.

"No, nothing like that," Drew said, briefly. She plainly wasn't going to get anywhere with this line of questioning. She realised that time was getting on. She would have to get back for the children. It was Olga's night off and there was no telling whether Bart would come home or not. She explained the position to Drew, who was sympathetic.

Showing her to the door, he gave her a little kiss on the cheek.

His parting words were, "Anytime you want to talk, just pop in. If I'm not here, leave a note saying what time you're coming back, and I promise to be here for you. In the meantime remake that appointment with the solicitor and see what the legal position is concerning a separation or divorce. Might help if you bounced some of your problems off on that vicar chap, Mark Glenville ... He seems a good egg."

As Sasha walked back with Bess at her heel, towards home, she felt for the first time in weeks both a sense of comfort and hope. Then she smiled to herself. She still knew no more about mystery man Drew Thorpe than anyone else in the village.

★ ★ ★ ★ ★

The following morning the Reverend Mark Glenville had his own problems. He had just finished breakfast when there was a ring of the doorbell. Answering it, he was surprised to find constable George Fenning looking rather bleary-eyed from last night's drinking bout.

"Good morning, constable. Can I help you?" George had put on his most serious and mournful face.

He replied, "I think you had better accompany me to the churchyard vicar. There's something I think you ought to see." Mark's wife, Mary, came scampering down the stairs to see who the early caller could be.

"Whatever's the trouble, constable Fenning?" she enquired.

"Strange going on down there last night apparently, Mrs. Glenville. I think your husband should come and see what's happened before I say any more." Mary looked at Mark, both equally puzzled.

"I'll come with you, darling." Together with constable Fenning they took the short walk up the hill to the church. Once in the churchyard both Mark and Mary gasped in amazement. "Who could have done this terrible thing?" Mary exclaimed.

The sight that met their eyes was indeed horrific. Several headless chickens were laying on some of the oldest gravestones and the blood from them had been daubed onto the granite headstones. On one of them was an upside down cross. Mark peered down at the carnage. George awaited his response.

"Children, do you think, Mark?" enquired a worried Mary.

"No way ... . Satanists did this," he exclaimed, turning back to face George. "Have you reported this, constable?"

"Yes," replied George. "Got on to Grantfield HQ just as soon as old Gudgeon reported it to me. They are sending someone down this morning to investigate."

"I'll get some hot soapy water and clean this mess up, Mark," said Mary.

"No ma'am, you won't. I'm sorry to say we must wait for the man from HQ. He should be here soon."

"As if we haven't enough trouble already without this happening," Mark whispered to his wife.

CHAPTER SEVEN

Not more than fifteen minutes had elapsed during which the vicar, his wife and constable Fenning had discussed the strange happenings, whilst being forced to witness the grisly spectacle. Mark and Mary were dying to get on with the cleaning up process but George Fenning would have none of it.

"I've been told it's a Special Branch job and we have to wait here for them."

"Oh dear, someone's coming," whispered Mary, jerking her head to the churchyard path from the road.

"What do we do if they see this, constable?" asked Mark.

"Nothing we can do, sir ... Can't stop them walking through the churchyard. The couple, for couple it was, were nearly up to them now. It was a young man and woman.

"It's the young man from Briar Cottage. Who's the blonde girl with him?" whispered Mary to Mark. The pair came on purposely straight up to them. The young man addressed all three, looking at each in turn and then at the grim surroundings.

"Last night, was it?"

George Fenning glared at him and said firmly, "Mr. Thorpe isn't it? I met you the other night, didn't I?" Drew nodded. George went on, "Well, sir, I must ask you to say nothing of this. We don't want to alarm the village folk ... The young lady, too," he said, looking at the blonde. He noticed she was carrying a camera and added, "I hope you aren't thinking of taking pictures miss. I couldn't allow that."

Drew smiled, producing a plastic card from his inside pocket. He handed it to George Fenning saying "That is exactly what Caroline, WPC Channing will be doing, officer." George, having read the card, handed it back to Drew with an apology.

"Beg pardon, sir." He turned back to Mark and Mary explaining, "This is Detective Sergeant Thorpe from Special Branch." Drew shook hands with both of them and introduced Caroline properly to the vicar and his wife. George gave Drew one of his most mournful looks, his bottom lip coming over the top and eyebrows drawing together. "I did wonder why you were asking all those questions in the Black Bull the other night, sir."

"Well now you know, constable and I must ask you all to keep 'stumm' about it. This is exactly what I'm in Saddlewitch for, working undercover. I hadn't intended to blow my cover this early but it looks as if they have forced my hand."

"But who are they? Who would do such a terrible thing, here?" cut in Mary.

"Not just here, ma'am. I'm afraid they are in several of the villages round these parts." Drew angled his head towards Caroline. "WPC Channing is living under cover in the next village, Endersby … The same thing happened there last week." Caroline nodded, as if in confirmation as all eyes turned on her. Mark addressed Drew, a grave expression on his face.

"For Special Branch to be dealing with this, I gather that this is very serious and not just a one-off then, Mr. Thorpe? I mean for them to send you both under cover."

Drew nodded.

"I can assure you, sir, it's very serious indeed. At the moment they are only sacrificing chickens … but who knows what is going to come next."

Caroline put in, "The fear is that these Satanists are gradually building up to something big for All Hallows Eve."

"But that's three months away, surely … October thirty-first … Halloween," interjected Mary.

"I'm sorry sir," said Drew, addressing Mark, "but I can't say any more about that issue at the present time." Drew changed the subject quickly, Mark felt too quickly. Obviously the Special Branch man knew more than he was prepared to tell. "Now if you will all bear with us, Caroline is going to take some pictures then you can feel free to clear up this mess when she's finished. In fact, we will give you a hand." Looking round at the headless bloodied bodies of the chickens and the blood-stained gravestones, Drew added, "It looks as if you will need all the help you can get."

"Thank you officer, that's very kind of you both," said Mary. Caroline moved around, taking numerous photographs of the carcasses and then, kneeling on the grass, of the graves and headstones affected. In all, she completed a full roll of film.

"I think that does it," she confirmed.

"Right, let's get this mess cleared up then, vicar. Can you find some rubbish sacks for the carcasses and some scrubbing brushes or something?"

"There's some cleaning stuff in the vestry, which the church cleaner uses," replied Mark.

"Good man," said Drew.

"I'll go back and fetch some more brushes and some Flash from the vicarage," said Mary, hurrying off.

In fact, it took them to nearly lunchtime, all five of them working vigorously scrubbing at granite and marble. Some of the stones were badly ingrained and fought stubbornly against being cleaned, but finally something like normality was restored. Mary stood back and thanked everyone.

"I'd like to get my hands on the heathen so and so's," she exclaimed. Mark smiled to himself. He could picture redheaded Mary doing it too. She invited everyone back for a bit of lunch at the vicarage. "There's nothing special, but you are all welcome." George Fenning accepted with alacrity, but Drew graciously declined, saying that Caroline and he would have to return to Briar Cottage and compare notes.

"Also a report will have to go to HQ," he added. As they broke up to go their separate ways Drew took Mark aside. "Don't go into too much detail, vicar, but I think you can make mention of this during your sermon. No mention of us mind ... We must remain under cover. It might help though, to know if anybody saw any of this last night. If they did, ask them to come and see you afterwards. If you hear anything, let me know ... Okay?" Mark agreed and they parted.

* * * * *

Back at Briar Cottage Caroline stretched out on Drew's sofa in her stockinged feet, having kicked her shoes off. Drew was in the kitchen rustling up a makeshift lunch for them both. The two of them carried on a conversation from lounge to kitchen. Their relationship was not one of senior and junior, or boss and underling.

Caroline was, in fact, only a year younger than Drew. At thirty, she had been divorced two years earlier. The two had been firm friends ever since first joining the police force as cadets, broken only five years ago by Drew's promotion to Special Branch. Two years later Caroline had followed him there too, which probably accounted for her divorce after only two years of marriage. Her husband, Barry, simply couldn't cope with the pressures of her job, which she wouldn't give up on any account, in spite of the pressures he put upon her. They had, however, parted amicably although she didn't see much of Barry any more. Caroline had been quite pleased to hear that he had recently got engaged to someone called Hillary. She felt a release of guilt, having blamed herself for the break-up of their marriage.

She had not bothered with any more serious relationships since the break-up. True, she had gone out on a few dates. What young and attractive girl didn't? She spent a lot of time with Drew, whom she secretly idolised, but she knew he only regarded her as the sister he never had. These days, because of her job, she wore her once long blonde hair in a short modern style. She worked out regularly keeping herself in perfect physical condition. She had toned up a lot, building firm muscles and stamina since joining Special Branch.

Drew came back into the room carrying a tray. On it were two rounds of cheese and tomato sandwiches, some chocolate biscuits and two steaming cups of hot coffee.

"Ah, that's what I like to see ... A man working." Pulling her stockinged legs up to her chin, she clasped her hands round her knees, to make room on the sofa for Drew. He placed the tray on the coffee table and sat down next to her, noticing that her skirt, which had ridden up, gave him an entrancing view of the underside of her thighs and lace stocking tops.

He smiled and said, "I always did say you had the best legs at Police College."

Caroline laughed. "I always did say, if you've got 'em – show 'em!" but nevertheless she stretched out her long slender legs and placed them in Drew's lap. "God, my feet ache," she moaned.

"After all that work I'm not surprised," quipped Drew, taking each of her stockinged feet in his hands in turn and massaging them.

"Ooooh, that feels great. You can do that all afternoon."

Then, over a sandwich, the mood changed dramatically as they discussed recent developments and compared notes, from what had transpired in the two villages of Saddlewitch and Endersby. Caroline had been studying a documentary book on the occult and was a mine of information to the much more practicably minded Drew.

"Do you believe any of this stuff – seriously, I mean?" he enquired. Caroline's ice blue eyes looked past him into an unseen no man's land. She was deep in thought.

"I don't know … I don't exactly rule it out. I'm sure even the vicar here would tell you that there is a great power for good and another for evil."

"Well, these Satanists certainly take it seriously," interjected Drew, "and we have to stop them before they do more harm. Somewhere they must have a leader, or high priest, and we have to find him before they turn to something else, other than chickens."

"I agree, but how?" replied Caroline.

★ ★ ★ ★ ★

John Durham, genial, middle-aged and portly, turned to his wife Betty, who was in the process of closing the local grocery store for the night. He had been employed in making up the books to date, the last customers having left the premises.

"This is really weird, Betty," he said, turning the pages slowly and meticulously.

"What is, love?" she enquired, looking over the top of her spectacles.

"Boxes of face paints," he replied.

"Nothing funny about that. Children adore having their faces painted, don't they?"

"Well, yes," he exclaimed, "but it's the quantities of the stuff we appear to have sold, and there's even a note here to order more."

"Penny must have left the note for you. I didn't," ventured Betty. Penny was the young village girl who helped part time in the shop. John continued to look puzzled.

"I'm not disputing that, but surely kids don't paint their own faces … Isn't it usually done at fetes and carnivals, and by adults having a stall painting the kids faces?"

"Yes," said Betty, "they usually paint cats faces and the like on the kids, to raise money for charity. Why do you ask, John?"

"Just seems odd – the quantities we are selling … After all, the village fete here was back in May, nearly three months ago." Betty looked pensive.

"Now you come to mention it, t'would seem rather odd, but then perhaps the kids enjoyed it and are buying the stuff themselves." John Durham shrugged his broad shoulders.

"The three packets I sold were all to adults, as it happens."

"So what? Buying it for their kids or grandchildren, I expect," came back Betty's reply.

"One was Barbara Lake the bank manager's wife, another was her friend Sally Greves and neither has any children or grandchildren, to my knowledge," said John, stubbornly.

"Who was the other? I expect she was a parent?" put in Betty.

"No, perfect stranger … Never seen him before … Dark fellow, tall and sallow complexion." Now it was Betty's turn to look puzzled.

"Hmmm. I sold two packets myself, come to think of it … Both to adults, and both strangers."

"There you are then. It is very strange – at least I think it is. I must remember to ask Penny when she comes to work in the morning whether she has sold any."

"Why worry as long as it's good for business, which it is," exclaimed Betty.

"I'm not worried, just curious," John replied.

"You always were an old worrier," Betty laughed. By the morning, however, both had forgotten about it.

★ ★ ★ ★ ★

They might possibly have attached more significance to the phenomenon had they witnessed a happening later that night.

Barbara Lake and Sally Greves were both alibis for one another to their respective husbands. As far as their men folk knew they were going to a lingerie party and were going to stay over.

Barbara Lake, called for Sally in her BMW. Unbeknown to her husband Ted, she was known as the village man-eater. The two women, both in their late thirties, made up and dressed in their most glamorous attire, and drove to Endersby, the next village. It was quite dark when they arrived but Barbara had no difficulty locating the big old house on the outskirts of the village. She had been there twice before. The BMW entered at the large wrought iron gates and slowly wended its way up the long undulating and winding driveway.

By the time the two women arrived at the house, they could see several other cars had arrived and were parked to front and rear of the old Tudor house. The door was opened to the two women by a short, but powerfully built, black man. He looked them both up and down coldly and requested numbers.

Barbara replied, "666 – 21 and 22." The first being the password for the meeting, the latter numbers their respective identities. Ushering them in without addressing them, he summoned someone called Desiree.

A young fair-haired girl appeared and conveyed them to an upstairs room. No word was spoken. She simply opened the door allowing them to enter then disappearing, closing the door behind her. Barbara looked at the rows of assembled rails. Some had long white cotton gowns suspended on hangers; others revealed an assortment of women's clothing on them.

Both women knew the score and immediately began to disrobe completely.

Sally joked and said, "What was the point of having put all this make-up on and dressed so meticulously?"

Barbara laughed and said, "Well, it's usually worth it, afterwards, isn't it?" Giggling, both women arrayed themselves in long white gowns, leaving themselves totally nude beneath. Opening her make up case, Barbara produced make up remover and set to work on Sally's face. When all was achieved to satisfaction and her friend's face back to its natural form, the roles were reversed with Sally working on Barbara. A final face wash and the transformation began.

Sally was the more artistic and attended to both Barbara's and her own. Producing a tin of face paint, she reduced each of their faces to a deathly white. Then, with black and red colours, she attended to lips and eyes. The end result was two daughters fit for a vampire. A last look in the full length mirror and they were ready. As they left the room, two more women passed them in the doorway, one tall and slender of about their own age, the other younger and chubbier, with a face quite pixie-like in appearance.

Barbara and Sally, in their long white diaphanous robes, glided down the wide double banister stairway. Awaiting them at the bottom stair was the solemn and dismal faced black man. He led the two women into a large hallway. The spacious chamber was dimly lit and they could just about make out several shrouded figures, but not clearly enough to identify anyone. Dirge-like piped music was playing and seemed to envelope the room in an air of expectancy.

As their eyes began to accustom to the light, or lack of it, they could see that several of the women were dressed as they themselves were. Other figures dressed all in black robes wore hoods and were obviously male.

Five minutes later, after several more people of both sexes had funnelled in behind them, the doors were shut. A strange aura seemed to descend on the gathering and somewhere above them a blue ethereal light glowed in the ceiling. The music faded to almost nothing, and a black velvet curtain became visible at the far end of the room.

At the base of the dark curtain, and in front of them, orange and red flames glowed, powered by small hidden gas jets.

Quite suddenly, the curtains slid back to reveal a hooded figure, dressed in red from the top of his head to his toes. The whole assembly let out a gasp of expectancy. The red hood was almost half as large again as the body. The reason became apparent when, with a slow movement, it was lifted and withdrawn to reveal a horned goat's head. A booming voice from within the animal's skull addressed the gathering. Barbara felt her flesh tingle, and she felt Sally's hand searching for hers.

"All you who are entered here, bear homage to me, the great disciple of Satan. I am the great goat of Mendoza." Behind the figure the flickering flames illuminated a massive star shaped design, its outline further lit by a cold blue light.

The goat, or unknown figure, continued to chant, this time in Latin. The two women, quite unable to understand the dialect, stood like the remainder, transfixed.

★ ★ ★ ★ ★

Concealed on a balcony above, an interloper watched the ceremony with baited breath, hardly daring to breath in case he gave himself away. Ray Grainger, hired by Ted Lake to check upon his wife, had followed Barbara and Sally to Endersby. Ray's usual occupation as a private detective concerned divorce, but this was something else again. He had crept in a back way and hidden before the ceremony had commenced.

A sixth sense now told him, that should he be discovered, things would not go well for him. On tailing the two women, he had expected the culmination to be a clandestine meeting, nothing like this wild happening below him. The goat figure had ceased speaking and wild abandoned music, with a backcloth of drums, had filled the whole chamber. The black and white figures below began pairing off and an orgy such as he had never witnessed was enacted beneath him.

In the gloom he couldn't make out Barbara or Sally. Everyone looked the same from his position up above them all. Nothing for it

Saddlewitch

but to wait until the gathering broke up. Perhaps then he could creep out undetected.

Little did he realise how long he would have to wait. The pale light of dawn was filtering in when the last couple left the arena. Of the goat like figure there was no sign. Ray made good his escape. On his way out he noticed Barbara's BMW had gone.

Gunning the engine of his old Ford into life, Ray smiled to himself. He knew just what to do now. After all he had never been bothered by scruples in his line of work. If a chance to make more money came his way, then he didn't see why he shouldn't take it.

CHAPTER EIGHT

Sasha, her ankle almost restored to normal, faced up to life in a more optimistic frame of mind. Talking to Drew had undoubtedly helped her. What was it people said? A trouble shared is a trouble halved. Bart's disposition, however, seemed to worsen, rather than to improve. He wasn't around the house very often and Sasha had to confess to herself her appreciation of his frequent absences. She found Olga the young Swedish au pair easy to get along with. The two of them instantly seemed to strike up a mutual rapport. The girls simply adored Olga which gave Sasha more free time to pursue her hobby of painting with watercolours.

Twice during the next two weeks she had accepted Drew's invitation to call on him. "After all," he had joked, "I can't come and see you, can I? Might stop a bullet for my pains, if you husband happens to be in." Sasha had agreed that it was obviously better that way. She would have liked to have seen more of Drew but didn't want to appear too eager or too pushy.

Sasha admitted to herself that she not only liked him immensely, but also felt very physically attracted to him too. So far he had made no move on her, other than to provide an ear to listen and a shoulder to lean on. Drew gave every indication of being relaxed with her, but the nagging doubt remained with Sasha, that perhaps he just felt sorry and was indulging her. She realised too, that in spite of their long conversations she still knew little or nothing about the man. He had said he was a journalist, but when she had been at Briar Cottage with him, she hadn't seen any evidence of this occupation.

Maybe he was just a tidy soul and didn't leave things lying around. One thing for sure, Sasha knew she had no right to probe further concerning his presence at Briar Cottage.

Then, one day, about a month later in early September, Sasha set out to call on him. She had left it for over a fortnight since her last visit and hoped Drew would have missed her.

Sasha packed a wicker basket with tomatoes and apples from her garden and some local blackberries she had picked in the woods, when out with Bess. The bitch was with her now, trotting obediently to heel. The animal seemed to enjoy seeing Caliph, Drew's dog, almost as much as Sasha enjoyed seeing Drew.

Her hand reached for the latch of the gate to Briar Cottage and instantly froze upon it. Drew was standing on the top step by the front door, only he wasn't alone. His arms were round an attractive blonde girl who was gazing up into his eyes. Neither was aware of Sasha's presence, as they seemed to be having a meaningful conversation.

Sasha's heart froze, her hand seemed locked to the latch of the gate. The moment was broken when Caliph burst past the pair at the front door and rushed down the path, tail wagging to greet Bess. Drew saw Sasha, then called out, "Hi, Sasha, nice to see you ... I wondered where you had got to lately."

The blonde girl turned and looked at her. Sasha could feel the girl, who looked about the same age, taking stock of her. Suspicion seemed to cloud the blonde's eyes, as she turned her gaze back to Drew, a question clearly written there. Drew released his hold on the girl's waist and beckoned a stunned Sasha forward, saying, "Caroline, meet Sasha ... Sasha, meet Caroline."

A feeling that Sasha had never experienced before assailed her. She knew she had no right to feel jealous. Obviously this attractive girl was a girlfriend, or worse, his wife. The thought hit her like a sledgehammer. The pair were obviously totally relaxed in one another's company. Hardly conscious of her legs moving, she forced herself to approach and held out her right hand to the girl.

"Pleased to meet you, Caroline," she found herself going through the motion of saying.

"Likewise Sasha," replied Caroline, responding with a firm handshake. A few inane pleasantries were then exchanged between the three before Caroline declared, "Well I must be on my way Drew. See you tomorrow."

"See you," Drew responded and waved as Caroline exited down the path. Turning to Sasha, he said, "Come in. This is a pleasant surprise."

Once inside Sasha said, "I hope I'm not interrupting anything?" Handing him the basket she added, "I brought you a few things from the garden ... Nothing much." Drew looked in the basket and slowly unpacked it.

"This is lovely, but you shouldn't have ... What would your husband say if he knew you were giving me vegetables and fruit from his garden?" Sasha looked indignant.

"It's not his garden, it's mine ... I do the gardening, apart from what the gardener does." Suddenly she felt ill at ease and like an intruder. Even the tone of her last remark was not the way she had meant it to come out. The surprise at seeing the blonde had clearly rattled her. Sasha struggled to remain coolly in control. She went on to say how she thought he might like the produce as there didn't seem to be any in the garden at Briar Cottage. "I could make you a blackberry and apple pie next time I'm passing," she ventured.

"Yum! That would be great. My favourite, but thanks for these anyway." Sasha was dying to probe about Caroline's relationship with Drew, but half of her didn't want to hear the answer.

Unable to contain herself further, she blurted out, "Caroline is a very attractive girl. Does she live in the village?"

"Yes to the first part ... . No to the second," Drew replied with a smile. It was obvious he wasn't going to elaborate further, so Sasha tried again.

"Have you known her long?"

"Oh simply ages ... She's always been around." This told Sasha nothing. Although she was champing at the bit to question him further, she sensed that it was wise to back off. "Sit down, I'll make you a coffee," he said and went into the kitchen.

Damn the coffee! Sasha was desperate to know all about the attractive Caroline. When he returned the questions turned on her once more.

Sitting down with his cup he enquired, "How's life with that bully of a husband these days? Any better Sasha?"

"It sounds awful, but he's not around much and I can't say I'm not glad ... Debbie and Annabel are happier too."

Saddlewitch 67

"Why don't you bring them next time. I'd love to see them. Five and three and a half, I think you said they were." Sasha responded to the warmth and interest in his voice.

"How clever of you to remember," she smiled.

"Why wouldn't I? You have a lovely smile," he said laughing.

"Like Caroline, you mean?" She realised she shouldn't have said it, but there it was, and she had, and she didn't care. She simply had to know about the girl's relationship with Drew and couldn't contain herself any longer.

Drew didn't show any anger at her probing, but smiling said, "Yes, Caroline is attractive, isn't she?" Sasha didn't quite know how to follow this. She simply made an inane remark about Caroline having beautiful legs. Drew remarked quite objectively, "Yes, most people seem to notice that about her ... They are rather good, aren't they?" Then, looking directly at Sasha he remarked, "Almost as good as yours, in fact."

Sasha blushed and attempted to pull the hem of her skirt towards her knees. Drew saw the gesture and burst out laughing.

"Caroline and I are old friends. We have been friends since college days. She's divorced and is living in the next village at the moment ... We meet up quite often ... There – does that satisfy you?" Sasha blushed, deeply embarrassed.

"I'm sorry, I shouldn't pry, should I?"

"On the contrary Sasha, I'm flattered. You look even lovelier blushing like that." Leaning across, he caressed her face with the back of two fingers. A gesture that made Sasha feel she was glowing all over. Their eyes met and held a moment too long. Sasha knew that if he made a move on her now she doubted she would be able to resist.

"Don't be idiotic," she told herself. "You are a married woman with two children, not a silly schoolgirl and you are behaving like one." Drew leaned over towards her, his eyes on her lips; her eyes were locked on his. This was the moment when their feelings could no longer be contained; but a knock at the door broke their intimacy. Both she and Drew straightened up and looked towards the door.

"I guess I'll have to answer that," he said, rising. Walking to the door, he opened it to reveal Caroline standing there, a serious look on her face.

"Sorry if I'm interrupting anything important, but something has just come up that we need to discuss urgently, Drew."

"But you only left a quarter of an hour ago, Caroline," replied Drew, obviously amazed at her quick return.

"Yes, I know. I was driving back to Endersby when this information came in on my mobile. I turned round and raced back here, post haste," said Caroline, looking pointedly at the seated Sasha. For the first time Sasha saw that Drew looked somewhat rattled and more than a little embarrassed. He turned to face her.

"Sorry Sasha, but I'll have to ask you to leave us … Come and see me tomorrow, eh?"

Sasha didn't know what to think. Had he been stringing her along and not telling her the truth about his and Caroline's relationship? All she could think of now was, well – he's shoving me out for her. In a dignified fashion, she rose to her feet.

"You will come back tomorrow, Sasha, won't you?" he exclaimed, looking agitated.

"Maybe," Sasha found herself saying. All the way through the village she kept asking herself the same questions. So preoccupied was she that she hardly noticed when Tom Bridges the publican at the Black Bull called a cheery greeting to her. By the time she arrived home she had convinced herself that not on any account would she call on Drew Thorpe tomorrow. Even Olga the au pair noticed that she seemed depressed, and offered to make her a cup of tea, an English 'cure-all'.

When she went to bed that night, she felt cross with herself. After all, she had a lot more to be thankful for than poor Olga, who had already told her that she had no family alive at all. At least she, Sasha, had the kids.

She looked in upon them. Both were sleeping peacefully, deep in untroubled repose the way only children can. She brushed a lock of hair away from Annabel's eyes and bent down and kissed her on the forehead. She undressed, took a shower, pulled a nightie over her head and slipped under the duvet. Sleep didn't come easily. She twisted and turned well into the early hours. She heard Bart come in about two. He came into the bedroom, undressed and slipped under the cover with her. Sasha pretended to be asleep. It must have helped. Shortly after that she was.

Several times the following day she thought about going to see Drew, but convinced herself not to. Bart stayed at home and was in a particularly bad mood constantly trying to pick arguments with her, so it would have been difficult to get away without a good reason, anyway. The next day was Olga's day off, and by the day after that she felt too self-conscious to return to Briar Cottage, not knowing how to handle the situation.

* * * * *

In fact, after she had left Drew with Caroline at Briar Cottage, she would have been surprised at their conversation. It appeared that the local constable at Endersby, who knew that Caroline was working under cover, had telephoned saying a local man had been seen in the churchyard there, behaving strangely. Apparently laying on top of one of the old granite vaults dating back to the last century. When questioned by the constable, he had said he was communing with the dead.

"Sounds more like Necromancy than Satanism," suggested Drew.

"Well, that's as maybe, but I said we would go and see the constable. He has the man's name and address, but he wouldn't tell me over the 'phone. I wondered if you would come with me now, then after we've seen him we could go on and interview this other chap ... . What do you think, Drew?" Drew looked thoughtful and when he didn't instantly reply, Caroline said, "Or perhaps you would rather go chasing after that brunette. What did you say her name was?" Drew couldn't help picking up the note of animosity in Caroline's tone.

"Her name is Sasha Paget," he said, matter of factly.

"Hmmm! I see she has a wedding ring on her finger," said Caroline, pointedly.

"So — what of it? Just what are you implying, Caroline?"

"Nothing," said Caroline, softening her tone. "I just wouldn't want to see you jeopardising your career and getting involved with a married woman here in the village."

"Who said anything about me getting involved?" snapped Drew.

"We shouldn't forget that we are under cover here, and we have a job to do ... Neither of us can afford attachments," Caroline pointed out. Drew's hackles rose.

"I don't need you, Caroline, to remind me of my duty and I would remind you that I am senior to you and call the tune here."

"She's getting under your skin, I can see that. This Sasha girl, I mean," Caroline jabbed away further.

"If she was, which she isn't, it's no damn business of yours Caroline," snapped Drew. "I'm quite capable of knowing where my duties lie." Caroline switched her attack; moving in close, she put her arms round Drew.

"It's only because you're my friend and I'm very fond of you, Drew. I wouldn't want to see you make a fool of yourself ... Really I wouldn't. I mean, she's very attractive, and ......" her voice tailed off.

Drew, recovering his temper, never being able to bear malice for long, gave Caroline a playful slap on her curvaceous rear and with a meaningful look, said, "I think you're jealous."

"No, just looking after my friend's interest. You are my best friend, you know, number one and all that."

"It's rude to number people ... Come on, let's get off to Endersby and see this constable bloke," quipped Drew. With his arm round Caroline's shoulders, the pair left the cottage to locate Drew's car.

★ ★ ★ ★ ★

Ray Grainger watched the Lake's house. It was nine a.m. in the morning. It had taken him a little while to work out his strategy. The day before he had visited Ted Lake at the bank in Grantfield to report on his assignment. He had watched Mrs. Lake, he told the manager, for one whole month, and he had seen nothing suspicious in that time. She was, he reported, an exemplary wife and had not presented him with a moment's doubt. Ted Lake, of course, beamed with pleasure. This was exactly what he had hoped to hear from the private detective. All his fears and the rumours circulating the village were indeed groundless.

Delighted with the report, he reached for his chequebook and wrote a substantial cheque for Grainger, there and then.

That had been yesterday. Now Grainger sat in his car watching the Lake household. He saw Ted Lake leave for the bank just after nine. He knew that the man always arrived at the bank in Grantfield by nine thirty. He waited for a further ten minutes, just in case Ted Lake had forgotten anything and returned to the house. Then Grainger telephoned the house. Mrs. Lake answered. He introduced himself and said that he needed to see her.

She was quite rude at first and said she didn't know him, and no, she didn't want to buy whatever he was selling.

"I think you will want to buy this, Mrs. Lake." She was about to hang up, when he said the address of the house where the Satanists orgy had taken place.

Silence greeted him on the other end of the line and he could sense the stunned shock … He waited, a smile on his cunning face.

"W..what's all this about?" Barbara Lake stammered.

"Probably better if we don't talk over the phone, don't you agree, Mrs. Lake, or may I call you Barbara."

"No, you're right. Where shall I meet you?" She sounded worried but slightly relieved.

"Shall we say at your front door in about a minute from now … I'm sitting outside now," Grainger affirmed.

"Very well." The line went dead. Grainger got out of his car, locked it, and walked boldly over to the Lake's front door. The house was large with two colonnades supporting a central archway. He reached for the bell, but the door opened before he could press it. Barbara Lake stood there, dressed in a low cut floral negligee. Even at this early hour not a hair was out of place and she was heavily made up, although the high heels looked strangely out of place with the negligee.

"You had better come in," was all she said. He stepped over the threshold and she hurriedly closed the door behind him. She led him into the lounge. "Well, what do you want?" She tried to make her voice sound in control and authoritative.

Without being asked, Granger sprawled insolently in a large leather armchair, his eyes literally undressing the well-endowed woman before him.

"When I came in, I was only thinking about money, but, I mean ... well!" Again, his eyes swept up and down her. "Maybe we can start with twenty thousand pounds ... I mean, I'm not a greedy man ... That's if you're nice to me, Barbara, otherwise say, twenty five grand?"

"Why should I give you anything, you slimy, horrible, little man?" said Barbara.

"Listen!" was his next word, more like a command. She did, and he related the details of the Satanists' orgy that he had witnessed. He let her think that he had seen her part in it, although it had actually been too dark to pick out individuals, Grainger knew that her own guilt would do the rest of his job for him. "You wouldn't want your good, kind, husband to know about this, my dear, would you?"

Barbara knew she was trapped. She shifted uneasily from one foot to the other.

"It wasn't just me, you know. Sally Greves did it too," she pleaded.

"Well, aren't we the loyal friend, Barbara. I suggest you ring her and get her over here pronto…"

CHAPTER NINE

The Reverend Mark Glenville had just completed the Blessing for the dismissal of the Sunday Morning Service. During his sermon earlier, he had made mention of the serious vandalism in the churchyard that had occurred during the week, taking particular care not to mention Satanists. He had no wish to alarm his congregation unnecessarily, so merely said that if anyone had seen or knew anything about it, to let either himself or the police know.

At the end of the service, as was his usual custom, he moved to the outside porch of the old church. This way he could always have a word and shake hands with parishioners as they left.

The first, as always, was Hortense Hyde-Potter, chairperson of the Parish Council, chairperson of the Parochial Church Council, and president of the local W.I. With finger and thumb, she pulled her pince-nez glasses a shade further down her long bony nose and looked at him sternly over the top of them.

"I see you are still choosing the wrong hymns, vicar," she retorted tartly.

"Actually I only choose one of them, which fits in with my sermon, Mrs. Hyde-Potter. The rest are chosen by Mr. Finch, the choirmaster." Why he needed to defend himself, Mark didn't know, but Mary had said, "Try and please the old biddy."

"I shall speak to him, then," she replied in the same acid tone.

"Yes, I'm sure he will be happy to include a hymn of your choice," said Mark, trying to pour oil onto troubled waters.

"Oh, and another thing, vicar."

"And what would that be, Mrs. Hyde-Potter?"

"These goings on in the churchyard. We never had anything like that when the Reverend Wesley Pendale-Cummings was here." Mark nearly choked. This shrew-like martinet was actually blaming him for that, too. He counted to ten.

"I can assure you I am equally disturbed about such happenings, madam."

"Then I hope you are going to do something about it!" With that, Hortense wielded her brolly as if she was conducting an orchestra and departed without as much as a goodbye or a backward glance.

Karen Thomkins, the local doctor's receptionist, was next in line. An altogether more pleasant sight thought Mark, turning to greet the bright and breezy girl who was blonde and in her mid twenties. The girl, of course, had heard the discourse between himself and Hortense.

"Take no notice, vicar. A lot of us younger ones think you are doing a grand job here. A breath of fresh air and that goes for your wife, too," said Karen.

Mark smiled.

"Thank you Karen, very nice of you." He must be doing something right.

People continued to file by and it was Kate McLean, the local primary school mistress, who brought up the rear. A smart young lady, perhaps a little older than Mark – mid thirties, he thought, slim and dark and a wonderful way with children, he had noticed.

"About what you were saying happened the other night, vicar," she said.

"Yes, Kate." His interest immediately aroused. "Did you see anything?"

"Well, not what happened in the churchyard, but you know where I live? Just along the lane from the church," she went on.

"Yes," Mark prompted.

"Well, my husband and I had been to the theatre in London. By the time we got back to Grantfield on the train and drove on home to Saddlewitch it was about one a.m." Mark was all ears by now. Mary, his wife, had joined him. Kate went on, "There were several cars parked along the lane, which seemed unusual at that time of night. People were in the lane and getting into the cars. The odd thing about it was they were all hooded … The people, I mean … I wanted to ring the police about it, as it looked highly suspicious to me. David, my husband, said not to be so daft – not to interfere and not to get involved. . I wish I had now, after what you said in your sermon ... Do you think they could have been the ones in the churchyard that did the damage, vicar?"

Mark looked pensive.

"As you say they were all hooded, it's not possible you could recognise anybody then Kate?" cut in Mary.

"No, but I did recognise one of the cars."

"You did!" said Mark, excitedly.

"Perhaps I didn't ought to say ... . I mean, I don't want to get anyone in trouble. It could be nothing," replied Kate nervously.

"If it's innocent then the person would have nothing to fear, would they, Kate?" reasoned Mark.

"I suppose not ... Well, it was the BMW that the bank manager's wife, Barbara Lake, drives. I remember the registration number. It's one of those personalised ones." Mark and Mary looked at one another, then Marked turned back and addressed Kate again.

"Okay, Kate. Don't mention this to anyone else, and I'll see that it is discreetly checked out. Thanks for telling us, it could be nothing, but we will see." The couple shook hands with Kate McLean and watched her depart down the churchyard path.

"What are you going to do about this, Mark? After all you don't want to stir up a hornets nest," said Mary, to her husband.

"What do you mean, Mary?"

"Well, I gather from rumours around the village that Barbara Lake has quite a reputation as a man-eater. Suppose she was just involved in a clandestine meeting with someone. We don't want to be the cause of a family dispute do we, Mark?"

"No, but on the other hand, we do have a duty to pass this information on, I think," said Mark.

"To the police, you mean ... Not George Fenning, surely?" replied Mary, incredulously.

"Oh George is not a bad egg ... but I think I'll have a word tomorrow with that chap Drew Thorpe at Briar Cottage ... Might be more in his line, and I'm sure he can be relied on to be discreet."

★ ★ ★ ★ ★

Sasha continued to tie herself in knots over Drew's possible relationship with the blonde Caroline. After all he had admitted to her that the girl had always been around. Yes, that was exactly the term he had used. Drew had said for her, Sasha, to bring the children round next time she called to see him. She even wondered if that remark from Drew had been a way of warding her off. Yet, just before Caroline had returned, things seemed to be going so well between her and Drew. She supposed, as a married woman, she should be feeling guilty at even wishing for something to happen. One thing for sure, Sasha had her pride. Drew had bundled her out quick enough when that girl had returned. There was no way, she told herself stubbornly, that she would call again at Briar Cottage.

Let Drew come to her if he wanted to see her. She knew that she was being unreasonable, but as far as she was concerned that was an end to the matter. Or was it? As the days crept oh so slowly by, she missed his warmth and understanding manner more and more. It was the way his eyes lit up when he smiled that she missed most of all.

In her walks with the dog, Bess, she more than half hoped she would accidentally bump into Drew. Surely he must have to go into the village sometimes, to do his shopping and post letters, etc. She hadn't ever seen the girl Caroline around either. Perhaps they had gone away together. It infuriated Sasha beyond belief that she knew so little about him.

Gradually, as one week progressed into two, realisation began to sink in. He wasn't coming to see her... How could he? The way Bart had acted in the past towards him, Drew would probably be expecting a shotgun welcome for a repeat visit to the Paget household.

Happily, Bart wasn't around very often, and when he was, he continued to act strangely. She found several books on the occult, which he seemed to have suddenly taken an interest in. In happier days of their early marriage, he had even poured scorn on the astrological charts she read, yet now this strange pursuit.

The other day she had even caught him watching the au pair Olga. The girl, like many nineteen year olds, wore very short skirts. On this occasion, she had been bending over, looking at the fish in the ornamental pond. Her skirt, which had ridden up even higher at the back, revealed a glimpse of white panties. From the kitchen window, she could see Bart studying the girl. He was half concealed behind clumps of rhododendron. Normally this wouldn't have worried Sasha too much, but it was the expression on his face that caused her more than a little anxiety. It wasn't even so much of lust, but more one of hatred.

When he saw Sasha had seen him, he pretended to stoop and pick up something, but continued to watch Olga. On the pretext of something, Sasha went out and called Olga in. Bart disappeared and she didn't see him again that day……

When Ray Grainger had ordered Barbara Lake to ring her friend, Sally Greves, telling her to come to the Lake's house immediately, Barbara had been quick to recover. She knew she must play for time. After all she had powerful friends.

"No can do," she said.

"No such thing as can't, lady. You do it, and do it now, or I tell your husband all about you!" The menace in Grainger's tone was very clear.

Barbara smiled provocatively at him and went on, "No, I don't mean I won't telephone her … It's just that she won't be there. Gone shopping in London today. I know that because she told me last night that she was going to." Grainger said nothing, just glowered and reached for the telephone book. He thumbed through the pages and finally punched in a series of numbers on the handset.

"I'll just check this out, lady," he exclaimed as he listened to the ringing tone.

Barbara kept her fingers crossed behind her back. With any luck, Sally would be out with her dog about this time. Obviously this proved to be the case, the phone continued to ring, no-one answered.

Grainger replaced the receiver, giving Barbara a pointed look. "Looks like you're telling the truth," he said, then went on again, "This is the deal, lady. Do you know the Highway Motel on the Grantfield London Road? It's about ten miles out of the town." Barbara said that she did.

"Why?" she questioned.

"Because this is what you are going to do. I want both you and this friend of yours, Sally, to be there tomorrow night at eight o'clock. With you, you will have twenty thousand pounds, in cash, mind!" Grainger gave Barbara a cunning smile at this stage and added, "You will recall I said that if you were nice to me I would let you off at twenty grand instead of twenty five."

Leaning forward, he suddenly reached out and parted the flimsy negligee revealing Barbara's well-rounded and ample thighs. She took an involuntary backward step and the garment fell back into place. Grainger laughed.

"Weren't so coy at the little party, were you luv?"

"You disgusting, slimy little man," she snapped.

"Right – that's settled then. Twenty thousand in cash and both of you tomorrow night ... I always did fancy a 'ménage a trios'."

By this time, Barbara already knew what she was going to do. The end result might be quite fun, but she would let this slimy little man think for the moment he had the upper hand. She would play the frightened lady for just a little longer.

"Where do you think I can just get hold of twenty thousand pounds in cash from, by tomorrow night, for goodness sake?"

"Goodness has nothing to do with it, lady. Either you get it or your husband hears about your activities."

"Will you take a cheque?" Barbara enquired. Grainger laughed, a horrible cackling sound from deep in his throat.

"What do you take me for – a fool? You'd have it stopped long before I could cash it. No, lady – cash. Borrow half from your friend Sally if you like."

"I don't think I can raise it in the time," whined Barbara.

"If you can't lady, then you can make it out to cash and I'll hold you and your friend overnight. Then you will accompany me to the bank in the morning to see the cash handed over." Grainger finished this statement with another cackling laugh. "Somehow I don't think you'll care for the latter idea."

"Very well, then. I don't know how but I'll raise the cash somehow," said Barbara in a hurt voice.

"You can bet your boobs on that lady ... Remember, eight o'clock tomorrow night at the Highway Motel, and don't be late. I've booked the room already," Grainger said with a leer.

On his way to the door, he had to pass her. Suddenly he reached out and grabber her by the hair. Twisting her round he pulled her back against himself. With his other hand he reached down the front of her negligee and fondled her breast.

"Just an aperitif to keep me going until tomorrow night lady, and don't even think of going to the police or trying a double-cross." He pinched her right nipple hard and she cried out in pain. Grainger laughed, let her go and made for the door. With his hand on the brass doorknob, he turned again towards her. "Until tomorrow night then." A moment later she heard the front door close behind him. Barbara crossed to the window and watched him cross the road towards his car. She saw him drive off then, smiling to herself, she reached for the telephone. She dialled a number.

She would teach the slimy little toad not to threaten her, Barbara Lake. Twenty thousand pounds plus Sally and herself! He'd be lucky!

★ ★ ★ ★ ★

Young Billie Tate's mother was doing the washing on the Monday morning. She went through his pockets as usual, otherwise there was no telling what the boy would leave. She had damaged the drum of her washing machine before with stones and metal objects left in his clothing. She pulled out a snail with a striped coloured shell and piece of half chewed chewing gum and then, to her astonishment, a piece of folded black silk.

She unfurled it to reveal a black hood with eyeholes and cut away mouth section. Where in blazes did he get this? She resolved to question him when he came in. She put the article in a drawer and unfortunately forgot all about it by the time she had taken the snail and chewing gum to the outside dustbin ... ..

★ ★ ★ ★ ★

Mark Glenville was sitting in Drew's lounge. He had just acquainted him with the information passed to him by the schoolmistress Kate McLean. It was two days later.

"Do you think there is any significance? I mean this is a rather delicate matter, Mr. Thorpe. The Lakes are local dignitaries and we don't know that Mrs. Lake had anything to do with the churchyard incident ... I mean, just because Mrs. McLean saw her car in the lane." Mark let the sentence tail off and looked somewhat embarrassed.

Drew replied, "We don't know that it hasn't any significance, vicar. You really shouldn't have waited two days to acquaint me with this information. I'll get on to it straight away."

"You will be discreet in your enquiries, won't you, Mr. Thorpe, and perhaps you needn't mention to Mrs. Lake that the information reached you from me?" Drew smiled and patted the vicar's arm.

"Don't worry. No need for you to be mentioned at all. The police never reveal the source of information."

"Nor Mrs. McLean either. I mean, I wouldn't want her involved."

"No. Anything you tell me is confidential, as is what I tell you," said Drew.

"That's reassuring, anyway," said Mark looking relieved. "What are you going to do now, or shouldn't I ask?"

"I'll probably get Caroline to have a quiet word with Mrs. Lake."

"Caroline?" queried Mark.

"Yes, WPC Channing. You remember, you met her in the churchyard," Drew explained. "Probably be more discreet than I could be. We wouldn't want to put Mrs. Lake in an awkward situation with her husband if she's, as may well be, completely innocent."

Mark coughed.

"Very considerate of you, Mr. Thorpe. I see I came to the right man."

Drew smiled.

"Even if a trifle late, vicar."

Later that day Drew discussed the delicate situation with Caroline.

"So will you go and see her?" he concluded. Caroline laughed.

"Chicken?" she queried.

"Not at all, but think about it. If I go blundering in and her husband is around, and it turns out that she was having some clandestine assignation with a boyfriend … .You see what I mean … ." Drew let the sentence tail off.

"So how do you want me to handle it, then?"

"You could make an appointment to see her … Say in the daytime, when her husband should be at the bank. If he does turn out to be at home – make out you're a market researcher or something … You'll think of something, love." Caroline laughed.

"As I said – chicken!" she repeated.

"No – discreet," answered Drew.

*****

At the same moment in time at Rangeways farm, Rachel Steel answered a knock at the farmhouse front door. A man dressed in a smart city suit and wearing a bowler hat stood there. Rachel immediately thought that it must be someone to see her father, farmer Burgess Steel.

"Yes?" she enquired when the smartly dressed man didn't speak. She adjudged him to be middle-aged. He was well spoken and polite when he replied.

"I want to purchase a goat," was all he said. Rachel laughed.

"Sorry, I don't understand. We do have a few goats but my father doesn't sell them. He keeps them for milk."

"Ah, I see," said the caller. "It was a billy goat I was interested in."

"Well, I'm sorry. We do have a billy but my father certainly wouldn't sell him. He's a pet, you see."

"When will your father be in?"

"Could be anytime. I suggest you phone, but I'm telling you he won't sell."

"Very well miss. Sorry to have bothered you. I'll telephone later. Goodbye." Rachel watched him depart to his car and drive off in the direction of Grantfield. When her father came in later, she told him about the caller.

"Can't think why anyone would think we sold goats," remarked Burgess Steel. Neither Rachel nor her father ever heard again from the caller, but the next morning the goat was missing from his compound.

Burgess Steel sent for Constable Fenning.

CHAPTER TEN

Ray Grainger arrived at the Highland Motel, parked his car and switched off the engine. He virtually licked his lips with the anticipation of what was to come. He had organised everything perfectly; rang and booked a room for the night, earlier that day, then telephoned Barbara Lake to tell her to wait in her car in the motel car park with her friend until he came for them. That was to be a quarter of an hour later than his arrival. First he wanted to go in and register under a false name and get the key of the room he was to use.

He registered under the name of Johnson, collected the key from the clerk and went to check the room. Ideal – its entrance was directly off the car park and ground floor to boot. Everything was going so well, thought Grainger, he wouldn't even have to take the two women in past the reception desk. It was possible to watch from the window and see when Barbara Lake's BMW arrived outside. Grainger turned on the television, opened the mini bar and poured himself a whisky. Then he lay back on the bed contentedly thinking which one of the two women he would have first and collect twenty thousand grand as well. Smiling smugly the detective thought with relish that he had also been paid by her poor sap of a husband for giving him a negative report on the bitch.

Ten minutes later a car drove onto the forecourt. Excitedly, he put down the half empty whisky glass, leapt off the bed, crossed the floor and eased the curtain back.

Stepping back, he rubbed his hands gleefully. Let them wait a minute or two then go out, he thought. In point of fact he had only to open the door and look out. The two women in the BMW saw him at once in the lighted doorway. Instead of going outside, he jerked his thumb over his shoulder to indicate to them to join him. With that, he retreated into the room. A minute or so later the two women joined him, Sally Greves closing the door behind her.

"Turn the key!" he commanded. Sally appeared to comply.

"That's better. Makes you feel safe, doesn't it?" said Barbara, giving Sally a sly grin. Grainger ignored the barb.

"Let's keep this sociable, shall we? Would you like a drink, ladies?"

"Mine's a G and T," said Sally Greves.

"And you?" he exclaimed, eyeing Barbara.

"Dry sherry," came back the reply. He poured the two drinks and topped up his own whisky.

"Now that we are all nice and cosy, let's see the money first," said Grainger.

"Oh, you will get what's due to you, Mr. Grainger," replied Barbara. "But, first things first." Turning her back on Sally, she said, "Would you oblige?"

Sally Greves undid the zip at the back of Barbara's black satin dress and the latter slid out of it, like a sensuous snake shedding its skin. Grainger's eyes nearly popped out of his head. Barbara did a twirl dressed in a matching satin basque, panties and black stockings.

"You sure are some classy dame," he said, with a smirk on his face that would have done justice to a Cheshire cat. Sally slipped her own dress over her head to reveal a natural coloured full-length body stocking. She winked at Barbara.

"I wonder which he likes best?"

"I wonder," quipped Barbara, emptying her glass at one go. "Considering he's not getting either, the slimy little toad." The sudden change in her tone alarmed Grainger. Something was desperately wrong here. These two women didn't seem at all worried. In fact, both looked confidently in command of the situation from the moment they had entered.

"He can have a good look at what he's missing," laughed Sally, pirouetting on her high heels theatrically, her glass of gin at arm's length. Thoroughly alarmed now, Grainger grabbed Barbara by the throat forcing her back against the wall.

"I'll see that money now," he snapped. Sally walked calmly to the door and flung it open wide. "You will see the Devil, my friend," she retorted. Grainger had released Barbara in a futile attempt to stop Sally opening the door, but it was all too late.

A huge cloaked figure stood in the doorway and Grainger could see another behind him. Both were hooded. He could see their eyes glinting through the eyeholes of their masks, as the light from the room hit them. After the second man had entered, he closed and locked the door ominously behind him.

Grainger, like a scared rabbit, swept his eyes from one to the other. The two women laughed.

Barbara said, "I think you are about to be laid in a different way than you had planned, scum!"

Grainger backed away until his progress was halted by contact with the far wall. The larger of the two figures gave a throaty laugh, watching him through the eyeholes of the mask like a cat watching a mouse. The smaller nodded to the two women.

"Get your clothes on ladies. This won't take long."

The women reached for their dresses, whilst Grainger, wide eyed and terrified, looked from one to the other of the hooded figures.

"W…what are y…you going to d…do?" he stammered.

The smaller man spoke. His voice was icily cold.

"We are going to teach you a lesson you won't forget in a hurry. Grab him, number four."

The huge figure stepped forward and advanced on Grainger, who threw his arms up to protect himself. A fist, the size of a small melon, smashed through Grainger's guard and the women, in the act of dressing, could hear the smashing of bone. Blood spurted forward in a crimson flood from the middle of the victim's face. Grainger doubled over, but a vicious uppercut jack-knifed him straight again. The giant spun him round, locking his arms behind his back.

"Your turn now, number three." Through a mist of blood Grainger watched the smaller man fit knuckle-dusters to both hands. The whole process was very slow and menacing for effect. Effect it certainly had on poor Grainger.

"I'll go! I won't say anything to anybody," he whined.

"You're damned well right you won't … Be lucky if you can talk at all after we have finished with you," chuckled the man holding him.

Without more ado, the other man, his knuckle-duster covered fists a blur of action, exploded blow after blow into Grainger's face and body. Only when he was exhausted himself, did he cease. The large figure released his victim, who slid down the giant's body in a crumpled heap to the floor.

Only the fact that he was still groaning showed that he was alive. Both men gave him a final vicious kick in the ribs before number three said, "If you should live, I would remind you that, tell anyone about this and we will come back and finish the job. You got off lightly, this time."

Grainger didn't answer, but continued to groan.

The two women left with the cloaked and hooded figures. As they filed out, Barbara, the last to vacate the room, put the light out saying, "Sleep well, Mr. Grainger."

He was found, still unconscious, the next morning by the maid employed to clean the room. The manager called the police.

The police arrived and called an ambulance immediately. Grainger's face was so swollen and bloodied as to be virtually unrecognisable. The unconscious Grainger was then transported to hospital and attended to in Casualty. He was still comatose. Finally, after a thorough examination, he was taken to Theatre and worked on for two hours. Amongst his injuries were, together with a broken nose, depressed fractures of the cheekbones, a fractured jaw and three broken ribs. He was then taken to an intensive care ward and placed on a drip.

The two policemen waited in reception for the surgeon in charge – when the senior registrar finally appeared, he looked grave faced.

"Don't think there's much point you people hanging around ... It's no more than fifty-fifty whether he makes it or not, let alone talks to you. Do you know who he is? There's no identity on him."

"No we don't," replied the police sergeant from Grantfield. "We thought of sending for the constable from Saddlewitch – George Fenning – been around for years and knows everybody hereabouts ... Maybe he might know him."

"If he can recognise the poor devil, sergeant …. somebody sure didn't like him. Never seen such deliberate injuries," replied the registrar.

"Well we'll send for Fenning anyway. If he doesn't know the guy, we will have to see if anyone is reported missing fitting his description … Sorry doctor, but I'll have to leave my man here, just in case he recovers consciousness and can tell us anything."

The registrar shrugged his shoulders.

"Very well sergeant … but don't hold your breath."

When left on his own with the unconscious man, the constable eyed the patient who had a tube up his nose and drip in his arm, then drew up a chair. Shaking his head, he said aloud, "This looks like a bloody waste of time……"

WPC Channing, as requested by Drew, had called to see Mrs. Barbara Lake. The latter had opened the door dressed in a light grey two-piece suit elegantly tailored to accentuate her fulsome figure. Until Caroline had produced her warrant card, Barbara had been quite hostile. On production of the said object, her manner changed.

"Oh, I see you have come about my stolen car, constable … Have you found it yet?" Caroline was quite taken aback.

"I didn't know that you had reported it stolen, Mrs. Lake."

"Why are you here then?"

"Your car was seen in the lane the night before last and we have reason to believe its presence could be related to strange goings on in the local churchyard."

"Goodness, gracious, my dear. So the thief must have taken it there …. Whatever for, do you think?" Barbara was all innocence. Ignoring this, Caroline enquired when Barbara had first reported it missing. "Not until yesterday when I wanted to go into Grantfield … I rang the police immediately."

"So you wouldn't know anything about its presence in the lane, then?" Caroline watched Barbara's face keenly for any reaction.

"No my dear ... Obviously the thief, when you catch him, will. Then you can ask him, can't you?" Barbara smiled smugly. Caroline tried again.

"If your car was stolen some time the day before yesterday, why did it take you so long to report it to the police?" Barbara now began to switch her mood to one of annoyance.

"Look, WPC Channing, or whatever your name is, I've already explained that. Why don't you get on trying to find my vehicle for me instead of bothering me with silly questions."

"Then you weren't in the churchyard the night before last?" said Caroline, deliberately trying to rattle Barbara.

"Certainly not, young woman and I resent your implication. I'm a respectable married woman ... My husband's a bank manager, you know."

"Yes, we are aware of that Mrs. Lake," said Caroline. She was getting nowhere, and yet she had a hunch that the woman was lying. She tried a bluff. "That's strange, because you were reported being seen there."

"Who saw me? I mean – that's impossible. I wasn't there so nobody would have seen me. I..." Barbara was clearly flustered and her reaction clearly showed that she was indeed lying.

"I'm not allowed to say who reported you there, madam, that's privileged information."

"Well, whoever they were, they are obviously lying, and I don't like your attitude WPC Channing ... In fact, I shall report you to the superintendent at Grantfield ... He plays golf with my husband, perhaps you would like to know," said Barbara, looking smugly superior.

"Nice for him, I'm sure, Mrs. Lake," replied Caroline politely.

"Now if there's nothing else," snapped Barbara, showing Caroline the door. "Perhaps you will let me know when they find my car."

"Oh, we will," said Caroline, as she departed through the front door. "And who was in the lane too, that night. I'm sure you will be interested in that, too." She smiled as she heard the door slam behind her.

Saddlewitch

At least she had succeeded in rattling Mrs. Lake. She went round to Drew's and telephoned Grantfield police from his place.

It was true that Mrs. Lake had reported the BMW stolen yesterday morning, but it had been nearer lunchtime. Stranger still, the car had just been found … Only ten minutes ago and would you believe it, only two miles away from the Lake's house up a farm cart track completely undamaged. Apparently young Rachel Steel had found it whilst out riding and notified the police.

Caroline relayed this information to Drew whose first reaction was, "I think that proves your theory, Caroline. No thief in his right mind steals an expensive car to drive half a mile to the churchyard and then dumps the car two miles away from where it first came from without taking anything from it."

"She's obviously involved with this cult although, to look at her, you wouldn't think butter would melt in her mouth," said Caroline.

"Well, at least, thanks to you, we have a lead. We can watch her like a hawk. Sooner or later she is going to make a slip," replied Drew.

"Trouble is, she will now have rumbled my cover," put in Caroline.

"True. She will no doubt, when she reports you, find that you are not attached to Grantfield police," Drew mused.

"Do you think she will go ahead and report me?" asked Caroline.

"Sure to, if only to make herself look good. Her kind always do," responded Drew.

"We need someone who could gain her confidence and get in with her and hope she will give something away," said Caroline.

"Yes, but who? If we don't turn up something soon, Special Branch won't keep us on this case for ever, let alone give us another agent." Both scratched their heads, deep in thought.

★ ★ ★ ★ ★

As time went by, Drew experienced regret that Sasha had obviously ceased to call on him. He was aware that he had somewhat bundled her out on Caroline's untimely return. It was all very well for the latter to say that he had a job to do and shouldn't get involved. Damn it all, thought Drew, I do have a life. He knew now, that it was up to him to make the next move. Sasha obviously thought his relationship with Caroline was something more than he had said. In fact, he respected and admired Sasha's pride. Anything else now was up to him.

If he called, and her husband was there, he knew Bart would make life difficult for her and he agonised for a long time on what to do next. His final decision was to dial 141, then her number. If Bart answered, he would put the phone down promptly.

In point of fact, it was the au pair who answered. Drew guessed correctly that this was the case, hearing the strong Scandinavian accent.

"Yes, Mrs. Paget was in," she said. "I go fetch her, yes?" Drew thanked her, and could hear her go away, calling for Sasha. A minute elapsed before Sasha came on the line.

"Can you talk?" he enquired very quietly. She recognised his voice immediately.

"It's Drew, isn't it?" He affirmed that it was and then asked if she was alone. "Bart's at the London office today." He thought he detected a slight nervous tremor in her voice.

"I was wondering if I could come round and see you this morning, Sasha … It's been a long time…" Drew's voice tailed off uncertainly.

Sasha seemed to recover her poise having got over the surprise of his call.

"The way you dismissed me, the last time I saw you….." Sasha began and tailed off.

"I know, I'm sorry about that. That is one of the reasons I want to see you and explain."

"You don't have to, you know," replied Sasha. "I mean, you don't owe me anything." Drew wondered if she didn't want to see him.

"If you would rather I didn't call, I understand," he said.

"Oh no. I'd love you to call, Drew."

"Great," he said, enthusiastically. "In about half an hour, then. Bye for now." He replaced the receiver, a satisfied smile on his face.

True to his word, he arrived half an hour later and was let in by the au pair, Olga. The pretty young Swede led him to the lounge and bid him take a seat.

"I fetch Mrs. Paget, yes?" With a backward glance at him, she departed. A few moments later Sasha appeared, dressed in a little black dress, high heels and just the right amount of make-up. Drew gave a low whistle of appreciation.

"You look great for ten a.m. in the morning."

Sasha smiled.

"Actually I was just going in to Grantfield shopping when you rang ... I don't always walk about the house like this."

"Oh, I'm sorry if my call has upset anything." He made as if to get up.

"No, don't. It's quite all right," Sasha said, hurriedly. "It can wait. Any time will do for shopping. Anyway it's lovely to see you. I'll get Olga to make us some coffee." Sasha vacated the room and returned a few moments later.

For a while the two of them discussed the weather and recent events. The sort of small talk that people, a little unsure of themselves, make. Olga brought in the coffee and some biscuits and it was whilst sipping this, that Drew tried to explain about Caroline. Like many men he wasn't very good at explaining a relationship that didn't exist, when someone else thought it did. He ended by saying, "We are just good friends, you see."

Sasha quite enjoyed his obvious embarrassment and jokingly replied, "You might see it that way, Drew, but I saw the way that Caroline looked at you – and at me for that matter."

"No, no, you're wrong, Sasha. You see, she works with me and she's just worried I might get involved." Sasha gave him a sideways look.

"I don't really know much about you, do I Drew? What is it you do here and how is Caroline involved?"

Drew saw that he had manoeuvred himself into a corner. There was a pregnant pause before he replied, "I think I owe it to you to tell you, but I could be out on my ear if anyone talked. Can I swear you to secrecy?" Sasha leaned forward on her chair, intrigued.

It took about fifteen minutes to tell her all about the Satanic cult that they were trying to expose and bust, and his own and Caroline's involvement. He ended by saying, "So it's only PC Fenning and the vicar and his wife who know about this .... and now you, of course."

Without realising what she had done, Sasha had reached out a hand placing it on Drew's knee. It had just seemed such a natural reaction. Drew didn't move away but simply covered her hand with his own.

"I'm so glad you've told me, Drew, and I can promise you it won't go any further."

Drew stayed talking for about an hour and then on leaving said, "So you will come and see me again? Very soon, won't you?" he enquired.

"You can bank on it and if I can be of any help, let me know."

Drew was wondering if he should kiss her, but his mind was made up by the appearance of Olga. He just gave Sasha a polite kiss on the cheek and left…

CHAPTER ELEVEN

Sasha felt a sense of guilt, not because of any thoughts of disloyalty to Bart, but rather because the school holidays were over tomorrow. It was early September and the long six week vacation was coming to an end. She realised that with Debbie going back to school and Annabel to playgroup she would have more time to herself.

The situation between her and Bart had worsened. They had become like two strangers and hardly talked at all. She would have had to admit, if only to herself, that she was as much to blame. She had simply given up trying. The more he was out of her hair the more Sasha liked it. In the early weeks of their estrangement, if such it could be called, she had suggested a marriage counsellor. Bart's reaction had been to storm off, swearing that he didn't want any damned busybody prying into his private life.

Somewhere, tucked away, Sasha decided, he must have a mistress as quite a few nights he never returned home. At times he would be missing for forty-eight hours at a stretch. She supposed that she should have confronted him with her suspicions and not let things just go on. The plain truth was that if he wasn't around, he was out of her hair and for this she was thankful. Physical relations between them were non-existent and Sasha certainly had no plans to make any overtures towards him. He took no notice of the children either.

Most of the time he would behave like someone possessed and retire within himself in a sombre dark, foreboding mood. Twice since the first time she had seen him watching Olga, it had happened again. The expression on his face was not, however, pleasant to see. Had it been simple lust, Sasha might have understood, for Olga was a pretty girl and very provocative with her blonde hair and short skirts.

Why would he hate Olga, Sasha wondered. She had done nothing to him and he hardly spoke to the girl anyway. In all, Bart's behaviour grew more mysterious by the day. Sometimes Sasha would catch him on the telephone and he would quickly hang up, without an explanation.

When she would quite naturally enquire who it was on the phone, Bart would reply, "Oh, another damned wrong number," and march off looking very guilty, having slammed the phone down.

The time was fast coming, Sasha knew, when she would have to take legal advice about this intolerable lifestyle, even if only for the sake of Debbie and Annabel. At the end of October she had arranged for her favourite aunt, Jennifer, to have both children stay with her down in Bournemouth, but half term was still seven weeks away. She had originally planned a holiday in the Lakes for Bart, herself and the children, but had recently found out that Bart had cancelled the booking.

He hadn't even had the good grace to inform her and when she confronted him with that fact, he had flown into a rage and stormed out.

Since Drew's visit to her house, a new meaning had suddenly seemed to come into Sasha's life. She felt alive again. It wasn't until then, that she had realised how crushed she had felt, at what she imagined had been the rejection of herself for Caroline. He did care and he had come to see her, and yes, she would certainly now go and visit him. What if somebody did see them together at Briar Cottage? Why not, she had a right to a life didn't she? All these thoughts crossed and re-crossed Sasha's mind as she looked forward to the next opportunity to be with Drew.

After Drew had left, Olga had questioned Sasha, but not with any ulterior intent.

"Good looking man, yes? You like, I think."

"Yes Olga, I like," Sasha had replied.

"I like, too," Olga had enthused, rolling her eyes suggestively. They had laughed together.

★ ★ ★ ★ ★

In the middle of September another Satanic happening occurred.

Two miles north of the village of Saddlewitch, high on a hill overlooking the valley was an old ruined Norman monastery. Not much of it stood any more and apart from the occasional very dedicated tourist, few people visited it. Grass had grown up throughout the old interior courtyard and thistles and moss sprouted up between the edifices of the crumbling stone walls. The only way up from the village was a bumpy old gravel cart track that wound and twisted its way to the summit. From the top of the ruined tower, an excellent view of Saddlewitch presented itself.

On this warm night in mid September, two young lovers from the village had made the two mile trek and climb to the old monastery. Although it was dark, a full moon illuminated the remains of the old building, giving it a quite spectral and eerie appearance. The crumbling walls were bathed in a silvery glow contrasted by shadows where the moon's rays failed to reach.

Kevin Dale – a tall, gangly youth of seventeen, not yet clear of his adolescent spots, bent and felt the grass. Already a heavy dew had descended.

"Too damp here. Let's climb the tower," he suggested to his companion, Dawn Cummings. Dawn was a year younger than Kevin and a good foot shorter. Her long brown hair looked out of place with her short rather plumpish figure. Both youngsters were dressed in jeans, tee shirts and trainers. Kevin had a knapsack on his back and carried a torch in one hand.

"No, Kevin, that tower is dangerous … My dad said so," Dawn complained.

"Rubbish! It's safe enough if we take care … Come on, I'll help you," reasoned Kevin.

Although Dawn continued to grumble she went with him to the foot of the tower, where a crumbling stone staircase led in a spiral to the top. In places some of the walls were missing and Dawn could see clearly out into the night. Far below in the valley, the lights of Saddlewitch glinted and flickered. With great caution and continuing trepidation on Dawn's part the pair of young lovers climbed the centuries old worn stone steps, Kevin holding tight to his girl friend's plump hand and virtually towing her upward behind him.

At last to her relief, they arrived on the parapet, which was devoid of any remaining walls. Dawn peered down over the edge. She could see clearly down onto the old courtyard below. Everything was brightly illuminated by the silvery moonlight.

"Come away from the edge ... You're quite safe here," said Kevin, patting the ground and unbuckling the pack on his back. From it, he withdrew a car rug and laid it on the uneven stones.

"Where'd you get that, Kevin Dale?" queried Dawn, suspiciously.

"Took it from my dad's car. He never uses it so he won't miss it. Come over and lay down," Kevin added, making himself comfortable on the blanket.

Dawn looked doubtful, but she moved away from the edge and joined him on the black and red chequered rug.

"Okay, take 'em off ...cos you said we could try it tonight," urged Kevin excitedly, reaching for the top button on Dawn's jeans. She slapped his hand away crossly.

"You mind your manners, Kevin Dale. I read in my mum's magazine that there should be loving foreplay first ... 'Sides, I'm not sure I want to do it now ... How many times you done it, with other girls, cos I've never done it?"

"There you are then, Dawn ... You should try it now. I'm sure you will like it," reasoned Kevin. Reaching up inside her tee shirt, he fumbled about looking for the catch on her bra.

"You won't find it ... It's a front loader," she informed him.

"What's a front loader?" Kevin enquired.

"I don't think you're as experienced as you make out, Kevin Dale, if'n you don't know that," replied Dawn, giving him an old fashioned sideways look.

Kevin, taken out of his stride responded, "Course I do know, but better you take it off, then I shan't damage it, will I?" Dawn snorted derisively, pulled up her tee shirt and unhooked the white satin bra. Two large round breasts flopped out to freedom.

Kevin's eyes nearly popped out of his head, his gaze homing in on her rose pink nipples. Then he made an instant grab. Dawn knocked his hands away.

"'Ere, you go steady ... That's me you're pulling about." Now Kevin fingered the objects of his desire as if they were Dresden. "You don't have to go that steady, Kevin," laughed Dawn, undoing the top button of her jeans and wriggling out of them. Underneath she wore matching white satin knickers and black hold up stockings.

"Cor blimey, Dawn! Where'd you get the money to buy that sort of stuff? That's expensive," enthused Kevin, stroking the white satin across her plump abdomen.

"Didn't! Nicked my mother's. Thought you might like them."

"You shouldn't have done that, Dawn. She might find out and stop us seeing one another," said Kevin.

"You nicked your dad's blanket."

"Well, that's different."

"No, t'aint."

"Anyway they don't go very well with trainers. Makes you look like Minnie Mouse," argued Kevin.

Dawn eyed the bulge in Kevin's jeans.

"Well, it seems to be having the desired effect on you, whatever you say." She reached playfully for the zip of his jeans. "You'd better have brought some French letters with you," Dawn said, giving him that searching look that he hated so much.

"You don't need 'em. Girls all take precautions these days ... Easy like, pills and the like."

"Well this girl doesn't so that's your lot, Kevin Dale." With this she reached for her jeans. Kevin, now feeling considerably sulky, eyed her as she struggled into the jeans.

"Why do your thighs bulge over the top of your stocking tops? Bet they don't do that on your mother?" Dawn poked her tongue out at him.

"You keep my mum out of this," she retorted.

"Bet she takes precautions and your dad isn't expected to use rubbers," said Kevin.

It was then that they heard the noise. Several motor engines approaching and getting louder. As one, they crawled onto their knees and peered in the direction of Saddlewitch. Wending their way up the dusty cart track were no less than four, four wheel drive vehicles. They watched the headlights cutting a swathe across the grass covered hills.

"My God, Kevin, they are coming here," gasped Dawn, struggling to complete dressing.

"Looks like it," said Kevin, flattening himself on his belly, peering over the parapet at the oncoming vehicles.

"Are they looking for us, do you think?" whispered Dawn, nervously.

"Don't see why they would be, but we had better stay put in case they see us ... Perhaps we shouldn't be here," whispered Kevin, his eyes still fixed on the advancing headlights.

"Fine time to tell me that," said Dawn, digging him in the ribs.

Two minutes later, the four vehicles arrived and parked on the outer side of the old monastery just out of the young couple's view. A babble of voices greeted them, both male and female.

"Perhaps it's a gang bash," whispered Kevin.

Dawn looked quite petrified. He could see her face in the moonlight.

"Suppose they get me." She was close to sobbing.

"They won't know we are here if we keep still and quiet ... No reason for them to come up here, anyway."

A few moments later from their position high above, they saw a column of people, all carrying burning torches, file through into the ruined central courtyard.

Kevin counted under his breath, twenty people in all – everyone cloaked and hooded. The last one into the square led, of all things, a goat on a leash, which he took to one side. The animal was bleating loudly. After parading it around the courtyard it was then led out through a crumbling doorway. The group then formed themselves up into a circle, the centre of which was occupied by another cloaked character, wearing the mask of a goat on his head.

Dawn squeezed up beside Kevin, peering down from their vantage point.

"W...what are they going to do, K...Kevin," she stammered. Kevin gripped her hand, too frightened to answer.

The figure in the centre began to chant in a deep bass voice, whilst the rest, facing in towards him, began to wail in response. Then all went quiet and one of the figures in the ring joined the goat-headed one in the centre. The latter then stepped forward and removed the newcomer's hood. Kevin and Dawn saw that it was a blonde woman.

Then, to their amazement, two others stepped forward and removed the woman's cloak, pulling it over her head. She was revealed totally nude. Each of them then supported an arm and held them outstretched on either side of her. Then something flashed in the reflection of the moonlight. To their horror, Kevin and Dawn saw that it was a large curved knife.

"My God, they are going to kill her," whispered Dawn. Kevin could feel his companion veritably shaking with terror next to him, where her leg touched his.

"Quiet," he hissed, "Or they'll do us in too." Horror stricken they watched, hardly daring to breathe, lest they be heard and discovered.

The goat-headed figure made several passes with the knife longitudinally and transversely across the woman's naked body, the edge of the pointed tip always just missing her bare flesh. She did not flinch. From the flickering fire of the burning torches, they could see that the central figure had a crimson red cloak, whilst the rest were in black. With each pass of the knife, the goat-headed apparition made a hideous hissing noise, such as a serpent might make, prior to attacking its victim. This would then be followed by a prolonged gasp from the whole throng of disciples.

Everything went quiet, and Kevin and Dawn saw another hooded figure enter through the archway, on the other side of the courtyard. To their amazement this one led the goat with a red velvet cord round its neck.

In spite of his terror, Kevin edged forward to obtain a better look at the goings on below. A small stone dislodged near the edge of the parapet and went tumbling down to the courtyard. To Kevin's intense relief it landed on a grassy patch between the well-worn stone. Even so, he edged back, totally out of sight from below and held his breath. After about half a minute, he realised it had gone unnoticed, and gingerly edged forward again.

The goat had been led up to the red cloaked, masked figure and now was being supported upside down by its back legs, one man holding each. The naked blonde woman, still supported by two others, remained next to it. The poor animal was bleating piteously. A deathly hush, broken only by the noise the goat was making, descended on the throng. This continued for about a minute, before the central figure renewed his chanting.

Then a tall wooden frame was brought in by two of the group, who had left a minute before, and now returned. The poor goat was suspended with leather straps by its back legs and cranked up by a handle mechanism, until its head was level with that of the goat-headed apparition.

"I dedicate this offering to you, oh my master, and death to all who do not follow your path." The deep tones of the central performer of the sacrificial rite floated up to the concealed pair above. There was a low moan of expectancy from the throng and then a prolonged sighing gasp. The goat's continually bleating was permanently hushed, as the red-cloaked apparition, with one savage slash, cut the animal's jugular. The animal continued to twitch for some seconds in its death throes, and then the blood started to flow in a steady stream onto the worn stones of the courtyard.

The woman was then pushed forward by the men supporting her. Still she showed no fear, only a trance-like acceptance of events. The goat-headed masked figure ceremoniously wiped the blade of the long curved knife in the fast increasing pool of blood, under the deceased animal's body. In the light from the torches, Kevin and Dawn watched in abject horror as a crimson stain dulled the shiny object. The leader placed the knife at the woman's throat and without puncturing her skin drew with the steel point, a line of blood, down between her ample breasts to where it stopped at her bushy pubic hair. Then, changing the direction, he circled each breast with blood and finally concluded by making a transverse pattern across the woman's abdomen.

The horrific sight was by no means finished for Kevin and Dawn. They watched powerless and transfixed as the goat-headed man produced a silver chalice of the kind used in churches and proceeded to fill it from the dripping throat of the dead tethered goat. Then they watched him drink from the cup, which was then in turn passed from one to the other of the entire group. Each would drink from it and hand it to the next hooded figure.

Worse was to come. At the invitation of their leader, every member of the large group filed up in turn to lick blood from the naked woman. When the last one had completed this foul act, Kevin and Dawn watched the figures pair off. There seemed to be an equal number of men and women.

The leader dragged the naked blonde into an area below them, hidden from their view and from the noises they could only surmise what was transpiring. If they were in any doubt it was soon removed. Couples began to copulate in the courtyard below them. This mass orgy continued until about one a.m. in the morning with couples continually changing partners.

There was nothing Kevin and Dawn could do but remain cold and shivering where they lay. Dawn threw up once, shocked and appalled at what she was being forced to watch. The noise of this bodily disturbance went quite unnoticed, due to the cacophony of sound from the courtyard, and the pair remained undetected throughout.

The mass orgy broke up a little later and everyone gradually began to disperse. It wasn't until Kevin saw the last of the car lights receding down the hill towards Saddlewitch that the pair felt confident enough to move. Cold and stiff from being still so long, they crept down from the old tower and began the long trek home.

"I won't half cop if when I get home. My mum says I have to be home by ten," moaned Dawn.

"Don't worry. I'll come with you and explain," explained Kevin.

CHAPTER TWELVE

Although the pair hurried, it was fully two a.m. when they reached the council estate where Dawn lived. As she had expected, both her parents were waiting up for her and flew into a rage, most of it directed at Kevin. It was ten minutes before either could get in a word of explanation.

Finally, Kevin managed to relate what had happened. Dawn's parents were horrified and, in spite of the late hour, called George Fenning at the police house. George, however, had had his usual skinful of beer and couldn't be wakened by his wife, Gladys.

To ring Grantfield, Gladys knew, would get her husband in severe trouble. She knew from George that the young fellow at Briar Cottage was something to do with the police. Yes, she would ring him.

She rummaged downstairs in George's makeshift office for Drew Thorpe's number. She knew he was new in the village and wouldn't be in the telephone book. After much searching and cursing of the sleeping George, she found it and rang the number.

Drew was woken from a sound sleep, but assured her he would go at once. He took down the Cumming's address and got dressed for quickness in a Dash tracksuit and trainers. As he set off on foot – it wasn't far; he mused, there goes my cover now. But what could he do? After all he didn't want to get PC Fenning into trouble.

He found the Cumming's home. A group were waiting for him at the front door, all in an agitated state. Apparently Mr. Cummings had rung Kevin's parents, and the Dales were both there too, as well as the neighbours from next door.

Drew introduced himself by showing his warrant card and was invited in. Everyone was talking at once, trying to tell him what had happened.

"Okay, hold it everyone. Let Kevin and Dawn tell me exactly what happened," Drew said, as calmly as he could. Between them and with several interruptions, Kevin and Dawn related the appalling earlier scenario.

Drew made a few notes in his book and enquired whether Kevin would go up to the old monastery now with him to show him exactly where this had all happened.

Mr. Dale objected fiercely.

"My son's only seventeen. I don't want him taking any further risks." This caused an outburst from Dawn's mother, Mrs. Cummings.

"Never mind your son ... It's him what's leading my daughter into bad ways. . What were they doing there in the first place, I'd like to know."

Drew stepped in – the last thing he wanted now was to be caught in the middle of a dispute between parents.

"I'm sure the youngsters merely went for a walk on a nice warm night. If this hadn't happened they would have both been home at a normal time ... I think, given the circumstances, they both did extremely well ... These people are very dangerous and you should be pleased the kids are both unharmed."

Kevin and Dawn both shot looks of pure relief at Drew, and the mood of the irate parents mellowed somewhat. Eventually they agreed to let Kevin go up to the old monastery with Drew. Kevin's father offered to drive them up there, but Drew suggested it would be better on foot. Unfortunately, Mr. Dale insisted on accompanying them and there was little he could do to dissuade him.

By the time the three of them arrived at the monastery Drew's watch told him, although it was still dark, the hour had reached four a.m. The moon had since set, although the stars still showed abundantly in a clear sky.

Both men had flashlights with them, which they shone in all the old ruined crevices and Kevin showed him where he and Dawn had lain watching the spectacle below. In the courtyard there was a pool of blood on the stones and the grass was stained crimson, but of the goat's remains there was no sign.

"It was here – honest it was," said Kevin. Drew patted him on the shoulder.

"Okay lad, no-one doubts you … Obviously they loaded the carcass and took it with them in one of the vehicles."

Drew, with his flashlight, went over the entire area with a fine toothcomb, but all he came up with were a torn piece of cloth, a cigarette packet and a disposable lighter. He carefully collected all three in a polythene bag and pocketed them.

"Probably not much help, but we will see what forensics come up with," he explained to Kevin and his father. By the time they left the site it was five and still dark. The tyre tracks of the vehicles still showed in the dew of the grassy slopes. He thanked Kevin and his father and they parted for their respective homes at the village perimeter. Drew asked them to keep this matter to themselves, but he knew he was wasting his time when he said it.

By morning it would be all round Saddlewitch. Drew knew from old that nothing could compare with a village gossip system. It could even rival the jungle drums for circulating news.

When he eventually reached Briar Cottage it was too late to go back to bed, so he sat down and wrote a full report for his superiors. By the time he had finished that, the pale light of a mid September dawn was filtering though the kitchen window. Later on he would ring Caroline and keep her up to date…

★ ★ ★ ★ ★

Sasha heard the news herself the next morning when she was buying groceries at the village shop from plumber Ted Sewell's wife, Maggie. The whole village was talking about it, apparently. This fact was confirmed when she heard it again later from Strimmer the postman. This followed a recounting of him and his partner Jethro's victory of 301 in the darts match at the Black Bull. Sasha couldn't have cared less about the darts, but she listened dutifully and patiently to how in one leg he had scored 151 in, and left Jethro 150 out. To everyone's amazement, including Jethro, who was a known duffer at darts, he had got it; a sixty and double top and a bull out. At this point he had then put his thumbs behind his braces, thrown his chest out and milked the applause. The Black Bull had beaten the George and Dragon from Endersby by four games to three.

Sasha was, however, interested in the part about the Satanists and that young fellow from Briar Cottage, turning out to be a C.I.D man. The village, Strimmer said, had never had such goings on. As usual there was no sign of Bart, so she telephoned Drew.

"Are you going to be in if I call round this morning?" she asked him.

"For you, always," he exclaimed, delighted to hear her voice. Twenty minutes later she was with him at Briar Cottage. "Thought I ought to let you know that your secret is out ... It's all round the village this morning ... As you had already told me about your purpose here, I didn't want you to think it was me who had blabbed," exclaimed Sasha. Drew confirmed that he knew it wasn't and after last night's meeting with the Dales, Cummings and their neighbours, he guessed it wouldn't take long to circulate. "What really happened last night, Drew? I've only heard the gossip version so far – or shouldn't I ask?" enquired Sasha.

Drew gave her a detailed account of Kevin Dale's story. Sasha listened with eyes wide open.

"Could he have made it up?" Sasha asked hopefully.

"No, there's no doubt about it, it's all perfectly true. The kids were scared out of their wits," Drew replied. The two of them continued to discuss the affair and were still involved when Caroline arrived. He had telephoned her earlier and informed her of last night's happening.

Sasha noted the instant displeasure on Caroline's face when she saw Sasha in the lounge with Drew. After pouring Caroline a cup of coffee he began talking about the events of the night.

Caroline cut in. "Should you be talking in front of her?" she said, jerking her head in Sasha's direction.

"Oh, it's all right. Sasha knows all about it," Drew said. "It's all round the village."

"I'll leave if you want," volunteered Sasha, embarrassed.

"No you won't ... You stay right where you are, Sasha," affirmed Drew, giving Caroline a hard look.

"Oh well, it's no skin off my nose, the rumour at HQ is that not having obtained a result we are going to be pulled off this case, anyway" snapped Caroline.

"After last night I wouldn't think so," argued Drew.

Sasha sat back and sipped her coffee, letting the two of them talk it through, but she sat up anew when Caroline enquired how he was progressing with Barbara Lake, the bank manager's wife. Drew looked a little embarrassed and felt he needed to explain to Sasha.

"Caroline's cover was blown first and we decided I should try and make contact with Mrs. Lake and get into her confidence ... as she was the only possible lead we had," said Drew.

"And he did, too," exclaimed Caroline, giving Sasha a smug look. When Drew said nothing, Caroline enquired, "Why don't you tell her how that went, as you seem to have told her everything else about this case." Drew shot another savage look at Caroline.

"The plan was for me to make her acquaintance and try to gain her confidence ... perhaps get an introduction to this group of Satanists, if she is involved ... We don't know for sure ... Anyway, it's all academic now, because the whole village, including Mrs. Lake, will know I'm a policeman by now. If she is involved she will be on her guard by this time," Drew looked crestfallen. "Where do we go from here?" He was virtually asking himself the question.

Caroline was not to be put off so easily. She addressed Sasha.

"Quite the ladies man, our Drew ... Tell her how you were getting on with Mrs. Lake, Drew."

"Nothing to tell. My cover is blown now," said Drew irritably glaring at Caroline. The latter was not about to let the matter go that easily.

"He even joined the local squash club at Grantfield where she is a member. Plays there every Wednesday evening ... Last week he played with her and he's gone to her house for drinks since, haven't you, Drew?" Caroline sat back and watched Sasha's face over the rim of her coffee cup. Sasha smiled sweetly at her.

"All in the line of duty," was all she said.

"She's quite an attractive woman, you know," put in Caroline, trying again to add fuel to the fire.

"Tonight, being Wednesday I was supposed to play her at squash again if you want to be brought up to date, Caroline," said Drew, his voice heavy with sarcasm.

Caroline, having failed to rattle Sasha, became resigned to developments. She added, "Well, with both our covers now blown, and her being the only lead, it looks as if we've had it, doesn't it? Head Office will have our innards for garters."

Sasha said calmly, "Not necessarily." Both turned to look at her. "Why don't I help?"

"Don't be ridiculous. How could you help? You're not a trained policewoman," snapped Caroline, glaring at Sasha.

"Shut up Caroline. Go on, Sasha, what were you going to say?" encouraged Drew.

"Well, I don't know the woman well, only to say good morning to, but she will have seen me about the village over the last two or three years, so she certainly wouldn't suspect me … I mean, I could, if you wanted, take it a stage further and sort of worm my way in."

"How in hell would you do that?" Caroline cut in. "These people are dangerous … Do you realise what you are getting involved with?"

"Just a minute, Caroline, if I may call you that, you said yourself that we don't know for sure whether Mrs. Lake is involved with the Satanists."

"It looks highly likely," retorted Caroline, twisting a lock of blonde hair round her finger.

"Okay, I accept that, but look here, if I can find out for you and locate where the next meeting of the cult is going to take place, the rest would be up to you," Sasha proposed.

"I don't see anything wrong with that, Sasha, provided you don't expose yourself to unnecessary risks," agreed Drew.

"Okay, that's settled then. I'll find out what I can and report back to you," confirmed Sasha.

"Or me – you can report to me," retorted Caroline.

Drew looked hard at Caroline and then pointedly at Sasha, before concluding, "Thanks for agreeing to help Sasha. Keep me posted and watch your step."

★ ★ ★ ★ ★

When the news of the monastery goings on reached the local paper, even the few people in the village that didn't know were made aware. Billie Tate's mother finally put two and two together and remembered the black silk hood she had found weeks before in Billie's trouser pocket. At the time she had stuffed it into a drawer, intending to confront Billie with it, but clean forgot. When she read about the events, she produced it and interrogated Billie with the details of how he had come by it. After much persistence Billie broke down and confessed that he and Dennis Madeley had broken into the old windmill and found it there.

"That Madeley boy will be the death of you, Billie. How many times have I told you not to play with him? Look what happened yesterday." Billie's mother was referring to an incident where as far as she could understand from Billie, his hero Dennis Madeley had taken careful aim with his air gun at Mrs. Barnes blue knickers as they hung out to dry on the line. The pellet had apparently lodged itself in the knickers and could be seen as a black spot from where the two boys hid behind the hedge.

Dennis had then instructed Billie to go and remove the pellet or, as everyone knew, he, Dennis, was the only one with an air gun and would get into trouble. Billie, who couldn't bear to think of his friend in trouble, had crawled through the hedge, ran across the lawn, picked out the offending pellet and returned it to Dennis. The latter inspected it and replaced it into the breach of the gun for future use. All this would have been fine if Mrs. Barnes hadn't been looking out at the back garden from her kitchen window at the time. Recognising the boy, she had promptly called on Billie's mother to complain.

"Then there was the other day when you and that Madeley boy threw a firework behind Mrs. Hortense Hyde-Potter. She claimed you could have given her a heart attack," grumbled Cathy Tate.

She dragged Billie round to PC George Fenning and took the black silk hood with them. She explained at length. George, never in the best of moods in the morning, before he could get to a pint of bitter, looked down his long nose, first at the evidence, then at young Billie.

"You say you found this at the old windmill, boy?"

"Yes sir, there were other things too ... Lots of these and black gowns and things and yes, a funny knife too," piped up Billie. George screwed his eyes up dramatically and pushed his bottom lip over the top one.

"That mill is private property ... Breaking and entering ... That's what it is, boy," George ran finger and thumb down his long nose and fixed his gaze on the boy.

"I'm s...sorry, sir," blurted out Billie, near to tears.

"I expect you are lad, but do you realise people go to prison for this sort of thing?" said George, in his long slow drawl. That did it. Billie burst into tears right there and then. George lent forward and patted the boy's head. "Well, being as how you have confessed, perhaps I'll overlook it this time ... You go home with your mum and be a good boy in future ... No more breaking and entering ... or shooting air guns at ladies knickers – understand?" George came as near to a smile as he ever did, his mouth curling up at one corner.

He kept the black silk hood and watched Billie go off down the road, still sniffling with his mother.

Half an hour later he was round at Briar Cottage with Drew Thorpe, acquainting him with developments.

"Come on, constable, let's get round to that windmill and take a look....."

Sure enough, they found what Billie had said was true. All the said articles were there. George asked what Drew wanted done with everything.

"We are going to leave everything here, just as it lays now. Obviously we can't spare a man to keep watch, so I'm going to have Special Branch install a hidden camera here. It should be interesting to see who collects this stuff ... I'll come and check each morning, because whoever comes for it probably does so after dark."

"Hmmm, you are probably right," agreed George, fingering the curved knife.

Drew rang through there and then on his mobile with his request to HQ then, turning to George he said, "They are coming straight away constable, so perhaps you can stay on here until they arrive. I've got to get over to Grantfield hospital. It appears that fellow they found at the Highroad Motel has finally recovered consciousness."

"I didn't know he was anything to do with this business, Mr. Thorpe," said George.

"We don't know for sure that he is, but two weeks ago when it happened, two hooded figures and two women were seen leaving the motel. It wasn't until the next morning he was found ... Been in a coma ever since, with a man at his bedside."

CHAPTER THIRTEEN

When Drew arrived at Grantfield Hospital, he was led through by a young nurse, to Intensive Care. He found a young constable seated by the patient's bedside. On seeing him the constable rose immediately and whispered, "Regained consciousness about two hours ago, but other than his name, which we already knew, nothing."

"Okay constable. Leave us for a few minutes, will you," said Drew. Drew pulled up a chair close to the patient who still had a drip placed in the back of one hand and a tube up his nose. "Can you hear me, Mr. Grainger?" he asked. The reply was barely audible, so faint was the man's voice. "Do you know who attacked you?" Drew asked, bending forward to catch the answer.

"Two m…men, m…masked," came back the weak reply.

"Any idea who they could have been?"

"No."

"Have you any enemies who might have done this to you?"

"D…don't think s…so."

"We know that there were two women with them. Did you know them?" The answer was a long time in coming.

"No."

"We think you do, Mr. Grainger. The clerk said you booked the room yourself and he saw the two ladies go directly into your room from the car park."

"No, n….no, he m…must have been m…mistaken."

"Are you saying that there were no ladies?"

"Only m…me. No l…ladies." Drew leaned closer.

"I know you are lying, Mr. Grainger. Did these men threaten to kill you if you said anything?" Grainger began to shake uncontrollably. Drew continued, "We can protect you … Take you to a safe house," he urged.

"Nowhere s….safe," came back Grainger's halting reply.

The man was clearly terrified and still in a critical condition. Drew was reluctant to push him any further.

"These are dangerous men and we want to get them behind bars," he said. At that moment a nursing sister arrived in her dark blue uniform.

"I'm sorry sir, but you will have to leave. I can't have the patient bothered further in his condition." Drew produced a card and laid it on the bedside locker.

"Very well, nurse. Call this number if Mr. Grainger wants to talk – day or night. I'll be back tomorrow anyway … Goodbye for now, Mr. Grainger," he said, turning at the door. He thanked the nurse and left the room and on the way out, saw the constable waiting outside. "Be on your guard, constable. The men who did this might take it into their heads to come back and finish the job…"

* * * * *

Sasha, quite fired up by the new challenge in her life, began to walk her dog Bess in an area where she had seen Barbara Lake walking her poodle in the past. It was a good week before she ran into the woman who, on seeing Sasha and Bess, scooped the white miniature poodle up into her arms.

"Oh, it's quite all right. My dog is quite friendly, she wouldn't hurt a fly," ventured Sasha. With this, Barbara Lake put her dog down on the grass, the meeting having occurred on a footpath across a grassy meadow. The sun shone down on them from a bright blue sky, although the first leaves were beginning to show signs of falling.

Sasha, dressed in jumper and slacks, positioned herself so that Barbara would have to leave the path, into longer grass, to pass her. She pushed home this momentary advantage.

"Beautiful day, isn't it? I do love this time of the year, don't you?"

Barbara, her face heavily made up and her hair carefully coiffured, was dressed in skin-tight leggings and pale blue Cashmere sweater. She responded in a cultured county voice.

"I've seen you around the village before, haven't I?"

"Oh yes, I walk my dog here two or three times a day." The conversation then went on to various small talk as often happens between strangers. At first, Barbara seemed quite stilted and aloof but gradually began to thaw out. After about ten minutes, with both dogs happily playing in the meadow, Sasha decided to push home her plan. "It's nice here in the village, very peaceful, but sometimes I wish there was a little more action … More people like you, my own age, I mean."

The ruse worked. Barbara's face showed that she was clearly flattered. She herself knew she must be at least ten years older than the girl before her.

"What did you say your name was?" she enquired.

"I didn't say, but it's Sasha."

"Well Sasha, mine's Barbara … You must come up and have drinks with us, some time … My husband is the bank manager at Grantfield, you know."

"Oh really," replied Sasha, effecting innocence. Barbara's eyes swept up and down Sasha almost as if she was seeing her for the first time.

"You're very attractive you know. I wouldn't have thought you're the type who would want to be buried in Saddlewitch."

Taking her cue beautifully, Sasha replied, "No, I must admit it is lonely when my husband's away, which is frequent, and I do find it rather boring."

"Oh dear, we can't have that, can we my dear … do you play squash?" Sasha admitted that she didn't. "Go to a gym or health club?" enquired Barbara.

"No, but I was thinking about it," replied Sasha.

"Great. Then you shall come with my friend and I. We go twice a week – tomorrow afternoon, in fact. Could you manage that?"

Not wanting to appear too keen, Sasha looked thoughtful for a moment or two, then said, "Why not. It would do me good. I could probably do with losing a few pounds."

"That's settled then. I'll pick you up at two p.m. tomorrow and we can go together," remarked Barbara.

"No...... no, I mean I couldn't put you to that trouble .... Give me your address and I'll call round to your place," volunteered Sasha.

"Very well .... if you don't want your husband to know, I mean. I quite understand." Barbara followed this with a conspiratorial snigger.

"No, it's not that at all. I just don't want to put you to any trouble." They continued to chat for a further five minutes before going their separate ways. On the way home Sasha smiled to herself and said out aloud to Bess, now on the lead, "I think I'm on my way."

★ ★ ★ ★ ★

The next afternoon took a long time coming, but eventually like everything, it arrived. Sasha, dressed in a red tracksuit with a leotard underneath and trainers on her feet, arrived at Barbara's house. Barbara introduced her to Sally Greves, her friend. Both women kissed her on the mouth, which she found quite distasteful, but tried not to show it. Sally, like Barbara, was dressed in a skin-tight poser type tracksuit. Sasha adjudged them to be about the same age.

"We will have a little aperitif before we go, shall we?" said Barbara, reaching for the sherry decanter. Sasha noticed, from the two empty glasses already residing on the coffee table, that both women must already have had at least one before she arrived.

"No thanks. Just an orange juice, if you have one. I'm reckoning on losing weight not putting it on," Sasha laughed.

"Isn't she good, considering she doesn't need to lose an ounce as far as I can see," remarked Sally Greves.

"We will soon alter that," said Barbara, pouring the required orange juice for Sasha, from the drinks cabinet. All three sat on the sofa with Sasha the sandwich in the middle. At nearly every opportunity Barbara kept placing a hand on Sasha's knee, which made the latter inwardly squirm. At any other time she would have made an excuse to leave. Once Barbara's hand strayed further up Sasha's track-suited thigh.

"I don't think she needs to lose anything, Sally … You should just feel how firm her thighs are," said Barbara, with a laugh.

Sasha gritted her teeth whilst Sally made the same experiment on the other leg. Sasha made a mental note not to get caught in the shower with these two. She realised with horror, that Barbara Lake's man mad reputation didn't only include the male sex. Sasha quickly finished her glass and looked at her watch. She rose quickly, eager to distance herself from the two women.

"Goodness me, look at the time. It's nearly two. Shouldn't we be going?" Sasha urged.

Barbara agreed that yes, she hadn't realised just how late it was. A few minutes later and they were on the way to Grantfield, the two friends in the front with Sasha in the back of Barbara's BMW.

"Your car will be all right in our drive," Barbara had assured Sasha.

The gym turned out to be an understatement. It was, in fact, a country club on the outskirts of Grantfield. An old beautifully refurbished Tudor mansion at the end of a long drive surrounded by a grove of chestnut trees. Everything about the decor reeked of money and sumptuous furniture complemented it. The separate modern gym had just about everything, complete with computer screens. Barbara signed Sasha in as her guest.

With considerable unease, Sasha removed her tracksuit in the communal ladies changing room, to reveal a trim black leotard. She felt, rather than saw, Barbara and Sally's eyes on her. As quickly as she could, she hurried through to the gym, Sally and Barbara following in her wake. Barbara introduced her to the male attendants.

An individual, who called himself Hugo, attached himself to her saying he would act as her personal trainer. Sasha disliked him on sight. He was one of those terribly good looking supercilious characters, who obviously thought he was God's gift to womanhood. At every opportunity he would run his fingers though his long blond hair in a most affected way and smile at Sasha in a patronising manner.

First he asked lots of questions, saying he knew best what would suit her. He elected to put her on the treadmill first, followed with the cycle. Then came some work with weights. At every opportunity Hugo would touch her, only briefly, but Sasha found it quite irritating. Some time into the session she noticed the absence of both Barbara and Sally. They were gone for about twenty minutes before reappearing, both looking like the cat that had swallowed the cream.

After putting Sasha through some leg exercises, Hugo suggested she might benefit from a general massage, which apparently he would do in a separate room for her. Sasha declined, saying she really wouldn't have time. Luckily Barbara arrived just after Hugo's invitation but Sasha's relief was short lived as the latter suggested a shower. Sasha was half expecting this, so she had her excuse ready.

"Actually I feel a bit wobbly after all this exercise ... I think I'll just sit down and rest for a bit ... You and Sally go ahead."

Barbara seemed quite concerned and flustered about her. Sasha reassured her that it was nothing really, and that she just wasn't used to that much exercise at once.

"Perhaps Hugo will fetch me a glass of water?" she asked...

Half an hour later, the BMW pulled into Barbara's drive. As they alighted from the vehicle Barbara invited Sasha to join them for a drink. Frankly, Sasha had had enough and would have loved to decline, but she told herself she owed it to Drew, to inveigle herself into Barbara Lake's confidence. She accepted.

In the plush lounge, Barbara poured three sherries, without bothering to ask. She handed them round. This time Sasha was careful to sit in an armchair. Over drinks Barbara and Sally extolled the virtues of the various physiotherapists and attendants at the club. Sally said that Bertrand certainly gave a lovely massage. Sasha caught a look between Barbara and Sally that seemed to say 'shut up and be careful'. She pretended not to have seen it.

"Perhaps you would like to take a shower here, Sasha, as you didn't feel like one at the club ... You are very welcome to use either the upstairs or downstairs bathrooms," offered Barbara.

Sasha declined graciously saying, no, she would wait now until she got home, it was time to see about the family dinner. "I've so enjoyed myself, today," she lied.

"Then you must come again my dear. But join us for drinks next Thursday evening … We are having a few friends in … Say about 7.30 p.m … .. Just nibbles, you understand, nothing grand … I think you mentioned your husband might be away … Bring your au pair, if you like, she sounds very nice."

"Thank you Barbara … I'll have to see about a baby sitter if I do … but I'll certainly try," replied Sasha.

After saying goodbye to both, she drove the short journey home through the village, feeling at least satisfied with her progress. Obviously it was going to take time to get Barbara Lake to trust her enough to open up …

Sasha might not have been so pleased with herself had she witnessed a scene that was being enacted in London's Neptune Hotel; in room 506 on the 5th floor. In the centre of the room stood a male figure clothed from head to foot in red. His entire head was covered by the horned head of a goat mask that reached down to his shoulders. On his feet were boots resembling cloven hoofs and in his right hand he carried a long black rawhide bull whip.

At his feet, a young black girl whimpered. She couldn't have been above nineteen. She was dressed only in a white thong. Placing his whip free hand on the girl's thick dark 'afro' curls, he pushed her head down towards the floor.

The girl cried out, "The agency didn't say anything about this. They said just straight sex." The only response the girl's complaint received was a stinging welt across her ebony back. With a cry of pain, she flung her hands up in a vain effort to protect herself.

The red-cloaked apparition threw down the whip and, reaching down, fastened his fingers into her tight black curls and pulled her to her feet. She found herself staring straight into the venomous eyes, through the slit eyeholes of the goat's head.

"P…Please, no!" she cried in terror. Still holding her by the hair, he twisted her round, so that she faced the double bed in the centre of the room.

"Down," was the only word he uttered, in a low menacing tone. She found herself forced down, her screams muffled by the pillow her head was pushed into. Almost numb with fright and shock she felt the flimsy thong ripped off her nubile body. Then the hands were back in her hair again, pulling her head backwards, causing an excruciating ache in her neck. The voice behind her was both deep and menacing.

"Submit to the master," was all it said.

Had Sasha been there, she would have recognised the voice of her husband, Bart Paget.

★ ★ ★ ★ ★

Ray Grainger continued to improve very slowly. Although off the danger list, he defied all attempts by Drew to get him to talk. No, he didn't know the men, or the women seen leaving the motel. He was plainly too terrified of receiving the same, or worse, if he talked. Drew suggested to Caroline that she might try the feminine touch, but the result was the same.

It was obvious to both that he knew a lot more than he was willing to tell, but they were powerless to extract anything tangible from the frightened private detective. His wallet and business cards found on him when the police arrived, had identified Grainger, but that was all they knew. He had a small dingy office in Grantfield and an estranged wife living on the other side of town.

Drew and Caroline went to see Mrs. Annette Grainger. She wasn't much help and, in fact, when they introduced themselves remarked, "What's that scum bag been up to now?" When they asked if he had any enemies, she replied, "Don't you mean, has he any friends?"

She was a large, rather coarse busty blonde, dressed in a leopard skin top and matching ski pants. Her accent was definitely from the midlands. After five minutes it became obvious that Drew and Caroline were wasting their time. She knew nothing and cared less.

"If I had one wish, it would be never to see that rat ever again, unless it's in court for the money he owes me," was her parting shot, as she showed them out …

* * * * *

Two weeks after the visit to Annette Grainger, Drew and Caroline were summoned up to Special Branch HQ in London. Drew drove them both up in his car. Both were under no illusions. Having got nowhere fast, they guessed that they were due for a carpeting. They were not wrong.

A WPC showed them through to Superintendent Dawson's office. He was seated at his office desk, working on some papers. He didn't look up when they entered and both were forced to stand uneasily in front of his desk.

A large mass of iron-grey hair was all they could see of him. When he did look up the head under the mane of hair gave the impression of being two sizes too big for his body. Thick, bushy eyebrows arched over severe brown eyes. His face looked like it had been carved from granite, with high cheekbones and forehead. The chin and jaw line were strong and equally robust.

Without speaking, he indicated the two chairs in front of his desk, by jabbing a broad index finger in their direction. Drew realised that they were deliberately being made to feel insecure, always a characteristic of Dawson.

When he finally spoke, it was one word.

"Well?"

Caroline looked at Drew apprehensively, the latter responded, "We are following the only lead we have sir … We believe it will take us where we want to go." Dawson's eyes bored through Drew who, to his credit, did not look away.

"You believe! … Not much for – let's see, how long is it you two have had these villages under surveillance? It's a good three months, I see," remarked Dawson, dryly thumbing through some papers on his desk.

Drew gave a full report of developments over the period and, at times, Dawson interjected with questions. As was the Superintendent's manner, they came like bullets from a gun, sharp and staccato. At the conclusion of Drew's report Dawson turned his attention on Caroline.

"And you, WPC Channing, have you anything to add?"

"No sir, I think Drew ... I mean DS Thorpe has covered everything."

"Which doesn't amount to much, does it, Channing? ... Friends from way back, weren't you?"

"Beg your pardon, sir?" said Caroline. Dawson didn't repeat the question – he just looked very pointedly from one to the other before continuing.

"A nice summer holiday for both of you in the country, some might say, and not a lot to show for the department's expenses concerning this affair ... Up to now, it's been chickens, vandalism and goats ... Do I have to spell it out to you both what's coming next? It's only a matter of time before we have a body and then it's murder. If you're right, Thorpe, we nearly had one with this Grainger fellow ... Lucky for whoever did it, that he's recovering ... Has he talked yet?"

"No sir, we are still working on him," Drew responded.

"Then you had better work a little harder, hadn't you Sergeant?" snapped Dawson. "I want results here. It's not just you two who are under pressure ... I have superiors too, you know," he went on.

"Yes sir," said Drew. Dawson switched his piercing gaze on Caroline. She nodded.

"Very well. Get out, both of you ... I'll give you one more month." Dawson reached for the calendar on his desk and, with a red pen, put a mark on Saturday, 31st October. With a mirthless laugh, he remarked, "Very appropriate – Halloween ... I don't need to tell either of you that this is not going to go down well on your c.v. if you fail me," Dawson concluded.

CHAPTER FOURTEEN

Sasha, over the last two weeks, had made considerable progress with Barbara Lake, who had invited her to coffee mornings and a drinks party at her house. She had even been introduced to Barbara's husband, Edward, known to all his friends as Ted. He was about ten years older than his wife with a waistline running to corpulence; bald on top with grey mutton chop whiskers and bushy eyebrows. A florid countenance suggested a liking for port and claret.

At the drinks party he made a beeline for Sasha and paid considerable attention to her all evening, showering her with compliments. He seemed a harmless enough individual, and Sasha felt quite sorry for him really. During the party, Barbara paid quite shameless attention to several of the male guests, never bothering at all about poor Ted's feelings.

It was on the first of October that the real breakthrough came. Sasha had been into Grantfield in the morning to see a solicitor about the deplorable state of her marriage to Bart. She had just arrived home when the telephone rang. It was Barbara Lake.

"Can you come round, my dear?" Barbara asked.

"When?"

"Now, or as soon as you can," urged Barbara.

Not wanting to appear too enthusiastic, Sasha replied, "In about an hour's time, if that's all right."

"Fine. I'll expect you then ... Bye." Sasha heard the phone hang up the other end. She waited a full minute, then rang Drew. He had formerly asked her to acquaint him of all developments concerning Barbara Lake.

He agreed that this could be the breakthrough they were waiting for. Perhaps Barbara now trusted her enough to admit Sasha into her confidence and innermost circle. Drew warned her not to run any risks and to play along with whatever Barbara suggested in name only. Anything else was up to him and Caroline. She was only to obtain information.

"I could never forgive myself if anything happened to you ... I wish there was another way, but unfortunately there isn't."

His tone made her feel quite warm inside, and Sasha resolved there and then, to do all she could for him. She had to admit to herself too, it was quite exciting playing the sleuth, a change from her usual mundane way of life. She felt better too, now that she knew the divorce papers for unreasonable behaviour were to be served on Bart.

She was already dressed for going out, having just returned from the solicitors, although she doubted that Barbara would approve of the smart two-piece light grey tailored suit. The plain skirt with a peplum was of respectable length. She debated whether to go and change but decided against it. If Barbara Lake had intentions that way, the last thing she wanted was to encourage her down that road...

An hour later, Barbara opened the door to her and showed her into the lounge.

"So glad you could come, my dear," greeted Barbara, clutching hold of Sasha's arms, she looked Sasha up and down, appraising her. "My, you do look smart ... good enough to eat, in fact," commented Barbara. Changing the subject, Sasha explained she had just returned from a business appointment in Grantfield.

Barbara poured dry sherries for both of them and sat down on the sofa with Sasha. After the usual small talk pleasantries had been exchanged Barbara's tone changed to a conspiratorial one. Sasha tried to ignore the hand the latter had placed on her stockinged knee.

"I couldn't help noticing last night how well my husband got on with you, my dear," said Barbara.

"Oh, ... I hope you didn't think ..." began Sasha.

"Oh no, no, nothing like that, Sasha. I didn't mind at all. In fact, had you been more responsive I would have approved."

"I'm sorry, I don't quite understand." Sasha was quite well aware that she was being deliberately obtuse, but she wanted Barbara's cards on the table.

"Well, you see, he tends to watch and prohibit what I do ... So, I mean, if he was distracted say, just a little? ... He does fancy you, he told me so last night … I mean, who wouldn't fancy you, Sasha?" The latter squirmed inwardly as she felt Barbara stroking her hair. "Such lovely dark hair."

No, and he's not the only one that fancies me, Sasha thought to herself, but she managed to control her thoughts and said, "What exactly is it that you want me to do, Barbara?"

"Well, shall we say I sometimes go to some very interesting meetings and have to always find an alibi for my husband; to stop him asking awkward questions … Do I need to say more?"

Sasha remembered her days at drama school and dug deep. She smiled coquettishly and twiddled a lock of her own dark hair.

"Well perhaps I might like to join you at one of these interesting meetings … I mean if they're that exciting.…" She let the words tail off, meaningfully.

"Did I say they were exciting?" queried Barbara. Was that a note of suspicion in Barbara's tone? Had she gone too far too quickly? Sasha recovered.

"Well, if you want to go to them, and you need an alibi, they sound like the sort of meetings I might be interested in." Sasha put on her most conspiratorial face, running one finger along her nose.

"You're a sport. I knew you would be when we first met," laughed Barbara. Then a thought seemed to occur to her. There was a pregnant pause before she continued. "How about your husband? You have never mentioned him. What's he like? Liberal I should think, to let a lovely wife like you out on the loose."

"I've just served divorce papers on him," remarked Sasha, dryly, deciding the truth might help in this instance.

"Oh, what a pity. We could have made up a foursome. I bet he's handsome to have captured a beauty like you, Sasha."

"Out of the question. I wouldn't care if I never saw him again." Sasha realised she had got herself into deep water again with Barbara's next question.

"But don't you have two children? I remember you telling Sally and me?"

"Yes, and I adore them, but they are better off without a father like him…" Barbara was like a terrier with a bone.

"But won't that make it difficult for you to get away? To play, I mean?" She accompanied the question with a crafty smile.

"No … Our au pair is very good with the children."

Barbara looked relieved and her hand found its way back to Sasha's knee once more.

"If my husband rang you and asked you out to dinner, would you go? One evening soon?"

Sasha thought quickly. This was all going wrong.

She countered with, "I'd rather go with you to one of these interesting meetings of yours." Barbara threw back her head and laughed before replying.

"Well you do have to be a member."

"Couldn't I join, or perhaps you could introduce me as a guest," Sasha queried enthusiastically. Barbara thought for a moment.

"I'll tell you what I'll do … You have a couple of dinner assignations with Ted to help me and then I'll take you along with me to one."

This wasn't what Sasha wanted at all, but there seemed little choice, if she was going to get anywhere, other than to agree. It occurred to Sasha, that it wasn't going to help with her divorce if she was seen out with the local bank manager. Come to that, it probably didn't help with her comings and goings to Briar cottage. That was a risk she was prepared to take, and nothing had happened between them yet anyway … Now this! Dinner with a man she didn't even find remotely attractive, even if she did feel sorry for him.

Nevertheless, she found herself agreeing to Barbara's proposal, which seemed, if nothing else, to delight the latter.

Sasha was intrigued just how Barbara intended to arrange these dates for her with Ted but when she questioned Barbara about it, she simply said, "Leave that to me." The crafty smile had, by this time, returned to Barbara's face, and it wasn't just Sasha's imagination, but the woman's fingers were definitely straying up from her knee. Out of the corner of her eye Sasha could see the hem of her skirt puckering.

"Good Heavens, just look at the time," Sasha said, glancing at her watch and rising at the same time. "The au pair will wonder where I've got to," she added. Barbara led to the front door and placed herself between it and Sasha.

"We could go out to dinner if you like, tonight … . just you and I," prompted Barbara. Sasha made an excuse of a fictitious prior engagement.

"I'd love to, some other time, if you're free," she added.

"Oh, I'll be free – I promise," said Barbara with a meaningful smile.

"Well, until then," Sasha said, offering her hand.

Barbara playfully knocked her hand away and made to kiss her, saying, "Not amongst friends, surely."

Sasha turned her cheek to receive a polite peck, but Barbara placed a hand under Sasha's chin and forced her head round so that she could kiss her full on the mouth. Sasha felt her stomach churn and she fought back nausea and forced herself not to resist. However, when the woman's tongue tried to force itself between her lips, she pulled hurriedly away.

"My, you are shy, aren't you," laughed Barbara. "Never mind, my dear, I'll soon cure you of that." Sasha tried to joke that she had led a sheltered life, and added a further inane remark as she pushed past Barbara and out through the front door. As she left, Barbara called a cheery goodbye and said, "You will hear from Ted in a few days, my dear … . or me," she laughed as she closed the front door.

On her way home a hundred thoughts were racing through Sasha's mind. What was she getting herself into here? She just hoped that Drew was right, and the woman was connected with the Satanists, otherwise she was enduring this sex mad woman's overtures all for nothing. She wasn't too worried about having dinner dates with Ted Lake. She had met his type before. All show and bluster. She would just make sure that his glass stayed full and hers empty. All she would need to do is make sure he didn't lose face and she was all right, Sasha told herself.

She was pretty sure from what she had seen at the cocktail party that he was one of those people who fancied himself as God's gift to womanhood. She sensed if he was that desirable then Barbara wouldn't want to 'eat ham out, when she could have steak at home'. No, she could handle Ted all right without having to 'come across'. However Barbara and her sex mad accomplice Sally Greves were another matter. The thought of even going through the motions with them made Sasha's flesh crawl. Obviously they weren't as much lesbians, as just hot for anything sexual. Sasha decided it would be unwise to go straight round to Drew and report. She didn't think for one minute that Barbara suspected her, but there was no point in taking silly risks. By now the whole village knew who Drew Thorpe was. Even to be going there, meant she could be connected with him if it got back to Barbara.

She found herself wondering just how Drew himself was now playing the Barbara Lake situation. Previously he had been playing squash and having drinks with the woman. If he suddenly baled out now, and had nothing to do with her, Barbara would surely suspect that he had simply suspected her and was on her tail. Sasha resolved to question him on the matter. Meanwhile it would be better if they weren't seen together. She would have to liase secretly with him.

Later that evening, she rang him and told him of her fears. He said that she was quite right, and they mustn't be seen together locally.

"However, we do need to talk about this … It's a lot to ask, but could you meet me at the Angel Hotel in Hogsworth? It's a couple of miles beyond Endersby … say tomorrow night at eight?" Sasha replied that she could and Drew said he would book a room under the name of Jones. "When you arrive just ask if your husband, Mr. Jones, has arrived … I'll be there waiting for you." Drew sounded somewhat embarrassed, and added, "We will need a private room to plan our strategy in case we are seen together in the bar … Is that okay by you?"

Sasha agreed and wondered whether Caroline would be there. She found herself hoping that she wouldn't be.

*****

Unexpectedly, the next afternoon before she was due to meet Drew, the telephone rang. It was Ted Lake, his voice all charm and honey. He wanted to know if she would have dinner with him at the Golden Picador restaurant in Grantfield.

"I often take my clients there, my dear, and after all, your husband banks with us, doesn't he?"

Sasha didn't know that Bart had an account with Ted's bank. Obviously one I don't know about, she thought, but all she said was, "Yes he does."

"Good, then a meeting there will be quite natural between us, I think, Sasha, my dear. Shall we say two days from now at seven thirty?" Ted's voice was very smarmy and self-assured. Sasha agreed and hung up, fairly quickly. The Golden Picador was a very expensive and exclusive restaurant in Grantfield, frequented by TV and film people. In happier days Bart had taken her there for her birthday. Sasha smiled to herself. At least she was sure of a good meal, if nothing else.

That evening, she drove to Hogsworth – about ten miles from Saddlewitch in all. She found the Angel Hotel, an old black and white Tudor building at the northern end of the village and pulled into the car park. It was a chilly October evening and had just started to drizzle again. It had been raining all day and there were several puddles in the hogging car park. Locking the car, she huddled her coat around her and, avoiding the puddles, headed for the door marked reception. A smart young woman about Sasha's own age was at the desk.

In answer to Sasha's enquiry, she said, "Yes, your husband arrived about thirty minutes ago. Go straight up – room 20. He's expecting you." She thanked the receptionist and slowly climbed the wide staircase to the residential rooms. She was relieved that she didn't need to go through the bar, from where she could hear a lot of merriment exuding – obviously a party, or something. She walked slowly along the corridor looking at the room numbers. She halted at No. 20 and knocked. Very quickly the door was opened. Drew stood there. He was dressed in an open neck shirt and slacks. His eyes lit up in greeting, when he saw her. Warmth exuded from the room into the corridor. He ushered her in, closing the door behind them.

"Let me take your coat, Sasha." He helped her off with the camel haired coat and hung it up on a clothes hanger in the wardrobe. "Let me get you a drink," said Drew, opening the mini bar. Sasha settled for a martini and lemonade, and Drew poured himself a brandy. Smiling, he looked her up and down in appraisal. "You look simply gorgeous."

Sasha was dressed in a little black cocktail dress, black stockings and high heels. She knew she had taken more care with her hair and make up than usual.

"Thanks," she said, demurely sipping her martini. She sat in the one armchair and Drew perched on the side of the double bed facing her.

"You know this is quite wonderful what you are doing for us … . After all, we were at our wits end, once our cover was blown," exclaimed Drew.

"I haven't done anything yet," said Sasha, with a smile. She then proceeded to give him a full report of her meeting with Barbara Lake and the invitation to dinner from her husband, Ted. Sasha had only given him brief details on the telephone of the former event.

Drew listened at length without interrupting, a worried expression on his face. When she had finished, he refilled her drink and his own before speaking.

"I'm not happy about this. I'm asking and expecting far too much of you … Supposing this Lake fellow tries it on? What are you going to do then?" Drew asked.

"Oh, it's not him I'm worried about. It's those other two female vampires," laughed Sasha. Drew rubbed his chin thoughtfully before continuing.

"I don't like this affair at all … Just as soon as you get any lead whatsoever … you pull out and leave the rest to us … Is that clear,

Sasha? These people are dangerous." With this, Drew reached out and caught hold of Sasha's arm. "I don't want to see you get hurt … Why, I'd never forgive myself if …"

Cutting in, Sasha reassured him that she wasn't about to take any unnecessary risks.

"Just as soon as Barbara agrees to take me to their next meeting, I'll let you know where it is and you and your people can do the rest."

"Supposing they switch it at the last moment and you can't let me know for some reason or other?" queried Drew.

"Hmmm, I hadn't thought of that." It was Sasha's turn to look worried. Drew seemed to come to a sudden decision.

"Once we know that Barbara Lake is going to take you to one of her meetings, I'll wire you." Drew went on to explain how he would tape wires to Sasha's body so that he could listen in and intervene at anytime. Sasha agreed that she would certainly feel safer knowing he was nearby.

"Carry a mobile phone in your handbag as a backup, too Sasha … Have you got one? If not, I'll get you one." Sasha confirmed that wasn't a problem as she always carried one.

With the pleasant warmth of the hotel bedroom and the effect of the two martinis, Sasha was becoming even more aware of Drew's physical presence. She noted the way his dark wavy hair curled round his ears and the way his eyes seemed to light up when he smiled at her. When he laughed a dimple appeared just above the point of his chin. She found herself wondering whether Caroline was suddenly going to show up. Unashamed at the thought, Sasha knew that if he made a move on her, she wouldn't resist. She supposed that the way things were with her marriage to Bart it wouldn't make much difference either way. Anyway the thought, she told herself, was purely academic as, technically, Drew was on duty and wouldn't want to get involved.

They talked for some time and ran though every eventuality, trying to offset even the remote possibilities of flaws in the plan. After a third martini, Sasha rose, saying she had better get back.

"Oh, my God, I quite forgot I drove here," she gasped. "Three martinis on an empty stomach … I'd better send for a taxi, I never reckon to drink and drive." Drew laughed and agreed that neither of them should. Having gone into such details and found her such delightful company, said Drew, he had quite forgotten where he was and that they both had cars outside.

"Come on, let's risk it and go down and get you a meal in the restaurant. It's the very least I can do," Drew suggested. Sasha, realising she was indeed quite peckish, agreed.

Luckily there was only one other couple, both elderly, in the restaurant, so there was little cause for worry on that score. Drew handed Sasha a menu to peruse and studying another himself, said, "Choose anything you like." She ordered duck in orange sauce and Drew ordered a steak. They complemented it with a bottle of red wine. By the time the meal was over it was ten p.m. Sasha could feel a warm glow all over, but reality struck her like a bolt from the blue.

"My God, Olga … my au pair … I must ring and let her know I'm going to be late … then ring for a taxi or she will wonder where I've got to." Suddenly she felt terribly irresponsible and guilty.

Drew smiled and held her hand over the table. The woman of the other couple smiled over at them both whilst her husband paid the bill.

"Do you have to go?" Drew whispered.

"What do you mean?" queried Sasha. "The children – I must get home."

"The room's booked for the night … Wouldn't your au pair be able to cope for one night … I mean if you stayed," Drew urged. "After all neither of us are fit to drive … You could have the bed and I'll sleep in the chair if you like."

Sasha didn't answer. She reached for her mobile and telephoned Olga. Two minutes later she put the phone down.

"Olga says she can manage perfectly," Sasha related to Drew.

Producing a credit card, Drew paid the bill and escorted Sasha upstairs to Room 20. Once inside, without switching on the light and with the October moonlight now streaming through the window it happened quite spontaneously. Drew reached for her and Sasha never quite knew how it happened, but she was in his arms. The sensation was not only exciting but warm and comforting. Their lips met, neither seemed to be able to get enough of the other. Drew's tongue was in her mouth and before she was even aware he had reached round behind her and unzipped the little black number she wore.

It slid easily down, over her satin briefs and silk hold up stockings to the floor. Without undoing her bra, Drew eased each of her breasts out over the cups and kissed each tenderly at first, then more wildly. Sasha experienced an exaltation of passion and fire she realised she had never felt before.

With Bart it had never been like this. With trembling fingers she undressed Drew, marvelling at his firm muscular torso, exposed in the moonlight from the window.

She could see that he was fully aroused and desperately realised she needed him inside of her. Sasha could feel the wetness between her own legs and the warmth at the pit of her stomach. With fingers and thumbs Drew hooked the waistband of her tiny black panties away from her hips, and they in turn slid to the floor.

Scooping her up in his arms her carried her towards the bed. As they reached the large double bed, Drew stood her up against himself and she could feel his manhood pressing into her. Transferring his grip under both her buttocks he lifted her literally onto him. Sasha felt a thrill of wild exuberance as he entered her. She hooked her long stockinged legs round his back, to obtain even more of him, almost bursting with desire and passion she gasped as Drew thrust to her very depths. When she thought she would melt with the sheer sensation, he eased her back on to the bed, and the wild thrusting joy began again.

Just when Sasha thought the world must end and she was in heaven, she climaxed, feeling Drew pulsating inside her as he, too, crashed over the top. They lay exhausted and contented, totally satiated in one another's arms. Sasha felt not one vestige of guilt.

CHAPTER FIFTEEN

From the dizzy heights of her night of sublime passion with Drew, Sasha came down to earth with a bump the next morning.

When she arrived home she was met by Olga, an anxious expression on the Swedish girl's face. It would seem that just for once Bart had returned home last night and demanded to know where Sasha was. Olga, bless her, had made up some plausible story that she was staying over with a friend, seeking to protect Sasha.

Apparently he had seemed to accept this story, but the real trouble had arrived with the morning's post. Sasha's solicitors had served the preliminary papers for divorce on him, for unreasonable behaviour. A visibly shaken Olga had been verbally abused and Bart had accused her of conniving with Sasha. He had finally rushed out of the house roaring.

"Well, you needn't think you are getting away with this, either of you. I'll be back in an hour."

"The hour," said a still trembling Olga, "is nearly up." Sasha gave her a hug and apologised profusely for having placed Olga in such a precarious and invidious position. Luckily, Olga had taken the children to school and play group before the scene with Bart had arisen. At least they had been spared that.

Sasha felt the guilt she had experienced earlier returning with a vengeance. She should never have left Olga to cope with everything, but then she hadn't expected Bart to return so suddenly. The trouble was she had grown accustomed to his long absences and had begun to take them for granted. A new worry assailed Sasha. How about this meeting with Ted that had been arranged? She couldn't now, in all good faith, go off and leave Bart in this sort of rage with Olga and the children.

Sasha rushed upstairs to change her clothes, better he didn't return and find her dressed as she was. She put on a sloppy sweater and slacks and some flat walking shoes. She was just lacing the second one when she heard the front door slam downstairs.

"Where is the bitch?" she heard him roar at poor Olga. Obviously he had seen Sasha's car in the drive, so he knew she was back.

A moment later, two at a time, Bart came racing up the stairs to confront her in the main bedroom. His face was almost black with fury. Coming straight at her, he waved a sheaf of papers in her face.

"What the hell do you mean by this?" he roared, so that poor Olga downstairs cowered against the wall in fear of what he might do to lovely Mrs. Paget. Sasha channelled her fear into cold anger.

"I should have thought it was obvious to you that things couldn't go on as they were," she exclaimed.

Bart pushed Sasha, a hand on each of her shoulders against the wall and hissed at her, "You belong to me and you will never escape … . Always you will be mine." Sasha met his furious glare with eyes centring on his.

"Nobody belongs to anybody. Each of us is our own person. We can give, we can share, but we don't belong." Sasha emphasised the last word deliberately.

Bart threw back his head and laughed, a mirthless sound, from somewhere deep inside.

"You are mistaken if you think I will ever release you."

"There's nothing you can do to stop me divorcing you," Sasha retorted, a trifle too smugly.

In blind fury Bart punched her viciously in the abdomen. Sasha doubled up clutching her stomach. A cunning smile on his face, Bart stepped back and let Sasha collapse in a heap at his feet.

"You see bitch, you will always be at the master's feet," Bart snarled, looking down at her writhing painfully on the carpet. Gritting her teeth through the pain and gasping for breath, Sasha still managed to meet his gaze defiantly.

"You may be able to knock me down physically but never mentally," she gasped out. The cunning smile returned on Bart's face.

"I will break you to my will as surely as a gale breaks a twig from a tree," then a sudden thought seemed to impregnate his mind. He bent down on his knees over Sasha and roughly pulled her chin up. Pushing his face into hers he roared, "So where were you last night?"

Sasha's first thought was to comment, 'That's for me to know and you to find out,' but she forced herself to refrain. A wild idea came to her. She simply responded with "I stayed over at Barbara Lake's house." She saw immediately the amazement on Bart's face. He even released the painful grip on her chin.

"I didn't know that you knew the Lakes ... I can check, you know ... It's not going to help your divorce petition if you're lying." Taken out of his stride, Bart's voice had returned to something like normal.

"Go ahead and check with Barbara. She will be only too pleased to verify what I have told you," said Sasha, still rubbing at her abdomen. She knew full well that Barbara Lake needed her for alibis and would doubtless substantiate what she, Sasha, had told Bart.

"I will," Bart said coldly, and immediately reached for the cordless phone in the bedroom and dialled a number. Sasha could even hear Barbara's cultured voice at the other end. The devious woman quickly grasped that her new accomplice needed an alibi and responded accordingly. After a few moments conversation Bart wished Barbara well and hung up. Listening to him on the phone, he had sounded quite his old charming self.

"Satisfied?" said Sasha, her voice heavy with sarcasm.

"For the moment," the venomous tone of his voice had returned.

Although her stomach and abdomen still ached miserably from the punch, Sasha pulled herself up to sit on the edge of the bed.

"Pack a case for me Sasha, will you? I'm going to be away on business for one week ... I'll need a suit, a couple of pairs of trousers, shirts, underwear, socks, you know the sort of stuff ... . I'll be back on the sixteenth of October." His voice was almost like any husband who might be talking to his wife.

Sasha decided discretion was the better part of valour. She rose painfully from where she sat, crossed the room and extracted a suitcase from one of the cupboards. Without a word, she went about packing the required articles. Bart sat in the bedroom armchair and watched her. She could feel his cold gaze on her as she moved around the room, selecting the various items. When she had finished, she closed the case, locked it and walked over towards Bart, handing him the key.

He raised his eyebrows.

"Quite the dutiful wife, aren't we? … Don't you want to ask me where I'm going?"

"No. I told you nobody owns anybody, and in fact, I don't much care where you're going." May as well say it as think it, reasoned Sasha.

It was a mistake … She realised it even as it came out. Bart leapt out of the chair like a coiled cobra striking at its prey. He seized her by the throat, with both hands cutting off her breathing, he forced her backwards until she was spread-eagled on the bed with Bart on top of her. The air was being forced out of her and Sasha fought and kicked to no avail. Bart was a powerful man and both hands were locked round her throat. Sasha could feel her eyes bulging with the pressure, but she was still conscious of the evil enjoyment in Bart's eyes. She realised then he was quite mad. Tighter and tighter he squeezed round her throat. A mist began to swim before her eyes, his face above her was becoming blurred. Somewhere far away she could hear a bell ringing, then voices. Was this death approaching? Sasha knew she was losing all grip on reality. Everything was beginning to go black, then, quite suddenly, the grip on her throat released. Spluttering and half choking, she hauled in large gulps of life giving air. Bart's weight had removed itself from on top of her. With reason returning, she heard Olga's voice downstairs and then constable Fenning's low gruff voice.

"'Ere, 'ere, what's going on up there?" Sasha, convinced that Bart had been going to kill her scrambled past the startled would be assassin and half ran, half fell down the stairs, collapsing into George Fenning's long arms.

It turned out later, that the loyal Olga had raced out of the house when she first heard Bart hit Sasha. She had run blindly through the street and, fortunately for her, nearly been knocked over by George on his bicycle. She had blurted out a cry of help and George had returned with her to the house. The intervention had been timely in the extreme.

Bart appeared at the top of the stairs glaring down at the three of them, suitcase in one hand.

George Fenning ran both fingers down his long nose, always giving the impression that he was going to pull it off his face. His lower lip came over the top one before speaking.

"Might I ask, what's going on here, sir?"

"Nothing constable, our au pair over-reacted. Just a dispute between husband and wife, I assure you." Bart's voice had switched instantly to a self-assured charm. Sasha clung on to George Fenning, her eyes pleading with the constable.

"He's lying, officer. If you hadn't arrived, he would have killed me." Sasha gasped, still fighting for breath. Only her desperation had got her down the stairs.

"It is right policeman. He try kill Mrs. Paget," burst out Olga in support of Sasha. George looked from one to the other.

"We don't usually get involved in domestics," he said dryly.

"Quite right too, officer," exclaimed Bart, coming down the stairs toward them.

"However," said George, holding Sasha away from himself and looking at her throat, "In this case, sir, I think you have some explaining to do."

"Policeman, you no leave us here with him .... Him madman," cried Olga, beginning to sob. George Fenning, never in the best of moods first thing in the morning, drawled in his most severe voice.

"I've no intention of leaving you ladies until I find out what's going on here." His eyes had centred on Sasha's throat where angry red marks were still apparent. Bart saw where George's interest had centred.

"She hit herself on a cupboard, constable," he blurted out.

"Those marks on her throat are finger marks, sir. I've seen enough of 'em before."

"I'm sure you're mistaken, constable," said Bart.

"I don't think so, and furthermore I believe I have good reason to arrest you for the attempted murder of your wife," said George, reaching in his pocket for a pair of handcuffs that he had never used before.

Before he could extract them, the three of them found themselves looking down the barrel of a snubbed nose automatic in Bart's right hand.

"You're only making things worse for yourself, sir ... Threatening a police officer in the line of his duties is a serious offence," added George.

"Stand aside constable, or I'll shoot all three of you," commanded Bart, jabbing the gun menacingly at each in turn.

"Best you do as he says," urged Sasha to George Fenning, who seemed about to argue.

"Good advice, constable ... I should take it if I were you," snarled Bart. As he edged past the three of them, he grabbed Olga by the arm. "You're coming with me ... If anybody tries to follow, she gets it ... Understand?" Sasha and George could only protest and watch in horror, as he handed his car keys to Olga. "You drive, girl – any tricks and you die."

"Help me Mrs. Paget," screamed Olga. A resounding slap across the Swedish girl's face from Bart silenced her. A moment later, in futile impotence, Sasha and George watched the car ease out the drive and pull onto the roadway.

"Where's the phone?" urged George, showing an alacrity of purpose she wouldn't have expected from him.

Whilst George phoned in for help and to arrange police cordons, Sasha raced out into the road, but the car had already disappeared round the bend. She stood watching, feeling totally helpless. Somehow Sasha felt she had let Olga down. Why hadn't she done more to stop Bart taking the girl as a hostage? She knew the reason was her own fear and felt bitterly ashamed.

She stood for something like five minutes watching the bend in the road. Did she expect the car to reappear? She didn't know. Finally, George came out to join her.

He explained, "Don't worry, Mrs. Paget. We'll catch him ... I've arranged for road blocks." Sasha shook her head sadly.

"I doubt it constable. He knows every road and lane round these parts. He's bound to keep off the main roads."

George ignored this and simply said, "Can I ring anyone for you Mrs. Paget? You've had quite a shock."

"No constable, I'm all right now, I assure you. Just catch him, that's all. If anything happens to that girl I'd never forgive myself," exclaimed Sasha. Nevertheless, whilst George was waiting for the police car to arrive, she went into the house and rang Drew at Briar Cottage.

"I'll be right there," he said, and hung up.

By the time the police car from Grantfield arrived, Drew was with Sasha. She had to make a report, through which Drew kept silent, then Drew took the senior of the two constables aside, whilst the other took George Fenning's account of things. He showed the constable his warrant card, which seemed to impress the man.

"Crumbs – I didn't know we warranted Special Branch in this part of the world, Sergeant Thorpe," he said. Drew impressed on him the need for secrecy here.

"I think it may very well be connected with something I'm working on ... Have you people put the road blocks into operation?" The constable confirmed that it was being attended to, but pointed out that this was the country, not London. He doubted how quickly and efficiently it could be done.

"Okay officer, you get an A.P.B. out on Paget and get descriptions and photographs of both him and the au pair ... No doubt Mrs. Paget will have them," exclaimed Drew, turning to indicate Sasha who was standing at the front door looking lost. Whilst this was going on, Drew had a quick chat with George Fenning, concluding by saying, "I'll stay on here with Mrs. Paget and see what can be arranged. Obviously we can't allow her to stay on here with the children, with this madman on the loose."

George nodded.

"Nasty customer if you ask me."

Ten minutes later, reports completed, the two officers left in the patrol car. George, his long mackintosh perilously threatening to get in the spokes of his back wheel, cycled off up the road into the village.

Up until now Sasha had kept a tight reign on her emotions, but once they had all left, she collapsed sobbing into Drew's arms. He was impressed that all her anxiety and worry seemed to be for Olga, in spite of the fact that she had very nearly been murdered herself.

After calming her down, he got her seated in the lounge, and made them both a cup of tea. For both their benefits he made her run through everything that had happened to her since returning home.

"Right Sasha," he said firmly. "It's obvious that you and the children can't stay here now. It's always possible the swine may come back to try and finish the job. We will put a man on the house to stand guard … In fact, I've already authorised it with the Grantfield chaps … Have you anywhere safe that you could go with the children and stay until we find Bart?"

"There's my aunt in Bournemouth. She would have the children, I know," Sasha responded.

"Yes, but how about you, love?"

"Oh, I'm not going. I promised to help you," stated Sasha.

"You surely don't think I'm going to hold you to that offer now, do you?" said Drew incredulously.

"You don't have any option Drew Thorpe. I'm meeting Ted Lake tomorrow night as planned … It's the only possible lead you've got, so you had better get used to the idea."

Drew argued back and forth with Sasha, but nothing could sway her. Finally he was forced to give in, but only on her agreeing to her being wired at all times, when she met up with any of the likely suspects.

With Drew's arm still round her, she rang her aunt Jennifer in Bournemouth and explained the situation. Jennifer tried to talk Sasha into coming as well, but Sasha was adamant in her determination to stay on. Finally it was agreed that aunt Jennifer would drive up tomorrow morning, stay for lunch and take the children back to Bournemouth with her after school.

After Sasha had replaced the receiver, Drew came to a quick decision, saying that he would stay on with her until her aunt collected the children.

"Just in case Bart returns," he added. "After that, you can come back to Briar Cottage with me."

Again Sasha argued but was finally won over. She was still shocked and dazed and still found it hard to believe that Bart, whatever he had done, would try to murder her. When everything was settled, Drew declared that he had better ring Caroline and put her in the picture in case she had been trying to reach him.

On receipt of his call, she agreed to come over immediately. He gave her the address to find him. Half an hour later, Caroline arrived. Sasha could see she wasn't in the best of moods by her expression and she was not proved wrong either.

Caroline pitched into Drew immediately. He had already told her on the phone what had happened.

In front of Sasha, she exclaimed, "What did you want to get involved for? I told you not to risk everything we've worked for. This attempted murder and kidnapping have nothing whatsoever to do with this case we are on … .. Let the police deal with it; it's nothing to do with Special Branch. Your feelings ….."

"Whoa there, Caroline. Shut up!" exclaimed Drew. "I don't want to pull rank on you, but I would remind you I'm in charge, not you, and I've a hunch that this has everything to do with this case we are on." At Drew's forceful tone, Caroline looked bemused and rattled.

"How do you mean?" she asked.

"Think about it. Why did he take Olga and not Sasha?" said Drew. Caroline became pensive.

"You mean …." She began. Drew continued at length.

"With the information Special Branch already have, which I would remind you, is why we are here in the first place, everything is leading up to a human sacrifice on All Hallows Eve, which is in two weeks time. The target we believe is a young blonde virgin in her twentieth year." At this point Drew turned to Sasha. "How old is Olga?"

"Nineteen," she replied.

"It would seem that several things are beginning to fit together here. From what Sasha has already told me, these mood swings and changes of character with Bart started two years ago when he became interested in the occult," Drew pointed out.

"Yes, his study is full of books about it … But, surely he wouldn't be involved in human sacrifice?" The horror was evident in Sasha's face.

"Why not? He would have killed you without a second thought if Olga hadn't gone for help and found George Fenning," Drew pointed out.

Caroline cut in, "Do you know if Olga is a virgin, Sasha?" Sasha looked surprised at the question.

"Hardly. She's Swedish, pretty and nineteen. What do you think?"

"Sexually aware, too," said Drew, with a dry smile.

"And you would know," Caroline remarked.

Drew ignored the remark and countered with, "The next thing, Caroline, for you to do, is go through the books in Bart's study. See if there's anything useful there for us to go on."

"But that could take the rest of the day," argued Caroline.

"Well, you're the so-called expert on matters of the occult, so best you get cracking right away." The reality of everything was finally getting to Sasha.

"My God, poor Olga … We must do something to save her," she cried.

Caroline gave her a hard look, then said, "This is all supposition on Drew's part for all we know a would-be killer has just taken a hostage to help him escape."

"Caroline – the books, please. Sasha can show you where the study is," snapped Drew. After escorting Caroline to the study, Sasha returned to Drew in the lounge. He was looking at his diary and then at the leaves drifting past the window. "We have two weeks left, that's all, to prevent murder. I'm sure of it." Sasha didn't say anything. Her fear paralysed her.

CHAPTER SIXTEEN

With a heavy heart, on the following afternoon, Sasha waved goodbye to her aunt and the children. Standing at the end of the drive, she watched the little Renault Clio disappear round the bend in the road, Annabel and Debbie gleefully waving from the rear window to the last moment. Mixed feelings of guilt and relief assailed Sasha. Guilt that she felt she should have gone with them and relief that they would both be safely out of harm's way.

Standing in the warm autumn sunshine, it was hard for her to believe what was happening to her life. The village nestling in the valley looked so peaceful and tranquil. A thin carpet of leaves was already covering the tree lined roads and gardens, and villagers were all going about their various ways of life, oblivious to the turmoil in Sasha's mind. Young Ron Head, the local cricket captain, rode by on his bicycle and gave her a cheery wave. Sasha tried to force a smile in return, but it was a pre-occupied half hearted affair.

She turned and walked slowly back up the drive to the house, her house where once she had been happy. Now it seemed the whole place had an air of foreboding doom about it. Inside she joined Drew, who was just marshalling the last of the bags she had packed for her transfer to Briar Cottage. He asked if she was sure that she had everything she needed. Sasha nodded, only half aware of what he had said. She realised that she would quickly have to pull herself together.

This evening she had to endure a dinner date with Ted Lake. The thought mortified her. Why had she volunteered, Sasha wondered.

Drew carried the bags out to his car, which was standing in the drive, whilst Sasha walked round the house, making sure that all windows and doors were shut. Earlier Drew and she had gone meticulously through Bart's desk, just in case anything showed up. The only thing they found of any use, was an address of the agency, from which he had obtained the au pair, Olga. Drew had rung them immediately. After a five minute conversation with the secretary, he had turned to

Sasha, saying that it transpired Olga was an orphan with no family. There was simply nobody listed for a contact address in Sweden or anywhere else.

Drew had commented that it merely firmed up his suspicions. Sasha had enquired what he had meant and he had said that if these Satanists were looking for a human sacrifice Olga was a perfect choice. Nobody to ask any questions if she disappeared, was his reasoning. It had been that which had finally strengthened Sasha's resolve to stay with their plan to infiltrate the Lakes' household … .

Driving through the village, they passed the post office from where they saw Nate Browning emerging. Nate was a regular at the Black Bull, and a runner for the bookmaker in Grantfield; on past the church and the village grocery store. John Durham's wife, Betty, was just arranging some merchandise outside for display and looked up to greet Bessie Pepper who was about to enter the shop. Everything looked so normal.

Some horses were grazing peacefully in a field and a tractor turned out of one of Burgess Steel's fields, depositing mud on the road from its large back wheels. The sun was still shining brightly, but all the trees showed clear signs of autumn, clothed in red and gold. Only the willows by the village pond were still green.

Drew parked outside Briar Cottage and collected Sasha's bags from the boot. Tom Bridges, the landlord of the Black Bull, passed by with more than a backward glance at what was going on. Sasha just smiled sweetly and followed Drew up the path to the front door. She was aware that Tom, hands on hips, had stopped to watch.

'Oh well, so what? Villagers would talk anyway,' she told herself. She had far more to worry about than village gossip. Only too well aware that she was probably Olga's best hope of staying alive. Inside, Drew showed her to the spare room, putting her cases on the bed and leaving her alone to unpack.

★ ★ ★ ★ ★

That evening, it was decided not to wire Sasha for her meeting with Ted Lake at the Golden Picador. Sasha assured him, in spite of

Saddlewitch

his concern, that she could handle Ted. It was agreed between Drew and Sasha that the former, would wait in his car in the restaurant car park. When Ted and Sasha came out, he would discreetly follow the bank manager's car, when he presumably would be taking Sasha home. They both decided that when Ted dropped her off, Drew would wait for him to drive off and then pick up Sasha. Drew ran through everything twice. He had earlier insisted that Sasha didn't dress too provocatively.

"Why?" Sasha had laughed. "Jealous or something?"

"Very," he had replied. "I sure hate the necessity for all this."

Sasha was dressed in a smart beige trouser suit and wore her dark hair up. Apart from lipstick and a little eye shadow, she had very little make up on.

"You still look gorgeous … Too damn beautiful, by half," complained Drew. Sasha wished now, that she had arranged to go in her own car and meet Ted Lake at the Golden Picador, but she had said that her husband was away and he could call and collect her. This, of course, meant Drew having to drive her back to her own house to be picked up.

"Next time, if there is a next time, I'll meet him wherever it is, and say it is because my husband is at home," said Sasha.

Twenty minutes before the appointed collection time, Drew drove Sasha back to her house. It looked very forbidding and gloomy in the dark. She went in with Drew and turned the lights on and they waited just inside the closed front door for Ted Lake's arrival. They didn't have to wait long. Ted turned up a full ten minutes early.

"Wait until he comes to the door and rings the bell," said Drew.

Sasha nodded. A minute or so later, the door bell still made her jump out of her skin, so on edge and uptight was she feeling. Drew flattened himself against the wall behind the door and Sasha opened it to the grinning Ted Lake. What hair he had left, was flattened down in strands across his near bald head, contrasting with the abundant mutton chop whiskers and moustache framing his ruddy countenance.

"What ho! You're a smart young filly if ever I saw one," he greeted Sasha. Sasha recalled the immortal words of Henry the Eighth, when he first set eyes on Anne of Cleeves. 'The jobs I've got to do for England.' She suppressed a laugh at the thought, and left with him, after turning off the light and pretending to lock the door. She had given Drew a spare key to lock up when he followed on.

As they were well aware of the rendezvous, Drew could take his time. It was when they left the Golden Picador, that he might need to be on his toes.

★ ★ ★ ★ ★

The Golden Picador was more of a country club than a restaurant, standing in open countryside on the outskirts of Grantfield. A long winding tarmac drive led to the main building, on either side was a well-kept golf course of eighteen holes. Sasha waited patiently whilst Ted parked his Jaguar. The large forecourt and parking areas were floodlit and she could see a wide balcony that led onto the lawns in summer. Taking her arm, Ted led her in, signing his name at reception. It was probably only Sasha's imagination, but she thought the receptionist gave her a funny look. A wide corridor with a sweeping spiral staircase on either side, led through to the bar, which was already quite crowded. Here Ted ordered drinks for them both, directing her to a seat in the corner. A moment or two later a young blonde waitress dressed in a very short skirt delivered the drinks to their table – a martini for Sasha and a whisky for Ted.

Sasha was pleasantly surprised. Ted made quite intelligent conversation on several subjects and appeared very gallant. Frequently he would glance round the room to see who was noticing him with such an attractive companion. He would give an expansive smile every time he recognised anyone and make a show of waving a greeting to people he knew.

He ordered both red and white wine with the meal. Something Sasha had not counted on, but she was relieved when he ordered a fish starter. She slowly picked her way through a Waldorf salad and took only minuscule sips of her white wine. Ted, on the other hand, sank three glasses with his whitebait starter. Sasha was glad that she had ordered salmon for her main course, because only a couple of glasses remained in the bottle of Chardonnay. With the arrival of Ted's steak tartare, he quickly began to demolish the dark red Burgundy.

The meal proved delicious, complemented by a lemon meringue for Sasha and a strawberry cheesecake for Ted. Then came the liqueurs. Sasha managed to tip hers into the table floral decoration whilst Ted frequented the gents. She was thankful that the vase was bone china. However, she waited for the orchids to wilt and was relieved when they didn't!

Ted returned from another cloakroom and polished off two more brandies. My God, thought Sasha, and he's going to drive me home? She was amazed at his obvious ability to hold his liquor. The fellow didn't even seem to be remotely drunk. She sneaked a glimpse at her watch, knowing she had spun out the meal as far as was humanly possible. It was ten fifteen, and Sasha thought of poor Drew cooped up in his car in the car park all this time. They took coffee in the lounge, which meant another brandy for Ted, Sasha, of course, declining.

At a quarter to eleven, they left the Golden Picador for the car. Now for it, wait until he hits the air, thought Sasha, hopefully. Then I can make an excuse and ring for a taxi. Again, she was surprised. Ted walked a perfectly straight course for his car and even opened the passenger door for her.

A little while after the journey home commenced, he laid his left hand on Sasha's thigh. She thanked her lucky stars that she had seen fit to wear a trouser suit. She gritted her teeth and put up with the presence of his podgy hand. A glance in the wing mirror, on her side of the vehicle, showed a car's headlights at a respectful distance behind. She felt sure it would be Drew, although she hadn't noticed his car in the restaurant car park. Perhaps he had been concealed in one of the dark shrub covered corners, she thought.

When Ted pulled up outside her house, she cursed herself for not telling Drew to leave the hall light on. If her senses had been working more effectively, she could have made some excuse about having to relieve the baby sitter. Now she knew that wouldn't wash with the now amorous Ted.

He leaned over and made a grab for Sasha's shoulder; pulling her roughly round towards himself in the driving seat. She could smell the overbearing fumes of alcohol on his breath. His right hand tried to come across and enter her jacket top. Pouring on pseudo charm that she didn't feel, Sasha made the most banal of excuses.

"Sorry Ted. I've had this appalling headache all day … It's been such a lovely evening, but can we do this some other time … . Us ladies, you know, time of the month and all that."

To her great surprise, Ted, although obviously disappointed, accepted her explanation, replying, "There's always next time, my dear. Allow me to escort you to your door." With that he got out and came round to open the passenger door for her, and then accompanied Sasha up to her front entrance.

Once inside, she turned on the light and gave him a kiss on the cheek.

"Just want to get my head down now. I'm sure I'll be all right in the morning," she said.

"I'll ring you and make sure you are. Perhaps you will come out with me again in a few days … Yes?" Sasha thought like mad. She couldn't afford to say no and yet she wouldn't be here if he rang her home.

"Yes, I'd love to," said Sasha. She gave him Drew's phone number at Briar Cottage. She was surprised after all the drink he had consumed that he picked up on it.

"But that's not the number I have down for you," he exclaimed, looking puzzled.

"No, that's right … It's my private number, you understand … My husband might answer the number you have," Sasha prefabricated.

"I thought you said he was away?"

"Well, yes he is, but he may be back tomorrow … I don't know for sure," she explained. After several more questions she had to endure a slobbery kiss tasting of a mixture of wine and brandy and was relieved, when in quite good grace, he left her, presumably to return to the Lake's residence.

Five minutes after his departure, Drew arrived, walking. He had parked round the bend in case any one was watching.

She related the events or non-events of the evening, adding, "So how do I stop him next time? This explanation won't wash twice, Drew … . The drink seems to have no effect on him."

Drew smiled.

"Don't worry. I've thought of that. I'm going to give you something to slip into his last drink." Sasha looked horrified.

"We can't do that. Supposing he loses consciousness and crashes the car."

"No, my love. He won't pass out. It will just make him feel very sick about ten minutes after drinking that last one. I can assure you that he will lose all interest in you and just about everything else," Drew explained. Sasha was still not too happy.

"And you can promise me there will be no permanent effects?"

"None at all," promised Drew. "Only a rotten hangover."

* * * * *

When poor Olga had been abducted at gun point by Bart Paget, she had been, quite naturally, in a state of terror. With a gun jabbed into her ribs by Bart, she had been forced to drive his car. Because of her nervous state she drove very erratically at Bart's snapped orders.

"Turn left here, right here, left again, left at the cross-roads, down this lane, turn right," and so on. Bart realised that the police would cordon off all the main exits but he knew too, that it would take time to implement. He hadn't very far to go. Everything, in fact, had been carefully arranged. By a system of back doubles and cart tracks, he reached Endersby and turned quickly into the driveway of a cottage. The garage had already been left open for him. He ordered Olga to drive straight in under the up and over doors. Almost before he had turned the car lights off, the garage door was pulled down and locked by somebody outside.

He ordered the terrified Olga out of the car and, indicating a connecting door through to the cottage, prodded her with the gun. It led through into an outhouse and from there into a kitchen.

An attractive blonde woman in her early thirties confronted the two of them.

"Everything go to plan?" she enquired of Bart, in a pleasant voice.

"Yes, but I didn't finish the bitch. That local constable Fenning arrived ... she fetched him." He jerked a finger at Olga, who was virtually cowering up against the kitchen sink.

"What are you going to d...do to me," sobbed Olga, finding her voice for the first time. The blonde walked purposefully towards her and slapped Olga hard, both sides of her face. The Swedish girl recoiled, grabbing with both hands to her reddened cheeks.

"Shut up! You are a commodity we need, which won't be for long. Behave yourself and do as you are told. You will be well fed and cared for, never fear ... Give any trouble and you will regret it, I can assure you," exclaimed the blonde, in an icy businesslike tone. She turned on Bart. "Why didn't you finish your wife as I ordered? She is a danger to us and should have been eradicated."

Bart tried to enlarge on his earlier explanation but was cut short by the blonde woman.

"It is of no matter ... She will put a noose round her own neck by meddling with us ... Now, tie the girl securely ... Bind her hand and foot and conceal her in the cellar. It will be a week or so before we have need of her ... Now that the police are looking for you, you will have to stay here, so she can be your responsibility – understand? Fail the high priestess Astarte and you know what to expect, do you not?"

"Yes, Caroline ... I mean, Miss Channing," blurted out Bart.

"I've told you before never to call me that. I am the high priestess Astarte, our master's right hand."

* * * * *

Two days later, Caroline Channing met up at Briar Cottage with Drew and Sasha and they discussed developments. Sasha found the previously hostile Caroline quite charming and sympathetic. Sasha even convinced herself that perhaps she had only imagined Caroline's previous hostility. The latter listened with avid interest of their plan to ingratiate herself with Barbara Lake, and of the meeting with Ted, her husband. Caroline even made some possible alternative suggestions, some of which they took on board. It was probably just as well for Sasha that she didn't see the expression on Caroline's face, when she drove off back to Endersby.

If ever an expression typified evil satisfaction, it was Caroline's.

* * * * *

The second meeting took place between Sasha and Ted Lake five days after the first encounter. Again, it was at the Golden Picador, with one vital difference. This time, over the meal, Ted informed Sasha that he had booked a room for the night. Right from the time she had met him at the restaurant, having driven herself this time, he was considerably more amorous. Sasha had once more dressed in a trouser suit, only this time it was of a rich purple. Drew had furnished her with a tiny yellow pill, which Sasha had carefully concealed in a pocket of her handbag. She was to be sure not to use it until he had imbibed sufficient alcohol. Leave it as late as possible after dinner is over, Drew had instructed her. She took some comfort from the knowledge that Drew was out there somewhere in the car park.

The dinner was quite excellent and she might have enjoyed it, but for the fact that Ted kept trying to touch her under the table. Also she couldn't get her mind off what had befallen poor Olga. There had, in spite of the lapse of time, been no word of the police having apprehended Bart or found Olga. He simply seemed to have disappeared into thin air, and poor Olga with him.

She had rung her aunt every day and spoken to the children. They, at least, seemed to be having a whale of a time. Only yesterday her aunt had taken them to the zoo and tomorrow they were going to see the New Forest ponies. She missed them terribly, however, and try as she might, couldn't get them out of her mind. At least they were safe down there in Bournemouth. By now Sasha had convinced herself that Bart had gone insane. If she had stayed on at their home with the children, there was always the possibility of Bart returning to harm them. She was brought back to reality by Ted's hand under the table groping her leg. With a smile on her lips that never reached her eyes, she removed it with a theatrical gesture, playfully slapping the back of his hand.

"Behave yourself... Time for that later," Sasha pretended to play the coquette, but inwardly squirmed. As the meal progressed she dreaded the moment when it would be time to retire to the room upstairs. Over the dessert she decided now was the time to use Drew's little pill. Unfortunately she couldn't seem to see an opportunity. Surely with all the drink Ted had consumed, he must visit the gents soon. She supposed because it was red wine followed by brandy, that it must be evaporating into his system, or something. She asked for coffee. May be she could find an opportunity to slip it into his. Horror upon horror, Ted declined and had yet another brandy. Sasha knew she couldn't put off the fateful trip upstairs much longer, but she also knew there was no way she was going to let Ted make love to her.

She made the coffee last as long as possible and could see that Ted had finished his brandy, and was getting impatient.

Sasha suggested a nightcap in the bar. Ted smiled in a crafty conspiratorial way and retorted, "We can have a drink upstairs in the room. After all, I'd like to see a little more of you."

Sasha could virtually feel her flesh crawl. The moment had come. She was only too aware that to stall longer was not an option open to her. From the reception area, they took the lift to the second floor. Ted fumbled in his pocket for the plastic card key to the room whilst still in the lift. To Sasha's further consternation, he found it, waving it gleefully under her nose. Down the short walk of the corridor to the room, Sasha's legs felt like lead. How had she got herself into this? She fought the desire to turn and run back for the lift. Somehow she must get a grip of herself. Stay in control – keep her head.

Fitting the card in the lock of the room, Ted watched for the green light, and then flung the door open triumphantly. Once inside he immediately made a grab for Sasha, crushing her to him.

"Steady on, buster," Sasha forced a laugh, extricating herself. "Let's have a drink first. After all, we've got all night." Ted, temporarily placated, opened the mini bar and asked what she would like. "A long drink I think … . perhaps a tonic," she responded. Ted obliged and poured himself another brandy.

Sasha was careful to sit in the only armchair and not on the bed. Ted brought the tonic over to her, gripping his brandy glass in the other hand. After handing it to her, he perched himself on the arm of her chair. With his free hand, he began to fondle her hair. Surely soon he must visit the bathroom? Sasha was physically willing him to.

"Why don't we sit on the bed … . We'd be more comfortable." Ted ventured. By now he was fiddling with the upper button of her jacket top.

Sasha again slapped his hand away playfully, saying, "Let me enjoy my drink first." She noted that Ted's brandy glass was now only a third full and suggested a refill for him. He declined and said that he needed to be excused for a moment.

No sooner had he gone to the bathroom than Sasha's trembling hands searched in her bag for the little yellow pill. She found it easily. Then horror of horrors, she dropped it on the carpet. She couldn't see it anywhere. Dropping to her hands and knees, she desperately searched. It must have rolled, she thought. In something like terror she ran her hands under the coffee table and the chair she was sitting on. Nothing! The bed, she thought. Pray God, it's there. Her hand sought frantically along its length in blind panic, conscious of the precious seconds ticking by. Then, there it was, by the rear castor. The tiny yellow thing and the only means of her escape. She rushed across the room and dropped it into Ted's brandy. At the same moment, she heard the toilet flush. Time was running out.

The tablet just sat there in the cognac. Nothing seemed to be happening, then it began to bubble a little and fizz, but oh so slowly. Perhaps there wasn't enough liquid in the glass? Sasha poured an equal amount of her tonic into the brandy glass. Hopefully Ted would be too excited to notice the increase in liquid level.

In terror she heard the tap turned off in the bathroom and a few seconds later the door opening. A glance at the glass showed her that it was fizzing fiercely now. Drew hadn't told her it would take this long to dissolve. If Ted saw it, even he, in his merry state would realise what she was doing. She got up to head him off putting herself between him and the glasses on the table. Sasha, biting back the revulsion she felt put her arms round him and crushed her mouth against his. Ted needed no encouragement. Instantly he pushed his tongue between her lips and Sasha was forced to accept it between her teeth. She held on and stuck the embrace for as long as she could, then broke away.

"Music, we need music," she murmured, anything to get his attention away from the glass on the table. Ted went over to the bed and fiddled about with the radio stations until he finally located some soft music. Whilst he was so occupied, Sasha watched the brandy glass. The pill had dissolved, but the liquid was slightly cloudy. She hoped fervently that he wouldn't notice the difference. She walked over and picked up his brandy glass, giving it a quick swirl on the way.

As he stood up from the radio, she handed it to him saying, "You finish your drink whilst I go and have a quick shower for you, Ted." Ted took the glass and finished it in a gulp.

"Well, don't be long. I've waited far too long already," he laughed. Sasha left for the bathroom. She waited a while after bolting the door, then undressed. She turned on the shower, but didn't bother to get in. She could hang this out for a few minutes more. Then she gauged the time it would take her to dry herself. The minutes ticked by, then she was startled by a knock at the bathroom door.

"Are you all right in there, Sasha? I'm getting impatient out here," Ted called through the door.

God, thought Sasha, the man must have a constitution like a horse. Obviously the pill hadn't taken effect yet; Drew had said ten minutes. It must be that already, she thought. Another thought struck

Sasha. Having taken a shower Ted would be expecting her to come out naked. Well, he could think again, thought Sasha, defiantly. She put back on her white bikini pants and bra. She had just fastened the bra when Ted called again.

"If you don't come out, I'm coming in." All right, Sasha knew the door was bolted and he couldn't enter, but she was equally aware that she couldn't postpone her absence much longer.

She applied some perfume and messed about with her hair, calling out, "Shan't be long." Finally, with a leaden feeling in her stomach, she vacated the bathroom. Ted was lying on the bed totally nude. He threw open his arms to welcome her. Sasha took in his drooping pecs and bulging abdomen and wanted to throw up – the sight revolted her.

"Just a moment whilst I finish my drink," she said, crossing to the coffee table and picking up what was left of the tonic.

"Hurry up you gorgeous creature," urged Ted. Sasha glanced at her watch. A full fifteen minutes had passed since she had doctored his drink. Why wasn't he retching and throwing up like Drew had told her would happen?

Suddenly, she felt Ted's arms around her from behind, crushing her back onto him. She hadn't even noticed he had got off the bed and crossed the room to her. He was fiddling with her bra straps. Sasha turned and kissed him again -anything to stall him. Why on earth had she undressed? She should have cut her losses and run and never minded the outcome.

All at once Ted recoiled and clutched at his stomach, muttering about a pain. He went and sat on the bed and his florid complexion had definitely turned pale.

"I'm sorry but I don't feel at all well," he muttered. A moment later he made a dash for the bathroom and Sasha could hear him groaning and then retching. Luckily she had brought her trouser suit and make up bag out of the bathroom with her.

Quickly, listening to his distress, she dressed herself. It was plain Ted was not about to re-emerge. She scribbled a note, left it on the pillow and departed. This way if he said anything to Barbara, his wife would merely think he had disgraced himself and she, Sasha, had left. With relief, Sasha closed the door behind her and gave a silent prayer of thanks to her Maker. She even felt a touch of sympathy for Ted Lake.

CHAPTER SEVENTEEN

The next morning Drew, Sasha and Caroline met at Briar Cottage to compare notes. Sasha had already related the events of last night's episode with Ted.

A report had come in, of a disturbance and suspicious lights being seen at an empty house on the outskirts of Endersby. The report was a direct one to Drew from Grantfield police. Drew stated his surprise that Caroline, who was living in Endersby, had no knowledge of this.

"Nothing to do with us … Just kids fooling about in an empty house, I expect," she retorted. Drew stated that she was probably right, but he would check it out, as he wanted to leave no stone unturned.

Caroline shrugged her shoulders and said he was wasting his time. However, she condescended to accompany him. Sasha asked if she could go too.

Quick to step in, Caroline snapped, "Of course not. You're not police … This is official." Drew ignored her outburst and addressed Sasha.

"Yes, you can come … In fact, it's better and safer than leaving you here on your own. Anyway, we already owe you a great deal, in view of what you have already gone through on our behalf."

Caroline glared and muttered, half under her breath, "and doubtless you will be repaid."

"What did you say?" barked Drew, raising his eyebrows at Caroline.

"Oh nothing, just an observation," said the latter with a grin.

★ ★ ★ ★ ★

The three of them drove to Endersby, Caroline in her own car. Drew and Sasha in his. The house on the edge of Endersby was locked when they arrived, but they found a window that had been forced and left ajar at the back. One at a time, Drew going first, they climbed over the sill and squeezed through. The house was, although empty, in a reasonable state of repair, and they had noted a For Sale board at the front on their way in.

An examination of the ground floor revealed nothing, but on venturing upstairs they found the main bedroom bedecked with strange symbols. On the floor, almost covering the whole room, was a five pointed star. Right in the corner was a small six pointed one where one person might have stood, certainly no more. On the wall was a large drawing of an Ankh. Even Drew, with his limited knowledge of the occult, knew this to be an Egyptian religious sign. On each of the other walls painted in red, were a boat like shape with a flame above it, a sceptre and another strange sign which meant nothing.

He questioned Caroline who had said nothing. She shrugged her shoulders and was non committal.

"I thought you knew about these things, Caroline?" said Drew, puzzled.

"Not in the sort of depth to understand this. Obviously some sort of ceremony was held here, but I'm at a loss to say what," she replied.

"Well, even I know about the Ankh, so I thought you might be able to enlighten us further," prompted Drew.

"Why don't you ask your ever present friend here, perhaps she's good for something other than an ornament," Caroline jerked her thumb at Sasha.

"Cut it out, Caroline," snapped Drew and he apologised to Sasha for the latter's rudeness.

With that, Caroline stormed out.

"I know when I'm not wanted, sort it out yourselves. Don't expect me to play gooseberry … I'm off home."

With that, she stormed off downstairs and they heard the window squeak as she exited. In actual fact, Caroline had simply worked the window back and forth to make the sound. She now lay pressed against the wall at the foot of the stairs listening to Drew and Sasha's conversation.

Saddlewitch

Sasha was apologising if she had upset Caroline in any way, but Drew had simply said that the latter was subject to moods anyway, and would have forgotten all about what was upsetting her by tomorrow.

Sasha guessed that she was obviously jealous but she didn't put it into words. Drew was still expounding on and examining the strange designs. He took his notebook out and made a quick sketch of them all.

"I would have sworn Caroline could have helped with this, after all she's made a study and hobby of the occult for years."

Maybe somebody just rubbed her up the wrong way," suggested Sasha.

Drew laughed. "Maybe, but it looks like a lengthy visit to Grantfield library for me … Want to come?" Sasha looked thoughtful.

"You might not have to go that far," she exclaimed.

"Why do you say that?" replied Drew, his interest immediately aroused.

"I think I know of someone who may help us."

"What are we waiting for then," said Drew. "Let's go."

Caroline, hearing this scrambled for the window and let herself out.

On the way back to Saddlewitch from Endersby, Sasha explained to Drew where she was taking him.

"It may be a long shot, but it's worth a try. Prepare yourself for something of a shock. She's an old lady of indiscriminate age, who lives on the eastern border of the village in an ancient dilapidated thatched cottage." At this point, Drew cut in.

"I'm sorry. I don't quite understand how she can help us."

Sasha laughed.

"You will, when you meet her … I'm about the only person in the village that ever talks to her. Local rumour has it that she's a witch and the young children are even advised to give her a wide berth. She appears to have been here for as long as anyone can remember."

"How come you met her then?" enquired Drew, whilst slowing down the car to avoid a rabbit running across the road.

Sasha digressed.

"Since you came to Saddlewitch have you ever heard the local legend of how the village got its name?"

"No," said Drew, his interest kindled.

"Well, on the eastern approach to the village is an old fir tree, tall and bent. When you look at its silhouette against the skyline at dusk, it doesn't take much imagination to visualise a witch, with her hat and broomstick, the cloak flowing out behind her."

"Where does the saddle come in, then?" laughed Drew.

"Oh, you can laugh, Drew Thorpe, but the old village inhabitants believe it, anyway. The saddle is the flat top above the witch. Look at dusk and you will see what I mean."

"And I suppose you are now going to tell me this old lady of yours lives under it?" chuckled Drew.

"No, but she lives at the bottom of the hill where the tree stands. I used to talk to her when I walked the dog, and she was very interesting .... Strange, mind you, but certainly interesting ... We pass the tree I spoke about on the way to her. I'll point it out and even in daylight you will see what I mean. We enter Saddlewitch by the eastern end anyway, from Endersby."

★ ★ ★ ★ ★

The journey didn't take long between the villages and soon Sasha was saying, "Here comes the tree now, on the right." Drew brought the car to a halt. The tree in question stood about a hundred metres from the road, with a continuance of the hill they were on. Drew gazed up at it. Even in this light he could see what Sasha meant. Dark storm clouds formed a backcloth, rapidly scudding by, outlining the dark green branches.

"Sounds like an old wives' tale to me, but I do see what you mean about the shape of it," agreed Drew.

"You may scoff, but don't go saying it to any of the old timers here. They all believe it. Take a look at dusk when the illusion is much more dramatic," urged Sasha. Drew smiled.

"Okay, just to please you, I will. Now come on, let's meet this old lady of yours." It was Sasha's turn to smile, something she hadn't done much of lately. She still blamed herself for what had befallen Olga, and no amount of reassurance from Drew seemed to help. She directed him down the hill, to where at the foot, stood a tumble-down cottage, the small front garden overgrown and uncared for. The roof too, looked badly in need of rethatching. Drew thought of the rodents probably crawling about in it.

He parked the car and locked it. Sasha led the way up the front path, stepping over the thistles and weeds, between the almost non-existent flagstones. The front door looked as if it hadn't seen paint for at least fifty years. Sasha struggled to make the rusty knocker work, but it had long since given up. Drew picked up a small rock and Sasha winced as he rapped the old wooden door with it.

"Put it down quick," urged Sasha, not wanting the old lady to see him holding it. Drew complied replacing it exactly as he had found it. For a few moments all was silent, then they heard a distinct muttering from the interior. A minute later the door creaked and opened just a crack. The inmate could only see Drew.

She muttered, "Go away, I don't want none ... Why can't you leave a body in peace?"

She was about to close the door when Sasha called out, "We are not selling anything. It's me, Sasha ... You remember, the lady with Bess the black Labrador." The door creaked again, on its rusty hinges and opened about a foot.

"Well, so it is dearie," said the voice from the darkness beyond the door. Now it opened fully giving Drew quite a shock. Revealed was a bent old lady with a discoloured lace shawl draped round her bony shoulders. She leant on a knobbly old stick that looked as if it matched her for age. Her face was more wrinkles and creases than skin, resembling that of parchment. It was, however, the eyes that startled one most, deeply sunken with the irises black like the pupils.

Never in his life had Drew seen eyes like those. Her nose was long and hooked and by her inturned lips, he could see that she was quite toothless. The voice that came out of her emaciated throat was more of a croak.

"What you be wanting, young Sasha?" Sasha explained that she had brought a friend to meet her and perhaps she could help them with some information. "You had better come in then," she croaked. After what seemed an age, she managed to turn round and hobbled off into the dark interior. Sasha indicated to Drew to follow. Smiling, he shrugged his shoulders and did so, Sasha closing the door behind her, bringing up the rear.

When Drew's eyes got used to the dark, he could see several cats' eyes looking at him. He counted seven at least, and then saw another emerge from under a chair. The old crone lit an oil lamp, which threw a subdued light on the room he assumed was her sitting room. The old blackened wooden furniture looked as tumbledown as the property. Even the curtains were hanging in rags.

"Don't believe in this new fangled 'lectric stuff ... . Now then, what do you want wi' me?" she shot at Drew.

Sasha said, "This is Mr. Thorpe. I've brought him to meet you, Esmeralda." Esmeralda cackled, a sound like rasping paper against a wall. She proffered a bony hand. Drew took it, half afraid of snapping it off, the hand and fingers appearing so frail and bony.

"Sasha here tells me you may be able to help us," Drew explained.

"'Elp you ... 'Ow?" came back the croak. Drew produced the notebook where he had drawn the symbols. The old woman peered at it, but plainly couldn't see well enough. Taking it, she shuffled over and held it against the light from the oil lamp. Drew watched her without much hope. Two of the cats, a black and a tabby one, were rubbing themselves against his leg.

Esmeralda turned slowly to face him.

"Where 'n you see these?" Drew explained, suddenly interested at her obvious agitation. "Don't have anything tur do wi' it. Be warned,"

Esmeralda croaked. Sasha reached out and gently laid a hand on Esmeralda's arm.

"We think somebody's life may hang in the balance. If you know anything we need to know, Esmeralda." The old crone looked from one to the other. Drew looked at Sasha, hopefully. It was clear the woman liked her. He would let her handle it. "Please, if you know anything, Esmeralda?" urged Sasha. The dark black eyes focused on Drew, then slowly turned on Sasha. The old lady's thin lips closed tightly together. "I can see that you do know, Esmeralda," urged Sasha again.

"Of course 'n I knows ... I'm gypsy stock," came the almost whispered answer.

"Will you tell us?" put in Drew.

"Depends," grunted Esmeralda. Drew put his hand in his pocket, thinking Esmeralda wanted her palm crossed with silver. Quicker than he would have thought possible she saw the movement and laid a hand on his arm restraining him. "At my time of life, I've no need a' silver ... . Depends on whether this person whose life you say is in danger be good or bad." Esmeralda followed the statement with a searching look at Drew. She followed this, "and also what be you?"

Drew, for once in his life, was quite lost for words, but Sasha intervened on his behalf.

"Mr. Thorpe is a good man, Esmeralda and the person we are trying to save is also good."

"Show me hand," said Esmeralda, jabbing an accusing finger at Drew. He held out his right hand, palm upmost. "No, the other," grunted Esmeralda. Drew offered the left, feeling rather foolish. Esmeralda held it up to her face, studying the palm. "Right hand, your destiny ... Left, what man make of it," she explained. After a while, she dropped his hand and said, "Sasha right ... You good man ... Policeman, I think."

Drew gasped. How could she possibly read that in his hand.

"Well, yes," he exclaimed.

"Esmeralda does not like police," croaked the crone. Sasha decided to try another line, much more drastic this time.

"Look, Esmeralda, you trust me, don't you?"

"Yes, dearie, I trust you."

"Well then, for Heaven's sake tell me what you know about those signs. A young and innocent girl's fate depends on us finding out," Sasha blurted out.

"Innocent you say? Virgin?" came back the answering croak.

"We think so ... Obviously we can't be sure," said Sasha.

"Then you have until All Hallows Eve ... After that, too late." Esmeralda clapped her hands together on the last word. Drew turned to Sasha.

"One week's time to Halloween," he whispered. She nodded and turned her attention back to Esmeralda.

"Please – the signs Esmeralda ... What do they mean?" Without more ado, Esmeralda shuffled off leaving Sasha and Drew alone. Both looked at one another in puzzlement. Two minutes later she shuffled back into the room, clutching an old battered wooden box. On it were strange hand painted designs, some of them faded by age.

"Runes ... My great grandmother's in Hungary," Esmeralda croaked. She tipped the box that she had opened onto the table. Several small polished stones fell onto the table. On each was a strange black mystical shape. Esmeralda studied the shapes in the order nearest to her. They reminded Sasha of some strange alphabet. She asked Esmeralda what they meant. Esmeralda said nothing at first, but continued to study the runes. Then, with her bony fingers she scooped them up and replaced them into the wooden box. She turned to face them both and explained that they represented ancient Theban Script, known as the Runes of Honorius.

"Some say that they may even have come from Atlantis."

"But how does this help us?" whispered Drew to Sasha. The latter held a finger up to her lips and questioned Esmeralda again.

"Why did you look at the runes, Esmeralda?" A strange crinkly smile appeared on the old crone's creased countenance. Drew almost felt her skin would split, but gradually it regained its erstwhile craggy state.

"The runes, dearie, tell me whether to tell you … . Fortunately for you they do." Esmeralda then went on to explain the drawings in Drew's notebook. "The five pointed star is a pentagram, an ancient pagan symbol drawn to give protection against evil spirits and more importantly to control them." Esmeralda went on to give an illustration of an old English song. "Green grow the rushes oh." She explained in her croaky old voice. "Five for the symbol at your door."

The six pointed star, she told them, stood for control of spirits and would be used during evocation rites. It was called a hexagram. Then she went on, almost gasping for breath between descriptions, to outline the other shapes Drew had noted.

The ankh, as well as being a Christian sign, was also a pagan one for penetration of the vagina, the flame over the boat was called an ouza and like the other two, ouser and dad, were Egyptian magical signs all to do with the union of man and woman.

Drew and Sasha listened intently at times bending forward to catch Esmeralda's voice, as she wheezed and gasped her way through the narrative.

"What I don't understand is why would they need protection from evil spirits if they are Satanists?" interjected Drew.

The old crone held one finger up and croaked, "Satanists can use evil, but they cannot control 'e. There is a deep rooted fear of the master, the anti-Christ, the son of Perdition." Sasha could feel goose pimples on her skin and wondered if her hair was standing up on end. "The runes show tragedy. A maiden will be sacrificed on All Hallows Eve unless …" Esmeralda left the sentence unfinished, gasping for breath.

"Unless?" prompted Drew.

"Unless you find the princess of darkness, Astarte, and her right hand, the goat of Mendes." Esmeralda clutched at her chest, clearly distressed with the effort of talking, her breathing coming in short wheezy breaths.

"I always thought the goat of Mendes was another illustration of the devil," said Drew.

"So be it young man ... but here 'e is controlled by Astarte .... princess of evil," croaked Esmeralda. "Find her and the danger is passed." The old lady, clearly exhausted, sunk down into an armchair coughing and spluttering.

"I don't think we can question her further, Drew," whispered Sasha.

"Just one more question," urged Drew. "As I came out of the building I noticed on the inside of the door a back to front swastika. What does that mean?"

Esmeralda, her already grey face turned even whiter.

"Death," she gasped. She went on to a spluttering explanation how in India it was the symbol of Kali the goddess of destruction and decay. "I can tell you no more ... You must hurry." With this Esmeralda seemed to collapse back in her chair with her deepset eyes tightly shut. The slow movement of her skeletal form showed that she was, however, still breathing. "Blessed be," she whispered. Sasha and Drew quietly left, closing the door behind them. Whether or not Esmeralda heard their whispered goodbye and thank you, was a matter for conjecture.

CHAPTER EIGHTEEN

Sasha accompanied Drew back to Briar Cottage to consider and work on the information Esmeralda had given them. For the life of him Drew couldn't understand why Caroline couldn't have told him most of this. After all, she had studied and been interested in the occult and astrology for years, since their college days in fact. He resolved to tackle her about it when they next met. From what Esmeralda had told them, Bart Paget, if he was involved at all was only an underling. It was a woman they were looking for … this princess Astarte, whoever she was. Despite all he knew, Drew was still cynical about the old crone's prognosis. After all how could she possibly know that a human sacrifice was to be offered up at Halloween, in a week's time.

Sasha, however, urged him to take it more seriously. She explained that little things Esmeralda had predicted had happened to her personally.

"Why, did you let her read your palm as well?" chuckled Drew. He could see by the annoyance in Sasha's face that she was serious.

"No," she retorted, "I mean things she told me when I was out with the dog, and stopped to talk to her at her garden gate."

"Such as?" enquired Drew, still cynical.

"Oh, you wouldn't understand … You're much too practical a person," replied Sasha, her hackles rising.

"I'll try … Give me an instance," Drew looked expectantly at her.

"Well I could give you several … Once she told me when I went home I would have a visitor waiting for me."

"And did you?"

"Yes, an old friend from university. She couldn't possibly have known." Drew looked unconvinced. "Another time she said I must hurry home because something had gone wrong."

"And had it?"

"Yes, a tap had been left on upstairs ... A few minutes more and the ceiling would have collapsed ... The bathroom was completely flooded."

"Anything else?"

"Yes, but I'm not going to bother telling you ... I think Esmeralda is psychic, anyway." Sasha gave Drew a defiant look as if challenging him to deny it. Drew's response at least was pensive.

"I'm not overlooking the possibility Sasha, but you must understand as a logical practical person it's hard to take in ... I can tell you one thing though, I am going to give Caroline one hell of a time when I see her ... She could have told us what those drawings were, I'm sure."

Sasha didn't respond to this statement, she considered the least she said about Caroline, the better for both of them. Sasha was firmly convinced the girl was head over heels in love with Drew, and therefore madly jealous of Sasha's presence with him at Briar Cottage.

"Come on Sasha, let's pay the library in Grantfield a visit ... Maybe they will have some stuff on the occult ... . Nothing much else we can do now, until Barbara Lake contacts you," said Drew.

"I've been thinking about that, of course we don't know what Ted will tell her about me walking out on him ... If she hasn't contacted me in the next three days I'll ring her and see if I can arrange something," rejoined Sasha.

Drew agreed and said that with Halloween fast approaching they dare not leave it any longer, as Barbara was the only possible lead they had...

★ ★ ★ ★ ★

Olga, as one would have expected was having a terrifying ordeal. She remained in the cellar of Caroline's cottage at Endersby bound hand and foot. She had seen little of the woman whose house it was, only Bart Paget, who had been left in sole charge of her. Three times a day he brought her food and drink and she was allowed to visit the toilet upstairs on request. At first she had thought that it might present an avenue of escape but that hope was soon shattered. The toilet window on the ground floor was securely boarded up. Once she had tried screaming and shouting in the hope that someone would hear her. All that had brought her was a beating from Bart, and she found herself gagged for the next twenty-four hours, as well as bound. Only when she promised not to shout again was the gag removed. At first she had refused to eat or drink, but Bart had simply shrugged and taken the food and drink away. Soon she became ravenously hungry and thirsty and was forced to give in and eat and drink.

The beating she had received from Bart for screaming was not only painful but humiliating too. With her hands and feet still tied, Olga had been bent over an old armchair in the cellar. Her dress was pulled up round her hips and her panties pulled down to expose her bare buttocks. Bart had then laid into her with a bamboo cane. It was one of the times when the blonde woman had watched the whole procedure with obvious delight. Olga's bottom had been sore for three days after that, and she could even feel the raised red welts across her buttocks. The only consolation was that no sexual abuse had been attempted on her person. It was Olga's only comfort. There were times when she caught Bart looking at her strangely. She couldn't explain it really. His expression seemed more one of hate, than any sexual desire.

One day the blonde woman whom Bart always addressed as princess visited the cellar and asked if Olga was a virgin. Although nonplussed by the question she thought it better to say that she was. Maybe then if they had a shred of decency they would leave her alone, Olga reasoned.

The woman seemed pleased with her answer but the respite was short lived. The blonde princess Astarte, as Olga was now forced to call Caroline, ran her hands all over Olga's body, and then turned to the watching Bart Paget.

"Good, she's not losing weight ... See that she keeps well and eats and drinks properly. She must be in perfect condition in three days time ... I shall prepare her on the day ... Do you understand?"

Bart bowed and replied in a subservient tone, "Yes princess, it shall be as you wish." When the woman had left, Olga was filled with a new terror. What was it they were going to do to her in three days time? Terrible visions of gang rape gave her nightmares, when she finally fell into a fitful and restless sleep. In her waking hours she tried to recall where she had seen this hateful blonde woman before. Somehow her face looked vaguely familiar. Then it came to her. She had only seen her vaguely when she had opened the Paget's door to them. She was the plain clothes woman with Drew Thorpe. Olga began to cry anew. Even the English police were her enemy …

★ ★ ★ ★ ★

After their visit to Esmeralda, Sasha and Drew spent the afternoon in Grantfield library. They found a couple of books on the occult and worked on one each. Sasha read of 'Adepts' that related to gifted magicians. Apparently there were different grades. Adeptas Minor, Adeptus Major and finally Adeptus Exemptus. Exacting and dangerous rituals must be, after long preparation, executed. Only then could the person claim to be an Adept and form an inner circle. She traced Devil worship back to the seventh century B.C. to something called Zoroastrianisns after its founder Zoroaster. She went on to read more about the goddess Astarte, the symbol of sex and lust, who could be summoned to evoke passion. Sasha remembered Drew telling her about what the young couple had witnessed at the old ruined monastery. That had apparently ended in a wild sexual orgy of free lust, rather than any pretension to love.

Drew read of a 'banishing ritual' which answered one of his own questions, of why the Satanists would need a Pentagram, the five sided star, to protect them from evil spirits. When a demon is evoked to work the will of the Satanist, that person, when the spell or ceremony is concluded, must conduct a ceremony to return the demon from whence it came. Failure to do this would cause the evil force to attach itself to the instigator. After taking in many other interesting facts he came to the ceremony of the Black Mass. Again his excitement mounted when he found reference to the term 'Blessed Be'. He recalled these as the last words Esmeralda had said to them. He learned that it was either the greeting or goodbye of a true witch. After quietly discussing their joint findings, Sasha and Drew left the library.

"I think we will call on Caroline," Drew said. They drove off for Endersby.

★ ★ ★ ★ ★

Caroline's response to Drew's accusations of withholding information, was as Sasha had expected, fierce.

"If you choose to spend all your time with her." Caroline glared in Sasha's direction. "How do you expect there to be time to tell you anything?"

A heated argument ensued between the two police officers belying their close friendship. Sasha thought it diplomatic to not only abstain from commenting, but to leave them alone for a while. She went out to walk in the garden.

The cottage was rented and nobody had done much with the garden – certainly not the present occupier. Weeds had grown in abundance, amongst those plants that had survived. A thick carpet of red and gold leaves were ankle deep on bedraggled lawn and flowerbeds. Wandering aimlessly Sasha felt miserable. She not only missed the children but also her dog Bess, (whom she had temporarily placed in the local kennels). She missed the walks; it just wasn't the same walking on your own! She allowed herself a smile – the time spent with Drew, especially the nights at Briar Cottage were a consolation. However, Sasha felt forced to admit to herself that Caroline was right. Since Drew had met her, his time with Caroline had been limited. It had been fairly obvious, right from the start, that Caroline's interest in Drew was far from platonic friendship. When Sasha had remarked on this fact to Drew, he had vehemently denied it by saying that they were just good friends. Maybe he honestly thought so, but she was sure Caroline had other ideas.

She had been in the garden for about five minutes when Drew re-emerged from the cottage.

"Come on," he exclaimed, firmly gripping Sasha's arm. "We are wasting our time here." He didn't say another word until they were in the car heading back to Saddlewitch. He told her then that they were going to see Mark Glenville, the vicar at St. Martins.

Mary, Mark's wife, was in the front garden when they arrived. She seemed surprised to see Drew with Sasha.

"Aren't you the lady whose husband has disappeared with the au pair girl?" she enquired rather bluntly.

Feeling rather guilty, not only about that, but perhaps more because she didn't go to church, Sasha said, "Yes, that's right."

Mary, who was cutting the last few roses worth capturing, gathered them up in a bunch.

She said, even more pointedly, "And I understand you have left your home and are now residing at Briar Cottage with ……" She left the sentence unfinished. Drew stepped in to finish it for her.

"That's correct, Mrs. Glenville. The police thought it safer to move her in with me at the cottage."

"Oh, I see, the police, yes." Clearly by Mary Glenville's expression, she didn't believe a word of it and Sasha could feel herself reddening.

Drew said, "She was very nearly murdered you know, and there's always the possibility that her husband could return." Changing the subject, he enquired whether the Reverend was in.

Mary said yes, he was, and she would call him. She crossed over to the front door, opened it and called, "Mark." A minute later he appeared wearing a pair of denims and in his shirt-sleeves. After greeting them he invited them through to his study excusing himself for his appearance.

"I'm a bit of a D.I.Y. enthusiast," he laughed. "Putting up some shelves at the moment." Turning, he indicated his labours.

"In that case, Sir, I'm sorry to disturb you, but there are a few things I'd like to discuss with you," said Drew. Mark Glenville waved them both to chairs.

"Fire away, Mr. Thorpe," he exclaimed, seating himself at his desk. Drew discussed the various things they had learned about the occult from the library and also the strange signs. He deliberately omitted any mention of the old hermit Esmeralda.

Mark listened with interest before saying, "Well, I've never actually studied the occult, but sometimes history has delivered some strange occurrences."

"Such as?" enquired Drew.

"Hecate for instance, the Greek goddess of witchcraft. It's even said her cult may have survived to the present day. It was said she haunted crossroads and graveyards. She was often invoked in ceremonies of necromancy. Her sign was always the crescent moon, the two points uppermost. Sometimes she would be depicted holding a key, apparently to exercise power over spirits."

"Any other instances," asked Drew, leaning forward expectantly.

"How about the Hell Fire Club?" suggested Mark.

"Surely that was a myth," put in Sasha.

"Surely it was not," said Mark, going on to explain at length.

"Ever heard of Sir Francis Dashword?" Both Drew and Sasha shook their heads. "Well, he was a rich young buck in the eighteenth century who, together with his friends, became tired of gambling, hunting and whoring. He formed the Hell Fire Club on the Thames, near Henley. Here they conducted experiments in Black Magic."

Sasha asked what sort of experiments. Mark went on to explain that they had caves dug into the hillside, which formed an underground chamber. Here, and also at a nearby ruined abbey, they carried out the most sinister of their experiments.

At this point, Sasha and Drew looked at one another, remembering the goings on at the ruined monastery in Saddlewitch, itself.

"What happened to them in the end?" enquired Drew.

"Well, even in that enlightened age their goings on were regarded by their peers as scandalous devil worship. Nothing more is known of what became of Sir Francis Dashwood, only that the club was eventually disbanded," Mark explained.

Sasha seemed to be lost in thought, then she asked a question of Mark.

"Do you believe in possession, Reverend Glenville?"

Mark smiled and looked surprised. "Why, do you ask me that Mrs. Paget?"

"Do you think it possible that my husband could be possessed? In the last two years his character has totally changed. He used to be kind and loving. Now he is violent, angry and always disagreeable."

"Such a change could be brought about by stress or worry or…" Mark left the sentence unfinished.

"Or?" Sasha probed further.

"Or, he could have become the instrument or tool of another person of stronger character. Possession by a demonic force is a possibility. Some people can draw down the power of an evil spirit, or another second person, could draw the force down upon them. Involuntary possession is more common than you might think."

"Go on, Reverend," urged Sasha.

"Well, say a person began by studying the occult … In the end, they can become so involved that they draw down an evil force on themselves, that they are powerless to resist. Thus we can say that they are indeed possessed. Liken it, if you like, to Dr. Jekyll and Mr. Hyde. Fiction I know, but the parallel is there for all to see. Sometimes exorcism is the answer. Even the demon fears possession, this explains the protective circle and stars they employ whilst invoking the spirits."

"As a man of God, do you honestly believe what you are telling us, vicar?" enquired Drew. Mark looked long and hard at each of them.

"I recognise a great force of good, so therefore there must be a great force of evil. I do, however, believe that good will always triumph in the end."

"That's reassuring, anyway," said Drew, with a smile.

The three of them continued to discuss like matters for a further thirty minutes. At which time Mary brought in a tray of tea and biscuits…

* * * * *

By the time Drew and Sasha arrived back at Briar Cottage they were surprised to find George Fenning waiting at the garden gate for them.

"Is there a problem, constable?" asked Drew.

"You won't have heard then, sir?" said George.

"Heard? Heard what?"

George Fenning was one of those men who always liked to talk in riddles and keep the listener in suspense. He raised his eyebrows and pulled on his long bony nose. The well-worn beige mackintosh fluttered in the October wind. George never seemed to button it.

"Murder, sir. Most horrible it was, sir. Blood everywhere."

"Can you get to the point, constable," exclaimed Drew, impatiently.

"The old lady, sir," retorted George.

Exasperatedly, Drew said, "What old lady?"

"Her as lives at the bottom of the hill on the edge of the village… Old hermit lady, even heard her called a witch by some in the village," said George, dryly.

"Not poor Esmeralda?" gasped Sasha, quite distraught.

"Urh, yes, I believe some called her that," said George.

It was Drew's turn to interject.

"Where, when, how?" he fired the questions like bullets from a gun.

"They found her this afternoon in her back garden … Throat had been cut clean through. Must have died instantly. Strange, though, nothing taken and no signs of burglary," George added.

Drew turned to Sasha and told her to go inside and lock the door.

"Don't open it until I return. I'm going down to Esmeralda's house now with constable Fenning to see what I can find out," exclaimed Drew.

Sasha went inside and put both lock and chain on the door. She leant against it and shuddered.

"Why would anyone want to murder a harmless old hermit?" she mused, then, recalling their visit to her, she thought she knew!

CHAPTER NINETEEN

Caroline Channing had, like most little girls, first become interested in witches at a Halloween party when she was only nine years old. However, with her the interest had far outgrown her peers. She began to collect books on the occult and by the time she left school at eighteen was quite an authority on the subject. Her bedroom was full of recipes for spells and love potions – even a collection of voodoo dolls and herbs brought back from holidays in the West Indies and Brazil.

All through her university days the obsession with the black arts grew and the bizarre studies continued, often at the expense of other things. If a friend or acquaintance displeased Caroline, she would, by fair means or foul, obtain a lock of their hair. Sometimes it would be nail clippings or an article of their clothes. Whichever item it was, would be used in conjunction with a doll she would fashion out of wax or clay. To enforce the spell further she would often acquire a photograph of the person. This would then be attached to the effigy or doll. Before attempting to cast a spell on the unfortunate victim, she would first soften them up by auto-suggestion of what might befall them.

When Caroline felt she had instilled sufficient fear within their minds she was ready to proceed. Uttering a string of incantations in private, with the clay or wax doll, she would slowly insert pins into it. The following day she would again work on the victim mentally. By this means the poor soul would be programmed into instability and come under her control.

Caroline was also obsessed with all things sexual. From the moment a new boyfriend dated her, she would seek to dominate not only their minds but their body too. All but the strongest personalities became totally subservient to her will, some even, like her ex-husband, a quivering jelly. Their marriage lasted only two years and the unfortunate Howard then ended up in a mental institution, having been sectioned.

Caroline obtained a divorce and went to police college, teaming up with the one man she had failed to dominate, Drew Thorpe. When Drew left to go on assignment with Special Branch, Caroline was forced to use all her overt and ever feminine charms in order to get the marks to follow him. Follow him, eventually, she did, using everybody on the way in reaching her objective. Probably the only person she had ever respected in life was Drew Thorpe. He hadn't the slightest incline that Caroline's mind was so warped. She had always taken the greatest care that he shouldn't suspect a thing. Patiently she played her cards, hoping that her friendship with him would develop into something more. She wanted him more than anything else in her thirty years of life.

In the past she had slipped love potions into his drinks and muttered spells in private to that end – all to no avail. Drew regarded her as a good friend and nothing else. Five years ago Caroline had joined a coven of witches near where she lived. She soon found the group too moderate for her beliefs. Mostly it was an excuse for a sexual orgy or glorified wife swapping. With all her knowledge of the occult, it didn't take Caroline long to undermine the leaders of the group. Within a year she was elected to high priestess and the activities of the coven went up a gear. Black masses and animal sacrifices became the order of the day. This sequence of events continued for the next three years becoming ever more daring.

It was then that, by accident, she met a new initiate, or rather a guest brought along by a friend. Tall, dark and around her own age with a handsome face, he was introduced as Bart Paget. Caroline immediately saw an element of weakness in his good-looking smile. After the coven departed the session, she invited him to join her for a drink at the local inn. Careful probing ascertained that he was married and had two little girls. He travelled in his business, often to where Caroline lived. His wife was named Sasha and his children Debbie and Annabel. The wife, he told her, was dark and attractive and three years younger than him.

Although on that first meeting they spent several hours together, Bart knew no more about Caroline than when he had met her. On the other hand, she had wheedled out of him his life history. By flattery and feminine wiles, of which Caroline was a master, or should we say mistress, she soon had Bart eating out of the palm of her hand. Caroline had been correct in her assumption that Bart had a weak streak and she played on it to maximum effect.

She arranged for him to become an initiate of her coven. At the very next meeting she saw to it that Bart was provided with an array of attractive women to choose from. When he left with a redhead of his own choosing, Caroline made sure she had one of her disciples follow him with a camera. The next time she met up with Bart she was able to show him some highly incriminating and very obscene pictures. The redhead, Gloria, he had left with, was renowned for her inventiveness. Bart was clearly very embarrassed and offered to purchase the evidence of his folly.

Caroline had smiled seductively and told him there was no need for that at all.

"After all," she said, "we in the coven protect one another. As long as you remain a disciple of the master your wife will never know. Simply do always as his handmaiden, myself, orders and you will come to no harm." Bart was terrified and instantly agreed. Caroline switched on her charm again.

Smiling she kissed him sensually on the mouth and exclaimed, "See, you are the favoured one."

From that moment on and for the next two years up to the present Bart became little more than an unpaid slave to Caroline. Always he must address her as the princess Astarte. In the last six months he had been forced to dress as the 'goat of Mendes' at all of the coven ceremonies. During this performance Caroline would invoke his presence and the members would gasp at his macabre and striking entry.

These impersonations of the devil had finally clouded Bart's mind. He became to believe he was such a creature. Unbeknown to Caroline he would book a hotel room, usually in the capital. Having dressed in the appropriate garb, he would ring an agency and send for a call girl. Always Bart would insist that they must be less than twenty years of age. For the entire night, he would then mentally and physically torment the poor creature, before releasing her in the morning.

Only in this way could Bart reassert his masculinity, Caroline having reduced him to a quivering jelly in her presence. In the early days he had hungered after her physically, casting an ambitious eye in the direction of her long and slender legs.

Caroline, however, was always careful to dangle the carrot, but never to deliver. The more she teased him the more enslaved he became until he was totally besotted with her and powerless to deny her anything she wished.

He had told her of his attractive wife Sasha long ago, and recently of their Swedish au pair, Olga.

Imagine Caroline's surprise when working for Special Branch with Drew, she was introduced to Sasha by him. Everything seemed to fit into place … . Sasha, Drew, the au pair, like a pre-planned solution to a puzzle. Caroline was sure that all was now being delivered to her by her master, Satan.

Drew was obviously besotted by Bart's wife, Sasha and she, Caroline, wanted Drew. Therefore only Sasha stood in her way. Caroline already knew that Bart and Sasha's marriage was in dire straights. A brilliant plan began to evolve in her mind to both get rid of her rival for Drew's love and to kidnap the au pair. At nineteen, the girl Olga could always be palmed off as a virgin to the coven. Now, because of that bungling idiot Bart, only half her plan was in position. If the Black Mass at Halloween was going to go to plan a new variation must be thought of.

Caroline's red lips drew back over her even white teeth in a cruel smile. She wasn't about to disappoint her master or his disciples. Pity about the old recluse Esmeralda, though. Once that damned Sasha had taken Drew to see the old woman her days were numbered. Caroline couldn't afford for Esmeralda to pass on useful leads to Drew, so she had had to go very quickly. Better that he remained in the dark. It had been very easy, really. Caroline had hung about until Drew left her house with Sasha at Endersby, then followed them to Esmeralda's. Later that day she had revisited the old crone and clinically cut her throat. So perish all traitors to the master, Caroline had hissed as she did the terrible deed. Then, driving back to Endersby she showered after burning her own bloodstained clothes.

"I've got Olga ... Now for that bitch, Sasha," she said, aloud.

Perhaps the most incredible thing about Caroline Channing, was her consummate ability to hoodwink and pull the wool over everyone's eyes. To all her colleagues in the police force she appeared as both talented and loyal, even when laughing secretly to herself behind their backs.

* * * * *

Bart Paget was a kind, caring husband and father, normal in every way until two years ago. It all started one night when he was away on company business. An acquaintance invited him along to a party, and as he was at a loose end in a strange place, he went. There he was introduced to Caroline Channing, and when the party broke up, went for a quick drink at the local pub. Bart had already drunk a considerable quantity of alcohol, which always had the effect of loosening his tongue. The quickie turned into several, in which he confided his life history to Caroline.

Nothing of a sexual nature happened, although Bart found Caroline to be an alluring and enchanting companion. Therefore, he readily agreed to accompany her to another party, when he returned on business a few days later.

This second party proved altogether different and Bart's first inclination was to split. It was weird in the extreme, with all the occupants dressed in strange erotic costumes. However, he was persuaded to remain, by an attractive masked redhead, who paid considerable attention to him.

She was heavy breasted and slim hipped, wearing PVC thigh boots and a short black skirt. Bart, always vulnerable to feminine allure, hung on the words of flattery she liberally poured out. More and more he wanted to see the eyes behind the mask she wore so bewitchingly. So enchanted did he become with his companion, that he barely seemed to notice the bizarre goings on around him.

Saddlewitch

Later that evening, the redhead, whose name was Gloria, suggested he accompany her to a more discreet place. Bart by now, his pulses raised to an excited level and well affected by the drink he had imbibed, accompanied Gloria upstairs.

Undressed, she looked even more enticing, her large breasts spilling out voluptuously from the black PVC bra. Having undressed herself, she proceeded to assist Bart to do the same. By now, he was far too excited to register that one wall of the room was totally a glass mirror. Unbeknown to him, from the other side of the trick mirror all the members of the coven were watching Gloria's antics with him.

Worst of all, one of the ladies was filming the whole performance, whilst another was taking photographs.

Bart continued to enjoy the amorous attentions of Gloria. There wasn't anything she didn't know how to do to perfection. He found himself oblivious to all but the pleasures she showered upon him. There was simply nothing that Gloria barred or disallowed. By the time he left for his hotel Bart was totally satiated, but he little realised that his life was about to change dramatically, and his troubles were just beginning.

The next morning before he left his hotel room to return home to Saddlewitch, he had a visitor – the delightful Caroline Channing. Opening the door to her, he beheld her smiling face. Bart's heart missed a beat with excitement. Could it be she had come to give him some of the same, like he had received from the redhead?

Bart invited her in and she immediately sat on the bed. She patted the duvet cover beside her, inviting him to sit there. It appeared that she had something he might like to see, she had said. With this, she reached into her handbag and produced a large white envelope. She tipped the contents onto the green duvet. Bart's elation began to turn into anxiety when he saw that all were photographs of him with Gloria. Every print had been superbly and professionally enlarged, clearly showing his and Gloria's face, besides other more private parts of their anatomy. He gasped and Caroline laughed.

"You can keep them, Bart, we have other copies," she had said, amicably enough. Bart's thoughts now raced. It had to be blackmail.

Should he go home to confess all to Sasha? Maybe she would understand, but then again, she might not.

Caroline sensed the indecision and playfully prodded him in the ribs.

"We have a complete film as well," she purred. "You were very good." Bart ground his teeth together, a habit he had when he was nervous.

"W…why?" he stammered. "Are you trying to blackmail me? I'm not a wealthy man you know." Caroline laughed.

"Blackmail … Good gracious, no. That's an ugly word to use for such a good looking man, now isn't it?"

"W…what then? I … I mean, what do you want of me?"

"Nothing, my dear. You are, after all, one of us now … .. The coven, I mean … There is no need for your wife to ever see these pictures, unless, of course, you leave the coven for some reason or other," exclaimed Caroline in a pleasant mellow tone.

"But I know nothing of covens and the like," babbled Bart, nervously, his right eye twitching uncontrollably.

"Have no fear. I shall give you books to read and you shall read them all – every word," laughed Caroline, happily enjoying Bart's misery.

"Is that all I will have to do?" Bart squirmed uncomfortably on the duvet.

"Good gracious, no. You surely don't expect to get off that easily," Caroline's voice was still friendly.

"What else then?" Bart tried to pick up his faltering courage. Suddenly Caroline's tone turned icily cold.

"You will attend whenever I command, and you will do what I order without question, wherever and whenever I say, or …" She let the sentence tail off.

Bart looked a picture of dejected misery. He continued to sit on the edge of the bed, his shoulders slumped and his head down. Caroline rose and crossed to the door.

With her hand on the knob, she turned back and said, "Be a good boy … Do as I command and the coven will be good for you … There are even rewards to be had." Then her tone once more turned to ice and she added, "Cross us and you will, I promise you, live to regret it."

With that, she was gone, closing the door firmly behind her.

★ ★ ★ ★ ★

That was the beginning of Bart's ordeal. Terrified of what Caroline had threatened him with, he complied with her every whim and command. He read every book that she gave him on the occult and attended every gathering of the coven. Whatever he did, it was never enough for Caroline.

Very early in his subjugation he was forced to address her as princess Astarte. Over the last six months, as his knowledge of the occult increased, she forced him to dress as the goat of Mendes, a form of the devil himself.

At coven meetings Caroline, attired as the princess Astarte, would then invoke him to appear. She would then control his actions to terrify the coven members and enhance her own standing in the group.

Bart was far too terrified of Caroline and what she would do to him to even think of disobeying her. Becoming ever more dependent on her he found himself lusting after her physically, but Caroline simply laughed at his desires and managed to put him down with derogatory comments on his manhood.

To combat this, and to hit back in his own weak way, he would dress in the goat of Mendes costume and terrorise hired call girls. That was, until Caroline found out about this also and punished him, accordingly.

By now, of course, Bart's self respect, fortitude and ability to function on his own, had totally deserted him. He was totally the devoted slave and servant of Caroline.

So when the day came that he was told to return home and kill his wife, who for some reason unbeknown to him, Caroline seemed to hate, he saw no reason why not. He was then to abduct the au pair girl, Olga, and take her to Caroline.

The second part of this mission he achieved, and but for the intervention of that constable Fenning, the primary order would have been carried out also.

When he had returned to Caroline with the girl Olga, he had expected to be rewarded. Caroline, however, was furious that he had failed in the first part and treated him woefully. Such now was the state of Bart's mind, that he gave not a thought for Sasha, Olga or his two children, Debbie and Annabel. Over two years Caroline had enslaved not only his body, but his entire mind too.

As a penance for his failure over the ordered destruction of Sasha he must be punished. Caroline placed a chair in the middle of the cellar, next to where Olga was bound hand and foot. Bart was ordered to sit in it and Caroline placed a handcuff on his right wrist, the other cuff was attached to the arm of the chair. It never even entered Bart's head to resist, so broken was his spirit and will to Caroline's.

Powerless to do anything, he squirmed and wriggled in the chair, whilst Caroline slowly and seductively removed all of her own clothing until she was naked. Standing in front of him but just out of range of his left hand, she proceeded to run her hands up and down her own body in a slow and sensuous fashion. She watched with delight the desire and lust in Bart's face as he tried in vain to reach for her. The bulge in his trousers was clear evidence of his state of mind.

Then, quite slowly at first, then gradually quickening the pace, she began to masturbate herself. Bart's eyes seemed about to burst from his face and his cheeks puffed and reddened with his efforts to escape his bonds and reach her.

Caroline rolled this way and that on the floor, a hand working wildly between her spread thighs, excited by the helpless condition of Bart. At last she came in a wildly gasping orgasm, and screamed with the sheer joy. Then, as a finale, she rose to her feet, took one look at Bart's protuberance and laughed. Caroline picked up a

Saddlewitch

bamboo cane from the table and brought it down hard across the offending member.

Bart screamed with pain and Caroline said icily, "That will teach you to lust after a princess." With that, she picked up the bundle of her clothes and vacated the cellar, leaving Bart still chained to the chair.

He turned to the bound figure of Olga on the floor next to him. She was watching him and her eyes expressed the terror she felt.

"What the devil do you think you're looking at, girl?" he snarled. Olga turned away so as not to meet his eyes.

Caroline left him chained like that with no food until the next morning. Bart fell on his knees and thanked her when she released him.

CHAPTER TWENTY

Olga was an intelligent girl who spoke four languages, therefore she was capable of putting two and two together and not making five. One, she knew her background, and as an orphan had no parents or family. Therefore, she could conclude, ransom was not the reason for her abduction. Two, the motive was not sexual, or she would have been raped by now. Three, she realised that Bart Paget could have escaped without using her as a hostage. Four, they were giving her good food and opportunities to wash and bath, even making her go through a form of exercises every day. There had been no talk of releasing her, so it didn't take a genius to realise that the evil pair needed her for something. From what she had seen of their joint behaviour, it was evident that the woman totally dominated Bart Paget. It was as if she had some hypnotic power over him. From remarks made, Olga deduced something was planned for Halloween. For some time now she had scratched tiny marks on the cellar wall, one for every day, conscious of the fact that if the ordeal went on, she would lose track of time. For this purpose she used a cheap ring she wore on her right hand. Every day she was untied for one hour to exercise and for some of this time, left alone.

Today, she counted the marks. If her calculations were right, from the day she had been abducted, October the thirty-first was only two days away. If ever she was to escape, now was the time to try. One thing was in her favour, her only other attempt to do so had been on the first day motivated by sheer panic.

Since then, she had accepted the hopelessness of her situation and hadn't tried again. Perhaps her captors were now a little complacent. Olga racked her brains. The hour allowed for her exercises was almost up. Soon Bart Paget would return to retie her. Whilst doing this he always locked the cellar door behind him and put the keys in his pocket. If she could only overpower him in some way, then take his keys and escape, locking him in behind her.

Desperately, Olga's gaze searched the room for some kind of weapon. If she didn't do it now, she would never find the courage again, and maybe tomorrow or the next day would be too late. Both her captors, Olga deduced, were quite mad.

Whatever they had planned for her, she guessed, was probably going to be terminal. The cellar contained only her chair, which was a fairly solid wooden one and a battered old table. Even if she stood behind the door and tried to wield the chair, she realised Bart would note both her's and the chair's absence before entering the cellar. She dismissed the idea and forced her mind to think again. To get his keys she realised Bart would have to be knocked unconscious in some way.

Olga's probing gaze swept round the walls ... Nothing. They had left her nothing. Then she noticed where the brickwork had slightly crumbled near one corner of the cellar. Maybe she could prise a brick out from the battered masonry. She rushed across and putting her fingers into the slight recess pulled at all four bricks surrounding the missing one. The first three were absolutely solid, but in the last, she sensed a touch of movement.

If only she had some sort of tool to use! Olga looked reluctantly at the silver bracelet round her wrist. It had been given her by a boyfriend back in Stockholm and therefore, had a sentimental value. She weighed the odds. It was all she had.

Coming to an instant decision, she tore it from her wrist and went to work on the battered brick. With a sawing movement she worked on the mortar between, using the bracelet's edge.

She was encouraged by fine particles of brick dust eroding away. A little heap of dust began to gather on the stone floor of the cellar. She stopped and tried to move the brick with her fingers. It definitely seemed looser. Then her heart sank. She could hear Bart's returning footsteps in the corridor outside.

She hurried back to the centre of the room trying to replace the bracelet on her wrist. It had gone out of shape and wouldn't go over her hand. Whipping her dress up, she hurriedly stuffed the twisted piece of battered silver down the back of her panties. The key was turning in the lock as she dropped her dress back into place.

Olga was still breathing hard as much as from fear as exertion. Bart noticed it, and said that at least he could see that she had done her exercises. As he proceeded to tie her hands and feet, she noticed the little pile of brick dust over by the wall. She prayed that he wouldn't notice it. When she had been secured and Bart had once again left her alone, she rolled over and over towards the wall. She had been lucky this time, but when he came back with her meal and stood over her, he would be sure to notice.

Rolling over and over on a stone floor with your hands and feet tied is no joke. When Olga arrived at the little pile of brick dust, she was still faced with dispensing it. Running her back up the wall, she managed to achieve a sitting position, wherein she was actually sitting on the little heap of dust.

Using her tied hands, behind her back as they were, she pressed against the wall. In this way she was able to scuff her bottom several times across the evidence of her labours. Whilst effecting this, the twisted bracelet scratched painfully and dug into her buttocks. Olga rolled away, and laying on her side inspected her efforts. God knows what state her dress was in. She knew it must be filthy, perhaps torn. By the time Bart returned with her meal, she had struggled back to the centre of the room.

The next twenty-four hours were probably the longest in Olga's short life. She found herself counting the seconds, let alone the minutes. She longed desperately for the time when she would be untied and left alone for an hour to do her exercises.

That morning dawned and she received a visit from Caroline who accompanied Bart. She was forced to stand up after being untied. Caroline walked round in a circle inspecting her. Then she berated Bart, saying how could be possibly have allowed Olga to have got into such a filthy state.

"Just look at her dress," she stormed. "What have you been doing to her?"

"Nothing, Princess Astarte," Bart cowered before Caroline.

During her captivity, Caroline had provided Olga with fresh underwear on a daily basis, but the dress she wore was the one she had been abducted in. Olga prayed that Caroline wasn't going to run her hands over her as she sometimes did. One thing for sure, was that the battered silver bracelet wouldn't remain a secret if she did.

Luck was with her. Caroline told Bart that she would give him a dress for Olga to change into.

"She can put it on before you retie her, after her exercise session later … Burn her old one," she commanded. Once more Olga was left alone with her thoughts.

After what seemed eternity, Bart returned with a red dress over his arm. Laying it on the table he proceeded to untie Olga's hands and feet. She rose painfully stiff from the long period of confinement.

"Take off that dirty rag and put the dress on I have brought you," Bart snapped.

"No," retorted Olga.

"What do you mean, girl?" bellowed Bart.

"I no undress in front of you. You go away," exclaimed Olga.

"Do it now!" snapped Bart. Olga played a wild hunch. It was plain the man was terrified of Caroline, and she knew he had orders never to touch her.

"Go away or I tell the princess woman that you rape me," Olga said, icily. She saw the terror in Bart's eyes instantly and knew that she had struck oil.

"You wouldn't?" he said nervously.

"You wait, see," Olga threatened.

"Very well," capitulated Bart. "I'll go, but just you see you put that dress on." With that he turned and left her alone, locking the door behind him.

Olga never even looked at the dress on the table. Retrieving the battered piece of silver, she rushed to the wall and went to work on the damaged brickwork once more. It was hard and laborious work. A hundred times she wished, if only she had a screwdriver or better still a chisel rather than this thin strip of bent silver. Her fingers were blistered and bleeding and she felt like crying.

Finally, she was forced to pull her dress over her head and tear it into strips. Using the strips of cloth, she wrapped them round her hands and continued trying to blot out the discomfort. She hadn't got a watch. They had taken it away from her quite early on in her captivity.

She stopped for a moment, pulling on the brick anew. It was definitely looser. Frantically she chipped away at it, then alas, the silver distorted to an unrecognisable shape and snapped. Olga was left with a tiny piece the size of a matchstick in her hand. Time was running out. The remainder was now firmly embedded in the masonry. Maybe she could use the heavy chair leg as a lever.

Rushing across the room she returned with the chair. Holding it with its back towards her, she inserted one of the thick legs into the hole she had made. Olga levered with all her strength. The brick moved, but only a little. Then there was a loud snap and the end of the leg broke with a sudden jerk, Olga nearly falling over. She recovered and thrust into the aperture the corresponding leg of the chair and levered with all her might.

This time there was a double commotion as both chair leg and brick sheered off and clattered to the floor. Olga held her breath and waited, fearful that either Bart or Caroline would have heard the noisy disturbance. Seconds, then a minute passed. At last she had a weapon.

Clutching hold of the brick, she tested its weight. No-one came. Now she must decide how best she should use it. First, she smoothed out the debris left on the floor using the torn segments of what was left of her filthy dress. Then, realising she was only dressed in bra and pants, she rapidly pulled the red dress over her head and reached round and zipped it up. She was surprised to find that it fitted perfectly, but on second thoughts, remembered Caroline was about the same size as herself.

The chair now had two short legs at the front where they had broken off, but there was little she could do to disguise that fact. Olga knew she would have to find some way of distracting Bart when he came in with her next meal, or he would notice the broken chair immediately. She propped it up against the table so that it looked as if it was just resting against the table top. Not perfect by any means, but nevertheless the best that Olga could come up with. She settled down to wait, feeling quite sick with apprehension. Some way or another she had to get Bart near enough to her.

There was only going to be one chance with the brick. If she didn't knock him unconscious with the first strike, Olga knew she was lost for ever. She gripped it in one hand, behind her back and lent against the wall. Then she heard his footsteps approaching again.

The door was unlocked and Bart entered, carrying her tray with food and drink. He made for the table to set it down. If he noticed the chair Olga knew she was sunk.

Just as he set down the tray, she exclaimed, pulling up one side of the red dress, "My knee, I hurt it. You take look, please?" She rubbed it with her free hand and effected a grimace of pain. Bart looked as if he couldn't care less but nevertheless crossed towards her. He stared at the exposed knee and ventured nothing. "You do something, it hurt bad" she pleaded.

Grudgingly, he bent to inspect the suspect knee. Just as he reached out with both hands to encircle her knee, Olga brought the brick crashing down in a roundhouse action to the side of Bart's head.

With a groan he slumped to the floor, blood welling from a vicious gash to his temple. Olga's first thought was that she had killed him. Putting the thought from her mind, she turned him over, going through his pockets for the cellar keys. She cursed herself for the delay. If she hadn't been so wound up, she would have watched which pocket he'd put them into.

Finally, she found them in a trouser pocket. Blood was streaming freely from the wound and some of it found its way onto Olga's fingers. Bart was emitting deep moaning sounds. She must hurry. Racing for the door she fumbled for the right key on the key ring. The first two she tried didn't fit. Then the third one did.

Opening the door, she scrambled through and closed it as silently as she could. The last thing she saw was Bart moaning, having raised himself to his knees, he was struggling to rise. The head wound still bled profusely. At least Olga knew she hadn't killed him as she had first feared.

She turned the key in the lock and crept off down the corridor towards the stairs leading to the ground floor. Now if Caroline wasn't around she was free. Tiptoeing up the stairs, she paused on each step for any sound from above. All was silent. Just as she reached the top step all hell broke loose, a thunderous crashing sound in the cellar behind her. Olga realised Bart had recovered and was yelling at the top of his voice and smashing the broken chair against the door.

No point in delaying now. If Caroline was anywhere in the vicinity she couldn't help but hear this racket. The stairs led to a door, which proved not to be locked. Olga rushed through and found herself in the kitchen. The door to the garden was locked, so she raced out into the hall and made for the front door. Bolts were on top and bottom.

She slid back the top and was stooping for the bottom when it all happened. Caroline came rushing downstairs from the first floor and taking a flying leap, landed squarely on Olga's back. The two women rolled over and over on the hall carpet, each trying to gain supremacy over the other. The noise from the cellar sounded like bedlam, but Olga was sure Bart wouldn't succeed in breaking down the sturdy oak door.

She had only to overcome Caroline now to escape, but she reckoned without the woman's unarmed combat and judo police training. Not only that, Caroline was honed to the last degree in physical fitness and worked out with weights daily. Olga herself was a fit youngster, but she sensed right away that her adversary was something else again. Caroline had a grip like a vice and forced Olga's head back, until she thought her neck would break.

The long shapely legs were wrapped round her and she was only too conscious of their deceptive strength. She punched wildly at Caroline's face, but was unable to get any power behind the blows. Bringing her knee up, she tried to hit her attacker in the abdomen, but didn't seem to be able to even dent Caroline's hard flat muscles there.

Saddlewitch

Gradually, although she struggled with everything she had, she felt Caroline's superiority gaining ascendancy over her. She was forced over onto her stomach and an arm twisted up behind her back. One of Caroline's knees in the small of her back pinned her to the floor.

Then Olga found herself being dragged along the floor by the ankles. She felt like a rag doll. All her strength seemed to have left her, even her will to fight on. Caroline stood with one foot on her back holding her down. She sensed rather than saw that she had been dragged into the kitchen.

She heard a cupboard door open and then the sound of a bottle being opened. Again she tried to struggle, but the foot increased its pressure on her back. Olga's ribs hurt and her nipples were sore where she had been dragged along. The little red dress was scuffed up round her hips.

Caroline knelt down beside her and pulled Olga's head backward once more. With the other hand, she put a sweet smelling cloth over Olga's nose and mouth. Twisting her head to left and right Olga tried to evade the pressure, but she could feel herself growing ever weaker.

There was a pounding in her ears and a mist began to swim in front of her eyes. She was dimly aware of Caroline's laughter. Then she seemed to be falling, falling ever falling and everything went black and there was nothing, only wild dreams.

★ ★ ★ ★ ★

When Olga awoke she found herself back in the cellar bound and gagged once more. Bart Paget was on his knees being berated by Caroline. He had a bloodstained hand clutched to his temple. For a full ten minutes he was forced to accept a vitriolic verbal assault, such as Olga had never heard before.

When Caroline finally ran out of breath, Bart complained about his head wound.

"Serves you right, imbecile," was all the sympathy he received from Caroline. Finally, she dismissed him and turned her attention on Olga. "And you, girl, did you think to escape the princess Astarte?

You are the property of the Master now. Can't you understand that?" She forced Olga's head back and gazed venomously down into her eyes. "You may be able to fool that dolt, but never think you can play games with me …" At this point Caroline's tone turned to all sweetness and light. "Never mind, tomorrow night you won't have to worry ever again, my dear … Shall I tell you what's going to happen to you…?"

CHAPTER TWENTY ONE

A deep shadow seemed to have enveloped the village of Saddlewitch. True, folk seemed to be going about their business in the same accustomed ways, but in some way or other, all were affected. The brutal murder of the poor old recluse, Esmeralda, coupled with the abduction of the Paget's au pair, had shaken the village to its very roots. The attempted murder of Sasha had also reached the ears of everyone. Rumours ran thick and fast around the Saddlewitch community, everyone adding their own two pennyworth of grist to the mill.

Most were saying that Bart Paget must have murdered Esmeralda, as it was well known he had tried to murder his wife. Another story was that he had run off with the au pair, because his wife was having an affair with that young Drew Thorpe at Briar Cottage.

Hortense Hyde-Potter had already informed everyone she met, which was a considerable number, that the shameless hussy was living openly with Thorpe in his cottage.

"Palmed the children off, she has, the dog as well," exclaimed Hortense. "I'm going now to complain to the vicar about their immoral behaviour." She didn't tell anyone about the Reverend Mark Glenville's reaction to her complaint, though!

Mark had said, "Before making judgement on people, one should acquaint themselves with the facts, and even then, desist from scurrilous remarks. Have a little compassion and charity in your heart for others, Mrs. Hyde-Potter."

"Well, really!" retorted the crinkly old spinster, staring at Mark over the top of her pince-nez.

"Be not a judge or jury if you want to enter the Kingdom of Heaven."

Without more ado, she flounced off down the lane from the vicarage huffing and puffing.

"Just wait until I tell Dorothy Sheridan, the postmistress, how rude this new vicar is." Ten minutes later she did tell Dorothy and got quite a surprise at Dorothy's answer.

"Well, everyone seems to think he's brought a breath of fresh air to the village. His wife, Mary, is nice too. A tower of strength at the W.I. Even the young ones seem to be going to church now .... Have you heard Mark play his guitar? Sings well too, asset to the choir, old Ralph Thoday the choirmaster says."

Hortense gritted her teeth and mumbled, "Guitar – that's all he's good for," and flounced out of the post office.

Maggie Sewell, the plumber's wife was buying some stamps at the counter and overheard the conversation.

"Miserable old busybody ... Live and let live, I say ... My Ted 'e says the same."

Dorothy smiled.

"It's a certain type and a generation, I'm afraid ... Time and circumstances won't change her ... I have to say though, there's a lot like her, Maggie."

"Well I can't say I feels sorry for 'er," laughed Maggie.

"I suppose you could say that she's a creature of the establishment," suggested Dorothy.

"Creature, yes ... The establishment, as you calls it – I wouldn't be knowing about ... It's Mrs. Paget, poor dear, I feel sorry for. My Ted did some work for her once – said she was very nice."

Dorothy nodded. "Yes she is very nice. Mind you, your Ted would like her, he's always been one for the ladies and she's quite a looker." Both women laughed.

"You're about right there, Dorothy," said Maggie, scooping up her stamps and change from the counter, as constable Fenning entered the post office. For once he was actually in his police uniform.

"Morning ladies," he said, touching the brim of his helmet.

★ ★ ★ ★ ★

Sasha had just returned from visiting Bess, her black Labrador at the kennels. She wondered if things would ever be the same again in her life. She certainly had no wish to ever see Bart again, but she longed to be reunited with her children and to have the dog back home. She realised that she couldn't have expected Drew to house Bess as well as herself, as he already had Caliph, the Alsatian. She was still desperately worried about Olga and couldn't seem to rid herself of the feeling of guilt and responsibility for the girl's abduction. No word had been heard of Bart or Olga since she had been taken. Sasha was sure in her own mind that Bart had completely flipped. Therefore, he was capable of anything. Hadn't he tried to murder her? But for Olga Sasha knew she would have been dead herself. Supposing he had since murdered the girl? Sasha shuddered at the thought. Thank God the children were safe down in Bournemouth. At least she could phone and talk to them every day. The one consolation had been the nights at Briar Cottage spent with Drew. Although even with this she couldn't rid herself of the feeling of guilt. She knew the village were all talking about it, and some people had even cut her dead, when she had met them in the village.

A few had been understanding and supportive which had helped in some small way, particularly the vicar and his wife. Caroline, Drew's police colleague, had returned to open hostility towards her. So much so, that she had suggested to Drew that she should return to her own house. He wouldn't hear of it, however.

"There's always the chance that your madman of a husband could return," he had said and she knew he was right. There had been no further word from Barbara Lake and it would be Halloween tomorrow. Maybe she had blown the chance with the last meeting with Ted Lake. She knew that Drew, who was under pressure from his superiors, was counting on this. After all it was the only lead they had.

Trying to put her worries behind her, she decided to take Caliph, for a walk. Drew had gone over to the vicarage to see Mark Glenville and wouldn't be back for some time. The telephone rang. Absentmindedly preoccupied, Sasha picked it up.

Her heart missed a beat. It was Barbara Lake. She could tell at once that the woman's tone was extremely friendly. She found herself wondering what Ted had told her. Barbara said how she had missed her, and whilst Sasha tried to curb her impatience, traded pleasantries.

Eventually, just when Sasha was thinking it would never happen, came the invitation. Barbara was very secretive about it.

"A wonderful Halloween party," she said. "Quite the most exceptional and spectacular you will have ever seen."

"Where?" enquired Sasha.

"Oh, don't bother about where, my dear. That's my little surprise for you … Just drive over to my place and leave your car here, then we can go on in mine. Sally's coming too … . Wear something glamorous, won't you." Sasha tried to probe without being too pushy.

"Is it inside or outside, Barbara?"

"Why?" Was that a note of suspicion Sasha detected in Barbara's tone.

"Oh, nothing. But just so I know how to dress … After all, it is nearly November."

"Inside, my dear … Wear as little as you like … I assure you, you will be warm and well looked after," purred Barbara. "Six-thirty then, tomorrow night. I'll expect you then." Sasha agreed and heard the phone click off the other end.

Oh well, at least she would have something to tell Drew when he returned from the vicarage. She would go for a walk through the village and into the woods with Caliph. The dog looked at her expectantly, as she took down the lead from the peg.

"Come on Caliph," she called. The Alsatian was with her in an instant. Outside in the road autumn was well and truly with Saddlewitch. Leaves of red and gold danced and hopped, whisked up by the fresh October breeze. Others glided down like falling snow from the numerous trees. Great colourful piles were forming in the gutters, some of them wet and matted from last night's rain. It was a bright and mild morning, with the wind coming in from the south west. A little way along the road she could see where leaves had blocked a drain and formed quite a pool of water that couldn't escape. A car went by and sent a great jet of water cascading from it onto the pavement. In this idyllic village setting Sasha and Caliph set off. On their way past the post office, village shop, church and war memorial several people were going about their daily lives. Sasha saw doctor Denzil Davidson with his black medical case. He had finished his morning surgery and was now on his rounds visiting the sick. He gave her a cheery wave whilst getting into his car. There was old Tammy, she had never known his second name. He was an ex-naval man and entertained at the local pub. Singing and vamping at the piano for any that would buy him a drink. She remembered listening to him with Bart in happier times at the Black Bull. The words of one of his monologues came back to her and she smiled to herself at the recollection. The song was called the 11.69 and was about an old boat train.

"And we came across the stoker and we thought that he was dead. For his body and legs were missing and we couldn't find his head."

Sasha stopped and chatted to Tammy for a few moments before proceeding on her way.

Burgess Steel, the farmer, waved to her as he went by in his car. Mrs. Ponsonby-Forbes cut her dead at the entrance to Park Meadows, an upmarket estate. She got the same treatment from Strimmer the postman, only for a different reason. Strimmer was weaving dangerously from side to side on his bicycle obviously still the worse from last night's beer. Sasha turned to watch his erratic course on his return to the post office.

In the woods she found peace and tranquillity. A good many leaves were down now and formed a golden brown carpet beneath her feet. The light breeze rustled the tops of the high trees disturbing the remaining leaves. A few floated their way on a downward spiral to the woodland floor. Not having had Bess to walk, it seemed ages to Sasha since she had walked through here. This was somewhere she had always found contentment and solitude. Here she had always been able to give thought and consideration to her problems. Now she tried the opposite, trying to wash from her mind everything that had happened. She stopped to listen to a woodpecker tap, tap, tapping, somewhere ahead of her. A squirrel darted down a tree and ran across in front of her. Caliph gave chase but was thwarted when it rapidly ascended another tree to safety. She came across an area where forestry people had been doing some logging. At another place a landslide had occurred and deposited earth and debris in the brook fifty feet below. She was startled out of her prepossessed state when a voice called, "Hello."

It was Job Parrott, the local poacher. Everyone knew him as Digger. He had a brace of pheasants supported by a piece of rope dangling from one hand.

"You wus so quiet, missie … Gave me quite a start, yur did … Thought as 'ow you wus Batchelor the gamekeeper, I did … Coming up quiet like that on me," exclaimed Digger.

"Not to worry, Digger. I won't tell on you," laughed Sasha.

"Good on yer, missie," exclaimed Digger, creeping off through the undergrowth.

Sasha continued, Caliph running ahead. Twenty minutes later she emerged on the northern perimeter of the woods. Meadowland and arable farmland stretched out before her, reaching down to the village a mile or so below her in the valley. The fields, even the grasslands, looked sad, she thought at this time of the year. Two or three months ago there would have been golden corn gently swaying its heads to the breeze. Now there was only the stubble, waiting to be ploughed in. The cattle had been taken in from grazing for the winter so the meadows were stale and damp looking. Grass was still growing a little, so an untidy image was presented at this time of the year. A grove of elm trees were already devoid of leaves and a colony of rooks appeared the sole denizens of their stark bare tops. Sasha stood with Caliph at her heels looking down into the valley. Smoke was already drifting up from some of the chimneys and she could hear the church clock striking eleven. There was another way down round the side of the meadowland and through a cemetery back into the village. Sasha took it. Going through the cemetery she stopped to look at the gravestones. There was one that always made her smile. For the umpteenth time Sasha read it.

"Remember as you pass me by, as you are now, so once was I.
As I am now you soon will be, prepare yourself to follow me."

It wasn't this so much that Sasha chuckled at but the inscription in chalk written underneath this.

"To follow you, I'd be content,
If I did but know which way you went."

She ambled through the cemetery, most of the graves were old, some of them dating back to the sixteen hundreds. Others, completely eroded and indecipherable, were probably even older. She turned out onto the road and ran into Bessie Pepper the young barmaid from the Black Bull. The girl was making her way towards the local for her morning stint there. She walked along with Sasha and Caliph until she turned in at the pub, chattering on most of the time about the recent murder of the old recluse and the abduction of Sasha's au pair. Sasha was rather relieved when the girl left, not wishing to be drawn too deeply. By the time she arrived back at Briar Cottage she found Drew waiting at the front door.

"I was worried about you until I found Caliph gone too, so I guessed you must have taken him for a walk," Drew said. Once inside Sasha told him about the party she had been invited to tomorrow night. Drew was instantly excited, but then his excitement turned to worry. "Really, I don't know whether I can expect you to do this for us ... Even with back up, you could be putting yourself in considerable danger."

Sasha reassured him and reasoned, "How can I be at risk? You are going to wire me up so you will know exactly what is happening at any time. If anything happens you will be handy and can jump in immediately. Surely the important thing is to capture these dreadful people before they can do more damage ... Anyway, we don't know for sure Barbara Lake is anything to do with them, do we?"

"I'd put my last pound on it," said Drew. Then he went on to tell Sasha how the meeting with Superintendent Dawson had gone yesterday. "Didn't want to say anything before because it involved you in a way."

"Me?" exclaimed a surprised Sasha.

"Well, er yes ... How he knew I don't know. Said I was too busy knocking off the suspect's wife to have my mind on the job."

"He said that?" gasped Sasha.

"Well, he actually said another word I won't go into, love, but that was the size of it … Gave me two days to wrap this Satanist thing up, then I'm off the case. It appears I should have had you installed in one of our safe houses and not moved you in with me. I knew that, of course, really," exclaimed Drew.

"I'm sorry if I've caused you trouble on my account … Could you lose your job over it?" asked a concerned Sasha.

"I could, but I don't think it will come to that provided we get a result … He has threatened me with a disciplinary hearing anyway – mind you, that won't hold much water if we come out on top," Drew explained.

"But how did they find out about me? Staying here with you, I mean? … Caroline's the only one that knows that. Could she …..?" Sasha left the question in the air.

"Oh no, I'm sure she wouldn't do that. I know she's not too keen on you but she wouldn't grass on us," said Drew. He changed the subject. "Had another long chat with the vicar chap today. He was really helpful … Wants me to meet a Brigadier Jessup – lives in the village – even written a book on the occult apparently. The Vicar has made an appointment for me to go and see him tomorrow morning."

Sasha smiled. "Halloween tomorrow … Very fitting for a chat about the dark forces." Ignoring this, Drew responded that the Vicar wanted to help in any way.

"He's really worried about seeking out these Satanists and getting the Parish back to normal … Seems some of the old guard here are giving him a bad time over it. He's actually volunteered to come along to see this old retired Brigadier chap tomorrow with me."

"Is Caroline going with you as well?" asked Sasha.

"Why do you ask?" enquired Drew.

"Oh nothing, just wondered." Drew looked puzzled.

"I haven't said anything to her about it yet," he said.

"It's only a hunch, but don't, Drew," advised Sasha. When he looked even more puzzled Sasha went on to explain her concern. "Look, I may be wrong but Caroline, by your own lips, is supposed to be up on the occult world."

"Well, yes she is b…" Sasha didn't give him time to finish.

"Don't you think she may be annoyed if you go behind her back, asking questions she ought to be able to answer?"

"Ummm, I see what you mean. Perhaps you're right, but I'll have to discuss and plan for tomorrow night with her. You, as well, of course, Sasha."

"I suggest we have a detailed meeting and plan tomorrow evening, when we wire you up to go to your party … I have to tell you I still don't like it, though. You are putting yourself at a terrible risk."

Sasha laughed. "Just make sure none of them get their hands on me and that includes that sex mad Barbara Lake."

"I won't let you down, Sasha," assured Drew.

Changing the subject Sasha said, "Well, I suppose I'd better see about rustling up some lunch for us." No sooner had she said it than the telephone rang. It was the police to say that Ray Grainger, the private detective, had asked to see him at Grantfield Hospital.

"Forget lunch Sasha, I've got to go out," said Drew.

CHAPTER TWENTY-TWO

Arriving at Grantfield Hospital Drew was led straight to a small side cubicle in the Intensive Care Unit. A police constable sitting outside, rose to greet him. After a short conversation with the officer Drew went in to see Ray Grainger. To his surprise the fellow was sitting up and all the equipment and tubes had been removed. He still looked drawn and deathly white, but otherwise the improvement was startling to say the least. Drew offered his hand and Grainger took it, offering a flaccid and limp grip of his own.

After Drew had pulled up a chair, he said to Grainger, "You wanted to see me, I believe?" Grainger looked furtively to left and right and then spoke in a low voice.

"I'm not blameless in this, you know, Mr. Thorpe."

"What are you getting at Mr. Grainger?"

"Well, I mean, if I told you anything to help you ... How would that go for me?" Drew looked thoughtful. He really hadn't the authority to offer deals. If Grainger had been up to something he ought to pay the price. On the other hand, the fellow had nearly died, surely punishment enough, he reasoned.

"I can't promise anything, but on the other hand, I don't have to tell anybody else, anything you tell me ... Do I make myself clear?" explained Drew.

Grainger looked relieved and began to blurt out the whole story in detail. At the mention of Barbara Lake and the ceremony of the Satanists, Drew craned forward. So they were right, Barbara Lake was involved. He listened avidly to every word, right from the time Grainger had followed Barbara and Sally to the coven right up until the man had been beaten up. What Grainger didn't say about his own activities and involvement, Drew read between the lines.

"So you tried to blackmail Mrs. Lake then, against her husband finding out? That way you got paid twice," said Drew, dryly.

"Only I got a beating instead of getting paid, Mr. Thorpe."

Drew smiled wryly.

"Some might say you deserved it … A pretty low life crime, blackmail."

Grainger looked terrified.

"But you said you w…"

Drew cut in. "No, I didn't promise anything, Mr. Grainger, and I don't like blackmailers. However, …" he let the word hang in the air. Grainger looked like he was going to cry. Drew continued, "However, as I was saying, in this instance your information is of great use to me, so I propose to take no further action against you." The relief was plain for anyone to see on Grainger's face.

"Thank you, Mr. Thorpe. I feel a lot better for getting this off my chest, I can tell you."

"It might have helped if you had told me some of this before … . Anyway, you have now. I just hope it's in time to save a certain young lady's life," said Drew, before changing the subject and continuing. "Now my advice to you when you finally get discharged from this hospital, is to find yourself a different job. You might find it easier to stay out of trouble that way."

"Oh, I will," enthused a relieved Ray Grainger.

Drew left the hospital and returned to Saddlewitch. Excitedly, he relayed Grainger's confession to Sasha. She was as exuberant as he was with the news which definitely showed they had been on the right track concerning Barbara Lake. After Sasha's first burst of excitement, Drew pointed out that they would have to be even more careful now.

"You will be literally going into the lion's den tomorrow night, Sasha. You don't have to do it and I won't think any the less of you if you pull out."

"Do you really think I would?" she whispered.

"I wouldn't think any the less of you if you did … I just want you to know that … In fact, in a way I wish you would. I hate to think of you subjected to these fiends," exclaimed Drew.

"Don't be silly, Drew. We have arranged it all … There's really no danger. You said so yourself. I will be wired, so you will be listening to everything, and just as soon as anything happens, your back-up people will descend on the whole gathering. We both know we have to get the evidence to convict them. This is the only way."

"I know, but I just wish it wasn't necessary," Drew said, as he reached for Sasha and pulled her to him, kissing her firmly on the lips.

The remainder of the afternoon was spent in wild abandoned love making in front of a warm log fire, and afterwards they lay contentedly in one another's arms. Sasha couldn't seem to erase the thought that maybe it was a portent of coming disaster. She could never remember being so happy with anyone. She was sure it couldn't last. Not only for Drew's sake, but she owed it to Olga to go through with everything. After a light evening meal, Drew declared that he had better drive over to Endersby and go through tomorrow night's plan with Caroline. Sasha agreed that it seemed a good idea.

She stood at the front door and waved him off. It was a chilly night and already a mist was rising from the valley floor making visibility poor.

Sasha called out to him to take care as dense fog frequently descended locally. With a kiss blown towards her from the car, he drove off. Sasha shut the door and locked it.

Half an hour later he arrived at Caroline's. He was surprised to find her heavily made up and wearing a slinky black dress slit to the thigh. He assumed that she must be about to go out and apologised for not calling first. Caroline, however, said that was not the case, and she had expected him, as obviously, they had a lot to discuss for tomorrow night.

A huge log fire was burning in the grate and the house seemed incredibly warm. He removed his jacket and commented on it but Caroline said it didn't seem that warm to her.

Over a cup of coffee he went on to elaborate the plan for Sasha's meeting with Barbara Lake at tomorrow night's Halloween meeting.

Caroline already knew much of it, as they had discussed it before, assuming that the coven would meet. Now it was *fait accompli,* Drew wanted to make sure every 'I' was dotted and every 'T' crossed.

"I am sure I can leave it to you Caroline to arrange Special Branch back up, as arms will have to be drawn and signed for, can't I?" asked Drew.

"No problem. You can leave all those sort of details to me … How many men do you want standing by?" Caroline enquired.

"I think six will be enough if they are all armed … They will move in on my say so. Is that clear?"

"Are you going to be armed yourself?" questioned Caroline.

"Yes, you had better draw a .38 for me and one for yourself."

"Where do you want me stationed, Drew?"

"With me, of course. We will be in hiding in my car nearby listening in to what's happening. At the first sign of trouble you call for back up and I go in … Clear?"

"Perfectly. We can finalise all this when Sasha leaves tomorrow night for the party."

The various scenarios were discussed in like vein until about 10 p.m. when Drew rose to leave. At the front door he experienced a severe shock.

During the evening, the mist had thickened into a dense fog even blanketing out the garden gate a mere four metres in front of him. Caroline came to look when he called her to see it.

"Well! That's settled then. You will have to spend the night here, and go back in the morning. The roads round here don't even have cat's eyes … There's no way you could see to drive. Probably finish up in a ditch somewhere," prompted Caroline. Drew argued, although he knew it made sense. "Give Sasha a ring, and tell her what's happened. She'll understand," urged Caroline.

Reluctantly Drew dialled his own number and explained the position. "What's it like there?" he asked, meaning the fog.

"Pea soup. I was wondering how you were going to manage … No, you stay over. I'll be fine. After all, I've got Caliph here with me."

After a few moments further conversation, Drew replaced the receiver.

"Looks like you win then, Caroline. It's agreed I'm staying over."

"Ah, that's cosy, Drew. I'll get us a real drink as you're not driving." She went through to the kitchen to prepare them. Afterwards Drew thought that he should have suspected something was afoot as the drinks cabinet was in the lounge where he was. At the time it didn't register. Caroline was gone some time but finally returned with a gin and tonic for her and champagne brandy for him. The latter was fizzing beautifully.

"There you are, your favourite, as you so rarely come to see me these days, Drew." She handed him the glass and said, "Cheers!" Caroline turned on some restful background music on the system and sat down next to him on the sofa. They sipped their drinks contentedly, discussing recent events and their likely conclusion. Gradually, Drew began to feel very warm and loosened his tie. Caroline brought him another champagne brandy.

"I got it in, in your honour," she informed him.

By the time Drew had finished the second drink, he felt strangely both woosy and high. He seemed to be finding it difficult to focus. Every now and then there appeared to be two Caroline's sitting next to him. He was even aware that his speech was slurred. Two drinks had never affected him like this before. He said as much to Caroline.

She advised him to go and lie down.

"I expect you have been overdoing it lately, and I'm not surprised with all these threats you are getting from Superintendent Dawson," Caroline went on, in a sympathetic tone. "The spare room's all ready for guests. Come on, I'll show you. No doubt you'll feel better in the morning after a good sleep."

Drew nearly fell over as he tried to rise and Caroline caught his arm. She led him to the small guest room and wished him good night with a kiss on the cheek. Drew felt strangely strong yet disorientated. With difficulty he struggled out of his clothes and climbed naked under the duvet. The room seemed to be spinning, yet he didn't appear to feel sick or have a hangover. He was very aware of the effect of cold sheets on his naked skin. He lay there, his mind wandering – wildly crazy ideas that he couldn't seem to control. Then he became dimly aware that he was not alone. Someone else was in the room.

The fog had given Caroline Channing a chance she never expected. She had always wanted Drew Thorpe and had been driven half mad by his acceptance of her only as a friend. Even when she had been married, it was always Drew she had wanted and not her husband. Tonight she had seen the chance and laced his drinks with L.S.D. Now she would get even with that Sasha bitch that had had him, as she thought, all to herself. From the moment Drew was safely closeted in the guest room, Caroline went to her own room and undressed completely. She covered herself with expensive perfume and donned a jet-black wig. She had even brought the same perfume that she had recognised on Sasha – 'Georgio'.

Ready now, and smiling cunningly to herself, she tiptoed along to the guest room and opening the door just a little, crept inside. She was aware of Drew tossing and turning under the duvet. An instant of doubt hit her, was he far enough gone that he wouldn't know what was happening? She had been practising, talking like Sasha, in her mirror, for days for such an opportunity as this. Such was her hatred for Sasha Paget, that she would don the black wig in the privacy of her bedroom, mimic her voice and then slap her own face, imagining that it would be Sasha that would feel the pain. She had turned the central heating up to full, to speed up the drug coursing through Drew's body. This, together with the lounge fire, made the whole house like an oven. A palace fit for the princess Astarte and her lover, mused Caroline.

Stealthily, her naked form glided towards the bed. Slowly she peeled the duvet cover back revealing Drew's slim and muscular body. She gasped with delight as he twisted and contorted his body from side to side. Kneeling on the floor besides the bed, she ran her fingers over his burning torso and down the long firm thighs. Caroline could feel already the wetness between her own legs. Tantalisingly slowly, she began to play with his manhood lying recumbent between strong hairy legs. She watched with animated delight as the item of her attention grew and grew into a perpendicular column. Slowly, never taking her eyes from her one focal point, she climbed astride the body on the bed. She ran her own body up the length of her victim's and could feel his hardness against her own belly. She began to kiss Drew's lips and her heart leapt with joy when she achieved an instant response.

She broke away and murmured, "It's Sasha, your very own Sasha." A moment later, unable to contain herself longer, Caroline spread her own thighs and guided Drew's wildly bucking manhood deep within herself. She cried out in elation and triumph and rode him like a maddened rodeo bronco wildly throwing her arms aloft.

The response from Drew was everything she had ever dreamed of. His body jack-knifed to meet her every abandoned movement. Pleasure was manifold as she knew she was stealing what was meant for Sasha. Soon Drew must surely come inside her and Caroline's pleasure would be complete. Clutched in her right hand was a tiny capsule of amyl nitrate for just that moment. If only she could hold out and defy nature long enough, she was so tantalisingly close to tipping over herself. Then it happened and she felt Drew pulsating inside her as he climaxed. Instantly she squeezed and burst the tiny capsule under her own expectant nostrils. Caroline dissolved in the most fulfilled and wildly exciting orgasm she had ever experienced. A moment later her body collapsed onto Drew, her mind temporarily obliterated.

★ ★ ★ ★ ★

It was just getting light, the first evidence of dawn seeping through the gaps in the curtains when Drew awoke. For a moment or two he wondered where he was, his throat felt sore, and his head throbbed like the hammers of hell. He turned over and reached out for Sasha. She was lying with her naked back towards him, her black hair spread out behind her on the pillow. Strange, he thought, I've never noticed that birthmark between her shoulder blades before. It resembled the letter '6'. Only once before had he ever seen anything like it, and that had been on Caroline, when they had gone swimming together back at university. Then it all began to come back to him. The last thing he remembered had been drinking with Caroline and then beginning to feel very strange indeed. Something was very wrong here. He sat bolt upright in bed, surprised to find himself naked. He turned and looked at the woman next to him and gasped. It was Caroline, only her hair was the wrong colour. Almost in a trance, he reached out and touched the lustrous black hair. A wisp of blonde hair protruded from underneath. Realisation hit him like a punch on the chin. Snatching the black wig off, he exposed Caroline's own blonde hair scrunched up underneath. At the same moment she awoke and her face slowly creased into a smile. The heavy make up was badly smudged round her eyes and mascara had run down her cheeks. Even her usually well-applied lipstick was all round her mouth.

Drew looked at her in stupefied amazement, his mind desperately trying to orientate. Caroline sat up and went to put an arm round him. Angrily he knocked it away.

"You were much more friendly last night, Drew," she purred.

"What the hell are you playing at, Caroline?" She watched his angry distress with obvious amusement. Her normally attractive face was a mass of distorted make up resembling a clown.

"I'll tell you what happened, shall I, Drew … then you can go and tell Sasha. I'm sure she will find it entertaining … Depends how you tell it, I suppose." Drew's usually cool demeanour was slowly turning to one of cold fury as Caroline expertly turned the screw.

"And I thought you were my friend," he said, in a low voice full of meaning.

"Oh, I am, Drew … and, if you let me, I'll be a lot more. I'm sure I could give you a better time than that Paget bitch."

Drew reached across and took a vice like grip on each of Caroline's biceps. He shook her savagely.

"You will tell me every detail of what happened here last night," he commanded.

"Willingly, my love," chuckled Caroline.

Drew's face remained stonily icy.

"Get on with it!" was all he said. Drew forced himself to listen whilst Caroline, obviously enjoying his suffering and embarrassment, related every minute detail. At the completion of the narrative she relaxed, propping the pillow up behind her and said, "So, if you don't tell Sasha, I surely will, Drew. I can't wait to watch her face."

Drew threw back the bedclothes and stood up no longer bothered or even aware of his nakedness. He focused his gaze on Caroline.

"You and I are finished as friends. I realise I have to work with you on this case, but that's it ... Is that clear, Caroline?"

"Perfectly ... but you will change your mind when Sasha rejects you, as I'm sure she will when I tell her with a little embroidery added," laughed Caroline. She threw back the bedclothes on her own side of the bed exposing her own nudity. "See what you can have anytime ... Can Sasha offer you this? A second hand married woman with two kids like her ... I don't think so."

Drew turned his back on her, throwing over his shoulder, "You disgust me ... I'm going to take a shower and wash the smell of you off." He slammed the bedroom door behind him.

Caroline hissed, "If I can't have you Drew Thorpe, nobody else is going to ... It's your own funeral ... So be it."

CHAPTER TWENTY-THREE

Drew left without speaking to Caroline again. His emotions were very mixed. How could Caroline, his best friend, have so betrayed and tricked him? He was still feeling very hurt and mixed up and quite a bit guilty himself. Had he led her on, he wondered. They had always been such good friends and now this. It was certainly going to make working together very difficult indeed. The worse aspect was that he simply couldn't remember a damned thing about last night after that second drink. What should he tell Sasha? Should he keep quiet and say nothing or tell her? From what Caroline had threatened, she intended to give Sasha her version either way. Drew deduced better Sasha should hear his version, but would she believe him? He slowed down the car and stopped outside Briar Cottage. Sasha heard the car and was at the front door to meet him.

She took one look at his face and said, "What's wrong?"

"We'd better go inside," said Drew, ushering Sasha before him.

Where do you start with something like this, he thought to himself, then he decided there was nothing for it, but to make a clean sweep. After they were both seated over a coffee and toast, he braved it. Even the start was awkward and embarrassing.

"Sasha, what I have to tell you, will probably disgust you as much as it does me, but if I don't tell you, somebody else will, so its better you hear the true version from me." The concern showed on Sasha's attractive face.

"You're frightening me, Drew … Who do you mean, somebody else?" she queried.

"Caroline," Drew replied. He then proceeded to relay the whole story, leaving nothing out, just the way that Caroline had related it to him. Drew watched the distress and horror in Sasha's eyes and felt terrible. She didn't interrupt and said nothing, even when he had finished. Embarrassed and worried by her silence, he added, "I only know what she told me happened. It's possible it didn't … I can't remember anything from the time I rang you to say I was staying over."

Sasha was concealing her distress well and trying to put a brave face on events, but this seemed like the last straw to her. When she finally found her voice, she spoke with a lump in her throat, very near to tears.

"If you don't mind, Drew, I just need to be alone for a while … . I think I'll take Caliph for a walk in the woods."

Drew tried to stop her and reassure her but Sasha was determined and called Caliph to go out.

Whilst she was putting the lead on the Alsatian, Drew said, "Well, I've got to go over and see this Brigadier fellow … I'll see you when you get back, love … Okay?"

"Maybe," murmured Sasha and left with the dog.

Perhaps I shouldn't have said anything. If I hadn't fallen in love with her I probably wouldn't have, Drew thought, whilst changing his clothes into something more suitable for the official visit to the Brigadier.

Sasha ran everything through in her mind whilst walking through the woods. Caliph, strangely sensing her mood, stayed close to her heel. When she had a problem in the past she would always seek the solitude of the woods to try and solve it. Drew had obviously been totally honest with her, but could she be sure he wasn't just trying to forestall Caroline's impending version of events. It just all sounded so far fetched, that he couldn't remember anything himself. Sasha knew that drugs caused a sense of diminished responsibility, but this, was it possible? With a woman's intuition, she had always known that Caroline was jealous of her, and that the woman obviously fancied Drew in a sexual way, this, even though he always insisted that they were just good friends. Sasha also had to admit that Caroline was very attractive. What man wouldn't fancy her, she thought. She desperately wanted to believe Drew, but the thought of what he had probably done with Caroline inwardly tortured her. She could almost feel and see Caroline's shapely legs wrapped round Drew. Her Drew. Tears began to run down Sasha's cheeks as she walked. Caliph looked up at her and whined. She patted him on the head and tried to put the vision from her mind. Now tonight she would have to face both of them, Drew and Caroline together, when they wired her up for her meeting with Barbara Lake.

Horrified, she registered that Halloween had arrived. It was actually here ... Could she go through with it, she wondered? Then, with reality she realised that she hadn't a choice, she owed it to poor Olga. Tonight she thought the world could end for the girl if their suspicions were right. Then, selfishly, she mused that it had already ended for her. It was in this state of depression that she emerged onto the road from the woods and ran into Kate McLean walking her dog. At first she was surprised to see the schoolmistress, but then remembered it was also Half Term. They walked along towards the village together talking. Sasha was hardly aware of what her companion was saying, she was so preoccupied with her own thoughts. Quite suddenly she found herself taking in what Kate was saying to her. About that chap they had found. So high on L.S.D. they say he had eaten through his own arm to the bone.

"What|?" said Sasha, aghast.

"Yes, apparently didn't feel a thing, thought he was fighting a monster, by all accounts ... Terrible, wasn't it?" went on Kate.

As they parted company at the end of the road, there was a new spring in Sasha's step. So it was possible. Almost ninety percent of the doubt was removed from Sasha's mind. She should have believed Drew and forgiven him. When she thought about it, the perfectly wretched look on his face should have told her something. She hurried the last few steps to Briar Cottage to tell him so. He wasn't there, but waiting at the front door was a perfectly groomed Caroline, a satisfied smile on her face.

* * * * *

Drew set out on foot for Brigadier Jessup's house. He lived in an unpretentious chalet bungalow near the war memorial. It was no more than five minutes walk from Briar Cottage. All Drew could think about at the moment was Sasha's reaction. Clearly she didn't believe him. What could he do to convince her of the truth? He was still thinking about it, when the Brigadier answered his half-hearted knock.

"Well, how do, young fellow. Nice to see you, come in," he greeted Drew. Silver grey hair with mutton chop whiskers and a walrus type moustache gave an immediate military impression. He was dressed in plus fours and woollen socks with heavy brogue shoes and a check jacket.

Drew was ushered into the lounge. The Brigadier had lost his wife five years earlier and now lived alone. Drew noticed a rack of shotguns on the wall and a bag full of gold clubs in the corner of the room.

"I expect you wonder why an old buffer like me should be involved in anything to do with Black Magic?"

Drew said that he was a bit surprised when the vicar had suggested that the Brigadier might be able to help. Jessup went on to say that it had started when he had been a young Captain in the Intelligence Corps. "Got sent out to Romania where there was a real problem at the time. They had requested help, and that's how I got into it in the first place … Can't tell you much about that though – bound by the official secrets act – what!" Drew was forced to smile. The old chap was so typical of one's imagination of a military man. "How can I help?" the Brigadier asked.

Drew looked pensive before replying, then said, "Everything we have seems to be centred on a build up to tonight's Halloween." His voice then took on a more serious and grave note. "I'll level with you, Brigadier … We have reason to believe that a human sacrifice is about to happen somewhere around here … Some sort of Black Mass ceremony … I wish I knew more but unfortunately I don't."

It was Brigadier Jessup's turn to look thoughtful.

"What makes you think so?" he enquired.

Drew outlined everything that had happened from the strange behaviour pattern of Bart Page, the attempted murder of his wife and the abduction of Olga, even the murder of Esmeralda. At the conclusion of the narrative the Brigadier slowly lit his pipe, never taking his eyes off Drew's. After a long pull, he exhaled a cloud of smoke, which spiralled up to the ceiling.

"Hmmm! It ought to be a baby, really," Jessup ventured.

"I'm sorry sir … . I don't understand," said Drew puzzled.

"A Black Mass lad – if it's to be authentic, would mean they use the body of a woman as their altar and then on top of her would be laid the baby."

Drew leaned forward.

"Which would they sacrifice – the woman or the baby?"

"Both," replied Jessup, "but not at the same time. The baby would be killed with a sacrificial knife and the woman …" Here he paused.

"And the woman?" prompted Drew.

"The woman would already be dead, or if she was alive, would be offered sexually to the disciples of the devil who were present."

"My god!" said Drew. "These people are fiends."

"Devil worshippers usually are, lad," affirmed Jessup.

"We have no reports of any missing babies," put in Drew hopefully.

"Doesn't mean a thing. They could be using one of their own."

"Surely not. Surely even a devil worshipper wouldn't allow his or her child to be sacrificed," expounded Drew in horror.

"Don't you believe it. These people are so programmed they could even be made to believe it was the proper thing to do … . By the way, they may not need a baby," added Jessup.

"What do you mean?"

Jessup continued, "You said this au pair Paget abducted was only nineteen. Was she a virgin, do you know?"

Drew shrugged and turned his palms uppermost.

"No way I would know Brigadier … It's possible, I suppose… Then it's quite possible that they will use her with someone else as the altar, Brigadier?"

"More than possible, I'd say."

"Do you think Paget is involved?" asked Drew.

"From what you have told me about his gradual mood changes it's highly likely, but he won't be pulling the strings, of that you can be sure."

"Why do you say that, sir?"

"Because he sounds like a weak character who is being used by a much stronger mind … . It always happens this way." Drew looked puzzled and Jessup continued. "He will gradually have been indoctrinated and programmed without ever having even been aware of it. By the time the devil or master, whoever they are, have finished with him, he won't know right from wrong. He will hate everything he ever loved."

Drew thought for a moment.

"That description would certainly fit in with what we know about Paget."

"Basically, as easily as I can explain it to you the answer is possession. The master or devil worshipper sees a chink in someone's mental makeup and gets him interested in the occult. Soon they are out of their depth and cannot deal with the forces they have unleashed … Take for example the story of Dr. Jekyll and Mr. Hyde … Here you see a good and honourable man turned into a fiend … Sometimes exorcism works, but only if the person involved is willing to let it."

"This is all very hard to take in," interjected Drew.

"I can appreciate that lad, but remember Satanists honestly believe that they rule the world. Think of Satan's temptations of Christ in the wilderness, offering our Lord the good things in life, if he will only worship him. Black Magic is practiced by Satanists, only they don't regard it as such. To them it is the use of their master's powers for his ends. Whereas we try to live by the Bible, such people live by the book of Shadows."

"What in hell is that?" queried Drew.

"Just what it sounds like," answered Jessup. "On the initiation of a witch or warlock she or he compiles their own book of spells, ceremonies and rites. This book of Shadows can be handed down and absorbed by the coven at her or his death. This way the power of the demon builds and grows."

"Does it always culminate at Halloween?" asked Drew. "The sacrifice, I mean?"

"Usually at All Hallows, but it can be Walpurgis Night – April the thirtieth," explained Jessup. The Brigadier continued on the same theme and Drew found it so interesting that he was almost made to forget his own problems for a short while.

Just before he left Jessup, Drew asked him if he had any idea where a coven might meet in the Saddlewitch area. The answer was somewhat guarded.

"I do have my own suspicions, but nothing I'd care to incriminate anyone with at this juncture ... Nothing I could prove, if you understand me." Then, changing the subject, he said enthusiastically, "If I can be of any help tonight young man, give me a call."

"Thank you sir. I'll remember that, and thanks for all the information you have given me this morning."

The Brigadier came to the door with Drew, and watched him walk off down the street.

"Dashed fine young fellow, that," he muttered, half to himself before closing the door...

* * * * *

Caroline was all bright and breezy charm as Sasha turned in at the gate. Sasha, however, decided to play her cards close to her chest. She was coldly polite, no more. She unlocked the door and let them both into the Briar Cottage.

"Drew's out at present, but he will be back soon," she told Caroline.

"Oh, that's okay, it was you I wanted to see really. Wanted to apologise for last night ... Spur of the moment thing really ... You know what Drew's like ... Rather hard to resist – you must have found this yourself," exclaimed Caroline, in a comradely way.

"Go on," said Sasha coldly. It would be interesting to see how Caroline was going to play this. By now Sasha had already, in her own mind, forgiven Drew having decided he was the victim of circumstances.

"Can I sit down?" enquired Caroline.

"Be my guest," said Sasha virtually shoving a dining room chair towards the other. Sasha herself sat on the edge of the table where she could look down on Caroline.

"Well?" she said.

"I expect Drew told you what happened. We just couldn't resist one another, you see," Caroline began. Sasha didn't answer but just kept a cold watchful eye on the other woman. Caroline didn't look so sure of herself now. Maybe he hasn't told her, she thought. Time to elaborate. Sasha, although she found the narrative distasteful, forced herself to listen. Of course, there was no mention of spiked drinks or drugs just unbridled passion.

When Caroline had finished relating her version of last night's affair she ended by saying, "Of course, I'm very sorry, Sasha."

Sasha eased herself off the sitting position on the table and stood up. She faced Caroline staring straight down into the blonde girl's eyes.

"Have you quite finished, Caroline? It so happens that I prefer to believe Drew's version and find you quite despicable ... Not for what you did to me, but for what you did to Drew, who until now believed you to be his friend. Just what sort of person are you, Caroline? Is this how you get your kicks?"

"Well, really Sasha. I only meant to tell you the truth. But if you prefer to believe Drew then there's no hope for you, is there?"

"Less for you, I think," retorted Sasha.

Caroline continued to try and assassinate Drew's character.

"There have been others you know. You're not the first – not by a long chalk, you're not."

"I didn't imagine I was," remarked Sasha, off-handedly, now beginning to enjoy Caroline's disappointment at her reaction. Just as she could feel Caroline's hate filled eyes measuring her for the next attack, Drew entered.

He looked from one to the other, guessing what had been going on and then, hopefully at Sasha. He was not disappointed. She walked over and kissed him in front of Caroline and whispered in his ear.

"The jury has just returned and found you not guilty," then aloud, "I'll go and make some coffee."

By the time she had returned, both Drew and Caroline were discussing the plans for cover of Sasha's meeting that night with Barbara Lake. Immediately, she noticed the cold detached way in which Drew spoke to Caroline whenever he addressed the latter.

Caroline herself seemed quietly resigned to having lost this round.

Over coffee Drew explained to Sasha what was going to happen, but first he offered her a last chance to pull out of the meeting with Barbara. Needless to say, she declined. Drew then outlined the plan to Sasha. Apparently Caroline would be the one to wire her. Sasha queried this, but Drew explained that it had to be done by another female.

"Otherwise some kind soul might report me," he said, ominously looking at Caroline. The latter stared coldly back at him. "Caroline will also arrange for back-up. Six armed men will be standing by to intervene, the very moment we pick anything up on our receivers."

"Where will you be, Drew?" queried Sasha.

"I'll be stationed in my car, so that I can see the Lake residence. I will see you arrive in your car and depart with Barbara Lake. I'll then follow at a discreet distance, so I'm going to be near by at all times."

"Where will she be?" asked Sasha, accentuating the she, and looking at Caroline, who said nothing.

"She, Caroline," said Drew, equally coldly, "will be secreted in a van with all the receiver equipment and six armed men. They will be positioned on a high hill, where they will best be able to pick up your wired conversation from the coven."

"How will you know when to come in yourself?" said Sasha, anxiously.

"Caroline will get through to me, and as the nearest, I'll be with you almost immediately … Caroline and her six-man back-up will be there just after. So, you see, nothing can go wrong, love."

Sasha looked doubtful.

"I'd feel better if it wasn't her. I don't trust her, Drew."

Drew looked hard at Caroline.

"I'm inclined to agree with you, but I'd have to admit she's a good policewoman. It's her job as well as mine that's on the line."

Caroline glared at Drew as if looks would kill.

"Don't you worry about me. Just keep your mind off of her for five minutes and do your job ... I'll do mine."

CHAPTER TWENTY-FOUR

At six o'clock that evening at Caroline's insistence, Drew left the two women alone in order for Sasha to be wired. He didn't like the arrangement one bit, but with Caroline quoting regulations at him, there wasn't a case for argument. He waited impatiently downstairs for their return. Up in the room hardly a word was exchanged between the two women, both observing a frosty silence.

Sasha secretly wished that her safety wasn't dependent on Caroline, but was only too aware that it did. Thankfully she would have Drew nearby to rush in and save her, should the worst happen.

A high wind had blown up towards evening, and a tentacle of undergrowth was rattling the windowpane. Sasha was conscious of it howling round the telephone lines outside. A fitting night for Halloween, she thought to herself, but said nothing to Caroline.

Sasha winced as Caroline pinched her, whilst fitting a small microphone to the inside of her bra strap. The appliance was totally flat and no bigger than a twenty pence piece. Without apologising, Caroline stood back and ran her eyes over Sasha, who was clad only in her underwear.

"Okay, you can put your dress back on now," said Caroline snappily. Drew had helped Sasha select a dress for the occasion earlier. It was a full-length royal blue creation with a high mandarin neck. The silky material was ankle length and split on one side to mid thigh. Small gold fleur de lys motifs contrasted effectively with the blue of the garment. Drew had said it was both sexy and yet concealing.

"No way anybody is going to see the microphone, and Caroline will hear everything in the technical van and relay it to me. I'll be in there just as soon as anything happens," Drew had reassured her.

When the two women came downstairs and joined Drew in the lounge, he let out a low whistle of appreciation.

Caroline snapped, "Anybody would look good in that dress." Both Sasha and Drew ignored the remark. Caroline said icily, "Well, I've got to join the technical people now, so I'll leave you."

"Just a minute," said Drew. "I want to run everything through once more before you go."

Caroline gave a long sigh of boredom.

"If you must."

Drew ran through every detail before releasing her, impressing on her the need to inform him immediately if Sasha was in any way endangered. With her back to them, as she went, neither saw the sly grin on Caroline's face.

At six twenty-five, the appointed time for Sasha to leave for the Lake establishment, she donned her coat and looked at Drew.

"Well, I guess this is it. Wish me luck, Drew."

Taking her in his arms he kissed her long and passionately. Finally stepping back he exclaimed, "I wish you didn't have to do this Sasha, but there really is no other way of infiltrating their midst."

"Don't worry, I'll be all right, I know you're going to be outside all the time." He went out with her to the car and watched her drive off. Somehow he couldn't seem to rid himself of that leaden feeling in his stomach.

Drew got in his own car and waited the agreed five minutes before following Sasha. When he arrived, he could see several cars in the Lake courtyard including Sasha's. Yes, there was Barbara Lake's B.M.W. next to it. As unobtrusively as he could, he parked down the road in the shadows. From here he would easily be able to see when Sasha left with Barbara and Sally Greves, for the meeting.

The minutes ticked by. One by one the other cars left. Only Ted Lake's Jaguar, Barbara's B.M.W. and Sasha's own car remained. Drew had watched the inmates of the cars as they had left, through a pair of field glasses. He knew for sure Sasha must still be in the house with Barbara. They hadn't left yet or he would have seen them…

✶ ✶ ✶ ✶ ✶

When Sasha had arrived she found quite a throng of people at the Lake household already. The women were all dressed in their finery, if a trifle ostentatious and rather provocatively. The men were

Saddlewitch

all in evening dress and several looked quite elegant. She was immediately offered a glass of champagne. Sasha made sure she took only small sips so that the level in the glass remained high as long as possible. She could feel her heart beating wildly and her chest felt tight with apprehension.

Several of the men attached themselves to her and she received many flowery compliments. Ted Lake seemed out of things and avoided her eyes. He wasn't even dressed like the rest and only wore a lounge suit. It was quite obvious to Sasha, that he was embarrassed by their last meeting, and therefore gave her a wide berth.

Gradually she noticed that the group was considerably smaller and that several people had already departed. Then, finally, there was only Barbara, Sally and herself.

"Come on then, girls. Time we left as well. We wouldn't want to miss out, would we?" All three put their coats back on and Sasha headed for the front door. "No Sasha," called Barbara, "not that way. We leave by the back way."

Sasha felt her heart miss a beat. Now Drew wouldn't know they had left. She reassured herself that Caroline, who would be listening in, would get in touch and tell him about the change in plan. All the same it did nothing for her nerves.

Going out through the back way Sasha found herself in a narrow lane. She remembered walking it once with Bess, but hadn't realised that the Lake residence backed onto it. A car, a black one, Sasha thought a Ford, was waiting there, a man in evening dress at the wheel. Sasha became alarmed. Why were they going a different way to all the other guests? She mustn't show her concern and tried to contain her apprehensions. Ted Lake accompanied them out and held the car doors open for them. She was invited to sit in the back with Barbara, whilst Sally seated herself in the front next to the driver. Ted shut the car doors and went back inside the house. As they drove off, Sasha asked if Ted was not going to the party.

"Oh no, we don't need him along," came back Barbara's reply.

The drive took only about seven minutes – Sasha carefully noted it. Finally, the driver who hadn't as yet spoken a word, turned into a driveway, with impressive wrought iron gates; a dragon emblazoned on either side of them. They proceeded down a long tree lined drive to a large Georgian styled house and parked in front of a wide stone staircase. At the top were two stone colonnades or pillars on either side of double oak doors.

A man in evening dress came down the steps, having emerged through the doors. He held open both front and back doors of the car for them all to alight. Once the women were out of the car it drove away and went round the house to the back. Sasha concluded the man who had brought them must be a chauffer or taxi driver, but when she said as much to Barbara, the woman said that he was another guest, but had merely gone to park the car.

Once inside, Sasha found herself in a large assembly hall, which had walls decorated by crests and suits of armour. Her party followed the butler down a long corridor with numerous doors going off it to an even larger chamber at the rear of the house. The room was long with a series of red and black velvet drapes with several bizarre pictures adorning the walls. It was already full of an assembly of chattering guests, some of whom she had seen earlier at the Lake household.

Barbara took her round, holding her hand possessively, introducing her to several of the men, but none of the ladies. Sasha remembered later, thinking this was rather strange. A glorious array of food was laid out on long tables on either side of the room, all on silver plates. Several bottles of champagne in ice buckets accompanied it. Two young girls dressed in French maids attire were bringing round plates of tit bits for the guests and two more were topping up their drinks. Sasha thought whoever owned this place must have a mint of money to lay on all this. A general hubbub made it quite difficult to discern the various conversations going on. At times it was hard to pick up the person's words next to her.

Sasha enquired from Barbara who owned the place.

"Come, you must meet her," said Barbara towing Sasha behind her through the crush of guests. It turned out to be a very strange elderly lady, who spoke with a strong heavy Eastern European accent. Romanian, it later transpired. She was introduced as the Countess Maria Bolsova. The woman was of indiscriminate age and very wrinkled. Her hair was coiffured to perfection with a blue rinse. She was extravagantly dressed and encrusted with diamonds on almost every finger. A long gold necklace terminated in a huge sapphire pendant. The woman craned her head forward in greeting, reminiscent Sasha thought, of a heron about to strike at a fish. She then offered her hand almost as if she expected Sasha to kiss it. Sasha accepted the end of the fingers and went through the motion of shaking hands, feeling very self- conscious with this affected gesture.

After inspecting Sasha from head to toe the Countess nodded and turned to Barbara.

"She will make a fine one ... The master will be pleased, I know." With this she turned on her heel and disappeared in the crowd.

"What did she mean – I would make a fine one and somebody would be pleased," asked a puzzled Sasha. Barbara leant across and pinched Sasha's cheek in an affectionate way.

"Don't worry, my dear ... It was the Countess' way of saying you're very attractive – but then I already know that, don't I?"

Sasha squirmed. It had been bad enough in the back of the car with Barbara's hand on her thigh. She was thankful the journey had been a short one.

She sensed by the way the assembly seemed to be reacting that something was about to happen. People seemed to be watching the far end of the room expectantly. Here two huge red and black curtain drapes obscured a raised stage. On them were emblazed two golden dragons, one on each side. Heavy ethereal music was playing somewhere in the background. A melody Sasha had never heard before. The air seemed strangely oppressive and smoky, like some form of incense burning.

Try as she might, Sasha could not rid herself of this feeling of apprehension and fear. It seemed to be gnawing at her like an invisible presence. Several of the throng of people already seemed the worse for drink or worse still, drugs. She saw a girl brush past her and noticed the girl's pupils were almost totally dilated. A man in evening dress unashamedly groped the girl right in front of Sasha. The girl seemed not even to be aware of this violation of her body.

Sasha fought down the impulse to turn and run. After all there was nothing to fear. The police with Caroline would be listening to all that was going on. Sasha would only have to shout one word and Drew would intervene. Then a new doubt assailed her. With all these people what could he do if he did rush in? It would take the police several minutes to back him up. In that time anything could happen.

She felt, rather than saw, the change in everyone. A deathly hush had replaced the general hubbub that had ensued before.

The curtains at the end of the chamber were ever so slowly drawing back to reveal a stage. Sasha could see it was quite large, and at the back was what looked like a church altar. The difference was the black velvet altar-cloth covering it portraying an upside down cross. She fought to prevent a gasp ensuing from her lips. The music grew louder and then the stage was filled with a strange yellow smoke. When it cleared the old Countess Bolsova was standing facing the assembly.

Now she had on a long black robe tied in the middle with a golden rope. She addressed the audience in a husky voice.

"We are here to celebrate our master's arrival. All who are true believers will rejoice."

Sasha felt her blood turning to ice water, she couldn't control an involuntary shiver.

* * * * *

Drew waited for one hour, growing ever more worried. He rang the number on his mobile for Caroline in the police van ... It continued to ring and there was no reply. Something was very wrong here. He rang Grantfield police station. There was only a young constable on duty. He told him there had been no request for technical assistance or any form of back-up. In fact, there was absolutely nothing in the book. Drew rang off and rang the number for his Special Branch contact in London.

No, they knew nothing about any wiring or surveillance operation and certainly no back-up had been ordered. Then came the final thing that sent Drew into near panic.

It appeared WPC Caroline Channing had requested special leave and had gone off duty that day.

Drew knew in his heart of hearts it was all too late now to order back-up. Whatever they did, there just wouldn't be time for them to get here. He left a quick message for Superintendent Dawson and got off the line.

He knew now beyond any shadow of doubt that Sasha was in terrible danger and prayed that they weren't on to her. He still didn't realise Caroline belonged to the Satanists. He just thought she had acted out of irresponsible jealous pique.

He must act and act quickly. He had seen most of the people go, but not Sasha and Barbara. Were they still in the house? In his notebook he had the Lake's telephone number. He rang it and asked for Mrs. Lake. By now, Drew was at his wit's end, feeling he had let Sasha down and that her life could be in danger.

He must know if she was still in the house. Impatiently he listened to the phone ringing. Ted Lake answered. No, Mrs. Lake wasn't in. She had left for a party with friends, he informed Drew.

"Why, who are you?" said Ted, somewhat suspiciously.

"Urr, just a friend. Name's Lennox," lied Drew.

"What did you want my wife for?" asked Lake. Drew thought quickly, his brain racing ahead.

"I'm supposed to be at the party with them all, but I know it's damned stupid of me, but I've lost the address ... . I thought, perhaps..."

Ted Lake sounded suspicious.

"It's where it always is, of course," snapped Ted, irritably.

"Oh, I see. Well, I've missed the last two meetings, so it's still at..." He left the end of the sentence blank hoping Ted would supply the address.

He didn't, and his mood turned ugly.

"Look, I don't know who the hell you are, Mr. Lennox, but get off the line."

Drew apologised and hung up. The futility of the situation rendered his brain impotent. They could have gone anywhere.

Getting out of the car he ran round the grounds to the back of the house, if Ted Lake saw him, it was just too bad. Sasha's – not to mention Olga's life was in danger. It was then that he found the lane at the back of the house and cursed himself for his incompetence. He just hadn't thought to check another possible exit. It was now obvious to Drew that Sasha must have been taken out that way.

The situation appeared even more serious. If they had left by a rear exit, when everyone else had left by the front, it was apparent that Barbara Lake did not wish that they should be seen. They could be just anywhere now, and with Caroline's treachery Drew had no means of knowing where.

Slamming his fist into the palm of his other hand in frustration, Drew thought of all the things he would like to do to Caroline, none of them nice. Somewhere, in the back recesses of his mind, he remembered something the Brigadier had said. It was a long shot, but it was all he had. Drew fired the engine, put the car into gear and raced off towards the war memorial, leaving rubber on the road. Three minutes later he was hammering on Brigadier Jessup's front door.

Jessup seemed to take an age before coming to the door.

Drew blurted out the basic facts of what had transpired and finished by saying, "So you're my only hope, sir. I seem to remember you said you had an idea where this Satanic coven met."

Jessup looked him up and down and seemed to come to an instant decision. He turned round and called out "Mark! The vicar's here with me at present," Jessup explained to Drew. A moment later the Reverend Mark Glenville's head appeared round the lounge door. "Come on vicar. There's not a moment to lose … Thorpe here, needs us. Just a moment, everyone." Jessup disappeared and reappeared a moment or two later with a double-barrelled shotgun.

Mark Glenville looked positively dumbfounded. Jessup pushed him out of the front door and locked it, still leaving all the lights on inside.

"Come on, if I'm right, we haven't a moment to lose. Young Thorpe can give us all the details on the way … Hurry, vicar!" urged the Brigadier. The three of them drove off in Drew's car, Mark still looked dazed. Drew explained in more detail, what had happened, mainly for the vicar's benefit. Jessup gave directions as the car sped through the village.

"Better pray that I'm right, young fellow, and it is where I think it is, otherwise we are going to look like a trio of real fools."

"You're the only hope I've got, sir," said Drew, taking yet another corner on three wheels.

"Wouldn't it be better, Mr. Thorpe, if we got there in one piece?" exclaimed Mark nervously.

Finally, after following Jessup's directions, they arrived at a pair of huge wrought iron gates, dragons emblazoned on both.

"Go past, and park in the shadows. We don't want to announce ourselves," exclaimed the Brigadier. Drew could sense the old fellow was revelling in reliving his old SAS days, but in spite of Jessup's age, he was glad he had him along. That shotgun would come in useful too. Mark still looked somewhat bewildered by his two comrades' actions.

CHAPTER TWENTY-FIVE

Sasha could hardly take her eyes off the wizened old Countess on the stage. Yellowish smoke still seemed to cover the lower part of her body. It was as though her head, shoulders and upper torso were detached and sitting on a cloud. The woman went on uttering an incantation, some of the words barely audible to Sasha and, as they were all in Latin, beyond her understanding.

Then, quite suddenly, the Countess switched to English and Sasha was only too aware of the gathering's intent. She was unable to control an involuntary shiver. The old woman's voice shook with passion.

"We are here to celebrate the Black Mass, the most powerful of all our master's ceremonies. We are his faithful disciples and we owe him homage. Beware any here tonight, on All Hallows Eve, who are not true believers."

At this point Barbara, who was standing next to Sasha, gave her a nudge and a knowing look. Sasha tried not to think too much of the meaning of the gesture.

"Together we will cry out and summon up the mighty princess Astarte … Only she can summon our master. She is the only one powerful enough, or worthy of such an honour, but first we must prepare the way for her arrival," went on the Countess. Raising both arms aloft the old woman cried out again in Latin and almost at once six nearly naked girls appeared. Each carried two huge black candles, which they set down, where the Countess designated. Each girl, none older than their early twenties, was clad only in a small red loincloth with their breasts bare. Having placed the candles, three of them lined themselves on one side of the stage whilst the others went to the opposite side. All six girls stood to attention.

"We summon ye –great high priestess Astarte, princess of darkness," crooned the Countess. The words were repeated in a deafening roar from the entire assembly except Sasha, who looked and felt terrified.

Saddlewitch

She tried to console herself. Caroline and the police must be listening. Any moment either Drew, or the armed back-up would come bursting in, Sasha mused.

All fell quiet again and then once more the Countess repeated the invitation. Again the multitude repeated it after her. Sasha glanced to left and right of her at Barbara and Sally. They too roared at the tops of their voices. She noticed the glazed look in their eyes.

Then, a third time came the request from the Countess. Again the audience responded. An eerie silence followed. After a pregnant pause a far away sound of drums could be heard.

Then there was a blinding flash that caused several of the throng to cover their eyes. More yellowish smoke filled the stage and a horrible pungent odour seemed to permeate the chamber. As near as Sasha, in her terrified state could tell, it was sulphur.

Then, quite suddenly the old Countess Bolsova had gone and in her place stood a young woman. Her face was entirely covered with a gold and black mask, and she wore a long black cloak, completely open at the front to expose her nudity underneath. She raised both arms aloft to the audience and the black cloak exposed even more of her pale skin. Sasha could see that the woman's fair pubic hair matched the long blonde hair on her head and either side of the full facial mask.

The entire throng, with the exception of Sasha, fell to their knees in worship, raising their arms up and down similar to Moslems. In the same action they cried out "Hail Astarte, princess of darkness. We salute you."

Everyone continued to remain in this subservient position and Sasha was totally conspicuous in her failure to comply. Astarte's eyes bored into her from the stage. Sasha could even see the glint of her eyes through the eyeholes of the mask reflected from the candle light. They were like pin points of fire.

Sasha wondered whether it would be expedient to fall to her knees as the others had done. Her reason prevailed against this compliance. Why should she succumb to these Satanists? Drew and the

Saddlewitch

police would be bursting in any minute and her ordeal would be over. She tried to channel her fear into anger and stared back at the cloaked figure on the stage.

Then came the worst moment of Sasha's young life.

A cold icy voice rang out from the masked lady on stage. Instantly Sasha recognised it as Caroline's.

"We have an unbeliever in our midst ... Take her," she commanded.

The grim reality sunk into Sasha's every fibre. If Caroline was here and obviously in charge of these Satanists, then she wasn't listening in, and neither were the police. Therefore there would be no armed back-up ...Worse still, Drew was waiting for a call from Caroline, which would never come.

Sasha had never liked Caroline, but she had never, even in her wildest dreams, believed her capable of this level of evil. The grim reality of it all sank into Sasha like a searing knife. There was no help coming. Drew couldn't possibly know where she was, or the dangers she faced. There was nothing anybody could do ... She was on her own.

Several of the group had raised their heads from their kneeling positions and were now staring at her.

Sasha knew she had to escape, and quickly. Some of the throng were struggling to their feet. Desperately her eyes sought every corner of the room. The door by which they had entered the chamber, was right over the other side. She would need to get past about thirty pairs of grasping hands to try that way. To her right, the other side of Sally Greves, was a staircase leading to a balcony. It was her only hope. Perhaps she could get up there and escape through an upstairs window.

Not a moment to delay or it would be too late. Barbara was already reaching for her. Sasha sent Sally Greves flying and jumped over her fallen body. Thank Heavens for her split skirt Sasha remembered thinking. She made the staircase and ran up it two at a time.

"Take her!" came the wild screech from Caroline on the stage. Several of the men gave chase.

At the top of the stairs Sasha found herself on a platform with surrounding railings. Probably for musicians at some remote time in history, she briefly registered. She picked up a chair and threw it down the staircase at her pursuers. The leading two were knocked off their feet and fell backwards into the hoard following. There was pandemonium on the stairs and below in the auditorium. She could still hear Caroline roaring orders from the stage.

"She's trapped. She can't get away. Get her!"

Sasha threw another chair and then another down the stairs. They crashed into the group, causing further disarray. Desperately she looked round her. There was a door to her rear.

Then a shot rang out and a piece of wood flew off the balcony railing. My God, they are shooting at me, thought the terrified Sasha.

"Don't shoot – you might kill her. We need her, you fool." Caroline's voice could be heard over the others.

Sasha turned and ran for the door at the rear. It turned and opened to her touch, although it looked quite a heavy wooden one. She slammed it shut behind her. The key was in the lock. She turned it. Bolts top and bottom. She rammed them home. Then she heard the clambering outside and raised voices. Someone was bashing on the panels of the door. Pray it holds.

Sasha was brought up by a moaning sound behind her. Her nerves were already at breaking point. She turned to face the new menace and had yet another shock. Olga was tied hand and foot with a gag in her mouth, over in the corner of, what was probably a storeroom, by the look of it.

The girl's eyes were riveted appealingly on Sasha and she was trying to make sounds. Sasha raced across and pulled the gag away from Olga's mouth.

Immediately Olga cried, "Help me, Mrs. Paget. They say they kill me ... They tell me ... yesterday."

The banging on the door and the shouting outside was getting louder. Quickly Sasha, all fingers and thumbs, worked at Olga's bonds on her wrists. As soon as the girl's hands were free Sasha shouted over the din outside, "I don't know how long this door will hold them … . Try and free your own ankles. I'll try to push this table against the door." Sasha pulled and pushed at a heavy oak table. If she could only get it to the door it might help to hold the pursuers off a little longer.

She had nearly achieved it when Olga, who had worked her feet clear, joined her. With their joint efforts the two women managed to lodge the table against the door. On top of it they stacked chairs and boxes. Sasha looked round again for some sort of weapon. There was an old umbrella stand in one corner. In it was a walking stick and an old umbrella. She took the walking stick and handed Olga the brolly.

"When the door goes, as it surely will, we may be able to keep them at bay for a bit longer with these," said Sasha.

"How glad I am to see you, Mrs. Paget," said an emotional Olga, grabbing at Sasha's arm.

"We are not out of the wood yet," replied Sasha, warily.

Sasha surveyed the room once more for inspiration. There was a small window at the back, big enough for either of them to have squeezed through, but it was barred. Sasha reached through with the walking stick and smashed the glass, using the stick like a billiard cue.

When she had punched out all the glass, she yelled through the aperture, "Help us! Get the police." Both girls yelled in unison. The coal black windy night however, seemed to mock them and threw back their voices, as a rubber ball bouncing on concrete.

The hammering on the door continued. Sasha saw with horror one of the panels had split. She could even see an angry face through the hole it had made as it had caved in. Then the panel next to it split and gave way. Sasha could see one of the men had an axe, and the press of faces behind him were straining forward expectantly.

She ran from the window and jabbed at the aperture in the door with the walking stick, trying to hit the axe-man in the face. Olga continued to cry for help at the barred window. Voices outside the room were baying for blood. Sasha realised even with the table and chairs propped against the door, she couldn't hope to hold them much longer. A heavy old chest of drawers stood against one of the side walls. Sasha shouted to Olga, above the roar of the wind from outside and the crescendo of noise from the mob hammering at the door.

Together they tried to move the heavy chest towards the door, but couldn't even budge it. Sasha pulled open one of the drawers. It was full of old books and papers. Olga could see at once what she was thinking. As quickly as they could the two women removed all five drawers. Now the chest moved. It was still heavy but they were winning. Unfortunately for them, so were the Satanists the other side of the door. Most of the upper part of the door, in the centre, had gone completely. They could clearly see the angry faces in the corridor being urged on by Caroline in the rear.

Once the chest was in place, reinforcing the table with the chairs upon it, Sasha and Olga rushed to replace the drawers. This done they reached across and jabbed at their assailants with the walking stick and brolly. A hand reached through and reached for the top bolt. Sasha succeeded in whacking the grasping fingers with the stick. The hand was withdrawn with a blasphemous oath.

Then, all of a sudden, the onslaught ceased and the mob withdrew. Still the gale outside howled through the exposed bars of the window.

"They have gone?" exclaimed a terrified Olga.

"No way … . They are up to something, you may be sure," retorted Sasha, trying to look over the chest and table at the now deserted balcony. They didn't have long to wait. A woman had appeared on the balcony outside. It was Barbara Lake. She approached the badly shattered door and addressed Sasha in a clear voice.

"You are only making things worse for yourselves, both of you. We don't mean you any harm. Give yourselves up and you can come and enjoy the party." The whole intonation was honey tongued.

"Just who does she think she's fooling?" whispered Sasha to Olga.

Olga shouted back through the door, "You not tell truth – I know you bad people. You kill me." She ended with a sob.

Sasha put a consoling arm around the Swedish girl's shoulders and called to Barbara through the enlarged aperture.

"Go to hell, Barbara."

"Willingly," came back the chuckling answer from Barbara.

Sasha, realising this was probably a bad choice of words added, "Go get stuffed."

"So am I going to have to go downstairs and tell them you both refuse to come out?" Barbara asked.

"Tell them what you damned well like, Barbara ... We are staying put," snapped Sasha.

As Barbara's footsteps receded they heard her mutter, "Be it on your own heads, then." Sasha and Olga didn't have long to wait. They heard the tramp of many footsteps approaching up the stairs. Caroline appeared at the head of a column of men in evening dress. The men were carrying a long bench between them. Through the ravaged and torn panels, Sasha could see that Caroline had fastened her black cloak temporarily together with a black silk cord.

It was obvious to Sasha what was about to happen. At Caroline's direction, the men were about to ram the well-battered door with the bench. She was proved correct. Using the length of the balcony, the eight men, four on either side, ran forward with the bench between them. There was a horrible rending sound of splitting timbers, followed by a cheer from the attackers.

Sasha couldn't see the damage, but guessed it was to the lower part of the door and was substantial. The impact had even moved the stacked furniture back a few inches on their side.

Two more charges like that and the devils would be in, thought Sasha in despair.

★ ★ ★ ★ ★

Mark was not at all happy about the action being taken by the Brigadier and Thorpe, and said as much as the three men got out of the car.

"You don't even know this is the place. We could get in terrible trouble if we just break in and the residents are ordinary peaceful folk."

"I'm dashed sure it's where these devils are. I've long suspected this Countess Bolsova ... Real weirdo," exclaimed Jessup. Drew looked from one to the other and came to a decision.

"Look gentlemen. There is no reason for either of you to risk or do anything as yet ... Let me go in alone and reconnoitre ... . If it turns out the Brig. is right, I'll come back and get you. How's that sound?"

"I say, old chap- you better dashed well had ... I mean, I want to be in at the kill," urged Jessup. Mark, however, looked relieved.

Without more ado, Drew scaled the low wall into the grounds, calling over his shoulder, "Wait for my return."

Once inside, he made his way through fairly thick undergrowth and then emerged into an orchard. The grass hadn't been cut by the look of it for an eon and was over knee high. Fallen apples were lying rotting everywhere. He felt several squash under his feet. He could see the house and courtyard clearly from there. Several lights were on in the house and there must be at least thirty cars in front of the courtyard. This lay between him and the front entrance. Drew could see the colonnades and stone steps going up to the house.

Stealthily, he worked his way, using all the cover and shadow he could, to the side of the house. Here several more cars were parked in an adjoining field. The number of cars, if nothing else, told him something big was going on here. True, it might turn out to be a private party but then again it might not. It was all he had to go on so he crept on crawling on hands and knees through the cars to the back of the house. Light flooded out onto the lawns at the rear from several downstairs windows. He could see several people milling about inside. They seemed to be all looking towards a staircase.

Taking out his field glasses, Drew crouched on the damp ground and scrutinised the scenario, the gale force wind howling around him. Apart from the men who were all in evening dress there were several elegantly attired ladies. Some others were scantily dressed. He could see several giant black candles and the room seemed to be lined with black and red drapes.

Of Sasha there was no sight, or Olga for that matter. Then he caught a glimpse of someone coming down the stairs. It was Barbara Lake. His heart leapt with excitement. The Brigadier was right after all, in spite of Mark's doubts. He must find a point of entry then return for the others. Using what shadow there was Drew closed in on the house. Gradually he worked his way round the large stone mansion. Every time he came to a window he crawled on his belly underneath the sill until he was safely past.

Eventually he came on a cellar flap. There appeared not to be any visible padlock. He attempted to lift one side and to his delight it moved easily. It was at this moment that he heard a commotion coming from inside the house. Several raised voices and a repetitive banging sound reached his ears over the sound of the gale blowing around him. Under the cellar flap were stone steps going down. All was in darkness. Once inside he closed the flap behind him and switched on his torch. The noise from somewhere upstairs was even louder now.

He appeared to be in a wine cellar. There were racks of bottles and a couple of barrels on a raised ramp. Stairs at the far end led upwards to a door. Would it be open, he wondered.

Edging his way up the stairs he listened at the door. The sounds seemed to be coming from much further away. Gently he tried the latch; the door opened a crack. Quickly he closed it again. If only he had a gun. Caroline was supposed to have acquired one for him, but she had been nowhere to be found. Irritated, Drew knew he must waste no time and return for the others.

Hurrying as much as he could, without taking any needless risks to expose his presence, he worked his way back to the road.

CHAPTER TWENTY-SIX

Another few seconds and Sasha knew the last vestige of their makeshift barricade must collapse. The assailants battery ram had virtually breached the door. Only the furniture the women had stacked, stood between them and the Satanists. Sasha reached at arms length with the walking stick, hopelessly trying to deter the latters efforts to break through. She was unable to achieve any power in the thrust due to her precarious position. One of the attackers made a grab at the free end of the stick and tore it from her grasp. Olga tried with the umbrella but was unable to even reach the door. Then it happened. Another full scale charge and the heavy chest of drawers moved inwards, and the table between with its chairs on top, turned over. Two of the Satanists broke through and scaled the chest of drawers. An instant later the first of them closed with Sasha. He was a powerfully built man of middle years. Olga jumped on his back to try and pull him off Sasha. The latter was beating at him with her fists, Olga too, was overpowered by the second man, whilst two more scrambled over the splintered debris.

Caroline shouted from the corridor, "Don't hurt or damage either of them ... We need them undamaged, particularly the young fair one." It didn't take long for the Satanists to clear the damaged barricade away. The two women were frog-marched out into the corridor to face a furious Caroline. In the scuffle her cloak had come open again, exposing her nakedness underneath. She glared firstly at Sasha then at Olga before virtually hissing venom at them with an icy tone. "You will pay dearly for delaying proceedings. Our master will exact his own punishment upon you both." She then summoned up a number of the women, telling them to take Sasha and Olga away. "Clean them up and prepare them for the ceremony," Caroline commanded.

They were taken to a large old-fashioned bathroom and ordered to strip and shower. Sasha refused but was told to either comply or have the clothes forcibly torn off her. It was obvious to her that all six of their custodians were going to remain, and there was going to be no privacy. As Sasha reluctantly undressed she was surprised to find that her dress was already badly torn and her tights laddered. Her carefully coiffured hair was also in disarray. She noted that Olga was in a similar condition. The two women, once naked, were pushed into the shower together. Olga was sobbing, and Sasha tried to reassure her with a confidence she certainly didn't feel.

"Hold on," she whispered. "Help will be here soon."

Even as Sasha said it, she realised how much worse Olga must be feeling. After all she had been a captive for ages, whilst Sasha's own position was only just developing.

The shower water was turned off and one of the women reached in with a towel to attempt to dry Sasha. The latter grabbed the towel savagely from her and went to work on herself. Olga took her cue from Sasha and did the same. The captors all laughed and one addressed Sasha.

"That's right duckie, you make the best of it whilst you can … Won't be much privacy left for you after the men finish with you." Then she turned her attention to Olga. "You won't have to worry … By the time they get to her, you will be long gone to join our master in hell."

Sasha tried to give herself strength by retaliating with a verbal onslaught of the mocking women.

She followed it by saying "When help arrives you will all go to prison as accessories." Unfortunately this simply caused more ridicule and merriment.

Once Sasha and Olga were dry, each was handed clothes, or more pointedly weird attire. Sasha's was a bizarre outfit consisting of a black leather mini skirt and top with thigh length red boots. Olga's was simply a white tunic. Again Sasha refused at first, defiantly facing them down. It was all to no avail. She was told if she didn't comply, she would be forcibly dressed by the men outside. Taking as long as she could, trying to play for time, she dressed herself in the way-out garb. By the time she had pulled the thigh high boots on she saw that Olga was already in the white tunic. Caroline arrived and asked what was taking so long. The woman captor who seemed to be in charge blamed Sasha.

"This bitch has been holding us up," she whined. Ignoring her, Caroline ordered them to bring Sasha downstairs.

"Leave the fair girl here until we are ready for her."

Sasha was forced out of the bathroom leaving the sobbing Olga in the custody of two of the women. Caroline walked ahead of Sasha down a sweeping staircase, with one of the women on each side of Sasha tightly grasping her arms. The remaining two brought up the rear.

Sasha could see the grinning and leering faces of the men in the chamber below, watching her descent. Several called out ribald comments, and made obscene gestures, when they saw Sasha's appearance in the erotic costume. Sasha's terror of what was about to happen to her made the lustful gestures even worse. As the little cavalcade of women reached the foot of the stairs several of the men made a movement to grab her. One of them actually ran his hands over the black wet look mini skirt. Sasha knocked his hand away and glared defiantly.

"Not yet!" called Caroline. "You will all get your reward for your devotion to the master, afterwards."

"After what?" snapped Sasha.

Caroline grinned and her eyes glinted with amusement through the eyeholes of the mask.

"You will find out," was all she ventured. Sasha was led through the group of leering men, up some steps and onto the stage, the centrepiece of which was an altar. Draped over it was a black velvet drape with an upside down red coloured cross edged with gold. She stood almost transfixed with terror looking at it, whilst crude whistling and jeering emanated from the gathered assembly.

They are going to murder me in cold blood, Sasha thought. She began to shiver and could feel her mouth drying up.

Caroline gave her a push from behind, and turned her round to face outward to the throng below.

"Turn round slowly, bitch," commanded Caroline aloud. When Sasha didn't comply Caroline jabbed her painfully in the ribs with the end of the whip she carried. Sasha glared back at her and turned slowly once. She poked her tongue out at Caroline in insolent defiance. More cat-calls ensued from the mob below stage. "Again, turn again. Twice more," commanded Caroline. This time she wrapped the bullwhip across Sasha's hips. Even over the leather mini skirt it hurt like hell. The Satanists all cheered with relish and delight at Sasha's obvious distress. She complied grudgingly with two more turns.

Whilst two of the women held Sasha by both arms Caroline addressed her disciples from the stage.

"Is she not a tasty morsel my followers? Once our master has satiated his desires with her, she will be given to all of you to enjoy as you will." Loud ribald cheering broke out from the eager faces pressing forward towards the stage. "Silence!" commanded Caroline. "First we have a serious offering to make. A virgin for our master." Sasha watched in horror as a tearful Olga was forcibly escorted down the spiral staircase and across the floor towards the stage. Even the lustful mob stepped back making a passage for her. As she was brought up onto the stage in her white tunic Olga looked appealingly at Sasha for help.

"Please stop them," pleaded the girl. Sasha felt a despair she had never known. The feeling of total impotence was all consuming. She offered up a silent prayer to God, for deliverance from evil.

Caroline crossed over to Sasha and whispered in her ear, "Don't think Drew or the police can help you. Nobody – but nobody – knows where you are ... This shall be your reward for taking my man ... When this lot have finished with you, I think you will pray for our master to end your misery ... Needless to say we shall oblige him."

"You are quite mad, woman," hissed Sasha through clenched teeth. Caroline ignored the retort and raised her hands high above her head, the cloak falling open to expose her nakedness.

"Let the ceremony begin ... Secure her," she ordered, pointing at Sasha. Two men came up onto the stage and Sasha, kicking and punching frantically, was carried bodily onto the altar. She was forced down onto her back. First her arms, and then her legs were spread-eagled and clamped down into leather thongs. These were in turn fastened to the altar. She was unable to move anything but her hips, however she might try and wriggle.

Caroline laughed aloud at Sasha's discomfort and looked down at her with an evil relish at what was to transpire. Then Olga was seized by the same two men and laid on top of Sasha, so that she too faced upwards. Further straps were placed across her to totally secure her above Sasha. With Olga's weight now on her Sasha could not even move her hips. Olga was sobbing and crying hysterically.

"The police will arrive in a moment, Olga. Bear up, Olga. These fiends will get their just deserts."

"No they won't...They kill us both," stammered the terrified Olga between sobs.

Sasha knew that there was little else she could say and what Caroline had whispered to her was probably true. Drew couldn't possibly know where they were. Barbara Lake and Sally Greves had seen to that, when they had left by the back way, before coming here. They were both doomed for sure. At least Olga's end will be quick, she couldn't help thinking.

In spite of her terror and despair she uttered the Lord's Prayer in as loud a voice as she could muster. Strangely she saw that Caroline shrunk back a few paces and for a moment or two looked uncertain and not totally in control. Even Olga managed an "Amen". Then Caroline recovered and stepped forward towards the front of the stage. She began to address the throng once more.

"Now is the time to summon the master. Only I, the princess Astarte, can do this for I am all powerful."

"You are the one, the only one," echoed the assembled multitude. Caroline, her cloak billowing out around her, raised her arms aloft. A sulphurous yellowish smoke began to engulf the stage. Sasha and Olga coughed and spluttered as it rose to the height of the altar. Caroline appeared like a legless apparition floating upon it.

"I call upon you, our master, to come forth. I call upon you once, twice and thrice. We celebrate the Black Mass in your honour, O master Satan. Show yourself in your earthly guise as the Goat of Mendes. Honour our Sabbat with your mighty presence."

More smoke, then an offstage roar of thunder. Sasha was aware of a strange odour. Afterwards she could only liken it to the aftermath of fireworks having exploded. A further cloud of smoke, this time blue engulfed the stage. Gradually as her eyes became accustomed in its clearance, she could see part of the draped backcloth had opened to reveal a horrific apparition.

Sasha, even with Olga's weight upon her, could feel herself involuntarily shudder. There, sitting on a huge carved wooden throne, his legs crossed under him, was the legendary Goat of Mendes. On his feet were cloven hooves and his legs resembled hairy shafts, thicker at the top that the lower part which tapered down. His torso was bare, but it was the head that horrified Sasha, as she turned her head to look at the apparition before her. It was the head of a ram, with the curling horns reaching up above it. Worse, between them was a third horn, at the top of which was a blazing torch.

Sasha remembered something that the murdered Esmeralda had told them, before her horrific end, about the Goat of Mendes, so named from the Egyptian city of that name. In this city was kept a goat, its purpose to mate with chosen women. Sasha was consumed with horror at the memory of Esmeralda's words. She had said that at witches Sabbats, witches were believed to have intercourse with the devil. Sasha was filled with terror. What ghastly fiendish things did these Satanists plan to carry out? Then she noticed it for the first time. In his right hand the apparition clutched a richly ornamented and curved dagger. He rose to his full height from the wooden throne. For a moment he seemed to waiver on his cloven hooves.

Caroline fell on her knees before him.

"Greetings O master. It is I your high priestess the princess Astarte, who has summoned you on this All Hallows Eve. We, your loyal disciples salute and greet you."

Then came Sasha's greatest shock of all. The Goat of Mendes spoke in a deep baritone voice that seemed to echo back from the very walls.

"I gladly honour you with my presence ... Who is it you wish to sacrifice in my name?"

It wasn't the words. It was the voice. Sasha recognised it as her husband Bart. Mortified with fear, she realised he had come back to finish the job. Olga's sobbing had ceased, and she had gone limp on top of Sasha, who realised that Olga must have fainted with terror at sight of the devil.

★ ★ ★ ★ ★

After explaining to the Brigadier and Mark what he had witnessed, Drew knew that there was not a moment to lose. He handed his mobile to Mark saying, "Get hold of Grantfield police and tell them to get here, yesterday!" He gave a worried looking Mark the number of the police station, then gave him another, adding, "Then ring Superintendent Dawson and tell him what's happening. The Brig here and I will try to slow things up in the meantime ... Come on, Brigadier."

Without waiting for any argument, Drew set off. Jessup, armed with his shotgun followed, but due to his advanced age, experienced more of a problem with the fence. Drew checked and helped him over. As they crept forward towards the lighted house Drew explained where they were going to enter the house. The old boy seemed to be relishing it and showed not a trace of fear.

"What ho, lad! What are we waiting for? Let's get to it."

Suddenly they heard a low growl as they began to cross the open lawn. Drew glanced to his left just in time to see a huge Rotweiller coming flat out for them. Damn it to blazes, thought Drew. He should have expected something like this. Before he could think further the dog sprang at him burying its teeth in his upper arm and knocking him to the ground. The two of them rolled over and over on the grass, then the dog let out a howl and rolled off him. The Brigadier holding the barrel of the shotgun, had brought the stock crashing down on the animal's head. It now lay prostrate and senseless.

"Sorry old man …Dare not fire for fear of alerting everyone inside," Jessup explained.

"You did very well, Brigadier …Let's hope no-one heard the commotion."

Jessup looked at Drew anxiously. The latter was holding his left arm with his right hand. Blood had already seeped through Drew's anorak between his fingers.

"You're hurt, man," said Jessup, coming forward.

"Leave it – we haven't time – come on." Drew set off again throwing caution to the wind, the Brigadier puffing along in his wake.

He was aware time was of the essence and he had let Sasha down. Now was the time to make up for it. Perhaps it was as well that they had left the vicar behind to telephone. Drew knew that bloodshed was hardly going to be avoided here. No place for a man of the cloth. Jessup was another matter. A real old warhorse, and he was glad to have the old fellow along. Drew could feel the blood from the dog's bite trickling down his arm and could see that the teeth had even severed the sleeve of his anorak. He gritted his teeth and forged on. With relief they reached the cellar flap and Drew threw it open. He assisted Jessup down the steps and this time didn't even bother to close the flap behind them. The wind had dropped now, and for a few seconds the moon broke through the cloud cover. No need for the torch. Drew hurried across the floor and up the steps the other side. He waited for Jessup to join him and quietly opened the door. It led to a darkened kitchen. Stealthily in procession, they crept across it towards a door. Drew tried it; thankfully it wasn't locked. It led, in turn, into a corridor. He had just emerged ahead of the Brigadier when a challenge rang out. A man in evening dress appeared from another door, and immediately seemed to take in Drew's bloodstained and battered grubby appearance.

"Who the hell are you and why are you not in evening dress? Look at you man, you're filthy," said the newcomer.

"I'm the gardener," lied Drew. The man peered at him suspiciously.

"You can't be. I was told all the staff had been given the night off," argued the man.

"Orders changed. I was told to stay on in case I was needed," Drew prevaricated.

"What have you been doing? You are all covered in blood ... I think you had better come with me and explain yourself to the Countess Bolsova."

Drew had no intention of doing any such thing. Picking his spot and putting all his weight behind it he landed an uppercut to the man's chin. The jar of it made his arm ache like hell and started the bleeding off again. The man, however, went down like a felled log. Jessup showed himself, having kept quiet whilst the argument had been going on.

"Well done, lad! We should tie him up or he'll raise the alarm." They dragged the unconscious fellow back into the kitchen and trussed him up as best they could, aware of the need for urgency, using clean tea cloths found in a drawer.

"It will have to do, come on," urged Drew.

The pair then progressed back into the corridor. A great deal of shouting seemed to be coming from one of the downstairs rooms. Just past it was the main entrance hall. They tiptoed up the corridor hoping no-one else would emerge from one of the numerous doors. On reaching the large entrance hall they were faced with the sweeping spiral staircase with its overhanging chandeliers.

"Let's go up and see what's happening from up there," whispered Drew. The Brigadier, firmly gripping his shotgun, nodded, and tiptoed stealthily after him, taking each step as it came.

At the top was another double door, the right hand side of which was just ajar. Noise and light was emanating from beyond it. Drew held up his hand and dropped to his knees. He crawled forward on all fours and eased the right hand door open enough to slide through. He could see at once that he was now on a balcony or landing, running down one side of the building. Across from him was another small balcony with a battered door beyond, which looked as if it had been shelled by a battleship. Damaged furniture was visible to its rear. The noise seemed to be coming from an area below him. Stealthily he edged forward on his stomach until he could see quite clearly through the rails of the banister. Such a sight met his eyes as he could never in his wildest dreams have imagined.

CHAPTER TWENTY-SEVEN

Looking down Drew saw a multitude of people of both sexes, all either elegantly or scantily dressed. As one their eyes were all riveted towards a stage. Drew's eyes swept round to follow the direction of their interest.

He almost gasped with the shock of what he saw. Firstly his gaze centred on the extraordinary sight of the goat-like figure with its terrifying horned appearance. So realistic was it that he had to shake himself and believe it was only a man dressed up. Standing next to him was a masked blonde haired woman, her black cloak open revealing her pubic hair. He remembered thinking afterwards that the small birthmark at the top of her left thigh resembled Caroline's. At the time he didn't connect the two.

The real horror of the situation was yet to hit Drew, when for the first time he focused on Olga, in her white tunic, strapped down with another body underneath her, on the altar. The one below was dressed in red thigh boots and a black mini skirt and top. He couldn't see her face as it was turned inwards towards the goat-like figure and the blonde woman.

A deathly hush of expectancy now seemed to envelope the gathering. Drew craned his neck forward for a better view. Maybe he could see Sasha down there somewhere? The blonde strode forward, the black gown flowing like a billowing cloud, accentuating the whiteness of her skin. She approached the front of the stage to address the throng. The lower of the two bodies on the altar turned her head to watch the masked woman. For the first time he could see the face.

"My God, it's Sasha," he gasped in alarm.

Jessup edged forward to join him and whispered in his ear.

"I knew these devils were functioning from here, but nobody believed me." Drew didn't answer; his mind was racing furiously. A greater shock was still to come.

"Let the Black Mass ceremony begin ...I, the high priestess, princess of darkness, Astarte – the handmaiden of our great master Satan so honour him with this offering of a virgin."

It wasn't so much the woman's words – it was the voice. Drew gasped with shock. It was Caroline Channing. For a moment or two, he was so confused as to almost believe himself dreaming.

Then, he took a grasp on reality. If he was to save both Sasha and Olga he must act quickly. What could he do? Jessup and he had one shotgun between them. Probably several, or all of these fiends below were armed. One thing for sure, he must act and quickly.

Jessup tugged at his sleeve and whispered, "Let me pepper the swines," and tapped the barrel of the shotgun purposefully.

"No, wait ... If you open up with that shotgun at this range, you will kill the two girls as well as the goat man with the knife ... . Caroline, too probably," Drew explained.

"Who the hell is Caroline?" whispered Jessup.

"It would take too long to try and explain. She's the masked blonde," muttered Drew.

Jessup gave him a strangely puzzled look, then followed it with, "So what do you suggest?" Drew put a finger to his lips and watched the stage. Caroline's incantations were coming to an end.

"We worship you in all your forms – Beelzebub, Set, Leviathan, Pan, Abigor, Bael..." She continued with what seemed to Drew an endless list and concluded with "I, Astarte, the goddess of lust and sex proclaim thee Satan."

Drew then couldn't believe his eyes as Caroline proceeded to openly masturbate herself in full view of the gathered assembly. He was having trouble believing what he saw and pinched himself trying again to establish reality. Could this really be W.P.C. Caroline Channing his long-time friend and confidante. True, he had been shocked at what she had done to him earlier, but this was something else again. Caroline must be possessed of the devil, or totally mad. Could jealousy have driven her to this? No, it had to be something else.

Drew looked at the goat-like figure, the curved dagger held menacingly in his right hand. If only he, Drew, had a rifle or a pistol and

Saddlewitch   253

not a shotgun. Now the goat figure moved forward approaching Caroline who was fast bringing herself to a climax. He could see the horror on poor Sasha's face, Olga appeared to be limp and unconscious mercifully fainted, Drew thought.

Caroline screamed in ecstatic delight as she shook with the violence of her orgasm. The goat figure lowered himself over her, with his horns, a good metre higher than her blonde head.

She buried her fingers within herself and offered the creature them to lick when withdrawn. The apparition took the fingers of her right hand and dramatically began to suck each one. The gathered throng of lustful faces pressed forward and cheered loudly.

"Satan accepts the offering of our princess," they chanted in unison.

Drew's feelings were one of revulsion and disgust, plus disbelief at what he was being forced to witness. Could human beings sink so low? The Brigadier, however, had witnessed it once before, in Eastern Europe, and knew what the next step would be. He whispered in Drew's ear.

"Now is the time lad, or we will be too late. The sacrifice of the younger of the two women comes next ... After that, the other one, the one underneath is given to the mob – when they have all finished with her, they will kill her too."

Drew couldn't think of anything else. He would be forced to try a bluff. He seized the shotgun from Jessup and leapt to his feet, just as a pregnant hush enveloped the hall below. The goat-like figure stood over Olga, the knife poised.

At the top of his voice Drew roared from the balcony above.

"Hold it right where you are or I'll blow your head off." It was like an animated moment in time. Almost every eye turned upwards to locate the intruder. Drew was even conscious of the goat-man's eyes opening and shutting behind the mask he wore. For a long moment silence reigned, then pandemonium broke out below. Angry voices shouted up at him. The Brigadier climbed to his feet and stood supportively beside Drew.

Caroline was first to recover.

She shouted, "Be silent everyone. I know this intruder, he is alone and cannot harm us. Satan will protect us and destroy him." A storm of abuse was hurled up at the pair on the balcony. Drew levelled the gun at the goat-like figure's head.

"Drop that knife!" he yelled, "or I fire."

Sasha cried out, "He's not Satan, Drew. It's my husband, Bart." Drew's first thought was, thank God, she's all right, then the words gelled on his brain. Bart Paget and Caroline – they were in it together.

"Free those women, Caroline," Drew ordered.

Caroline stared defiantly through the mask at him before coldly replying, "Whom do you address? I'm the princess Astarte, disbeliever."

"Cut it out, Caroline. I know who you are. Have you gone completely mad?" A shot rang out and with a shattering of glass, the balcony where Drew and Jessup stood, was plunged into darkness. So someone down in the audience was armed anyway, thought Drew.

Jessup shouted this time from out of the darkness, "Give up all of you, you're surrounded. The police are outside," he bluffed.

"Princess Astarte knows differently," said Caroline. Drew could see her mouth under the mask, which covered only the upper part of her face, the corners of which turned up and creased with the smirk.

Drew was at his wits end to know what to do next, conscious of his human frailty. He couldn't risk firing at either Caroline or Paget, for fear of the scattergun effect of the shotgun. Only too easily it could encompass the two trussed up victims on the altar.

Caroline turned back to Paget, dropping all pretence at humility.

"Kill the fair one," she commanded. Then events took a strange turn. A voice roared out from across the other side, on the small balcony opposite. It was the Reverend Mark Glenville. Drew realised that after making the phone calls he must have followed them in, but how had he found his way up there? Pray he had made those calls to Grantfield, thought Drew.

"Hold Satanists, lest you be like Lot's wife turned to everlasting stone," exclaimed Mark.

All eyes switched from Drew and Jessup to Mark on the opposite balcony. Drew grabbed his chance, shoved the rifle in Jessup's hands and disappeared down the stairs two at a time.

The Brigadier shook his head in dismay and muttered, "'Pon my soul. I never took the lad for a coward – he's run away."

In the commotion that followed, Drew ran from the house and round to the back of the house. Ascertaining the position of the action on the stage, he picked up a small branch from a tree that had been dislodged by the gale. With this he smashed out a window and climbed through, praying he would be in time. Making his way through the house without caution – there was no time – he found the side door leading to the stage.

Out of his pocket he pulled an all-purpose Swiss army knife. It was all he had. He eased the door open a crack and could hear that Mark Glenville still had everyone's attention. Mark, bless him, was preying on the superstition of the Satanists. Drew could hear his voice clearly.

"The Angel of Death is upon you all. He is known as Sammael. Whosoever summons him shall surely perish, for he will not return alone. Sammael is the fourth and most feared of the horsemen of the apocalypse, according to Saint John in his revelations."

Drew opened the door a crack more. He could see the altar with the girls upon it. Everyone's attention was on Mark. If he crept out he might just be able to hide behind the altar. Paget had moved forward to the front of the stage with Caroline, both had their eyes on Mark, high above them. The big danger was that someone in the audience might see him when he crawled out. Drew knew he would have about three metres to cross at which time he would clearly be visible from the auditorium. Nothing for it but to take the risk and hope everyone's eyes were still on Mark.

As luck would have it, the only one to see him was Jessup, up on the balcony. He had drawn a bead with the shotgun on Paget's horned head, and intended to shoot high so as not to harm the girls.

With his quick military mind, he realised what Drew was up to and knew that if the Satanists saw him all was lost. Switching his aim to the rear of the hall, he fired at a huge glass chandelier, which shattered into a thousand pieces and plunged that end of the auditorium into darkness.

This, just as Mark roared, "The fear of God be upon you," and made the sign of the cross by crossing his index fingers thrust out in front of him. A shot rang out from the floor and wood splintered above Mark's head. Gallantly he stood his ground.

Drew made the dash to the altar; Sasha turned her head on hearing a slight noise. She opened her mouth to speak. Drew raised a finger to his lips signalling her not to. He couldn't risk cutting her free at this stage. Somehow he must get to Caroline or Paget. Which – he wondered.

A wrong move now and everything would be lost. Three against this crowd wouldn't have a chance. He knew the Brigadier still had one barrel left, but he doubted the man had spare cartridges with him. There was no means of knowing how many of these devils were armed. He steeled himself to rush out and spring at either Caroline or Paget, whichever was nearest, while Mark still had everyone's attention.

"You see, the Lord has already given you a sign – He has plunged several of you into darkness – Repent and throw down your weapons, the horseman cometh and he will surely take the armed ones first."

At the back of the hall there was a low murmuring, some of the group were clearly unsettled and unsure at this turn of events. Two of their number even slunk out through the door. A somewhat braver disciple took a pot shot at Mark. The bullet tore through the sleeve of his jacket, but fortunately only grazed his arm.

Drew realised he couldn't let this state of affairs continue. Mark was a sitting target up there on the balcony. If he hadn't so rattled the Satanists, a bullet would surely have found him already. Luckily, where the Brigadier had shot out the lights at the back of the hall, had left Mark in semi darkness. That was probably all that had saved him so far.

Drew tensed every muscle readying himself for the spring, like a leopard about to seize his prey. Out he came from behind the altar, Swiss army knife at the ready. Out in the open he had only a split second to select his target. Paget was over on the other side of the stage and Caroline was the nearest. She was Special Branch trained, with reactions equally as quick as Drew's. Superbly fit and carrying not an ounce of extra flesh. Add to this she carried the rawhide bullwhip in her right hand. Drew, however, had the element of surprise on his side and Caroline probably believed him to be up there on the balcony with Jessup.

Drew took off and she spotted him coming, hurtling himself towards her. He was more than aware that he must close with her, before she could bring that murderous whip into play. The impact, with his greater weight behind it, sent them both crashing to the floor. All eyes swung back pinpointing the wild and furious scuffle for supremacy on the floor of the stage. The whip was flung from Caroline's grasp as she crashed to the boards. Drew lay on top of her pinning her to the altar steps. She punched at his face wildly with her one free hand. Drew brought up the knife and pressed it crossways across her throat.

"One more move and I'll kill you," he snarled, eyeballing her eye to eye.

Caroline remained smugly confident. She even smiled up at him and called out loudly for everyone to hear.

"He won't do it … I've always been his friend … He won't have the guts for it." She switched off the smile and glared defiantly at Drew. He knew if she called his bluff he wouldn't kill her in cold blood. The trouble was, Caroline knew it too.

"Get her, Satan," she called to Bart Paget, meaning Olga. It was a firm command, rather than any plea for help. The goat of Mendes moved forward menacingly still clutching the wicked looking curved dagger. He was making for the two women still strapped to the altar. Drew realised Caroline was ordering him to kill Olga, in spite of everything. It was her way of showing Satan to be all-powerful, and win back the support of any waning disciples.

Now he must leave Caroline and attack Paget, but Caroline knew it too, and clung on to him with her legs round his waist. Suddenly a loud explosion shattered the auditorium. Jessup, up on the balcony had had no choice, but to fire at Paget, or see the women, or at least one of them, killed. The Brigadier admitted to himself it was a terrible risk, but he reasoned the girl would die if he didn't anyway. He aimed high at the central horn of the goat's head, hoping the spray of shot would not engulf the women. The effect was both breathtaking and shattering. The goat of Mendes head virtually disintegrated. Where once there had been a face there was now just a bloody pulp, like a huge squashed tomato.

His entire body cannoned back against the altar and slowly slid down it onto the steps on top of Drew and Caroline. On its way an involuntary movement of the hand touched Sasha's leg above the red thigh boots. She screamed in terror. Mark, up on the little balcony, seized his moment. The throng below were now milling about like headless chickens.

"So ends all evil doers. The goat of Mendes is dead. He was but a pretender. Repent lest you follow him to the fiery pit." Several of the group were now making for the door. Mark pressed home his advantage using their uncertainty and uneasiness to his advantage. "You see how easily Our Lord has smitten your erstwhile leader. In one minute from now all here will join him in Hades."

There now followed a stampede for the main doors. In their eagerness to escape the wrath of God several of them trampled on their colleagues. In a minute the auditorium was emptied leaving only the main adversaries.

Paget's mutilated corpse was heavy but Drew managed gradually to slide out from under. Caroline's legs fell away from him and she cried tears of frustration. Ignoring her, he crossed to the altar and began to cut the bonds holding Olga and Sasha. The former was still out cold in a dead feint. Sasha was numb with shock. Drew lifted Olga off Sasha and laid her gently on the stage.

Then he assisted Sasha to her feet and put both arms round her saying, "I'm so sorry, my darling. I never expected it to end like this." She laid her head on his shoulders and broke down crying.

A loud commotion had broken out in the grounds. There was a lot of shouting, then a loud hailer was brought into play. Drew realised the police had arrived in answer to Mark's telephone call.

"The cavalry is a little late this time, but I guess it's better late than never." He turned to see the speaker, and realised it was Brigadier Jessup who had joined them. He was still clutching the empty shotgun. A moment later Mark Glenville arrived on the stage pushing the old Countess Bolsova in front of him.

"I think the police will want to speak to this one," he explained, matter of factly. Sasha was still grimly holding onto Drew and he was loathe to let her go. Caroline was still sobbing with frustration, her cloak open and torn, her legs wildly threshing about.

Mark removed his jacket and covered her nakedness with it. Drew looked down at her and shook his head sadly.

"I guess this occult thing finally got to her and she has completely flipped," he said. Caroline just lay there, still now, and utterly defeated. Mark put his hand on Drew's arm and said softly, "Maybe she can be helped if she gets the right treatment, Mr. Thorpe. I know she was your friend and colleague."

"Was, being the operative word, vicar," Drew replied, looking scornfully at the prostrate Caroline. Jessup removed the altar cloth and covered Paget's body with it.

"Less we see of that the better … I suppose I'm a murderer now," Jessup said, dryly. At that moment a police sergeant and a man in plain clothes walked in and proceeded across the auditorium towards them. The plain clothes man spoke first introducing himself as Inspector Johnson.

"Can someone tell me what's going on here?" he asked.

Drew handed Sasha over to Mark who tried to comfort her. Olga was just regaining consciousness and looked dazed. Jessup helped her up and put a consoling arm around her waist. Drew led the inspector aside, whilst the sergeant looked under the cloths covering Paget. He dropped it again, quickly.

"Phew!" was all he offered.

Drew explained at length. He had just finished when Superintendent Dawson from Special Branch arrived.

Left it late, didn't you, Thorpe? You would have been off the case tomorrow." Then he saw Caroline Channing still lying on the floor and exclaimed, "What in blazes are you laying there for, W.P.C. Channing, dressed like that?" Caroline didn't answer. "I think you had better explain all this, Thorpe," barked Dawson.

Drew smiled wryly. He had just given Grantfields's Inspector Johnson a full account now he had to do it again for Dawson. First, he turned to Mark Glenville.

"Do you think you could take Sasha and Olga back with you to the rectory, vicar? I wouldn't like them left on their own." Drew smiled at Sasha as he said this, but she gave no response.

"My pleasure, Mr. Thorpe," said Mark. "Of course I will." Gently taking both of the ladies by each arm he escorted them out. He turned at the door. "Oh, sergeant, do you have anything these two poor ladies could wear?"

The sergeant looked sympathetic.

"I'll find you some police capes or better still, some blankets, sir," he ventured. Drew continued to answer Dawson's questions with Brigadier Jessup's back up.

It was a good hour later before Dawson let them go and even then he followed it by saying, "I'll want a full report in triplicate on my desk in the morning, Thorpe ... . Oh, and Brigadier, don't leave the country, will you." Just as he got to the door, he turned with his hand on the brass handle of one of the double doors. "Oh, and well done, Thorpe," he commented dryly.

"It was as much or more the Brigadier and the vicar you should be saying that to, sir. I feel I let everyone down."

Jessup patted him on the back.

"Not a bit of it, old lad ... You were jolly brave. I wish I'd had a hundred like you in my Company – what!"

Dawson gave a wry grin.

"Be that as it may," he said then turned back once more. "By the way, you might like to know we caught most of these Satanists as they tried to escape. Quite a haul, in fact." He closed the door behind him.

While Johnson had been interviewing Drew, Caroline and Countess Bolsova had already been led away by the police. Now only Drew and Brigadier Jessup were left, other than a constable who had to stay with Paget's body. Already the outline had been circled in chalk for the police photographers.

"Come on Brigadier, let's go home, and thanks a million for your help," exclaimed Drew.

"Don't mention it, old chap. Come home with me for a nightcap, what!"

"Thanks a lot, Brig., but no thanks. I think I'll go round to the vicarage and check on the ladies."

"Just as you will, lad … Glad to be of service."

As they reached the main gate, Drew felt the old chap was almost sorry the excitement was over. Jessup dropped him off at the vicarage.

CHAPTER TWENTY-EIGHT

Mary Glenville opened the door to him at the vicarage, having been given the details by her husband Mark, when he had returned earlier with the two women.

She was very sympathetic to Drew and invited him through to the lounge, where Mark was having a conversation with Dr. Denzil Davidson.

On introduction, the doctor shook hands warmly with Drew and explained his presence there. It appeared Mary Glenville had immediately sent for him on realising how shocked the two ladies were.

"The vicar and his wife have kindly consented to let Mrs. Paget and her au pair stay the night. Both were severely traumatised and shocked," explained the doctor. "Mrs. Glenville was quite right to call me out even at this late hour."

"Can I see them?" asked Drew.

"Sorry, Mr Thorpe but that wouldn't be advisable. I have given both ladies a sedative and they have retired for what's left of the night." At this point the doctor looked at his watch and added, "I would suggest you call round in the morning and see how they are then."

Drew thanked doctor Davidson, as did the vicar and his wife who showed him out.

Whiles she was attending to this, Mark said, "Would you like a sherry or coffee, Mr. Thorpe?"

"No thanks, both you and your wife have done more than enough ... I can't tell you how grateful I am for all you did tonight, vicar."

Mark looked somewhat embarrassed.

"I did nothing – only carried out the Lord's work, Mr. Thorpe. It was all down to you and the Brigadier, really."

"I beg to differ ... Your courage in creating a diversion made the rest possible," Drew pointed out. Mary returned and renewed Mark's invitation again. Drew declined graciously, then added, "I'll get out of your way now. I have to sit and write a report out tonight for my superiors ... Will it be convenient if I call in the morning to see the ladies?"

"Of course, Mr. Thorpe. Come when you like – any time," Mary replied. As she showed him out, Drew turned back at the door.

"You should be very proud of your husband, Mrs. Glenville. He was a real hero tonight."

The smile and pride shown on Mary's face was all the answer required.

★ ★ ★ ★ ★

After working for the best part of the night on his report, he e-mailed it to Dawson at Special Branch. For their records he sent a copy to Johnson at Grantfield police station as well. By the time he tumbled into bed it was 4 a.m. on November the first. Exhausted he fell asleep almost as soon as his head touched the pillow.

It was ten a.m. when he awoke and the sun was shining brightly through a gap in the curtains. He rose, stretched and pulled back the curtains – there wasn't even a cloud in the sky. Even the birds sounded more cheerful. Water babbled musically in the little brook at the end of the garden and he watched a heron sitting on a rock scrutinising the rippling bubbles.

He went through to the bathroom and showered and shaved. By the time Drew had dressed and eaten a light breakfast of toast and marmalade it was eleven a.m. He walked Caliph for about half an hour then, after returning the dog to Briar Cottage, he set off for the vicarage.

Walking through the village everything seemed so peaceful. Drew found it hard to visualise what had taken place the night before. Maybe it had all been a terrible nightmare that was now over. He was brought back to reality by hearing two women in conversation outside the post office, one was Hortense Hyde-Potter and the other Mrs. Ponsonby-Forbes. Drew caught a section of the conversation as he passed them.

The former was saying, "And the vicar did it all single handed, you know. I always did say what a wonderful young man he was."

Drew smiled to himself and proceeded on his way. Everything was so tranquil and normal. A woman rode by on a bicycle and the milk float passed by on its way back to Grantfield dairy. On the other side of the road a man was approaching. As he got nearer, he saw it was the long tall form of P.C. George Fenning, in his almost ever-present lengthy beige mackintosh. The man wore his usual dismal expression. On seeing Drew he crossed over to speak with him. George's face creased in its nearest imitation and suggestion of a smile.

"High jinks I hear last night, Mr. Thorpe. I must say I was surprised you didn't call on me for assistance. Nothing against the vicar and the Brigadier you understand, but neither are members of Her Majesty's police force, are they, sir?"

"Sorry about that, constable Fenning, but I'm afraid there just wasn't time. They both just happened to be handy so I grabbed them."

"Fortunately for you sir it all ended as it did … I mean you catching that Paget fellow and finding the au pair he ran off with … won't look bad on your record will it? I should say they'll make you an inspector. Pity about your assistant, though. Nothing worse they say than a bent copper, is there?"

Drew found himself switching off. He was impatient to see Sasha. He found it quite incredible as a townie to understand how this village system worked. You could only liken it to jungle drums, he supposed. Just how did all this information get around so quickly?

George rambled on, "Mind you, Mr. Thorpe, who would have thought that bank manager's wife, Mrs. Lake, I mean, would have been involved? Excitement or boredom, I suppose makes 'em do it. Then there's old Brigadier Jessup – they say he shot Paget. You could have a problem there, sir, if you don't mind my saying so."

"Just so, constable but you must excuse me, I have a pressing appointment."

George was not going to be put off so easily, but Drew was rescued by the arrival of the plumber, Ted Sewell who, on seeing Fenning approached with "Excitement in Saddlewitch last night then George?"

Saddlewitch

Drew grabbed his cue and left them both talking about the affair.

He shuffled through the fall of red and golden leaves, enjoying the dry rustling sound they made. It somehow seemed to give a homely sort of feeling. Jake Cutter watched him whilst attending to someone's garden, leaning on his spade until Drew turned the corner. Drew proceeded up the lane to the vicarage. The chestnut trees on either side had now lost half of their leaves and the sun shone down in shafts between the branches. On the ground the leaves were six inches deep in places.

He arrived at the vicarage and knocked the door. Once again it was Mary Glenville who admitted him. By now it was nearly lunchtime. She showed him through to the lounge where Mark was sitting with the two ladies in deep conversation. Both Sasha and Olga looked white and drawn. Drew could immediately sense the tenseness in both as they greeted him. The meeting was stilted and strained. Drew found it impossible to do what he wanted and take Sasha in his arms with the vicar present. Unfortunately Mark didn't offer to leave. The conversation didn't seem to be getting anywhere so Drew decided to try and resolve things.

"So what plans do you two have now?" After he received no answer, he added, "Or does that depend on me, Sasha?" The second part of this was said in hope.

Sasha still looked dazed probably, Drew thought, from the effects of the sedative the doctor had prescribed. Mark looked from one to the other not understanding their relationship.

Mary, who had recently entered, was more perceptive and said, "Oh Mark, there's something I want you to look at for me and I think Olga would like to see it, too."

Drew was eternally grateful to her as she led them both from the room, leaving him alone with Sasha. He rose and sat on the arm of Sasha's chair. He placed a comforting arm round her shoulders and tried to kiss her on the cheek. To his distress she pulled her head away. The look she gave him was a trifle cold and detached and she didn't speak. Drew felt a growing impotence to reach her, but tried again.

"I will now be recalled to London. There's no way they will go on paying rent for me to stay on at Briar Cottage, Sasha."

"And?" was Sasha's cold and detached reply. Drew found himself unsure of the best way to approach her, faced with Sasha's detached response.

"Well, I mean, would you like to come with me, Sasha?"

"What do you suggest I do with the children?" Sasha said, quite snappily.

"Them too, of course. I love you, my darling … . When this is all over, the trial I mean, we can get married."

Drew felt he was making a totally ham handed mess of this. He hadn't meant to propose, at least not now, but Sasha's indifference seemed to have forced the issue. He loved her and he wanted her – that was all he knew.

Sasha jumped up and faced him, her white cheeks flushed and angry.

"How dare you, Drew Thorpe. You – you – totally let me down. If I helped you there would be back-up and I would be in no danger … That's what you said … Not much! I nearly got killed or worse, and then poor Olga … All this because of your arrival in Saddlewitch. My children have had to go away because of it … My dog Bess put into kennels. All this because of you, Drew Thorpe and your damned Satanists. If you hadn't been hoodwinked by your friend Caroline – who, as it turned out even got to poor Bart – sent him mad, she did. He was a normally happily married man before he got in with her lot. I have just witnessed his head blown to bits in front of me and you choose now to ask me to marry you! Well, no thanks!"

Sasha's outburst ended as she collapsed in tears. Mary Glenville rushed back into the room and put a consoling arm around Sasha.

"Whatever's the matter, dear?" she enquired.

"I'm sorry, Mrs. Glenville. It was me I'm afraid. I chose the wrong moment to ask her to marry me." Mary looked at him with a wry smile on her face.

"Not a very opportune moment, Mr. Thorpe, if you don't mind me saying so," she exclaimed. Sasha sank back in the armchair still crying. "Perhaps you had better leave. Sasha is still quite shocked – let me tell you what we have arranged this morning. She is going down to her aunt's where she will be with the children for a week or so. Then, after what has happened here, she feels she wants to come back to Saddlewitch to sell her house. All this distress, with her husband I mean, she couldn't possibly live there now," Mary explained.

"And Olga? What will she do?" asked Drew.

"Olga is going to live here with us. With the child, and another on the way, we can use her services."

"I see, so everything's arranged, then," said Drew sadly. He offered a goodbye to Sasha, but she didn't even look up. At the front door he said to Mary, "Say goodbye to the vicar and Olga for me, Mrs. Glenville."

"Yes, I will," replied Mary. Then as he was walking down the drive, she called him back. "Mr. Thorpe?"

"Yes."

"Don't give up on her – Sasha is not herself. Give her time. Try contacting her again, say in about a month or so, and I'm sure she may see things differently." Drew looked crestfallen and doubtful.

"She seemed very definite that she didn't want to see me again, and any way I won't have her new address, will I, so how am I going to get in touch with her, Mrs. Glenville?"

"Please call me Mary. It makes me feel so old – I will have her new address, Mr. Thorpe, I promise you," she said, with a knowing wink.

"Thanks, Mary … and it's Drew, not Mr. Thorpe."

"Leave it to me, Drew," she said and waved him goodbye from the door.

Drew walked sadly back through the village to Briar Cottage. Caliph greeted him warmly licking his hand.

"Oh well, at least someone's pleased to see me," he said aloud.

Just as he expected, there was a message from Superintendent Dawson on his e-mail screen. True to the man's nature it was short and to the point.

Thorpe – get everything together and return to London immediately.

Your report received.

See me Monday at ten hundred hours. We will take care of rent outstanding on the Saddlewitch cottage. Assignment complete.

Dawson.

Drew shook his head in disbelief but this was the voice of authority speaking. No time for congratulations, recriminations or sentiment. Just pack up and leave. Job finished and on to the next. Where to, he would be told on Monday, when he saw Dawson. Oh well, he thought, with Sasha letting him know she no longer valued him, why not leave. After all there was reason for him to stay. Firstly he rang Brigadier Jessup and told him not to worry about the trial of Caroline and the Satanists when it came up. There was no way anybody could blame him for having shot Paget. By so doing, he had saved many other lives. Drew thanked him for his assistance and promised full support at the trial should there be any accusations thrown at him.

Jessup thanked him and said, "I've had most of my life, lad. Do the same again, I would, if the occasion arose – what!"

Drew said goodbye and rang off, then he sat down with a sheet of paper and a pen. He wrote a short note to Sasha.

'My darling Sasha,
> Don't think too badly of me. Your help was invaluable in bringing these vile Satanists to trial. I can understand that you feel I let you down. I promised support which never materialised and but for the Brigadier's knowledge, never would have. For this I am guilty in my own eyes, as well as in yours. I trusted in Caroline, and it was my misplaced loyalty that nearly cost the life of both you and Olga. I can

understand if you never forgive me, and can assure you I couldn't possibly feel worse than I do now, having let you down so badly. I am leaving now on orders for London, but if not before, I shall see you at the Satanists' trial whenever that comes up. I am sorry that the authorities will not spare you giving evidence, Olga too, but that my love, is the case and there is nothing I can do about it.

I shall always love you and trust one day you will find it in your heart to forgive me and we can be united once more. Should you wish to get in touch with me, I have taken the liberty of including a card with my number on it.

My darling, whatever you decide,
Love Drew X

With a heavy heart he sealed it in an envelope and then placed that in a second one, c/o Mrs. Mary Glenville at the Saddlewitch Rectory.

It didn't take him long to pack his few personal things. One hour later, with Caliph in the back of the car, he set off for London, stopping only to post his letter at the Post Office.

* * * * *

Three days later a civilian clerk ushered him into Superintendent Dawson's office. The Special Branch chief indicated a seat, but did not look up from his paper work. Drew sat down and waited. Dawson did not look to be in a good mood, but then he never did.

After a further minute or so, he looked up and merely said, "Well?"

"Well what, sir? It's all in my report," Drew began.

"I know all about reports, Thorpe. It's the stuff that doesn't get said that I want to know about." Dawson's eyes bore into his, as if probing for answers.

"What sort of thing, sir?"

"Don't be clever with me, lad … Why, for instance, did you allow yourself to become involved with a married woman in Saddlewitch when you should have been on duty?"

Drew gulped. How did Dawson know about this?

When he didn't answer Dawson exclaimed, "Wonder how I know, do you? Well, I'll tell you … . Your good friend, W.P.C. Channing went behind your back to me, that's how I know. Think yourself lucky you're still on the payroll, lad." Drew was lost for words for a brief moment and could only manage a gulp. Before he could make things worse with an inadequate answer, Dawson resumed his interrogation switching tactics. "Could be awkward for you at the trial of W.P.C. Channing don't you think so, Thorpe?"

"I suppose so, sir … but I have to say whatever the outcome I would have done the same again."

"Oh, you would, would you, even if it meant you being thrown out of the Force?" By now Drew had recovered his composure and stared back at Dawson.

"I am considering resigning anyway, sir."

"Why in blazes would you do that, Thorpe?"

"Obviously at Caroline's trial my involvement with Mrs. Paget will come out. Therefore Special Branch will suffer embarrassment because of my actions." Suddenly Dawson's facial expression changed and he went into one of the longest pieces of dialogue that Drew had ever heard from him.

"You're a good officer, Thorpe and I would hate to lose you because of this … After all, you did bring this matter to a satisfactory conclusion … The whole lot of those devils caught in one night … I think if it hadn't been for Caroline Channing, your plans would have gone off without a hitch and nobody would have been at risk. There was no way that you could have known she was involved and therefore betraying you all the time … Nothing worse than a copper who's gone wrong, lad. No, everything considered, I think you showed yourself to be remarkably resourceful in the circumstances … Old friend of yours, Channing, I mean, wasn't she?"

"Yes sir, we went back a long way. I still can't believe she did what she did," mused Drew.

"Well she did, lad. You know what they say 'Hell hath no fury like a woman scorned'" remarked Dawson.

"I think there was more to it than that, sir. I think it was this dabbling in the occult that sent her over the edge."

"Well, we are still awaiting a psychiatric report ... Maybe at the trial she will be found to be of unsound mind, who knows ... Either way, she's up for murder and attempted murder. It will be life, anyway ... Only thing in doubt is where she will be spending it."

"And the rest of them, sir?"

"Anything from two to seven years, I'd say, but it's only a guess. The Lake woman could get longer for aiding and abetting, is my guess," replied Dawson.

"When do you think the trial will be?" asked Drew.

"Hard to say. Could be as long as six months," said Dawson. A silence ensued between the two men, broken finally by Dawson. "Take a week's leave, lad, starting from tomorrow ... I think you may have some unfinished business in other directions." He winked in a conspiratorial manner, then got up to indicate that the interview was at an end. "No more talk of resigning, lad ... When it comes to the trial tough it out ... I'll back you all the way."

Drew thanked him and left. The meeting hadn't been nearly as bad as he had expected.

CHAPTER TWENTY-NINE

Mark Glenville who, after all, was something of a shy young man, found himself something of a hero in Saddlewitch. His congregation doubled overnight, once the papers had got hold of the story. Miss Hortense Hyde-Potter became his devoted admirer and sang his praises all round the village. Much as Mark tried to keep to the background, he was in constant demand with the press. His words of 'no comment' seemed only to fan the flames of their desire to know more.

Mary laughed when he complained to her, and simply replied, "You grumbled before because nobody seemed to appreciate you, now you are moaning because they won't leave you alone."

Mark smiled.

"I guess you're right," he said.

"Well I rather like having a hero for a husband," exclaimed Mary with a laugh.

* * * * *

Brigadier Jessup managed to keep pretty much to himself. He wasn't over worried at having shot Bart Paget and didn't expect the jury at the trial, when it eventually happened, to be either. Superintendent Dawson, however, had insisted that he hand his passport over, but added that it was only routine.

Jessup had no wish to leave the country anyway. His travelling days were done long since. Truth to tell he had rather enjoyed the incident with the Satanists. Most excitement he'd had in a long, long time. It had been wonderful to feel useful once more, and it had given the old fellow a real buzz. That new young vicar fellow seems quite a lad. Maybe, just maybe, I might start going to church a bit more regularly in future, he mused.

* * * * *

Sasha had left Saddlewitch and was reunited with her children at her aunt Jennifer's in Bournemouth. Although she still felt quite numb and shell shocked from all that had happened to her, it was lovely to see the children once more.

Two days after her arrival in Bournemouth with all her belongings she received a letter from Drew. She recognised his handwriting on the envelope. Sasha handled the envelope turning it over and over for a long time without opening it. Sadly she came to a decision and wrote on it 'Return to Sender'. She posted it back when she went into town that afternoon. There was a lot for her to attend to which would keep her mind off things before the trial. How she dreaded that but the police had already informed her she would have to give evidence.

Then there was the matter of her late husband's funeral to be arranged. As yet the police wouldn't release the body until a post mortem and then an inquest had been held. Again they had said she would have to attend. She rang an estate agent in Grantfield and instructed them to put the Saddlewitch house on the market straight away. The furniture was to be put into storage.

Next she arranged for the children to go to a primary school in Bournemouth. They were to start next week. Her aunt Jennifer had kindly agreed to put them all up until Sasha could find a house. She had always liked the Christchurch area, so she began looking there.

After two weeks she found just what she was looking for, a small modern three-bedroom house, all double-glazed with gas fired central heating. Sasha had already transferred her bank account from Grantfield, so she was able to arrange a bridging loan without too much trouble. It was vacant so she and the girls moved in almost at once.

The inquest came up four weeks later. It was held in Grantfield. The whole thing was over very quickly. Everyone connected gave their evidence. Accounts all tallied and the verdict was a formality. It was the first time she had seen Drew since that dreadful night. He tried to speak to her before and after the inquest, but Sasha was only formally polite, no more. Somewhat embarrassed, Drew had left her alone after that.

With the formalities completed Bart's body was finally released to her. She made immediate arrangements for a cremation at Grantfield four days later.

Only one other person attended the short service. Sasha found herself surprised, considering how rude she had been to him. It was Drew Thorpe. Apart from shaking hands with him and thanking him for coming she hardly spoke at all.

After the service Drew said, "I came for you Sasha. I thought you might need me."

Sasha merely replied, "Thanks, but it wasn't necessary." She returned to Christchurch that same day.

Drew had sent three more letters but Sasha had returned them all unopened. During the weeks and months that followed Sasha began to rebuild her life. She got a job in a local solicitor's office, the hours fitting in nicely with the children's schooling. Debbie and Annabel both seemed happier now with their new school and play schools respectively, which was a great relief to Sasha.

As the months passed Sasha settled into a new routine. She was aware that something was missing but wouldn't admit to herself that it was Drew. After all he had let her down badly and she couldn't get that out of her mind.

She even accepted a dinner invitation from one of the young solicitors in the firm. It was a disaster. Sasha was aware that her heart was not in it, and when the young partner became a little amorous she put him down in no uncertain manner.

She told herself – I'll be all right once the trial is over.

It was fully six months later when the trial date came up. The whole thing, due to the nature of the affair, had been widely reported in all the national newspapers. As it was so high profile it had been scheduled for the Old Bailey in London.

Sasha managed a wry smile when she saw the date for the hearing, the 30th April. Surely that was Walpurgis? She remembered poor old Esmeralda telling her and Drew that the date was vitally important to Satanists and witches.

She found herself dreading the trial more and more, as it grew nearer. Why had it taken so long for the authorities to arrange? She, Sasha, had tried to wipe it all from her mind, now they were going to force her back into it. It had been hard enough for her to explain to the girls what had become of their father. With all the press coverage and people talking, there was no way she could have lied to the little girls. Down here, in Christchurch, for the last few months, nobody had known them and life had been easier. Now with the trial, it would all be brought out into the open again. She didn't mind so much for herself, it was Debbie and Annabel she was concerned with. Why should they have to suffer? Unreasonably she blamed Drew Thorpe. If she hadn't agreed to help him, none of this would have happened.

★ ★ ★ ★ ★

Drew was thoroughly miserable. He was in love with Sasha and she wouldn't have anything to do with him. She returned his letters unopened. Four in all he had sent and they had all been returned. First, he had thought when he saw her at the inquest he might be able to prevail, then at her husband's funeral he had tried again. Sasha had virtually brushed him off, quite rudely in fact.

Strangely he even missed Caroline Channing. Over the years they had had a lot of fun together. Drew still couldn't come to terms with what had changed her so. He had always thought her so normal until that night she had tricked him into having sex with her. Drew had never thought of Caroline as anything other than a very good friend.

Over the passing months he continued to carry out various assignments with Special Branch, but somehow there was never a day that passed when he didn't think of Sasha. He found himself wondering what she was doing.

He had her new address from the vicar's wife Mary. In fact he had become firm friends with her and Mark. Twice since the Satanists affair he had been to Saddlewitch and had dinner with them. This weekend he had been invited down to spend the weekend with them.

He went down to Saddlewitch on the Friday night. Everything was so different from when he had left on 1st November.

It was early April now, and the sun was showing its beaming face to Saddlewitch. Under its gentle spring warmth the young trees and saplings were richly endowed with blossom and there were pale green shoots everywhere, bursting out to meet the promise of another season.

He drove through the village to the vicarage. He recognised several people as he passed through. Old Gudgeon the gravedigger, doctor Denzil Davidson on his rounds, Kate McLean the schoolmistress and Burgess Steele the farmer. Two of them recognised him in his car and waved.

Drew almost felt like he was coming home. He passed Briar Cottage. Someone else, a stranger, was just going in, at the front door. Obviously let to someone else now. He thought of the times he had spent there with Sasha last year and became melancholy once more.

Up the lane and round a bend, he turned left under a chestnut tree in full blossom on the corner of Vicarage Lane. Further on along, he saw another, this time with a red blossom, contrasting with the white of the other.

Mary heard his car in the drive and came out to greet him. Drew kissed her on the cheek and gave her a hug.

"Lovely to see you Drew. Come in."

* * * * *

After dinner they talked of many things but eventually quite naturally finally centred on the oncoming trial.

"I'll be glad when it's all over," said Drew.

"I think we all will be," Mark put in enthusiastically. Mary changed the subject.

"Olga is still with us. She's a real treasure. Unfortunately you won't see her until tomorrow. It's her day off and she's gone up to London to see the sights. Staying overnight with a friend she met at a dance about three months ago … Have you seen anything of Sasha recently, Drew?"

Drew looked crestfallen.

"No, I'm afraid she returns all my letters and obviously doesn't wish to see me any more Mary. Not much more I can do about it …

She obviously feels I let her down over the Satanist affair, and I can't but agree with her, can I?"

"I think you probably saved her life … I fail to see how you let her down – risked your own, as Mark tells it," exclaimed Mary, hotly.

"So he did," enthused Mark. Drew just looked uncomfortably embarrassed.

"She just doesn't see it that way and I can't blame her," Drew added.

★ ★ ★ ★ ★

Later that night Mary and Mark had retired to bed and were discussing things. Mary thought that Sasha's reaction to Drew was terrible.

Mark laughed and said, "You're biased anyway, Mary … I know you like Drew, but you must see it from Sasha's point of view. She agreed to help and all the back-up Drew promised her failed miserably."

"Yes, but that was due to that horrible Channing woman letting Drew down," exclaimed Mary, hotly. Mark shook his head. Sitting up in bed in his pyjamas, he explained at length.

"Look Mary, I like the man too, but he was W.P.C. Channing's superior. Surely he should have seen it coming. The woman was supposed to be his friend, after all." Mary turned on her side with her back towards him.

She muttered, "Well you think your way and I'll think mine, thank you very much … Goodnight." Mark smiled and slid down the bed. He put an arm round his wife.

"Never let the sun go down on a cross word," he murmured in Mary's ear. She turned back towards him.

"Who said I'm cross?" she purred. "Time will tell who's right and who's wrong."

"Amen to that," laughed Mark.

The trial of Caroline Channing loomed, only one week away. The remainder of the Satanists were being tried following the main issue of Caroline for murder, and attempted murder. Drew had been told that the case was expected to run for a week or more. Most of the Satanists were on bail, other than Barbara Lake, Sally Greves and Countess Bolsova. Caroline herself was being held in a jail somewhere in the Midlands. Drew was never quite sure why he did it, but on one of his days off he decided to visit her in jail. Somewhere at the back of his mind he was severely troubled, as to why an apparently perfectly normal young woman had become so unhinged. He had mentioned his intention to visit her to Superintendent Dawson.

"Well, I can't stop you Thorpe … What you do in your time off is your own affair, but I would strongly advise against it … With her trial coming up it may not be a very opportune moment for you to choose. I realise of course that she was your friend, but I should have thought that after what she did to you, you would want to stay well away."

Drew didn't take the advice. He drove up to the Midlands to Raymouth Prison and after showing his identity card was given special privileges to see her. He was shown into a long cage like corridor and from there past a long line of barred cells. The prison officer escorting him led him to a visiting area where he was asked to take a seat. He had only to wait for about two minutes before another female officer brought Caroline into an area separated from him by toughened glass. Her appearance gave Drew quite a shock from the Caroline he had remembered. Her usually shiny blonde hair looked unwashed and matted. She wore no make-up, and was dressed in an unattractive grey smock like dress. She didn't meet his eyes and shuffled to a seat facing the glass partition. Drew crossed over and sat opposite her. Now that he was here, he was unsure of what to say to her, but it was Caroline who spoke first. Even the vitality and bounce seemed to have left her voice, when she looked up her eyes were dull and there were dark rings under them.

"You're the first visitor in nearly six months, and I certainly never expected to see you," she said, matter of factly without emotion.

"One word – why?" enquired Drew, trying to keep calm.

"Why what?" Caroline retaliated, showing animation for the first time.

"Why did you turn to Satan?" Drew tried to keep calm, although he felt anything but. A strange smile seemed to spread across Caroline's face although it didn't reach her eyes.

"Life got boring. It offered excitement, I suppose," she gazed past him at the far walls.

"Excitement is one thing, but you killed and were about to kill again," said Drew, this time unable to keep the emotion out of his voice.

Again the mirthless smile from Caroline, followed by "Well, you have no doubt read the psychologist's report on me – of unsound mind, it said."

"I've known you for years Caroline and I know you are as sound in mind as anyone else."

"So you are a shrink now are you? Know better than the professionals, do you?" Caroline's voice was heavy with sarcasm.

"I didn't say that," snapped Drew.

"Well, my Counsel will plead insanity and I shall get off lightly ... You just see if I don't," Caroline retorted.

"And the others? The other Satanists – are they all insane too?" Drew asked pointedly. Caroline made a gesture with her arms flung out, palms uppermost.

"Maybe, or more likely I dominated them. They just were weak and easily led. I gave them excitement and thrills and they lapped it up."

"How did Bart Paget become involved?" asked Drew, trying to check his fury at Caroline's indifference.

"He was weak. I promised him much and gave him nothing. It was easy to make the man my slave ... After a little while he would do anything I told him to, including kill."

"Was that what you wanted to do with me Caroline – make me your slave?"

Again a burst of emotion from Caroline as she replied, "Oh no, I wanted you with me. One day to rule beside me. We could have ruled the world you and I but you preferred that Paget woman … Are you with her now?" Drew ignored the last part of the question and answered only the first part.

"I think you are mad, Caroline … You must be, to have done this terrible thing." An evil smile, which this time made even Caroline's eyes dance with pinpoints of fire, followed Drew's last remark.

"That's right Drew. I am mad … Make sure you tell the court that, won't you, next week at the trial." The officer who had been standing watching moved forward and put a hand on Caroline's shoulder.

"Time is up, Channing," she said, coldly.

Drew on his side of the glass partition rose as well. He said nothing but just stood looking bemused and saddened. After all, this woman had been his long time friend.

As Caroline was led docilely away she turned and called back, "I love you Drew. I always loved you, right from the start." A moment later both her and the female warder had disappeared from his view. The officer on his side escorted him out to the main gates.

He realised on his way back to London in his car, that his visit hadn't been in vain. He now knew that Caroline was insane. She had shown no remorse at any time for the murder of Esmeralda the old recluse, or the kidnapping of Olga, and the intended murders of both the latter and Sasha as well.

He had had to know whether she was truly evil or insane. He now knew it to be both. Satan had entered her life and consumed her very soul sending her eventually round the bend. When he was called to give evidence next week he would, at least, be clearer in his own mind.

★ ★ ★ ★ ★

CHAPTER THIRTY

The day of the trial dawned bright and sunny in London. Traffic hooted and honked outside the great courts of justice whilst pedestrians scurried by in various directions about their respective business. Inside the court there was an air of expectancy. When the judge, resplendent in wig and gown entered, there was a deathly pregnant hush, broken only by the clerk's "All rise."

Caroline Channing was eventually brought up and stood in the dock. She was dressed in a pale grey tailored two-piece suit. Her hair was scragged back untidily and she wore no make-up. Sasha, watching from the assembled congregation thought that Caroline seemed to have lost a lot of weight since she had seen her last on that fateful day. Even now Sasha found it hard not to picture Caroline in her mask and black cloak, open to expose her nakedness.

She involuntarily shuddered at the memory that came flooding back as when she had laid there with Olga awaiting death on that altar.

The judge began his opening address in a grim foreboding tone his eyes ever on Caroline in the dock.

He went on to read the charges and ended by saying, "How do you plead? Guilty or not guilty?"

"Not guilty, your honour."

Then it was the turn of the witnesses. As the primary person involved in the investigation, Drew was called first. Sasha saw him step up into the witness box. He looked calm and handsome in a dark suit and tie. Sasha found her eyes drawn to him and waited with bated breath, whilst counsel for the prosecution questioned him at length. The interrogation lasted for fully thirty minutes, all the facts as she remembered them coming out, then it was the turn of the defence counsel. Drew was forced to go through it all again. This time, of course, the counsel for the defence was much more aggressive towards Drew. When he failed to win any points after another thirty minutes barrage he switched his attack in an attempt to discredit Drew. Sasha's heart went out to him, as he bravely tried to defend himself.

The counsel was an experienced, rather pompous middle-aged man by the name of Andrew Feathersby. He had a black beard, which contrasted strikingly with the white wig he wore. Every so often he would remove his spectacles and observe Drew as if weighing him up, then replace them before speaking.

"Would you agree, Mr. Thorpe, that you don't come out of this very well?" he asked.

"How do you mean, sir?" enquired Drew, knowing full well what was coming. Feathersby smiled quite benignly and turned to the jury.

"Well, were you not having an affair with one of the principal witnesses in this trial?"

Drew shifted uncomfortably and stuck a couple of fingers between his neck and collar. He could feel himself perspiring. When he didn't answer immediately, Feathersby reiterated the question.

Drew playing for time and trying to save Sasha, said, "Is it really necessary to answer that, your honour?" He turned hopefully to Judge Foley.

Although the judge looked sympathetic he replied, "You must answer Counsel's question."

Drew dropped his head and replied quietly, "Yes."

"Did you say yes, Mr. Thorpe? Perhaps you will reiterate that for the jury's benefit."

This time Drew looked him straight in the eye and answered boldly, "Yes, but it wasn't an affair. I loved her and still do." Drew shifted the direction of his gaze to where Sasha sat in the courtroom. The smirk on Feathersby's face riled him, but Drew knew he must not lose his temper.

"Do you see that lady in court, Mr. Thorpe? Perhaps you will point her out … for the benefit of the jury, you understand." How did these people live with themselves, Drew wondered, but was forced to point out Sasha. He saw her blush when all eyes were turned on her. Then she dropped her eyes. Feathersby continued in the same vein. "And was she not the wife of one of the deceased so called Satanists, when you began this affair with her?"

"It wasn't an affair, I told you, I love her," retorted Drew hotly.

"Objection your honour," said Haroldson, the prosecution's counsel. "Surely, your honour, this line of questioning has no bearing on this case."

"Objection overruled," said Judge Foley. Feathersby continued with a smug look on his face with more of the same.

"And was this lady — this Mrs. Paget's husband not still alive when you began this clandestine involvement with her?"

"No and yes," replied Drew.

"One or the other, Mr. Thorpe. You can't have both."

"It wasn't clandestine and yes he was alive. He even tried to murder Mrs. Paget." Drew managed to get the last part in before Feathersby could cut him short. Feathersby switched his attack, catching Drew off guard.

"You say you loved the lady, but do you deny that you had sexual relations with my client, Miss Channing, on at least one occasion?"

"It was against my wishes ... My drink had been spiked with LSD at the time and I was not in control of the situation," Drew began but was cut short by Feathersby.

"Quite the ladies man, aren't you, Mr. Thorpe?"

"Objection," said Haroldson, leaping to his feet. "Defence is deliberately trying to discredit the witness, your honour."

"Objection sustained," said Judge Foley. "Mr. Feathersby, kindly refrain from that line of questioning. The jury will disregard defence counsel's last remark."

Feathersby smiled benignly, accepting the rebuke and tried a new course of questioning.

"Would you say my client is an attractive lady?"

"Yes, anyone can see that," replied Drew, wondering where this was going to lead.

"And you had been friends for a long time, hadn't you? In fact you were assigned to this investigation together?"

"Correct," said Drew.

"I put it to you that you had been having an affair with her for a long time and when she spurned you, you decided to get even."

"Objection, your honour!" Haroldson sounded really hot under the collar.

Before he could outline his objection, Judge Foley remarked dryly, "Sustained ... Mr. Feathersby, I have warned you once. You are deliberately trying to discredit the witness. Any more of this and I will hold you in contempt. Do you understand?"

This time Feathersby looked less confident and after again accepting the rebuke, sat down, saying "No more questions."

After the battering Drew had received, he sat down, relieved that his ordeal was finished — at least for the moment. The next witness, Brigadier Jessup was called by the prosecution, Joseph Haroldson. His interrogation was short and to the point, Jessup replying boldly and confidently to his questions.

Then it was Feathersby's turn to grill for the defence. He began in his usual antagonistic manner.

"Do you usually go round shooting people, Brigadier?"

"Of course not. I shot the man because he was about to kill either one, or both of the ladies, these devils were about to sacrifice," exclaimed Jessup, hotly.

"You know that, do you Brigadier? I put it to you that if you hadn't acted as you did, Mr. Bart Paget would be alive today."

"Yes and one or both of the two ladies would have been dead," snapped Jessup.

"You are a military man with a distinguished war record and therefore used to killing, are you not?"

"In times of war it was a necessary evil," replied Jessup.

"Killing is therefore commonplace to you ... You would probably think no more about killing a man that I would on squashing a wasp in my window," prompted Feathersby.

"Objection," called Haroldson. Even Judge Foley's face reddened with suppressed anger.

"Mr. Feathersby, I will have no more of this — the court is adjourned. I will see you in my chambers — now! You too, Mr. Haroldson." The two men left with the judge and the court was patiently forced to wait for their return. Fifteen minutes later all three returned. Feathersby looked somewhat chastened, Haroldson much happier. The defence again questioned Jessup, but this time much more routinely. After a while Feathersby sat down.

"No more questions for this witness."

Next to take the stand was the Reverend Mark Glenville.

Haroldson questioned him very sympathetically and finished by saying, "In short Reverend Glenville, you acted very bravely, and as a man of the cloth, far more directly than could have been reasonably expected of you."

"If you mean I helped — yes, I did my best to help Mr. Thorpe."

"Indeed you did, sir. You may be heartily commended."

"Objection," snapped Feathersby. "It is not for prosecution to say what the witness should or not have done."

"Overruled," snapped Judge Foley.

"No more questions, your honour," remarked Haroldson dryly.

Mark underwent a short interrogation from Feathersby, but at least this time the defence counsel kept to the point.

Then it was the turn of Sasha in the witness box. Prosecution brought out all the relevant points in his questions to her. By the time he had finished with her, his sympathetic approach had the jury looking very favourably upon her. It was obvious she had faced a terrifying ordeal at the hands of the Satanists. When Feathersby's turn arose to question her he was very aware of not appearing to bully her. His tone was unusually mild. The last thing he wanted was to alienate the jury at this stage.

Drew, sitting in the courtroom, was immensely proud of the way that Sasha bore up through it all. Finally she was allowed to leave the stand. Then came Olga. Haroldson brought out to the jury all the horrors of her captivity at the hands of Channing and Paget. At one time she became overcome with grief and was allowed by the judge to sit and was given a few minutes in which to compose herself.

Then the prosecution outlined her ordeal on the Satanists' altar and added, "Not only this, but you were told the day before what was going to happen to you, weren't you, miss?"

"Yes, sir," whispered Olga in a hushed voice.

"All this in a strange land. Imagine this young lady's terror when tortured by these fiends," said Haroldson to the jury.

"Objection, my lord," began Feathersby. "Prosecution is assuming guilt by my client."

"Sustained. You know better than that, Mr. Haroldson." The judge's rebuke was quite mild.

"Apologies, my lord, but I was quite overcome by this lady's ordeal."

"Quite so. Accepted – proceed."

"No more questions," said Haroldson and sat down.

Feathersby glowered at him as he got to his own feet to question Olga. He knew the prosecution man had him beat here. If he verbally tried to abuse or discredit the young au pair he would lose all hope with the jury. Such was his nature that he couldn't resist one barb, however.

Relating to Olga's very short mini skirt, he said, "We note that you dress very provocatively, young lady … . Would you not say this caused some of the problems you were faced with?" Before Olga could answer, Haroldson was quickly on his feet.

"Objection, my lord. How the young lady dresses is entirely fashionable to the young and of no concern of anyone other than herself."

The judge put a hand over his mouth to hide a smile. "Sustained," he said.

With nothing more he could ask Olga, Feathersby sat down.

It was the end of the first day. Drew had hoped to have spoken with Sasha but by the time he reached the waiting area, he found she had left for the day. In fact he saw the taxi pull away with Sasha in the back seat.

The second day began with firstly Barbara Lake and then Sally Greves being put on the stand. Here Feathersby began to win back some of his lost ground. Barbara Lake confirmed that Sasha had dated with her husband and that it was all a conspiracy to trap her, Barbara, and involve her with the Satanists. Sally Greves, Barbara's friend, confirmed this and several of the jurors looked suspiciously at Sasha in the courtroom. Barbara said when questioned by Feathersby that Sasha had entered quite freely into an arrangement with her.

"And you used no force or persuasion, Mrs. Lake, to encourage her in this?"

"No, she asked me … Quite keen on my husband she was … Shamelessly so, I would say," said Barbara.

"And you are a bank manager's wife, are you not, Mrs. Lake?"

"Yes, we are very respectable people," exclaimed Barbara sanctimoniously.

"Quite so, dear lady … No more questions. You may step down."

Feathersby walked smugly back to his seat. There was uproar in the court, with reporters dashing out for the telephones.

"Silence in court – or I shall clear it," roared Judge Foley, hammering his gavel down several times.

The next witness called by the defence was Jake Cutter, gardener at Saddlewitch. He confirmed that he had seen Mrs. Sasha Paget on several occasions with Mr. Thorpe. Once he had even seen her going into Mr. Thorpe's cottage late at night.

Another witness, someone Sasha couldn't even remember having seen before, one Henry Stover, said he had seen Mrs. Paget having dinner with Mr. Ted Lake. After dinner he had seen them go upstairs. He hadn't seen them come down again. Ted Lake was called by the defence and backed up his wife's story. Yes, he and his wife had an open marriage and he frequently had had sex with Mrs. Paget, he affirmed. The court tittered.

Sasha looked across and caught Drew's eye. She could see understanding and sympathy there. What was this court trying to do to her? Surely it was Caroline who was on trial, not her. Why were they saying all these lies?

It was to get worse. Another witness, Max Stanislav, affirmed to Feathersby that he had driven a car in which Mrs. Paget had sat between the two ladies in court. At this point he pointed out Mrs. Lake and Mrs. Greves.

"She was in the middle of them sir, and they was fondling her sort of. I could see them in my rear view mirror."

"How do you mean, fondling her, Mr. Stanislav?" asked Feathersby turning once more to the jury.

"Stroking her legs and things like that," retorted Stanislav.

"And did Mrs. Paget object to this attention, Mr. Stanislav?"

"No sir. She didn't say anything. Just let them do it to her as far as I could see."

"Thank you. Your witness, Mr. Haroldson," said Feathersby, positively beaming. Haroldson got gravely to his feet and began his own interrogation of Stanislav.

"Would you say you are a good driver, Mr. Stanislav?"

"Oh yes, sir. Been doing it all my life."

"Are you in the habit of watching people in your car through your rear view mirror? Shouldn't you have your eyes on the road?"

"I do, sir."

"And yet you have time to see all this happening in the back of your vehicle?" Stanislav looked rattled.

"Well sir, the lady was quite a dish, sir." Again the court tittered. Haroldson himself smiled, a trick he often used to disarm a witness.

"What colour were her stockings, Mr. Stanislav?" The man looked rattled.

"Black, sir ... I believe."

"Black you believe. You had time to see all this and you only believe ... I put it to you, sir, that she was not wearing stockings at all, but in fact wore slacks at the time in question." It was a giant bluff but it just might work. Certainly Stanislav looked thoroughly rattled. Haroldson followed up, "I want you to turn to your right then look at me, then back to your right again. Understand?"

"Yes, sir."

"Then do it, Mr. Stanislav. Do it." When Stanislav turned back to face him, Haroldson held up seven fingers and shouted, "Look away! Now turn back." When the man again faced him he asked mildly enough having replaced his hands by his side, "How many fingers did I hold up, Mr. Stanislav?"

"Uhh, I'm not sure."

"Well, how many do you think?"

"Four, sir?"

"Are you certain about that? Four, you say?"

"Might be five, sir."

"Actually it was seven, Mr. Stanislav. Sit down. No more questions."

This time it was Haroldson who returned to his assistant with a smile on his face. Nevertheless at the end of the second day there could be little doubt that the defence had gained a marginal advantage.

Sasha returned to her hotel thoroughly depressed. Why were they trying to discredit her? All she had done was try to help and had nearly got gang raped and killed afterwards for her pains. At best, she was being portrayed by the defence as a wanton tart, hell bent on sexual excitement; at worst in collusion with the police to frame an innocent woman. Surely it was Caroline who was on trial. Why couldn't they see that? Why was she being persecuted like this?

The bedroom phone rang, shaking her out of her self-pity. To her surprise it was Mary Glenville.

"I wondered if I could come round and see you? I'm staying in the hotel next door to you … Is now a good time?" asked Mary.

Sasha, surprised, said it was, and Mary affirmed that she would come straight away.

"Okay, I'll meet you in the lobby downstairs in five minutes," said Sasha, wondering what the vicar's wife could want with her...

By the time Sasha had tidied herself up and applied some fresh make-up and gone downstairs Mary Glenville was already there. The first thing that struck Sasha was that Mary did not look a bit like the archetypal rector's wife. She looked very attractive in a modern plain and simple purple two-piece suit, well cut to show her figure off to good advantage. Mary was tastefully made up with just the right amount of eye make-up. Her hair was done up in a Tom Jones bow with a matching purple ribbon. The two women shook hands and went through to the lounge. Sasha ordered coffee for them both.

When the waiter departed after delivering it, Mary said, "I expect you wonder why I've come to see you?"

"Well I did rather. It won't do your reputation much good if you are seen with a wanton sex mad woman like me." The latter part of the sentence Sasha said with real bitterness.

Mary laughed.

"Oh really, Sasha! Nobody believes that, least of all the jury .... The defence is clutching at straws."

"Listening to it in that court I almost believe it myself," said Sasha.

"You will see – tomorrow will be different," reassured Mary.

"Why have you come, Mrs. Glenville?"

"My husband Mark wanted to, but as a principal witness you obviously realise he couldn't."

"That I understand, but ..." Sasha left the sentence unfinished.

"He wanted you to know that he was quite horrified at the way the Satanists defence has been allowed to attack and try to discredit you ... He feels you are a very brave lady and wanted me to tell you so."

"You could have told me that on the telephone, Mrs. Glenville. What did you really come for?"

Mary laughed.

Saddlewitch

"You are a very perceptive lady, Sasha – by the way please call me Mary. Mrs. Glenville makes me feel so old … I'm not much older than you – you know." Sasha said nothing but just gave her a quizzical look raising her eyebrows in an unsaid question. "Drew Thorpe … That's what I've come about," exclaimed Mary.

CHAPTER THIRTY-ONE

"Since you left Saddlewitch nearly six months ago my husband and I have become great friends with Drew ... He has even been down for the odd weekend ..." Mary paused in full flow and watched Sasha's reaction to this, then continued, "He has told us quite a bit about the way he feels about you ... Tell me it's none of my business, if you like, but I feel so sorry for him ... I don't think that a day goes by when he doesn't think about you."

Sasha cut in. "Did he send you to see me because I returned all his letters?"

"Good heavens no ... I'm sure he would be very cross if he knew I'd come here at all," said Mary.

"It was all his fault you know. After I volunteered to help, he promised full back-up ... Nothing could possibly happen to me, he said ... Then today was the last straw in court. Anyone would think it was me who was the criminal, the way that horrible Feathersby man attacked me." Everything came out in an outburst of passion from Sasha.

"Do you really believe that, Sasha? Drew didn't have an inkling that it was Caroline behind it all ... He had put in place everything for your protection and was as much betrayed by her, as you feel by him ... Surely you see that?"

"I don't know anymore. I just want this ghastly trial over and done with and to get back to my children," retorted Sasha. Mary argued long and hard on Drew's behalf, until Sasha became over emotional and virtually ordered her to stop. "You sound as if you are almost in love with Drew yourself," accused Sasha.

"If I wasn't in love with Mark, then I think I could easily fall for Drew" said Mary, honestly. Sasha looked astounded. Mary laughed at her expression of astonishment and said, "Just because I'm a vicar's wife doesn't mean I'm not human and have normal feelings for people."

"Oh, I'm sorry. I shouldn't have said that," apologised Sasha.

"On the contrary, you had every right ... I'm just sorry about the split between you two – you are so obviously made for each other," urged Mary.

"Thank you for coming anyway, even if it doesn't make any difference. Perhaps too much has happened to mend now," said Sasha, rising to show the conversation was at an end. She walked with Mary to the front door of the hotel.

At the door Mary's parting shot was, "It's never too late to mend. Opportunity only knocks once remember ... Don't let it slip through your fingers, my dear." Ignoring this last remark Sasha replied by saying that she would doubtless see Mary in court the next day.

★ ★ ★ ★ ★

The third day began in a totally different way. It was plain for Sasha to see that Haroldson's little bit of trickery had disconcerted Feathersby's method of questioning witnesses. His last one yesterday, Stanislav, had been made to look like an unreliable fool and he couldn't risk that happening again. Several fairly obscure witnesses were produced during the day, by both sides, without any vital points being won by either of the antagonists.

The prosecution's last witness, however, plainly made a vivid impression on the jury. It was Ray Grainger, the private detective. He related how he had almost been beaten to a pulp by the Satanists and was surprisingly quite honest about his own blackmail involvement with Barbara Lake. A doctor, called to conclude the day's witnesses, affirmed that Grainger had indeed been near death on arrival at the hospital and on the danger list for some weeks afterwards.

The fourth and fifth days more witnesses were introduced for both sides and some of the earlier ones recalled to the stand. The sixth day the other Satanists were brought in and duly charged with their crimes. Every one of them pleaded guilty hoping for a lighter sentence. On the seventh day it was finally time for the summation by the two counsels.

First it was the turn of the prosecution and Joseph Haroldson rose to his feet. He wore a serious and grave expression fitting the moment. An older man than Feathersby, he wore a black bow tie as was his custom. Usually his countenance was inscribed with a genial expression but today was an exception.

He faced Caroline Channing in the dock and then turned to the jury. A cough to clear his throat and he began. Caroline glared malevolently at his back throughout as he addressed the jurors.

"Ladies and gentlemen of the jury, you have listened over the last seven days to horrific accounts of Satanism perpetrated by this woman and her disciples, if I may flatter them with that description. My learned friend Mr. Feathersby has attempted to divert the course of justice, by attempting to throw doubts on the characters of both Mr. Thorpe and Mrs. Paget. I am certain that fair minded people, such as I am sure you all are, will see through this smokescreen. Mr. Feathersby has attempted to pull the wool over your eyes with irrelevant accusations against witnesses' characters. Mr. Thorpe has a fine record with Special Branch and he was instrumental in bringing Caroline Channing and her cohorts to justice. This was made particularly difficult for him by the fact the woman you now see in the dock was his assistant in the investigation. Mr. Feathersby would have you believe that Mr. Thorpe coerced Mrs. Paget, into inveigling herself into the Satanists' ring. He tells us this is illegal. Yes, I would agree with him, if Mrs. Paget had been employed by the police force. She was not. Mrs. Sasha Paget was a friend who volunteered to assist Mr. Thorpe, and I would emphasise to you that this is in no way illegal. Further you should understand that Mrs. Paget, who has been shown by the defence, as a wanton exhibitionist or worse, is in fact a very brave, young woman. She was married with two children and was forced to watch the destruction of her, up to then, normally mannered husband. Before her eyes he became almost hypnotised by these vile Satanists and the occult.

"The woman you see before you, Caroline Channing, consumed his entire soul, manipulating him to the extent that he even tried to murder Mrs. Paget, his own wife. If that wasn't dreadful enough he kidnapped his own family au pair, on the instruction of this woman, this Caroline Channing. They intended to use her as a human sacrifice to Satan. In spite of all this – this brave woman, Mrs. Paget, exposed herself to terrible dangers to both help Mr. Thorpe and to save the au pair girl, Olga Sorensen ... You see, both these women in court today – I ask you, ladies and gentlemen, look at them. Do they look like the sort of people Mr. Feathersby has portrayed them as? No ... They are normal human beings trying to live respectable lives. Whilst, on the other hand, you see the woman in the dock, Caroline Channing, a being so appalling that I will not even credit her with being a member of the human race.

"Without a second thought she was prepared to murder and torture and encourage others to do likewise. It was this woman ... . this creature, ladies and gentlemen, who murdered a defenceless old lady, a recluse who never harmed anyone. It was this woman who was prepared to kill a young nineteen year old , Olga Sorensen and Mrs. Paget, also. You will also recall one of the Satanists in the witness box telling us what they intended to do to Sasha Paget, before she too was killed. You must not be distracted from the real purpose of this trial. You are here to dispense justice, not listen to titillation and defamatory views on a person's character. Caroline Channing stands before you accused of these hideous crimes. She has pleaded not guilty although all her followers have admitted their guilt. Strange, don't you think? You may believe Caroline Channing to be insane – a distinct possibility, but that is not for you to decide. Your joint responsibility here is to return a verdict of guilty. Whether she is insane or not does not concern you. Other professional minds will decide that.

"In closing today I urge you to consider not only the gravity of this woman's crimes ... Murder most foul, but the fact that she has influenced so many other minds into her evil designs. We have even seen how she tricked her own senior investigator in so many ways ... . Mr. Thorpe believed her, like so many other people she took in. Superintendent Dawson listened to her, and even considered her for promotion. Mrs. Paget, although she has admitted not liking her, trusted her.

"Do not therefore become hoodwinked and taken in like so many before you by Caroline Channing. Remember the terrible crimes she has committed.

"If there was a death penalty in this country today, then I would be demanding it. I ask you therefore to find Caroline Channing, who stands before you now, guilty one hundred percent. She deserves no better."

With that Haroldson turned and gave Caroline a cold stare before returning to his bench.

"Mr. Feathersby, your summation please," called Judge Foley, to silence the response of the courtroom occupants. Feathersby edged his collar away from his neck and rose slowly. He crossed the floor to address the jury. Jurors would have noticed that he had recently been in earnest conference with his accompanying solicitor and his client Caroline Channing, even before Haroldson's summation had been delivered. Instead of facing the jury he turned to Judge Foley.

"At this late stage my lord my client wishes to change her plea," he began. Judge Theodore Foley showed surprise.

"You are right Mr. Feathersby it is a very late stage for such an adjustment to be made but nevertheless go on."

Sasha could feel the almost electric excitement in the courtroom as tension mounted expectantly. Two of the jurors leaned forward visibly. Reporters reached for their pens in the gallery.

"We wish to plead guilty but with mitigating insanity," exclaimed Feathersby.

"Do I take it then, Mr. Feathersby, that you do not wish to register a summation?" asked Foley.

"That is correct my lord. My client now wishes to throw herself on the court's mercy." Almost to excuse himself, Feathersby added, "My client has so instructed me."

Judge Foley looked very grave when he said, "You may sit down Mr. Feathersby." When the defence counsel had so done Foley addressed the jury. "In the event of the defence withdrawing its plea of not guilty and changing and amending it to one of guilty due to being of unsound mind, the defence counsel Mr. Feathersby has elected to not exercise his right to a summation and has forfeited that right given him by the legal system of the state. However, it is

Saddlewitch

now my painful duty to advise you, the jurors in this trial, to retire and weigh the evidence before returning your verdict.

"The defendant Caroline Channing has chosen to change her plea as you have heard. It is not for you to judge her sane or insane. We have heard over the last seven days conflicting evidence as to her sanity from medical experts better qualified than you or I. What you must decide is whether you hold her guilty or not guilty of these hideous crimes based on the evidence you have heard here. You may consider that the defence has at times tried to incriminate others, but I would remind you that the person on trial here is Caroline Channing. You must elect a foreman and so deliberate plainly and simply on her guilt. The other so-called Satanists have all pleaded guilty so no deliberation is needed from you on that score. They will await sentence from me at the conclusion of this trial. Consider carefully whether Caroline Channing, whom you see before you, is guilty or not guilty. You may now so retire and deliberate on your decision."

The jury of twelve, six men and six women, rose quietly and, led by the bailiff, filed out.

Only half an hour elapsed before they re-entered the court and took their places on the jurors' benches. Judge Foley turned to them.

"Have you elected a foreman?"

"We have my lord," said a small bespectacled youngish man who looked painfully thin and emaciated. In spite of this, his high forehead and pointed nose made him look very knowledgeable.

"Have you reached a verdict upon which you are all agreed?"

"We have, my lord."

"Do you find the defendant Caroline Channing guilty or not guilty?"

"Guilty my lord," returned the foreman.

Uproar broke out in the courtroom, mostly from the public gallery. Reporters jumped up and rushed out to be first to the telephones with their stories.

Sasha drew a deep breath of relief for at last it was all over. She was brought back to life by the judge's gavel banging loudly for order.

When the hubbub had died down Judge Foley once more addressed the courtroom. It was now four-thirty in the afternoon.

"I shall now adjourn for the day. At precisely ten a.m. tomorrow morning, I shall pronounce on my sentence on the accused Caroline Channing and also the others accused."

Caroline was escorted away by two policemen, to be returned to her cell.

Everyone stood whilst Judge Foley, resplendent in his robes, vacated his high chair of office and left the court for his chambers.

Sasha hurried out and went back to her hotel without waiting to speak to anyone.

The following morning Sasha was seated in court in good time for the sentencing. Somehow she felt things would look brighter once Caroline was behind bars, although what harm the woman could do now to her she wasn't sure.

The courtroom was crowded to capacity with reporters everywhere. The public gallery almost looked dangerously full. Such had been the interest nationally in the case, that almost every paper was represented.

The judge arrived and took his seat whilst everyone stood respectfully, at precisely ten a.m. Sasha saw Drew a few rows away. He tried to catch her eye but she quickly looked away. Then Judge Foley was speaking.

"Bring in the defendant Caroline Channing." The clerk repeated the call which was relayed.

A minute or so later she was led in, this time by an armed escort of two policemen and a policewoman. 'Could it be that the authorities were expecting trouble, or was this just a precaution,' Sasha thought.

"Turn and face me," ordered the judge. "Have you anything to say before sentence is passed on you?"

Caroline turned defiantly towards him, saying nothing. Sasha noticed she had done something with her hair and had applied make-up expertly. She was dressed in a plain black dress nipped in tightly at the waist, to accentuate her bust line. Sasha wondered if Caroline really expected to influence the judge with her sexuality.

Well why not – hadn't she influenced and fooled almost everyone else, mused Sasha.

"Caroline Channing – you have been found guilty of murder premeditated and further of attempted murder, and abduction of persons against their will. If it were in my power I would sentence you to death, for these hideous crimes. Alas it is not. Whilst contemplating and effecting these dastardly deeds you gave never a thought for your poor victims' suffering. Therefore you are to be retained indefinitely at her Majesty's pleasure in an institute of maximum security. There you will also undergo medical reports as to your sanity as I am by no means convinced of your insanity and feel you to be positively evil in the extreme. Take her down," Foley added to the court bailiff.

Without a word Caroline turned, glared almost directly at Sasha, and then allowed herself to be led away. To everyones surprise Judge Foley quoted a passage from the Bible.

"Revelation chapter 18, verse 23. And the light of a candle shall shine no more at all in thee, and the voice of the bridegroom and of the bride shall be heard no more at all in thee, for thy merchants were the great men of the earth; for by thy sorceries were all nations deceived."

Caroline turned back at the courtroom exit, a strange puzzled expression on her face. A moment later she was gone, leaving the crowded courtroom to contemplate the judge's words.

Then everyone rose as Theodore Foley strode in dignified fashion from the court.

★ ★ ★ ★ ★

Outside Sasha heard someone call her name. She turned and saw it was Brigadier Jessup. She waited for him to catch her up, then immediately apologised for not having thanked him before for saving her life.

"Very remiss of me, Brigadier, not to have done so before, but as you will no doubt have realised I was in a very shocked state at the time."

Jessup smiled sympathetically.

"Of course you were, my dear, but after all it's not me you should be thanking, it's that young fellow Thorpe ... .. Dashed brave young man. It was he who acted on his own initiative and came to me. Risked everything he did. Had he been wrong he would most certainly have been sacked, and you wouldn't be here now, or that young au pair of yours."

"I don't quite understand you, Brigadier," Sasha replied.

"Well he had everything nicely arranged to catch the lot of them. There was no way he could have known that his partner was the leader of the Satanists. Probably the last person in the world he would ever have suspected. He had trusted her with the back-up operation, so was left right out on a limb. Thank heavens he remembered an earlier remark I had made about my suspicions. Initiative, that's what I liked about the chap ... . Went right in he did, without a thought for himself. One minute he was up there on the balcony with me, the next down there tackling the devils ... By jove I could have done with twenty like him with me in Korea."

Sasha stood quite numb. If only Drew had told her all this, but then, perhaps he had. Mary Glenville had certainly tried to tell her, but she hadn't listened to her either. Maybe it had been explained in Drew's letters, she had returned so rudely unopened. She could at least have read them.

Suddenly Sasha felt quite overcome with guilt, at having judged Drew so out of hand. Was it too late to say sorry, she wondered? Perhaps, given the way she had treated him, he would have long since given up on her. Truth to tell she had missed him terribly, but up until now she had always believed him to have let her down.

She kissed the old Brigadier on both cheeks and wished him well.

He gave her a warm hug in return saying, "All's well that ends well. Nobody believed that stuff Feathersby was saying about you in there, you know, young lady, least of all me. The fellow's a bounder of the worst kind."

Sasha excused herself and went in search of Drew. If nothing else she must say sorry for the way she had treated him. She was just in time to see him board a taxi and drive off through the London streets.

She watched the rear of the black city taxicab disappear into the traffic in the distance. Sasha's heart was heavy and she suddenly felt very alone.

CHAPTER THIRTY-TWO

Once Sasha had returned to Christchurch, life settled into a routine. She had Debbie and Annabel to look after and then there was her job in the solicitor's office. She supposed she should have been happy, but constantly nagging on her mind, was the fact that she owed Drew an apology. At least Sasha tried to tell herself that's all it was, the need to apologise. After all, if it hadn't been for his intervention, she wouldn't have been here now and the children would have been orphans. A month went by; the fuss about the case had died in the papers and media.

Finally she decided to do something about Drew. The problem was she couldn't write to him as she had no notion of where he now was. Perhaps, given her ungrateful attitude, he wouldn't want to hear from her ever again let alone see her. The thought disturbed her even more than she would admit. I know I'll phone Mary Glenville, Sasha thought. She obtained the telephone number from directory enquiries and rang whilst still motivated. The Reverend Mark Glenville answered and after enquiring about her health handed her over to his wife.

Mary Glenville said how lovely it was to hear from her.

"How can I help?" she said. Somewhat embarrassed Sasha explained that she wanted Drew's telephone number as she felt she needed to apologise to him. "Hold on a minute and I'll go and find it for you," replied Mary.

Whilst waiting, holding the receiver to her ear Sasha could hear whispering and laughter the other end, which only heightened her sense of embarrassment. Finally Mary returned and read the number out to her. Sasha thanked her and was about to say goodbye, when Mary offered an invitation.

"Saddlewitch is looking lovely this time of the year, how about coming up and spending the weekend with my husband and myself?"

Quite taken aback, Sasha replied, "Oh, I couldn't possibly put you to that trouble on my account."

"Nonsense – no trouble at all. We'd love to have you stay for the weekend." Sasha continued to argue raising obstacles as to why she couldn't.

"I … I just don't think I could face Saddlewitch again … just yet after what happened…Don't think I don't appreciate your invitation though."

Mary continued to argue away her objections and then said quite suddenly, "My husband is making signs he wants to talk to you … I'll put him back on." Again there was a short break, and Sasha could hear whispering once more, then Mark came on the line.

"My wife has explained to me your reluctance to come down to Saddlewitch and I do understand how you feel Sasha," he began. Sasha heard him clear his throat before continuing, "However facing up to what happened and revisiting Saddlewitch, can only help to get the memories out of your system. You need to see the village as it is now with the early summer blossoms. Those dreadful people were only an episode that is past and they have all received their just deserts. Sometimes a problem or memory faced up to is a problem halved or even banished. Will you come, Sasha, we would love to see you….. Bring the children if you like."

Against such hospitality Sasha found it hard to refuse their kind invitation. She laughed.

"Very well vicar, but I won't burden you with the children … My aunt won't mind having them for the weekend. In fact she'd love it … always complaining she doesn't see enough of them, although Christchurch is so near to Bournemouth."

"Wonderful – I'll put Mary back on and you can arrange it between you, bye for now."

It was agreed between Mary and herself that Sasha would travel up that Saturday morning and arrive in time for lunch.

After Sasha replaced the receiver she wondered just how she'd come to agree. Secretly she dreaded a return visit to Saddlewitch, but maybe Mark Glenville was right and that was what she needed to rid herself of these terrible memories. She still had nightmares about them. Several times during the week she telephoned the number for Drew that Mary had furnished her with. Always she received no answer, only a ringing tone. Then Sasha agonised that maybe he had one of those phones that displayed the number of the caller. Perhaps, as he knew she had gone to that area, recognising that it might be her, he hadn't wanted to answer? Yes, that was it. Sasha sadly convinced herself he didn't want to know, and stopped ringing the number.

She took the children and her dog Bess over to her aunt's on the Friday evening, and stayed the night herself. Early the next morning she left in her car for Saddlewitch.

Sasha arrived in the village at round about noon. Mary was right; it did look beautiful. Even the Saddlewitch tree on top of the hill seemed to reflect the morning sunlight. It was the first of June and indeed June was busting out all over. The hedgerows had rhododendrons in full bloom. Red, pinks and whites interspersed the greenery of the hedges. The trees were fresh with an amazing array of shades of greens. The road through the village had been newly tarred. Everything looked so spick and span. A new sign had been erected near the war memorial to designate the county's prettiest and tidiest village. She noticed the post office too, which had had a new coat of paint. Even constable George Fenning came cycling down the road in uniform for once in his life.

There was young Rachel Steel, the local farmer's daughter, trotting her thoroughbred chestnut through the lane past the church. Sasha was forced to smile. Rachel's jodhpurs were so tight, the girl looked as if she had been poured into them. The horse had quarter marks on his rump and was beautifully turned out. He held his head proudly looking to neither right nor left. Sasha slowed right down as she passed and Rachel put up a hand in acknowledgement, then smiled and waved as she recognised Sasha.

Jake Cutter, the gardener, ambled down the road, a spade carelessly slung over his shoulders like a rifle. When he saw Sasha, he stopped dead in his tracks and watched her go by. When she turned the bend he was still standing watching her car disappear from view.

Strimmer the postman was cycling on his way back to the post office. He looked even more red-faced than usual. Then she saw a couple of hikers who had stopped to look at a map. Soon, almost without realising it she was turning into Vicarage Lane and into the vicarage drive itself. She parked the car and removed her small overnight case from the boot.

Mary must have heard her and already had the front door open to greet her. She gave Sasha a warm hug and a kiss on the cheek.

"Leave your bag in the hall Sasha and come through to the lounge and have a drink. It's such a lovely day. Perhaps we can all go into the garden after lunch," said Mary.

Then came the shock. As Sasha was ushered into the lounge who should be there but Drew Thorpe, looking very elegant in a pale grey lounge suit. He was in conversation with Mark and they were discussing the current test match against Australia. Drew turned his head as they entered. It was very plain to see that he was as shocked to see her as Sasha was to see him. For a moment both were lost for words.

Mary said, "No need to introduce you two, is there?"

They self-consciously shook hands, each as clearly embarrassed by this unscheduled meeting as the other.

No sooner had Mark poured Sasha a dry sherry and refilled Drew's martini than Mary said, "Oh Mark, can you help me in the kitchen for a moment please." He left Sasha and Drew alone in the lounge and followed Mary out.

"Look, I'm sorry about this ... I really had no idea you would be here," explained an embarrassed Drew.

Sasha, recovering her poise, smiled and said, "Neither I, you ... but it looks as if Mary Glenville is trying to do a little matchmaking."

It was Drew's turn to smile now.

"I guess so, but somebody should have known you didn't want to see me any more and I would like you to know I don't blame you one bit ... I really let you down ..."

Sasha cut in.

"No, you didn't Drew. I can see that now. It was Caroline Channing who let both of us down, and everybody else as well."

"So do I take it you don't mind me being here then?" asked Drew.

"Not if you don't mind me," laughed Sasha happily.

Drew's face took on a serious expression.

"Mind you? There's no one I'd rather see than you ... I've missed you a lot more than you will ever realise, Sasha."

Looking puzzled, Sasha replied, "When you didn't answer your phone all week I assumed you didn't want to hear from me ever again."

"I haven't been home all week ...Been on an assignment up north ... In fact, I came straight here from Leeds ... The Glenvilles invited me for this weekend three weeks ago ... When did you get invited?" asked Drew.

"Only earlier this week," Sasha responded.

"Oh!" exclaimed Drew.

"Oh, indeed."

They both laughed, the ice broken between them. Drew enquired why Sasha had been ringing him. She explained that it had been to apologise for her past conduct.

"Nothing to apologise for. It's me who needed to apologise ... I tried in my letters, but you always returned them unread."

"I'm sorry Drew, but ..."

Before she could go on Drew cut in, "Can we both stop apologising and get on with our lives," he exclaimed.

After laughing happily together, Drew pulled Sasha to him and hugged her as if there were no tomorrow. They were still in one another's arms when Mary Glenville entered with a polite cough, followed by a chuckle.

"Lunch is served, if you two can tear yourselves apart long enough to eat it," Mary said happily.

As Sasha and Drew broke away each had a happy embarrassed expression on their faces, which told its own story.

As they entered the kitchen Mark was opening a bottle of champagne. He took one look at the faces of all three of them and commented, "I see Mary's little ruse worked to get you two together once more. All's well that ends well, as they say."

He that sacrificeth unto any God, save unto the Lord only, he shall be utterly destroyed.

Exodus chapter 22, verse 20.